Kerry Barnes, born in 1964, grew up on a council estate in south-east London. Pushed by her parents to become a doctor, she entered the world of science and became a microbiologist. After studying law and pharmaceuticals, her career turned to medicine.

Having dyslexia didn't deter her from her passion for writing. She began writing when her daughter was born thirty years ago. Once her children had grown up she moved to the Kent coast and now writes full time.

The Choice

Kerry Barnes

ONE PLACE. MANY STORIES

HQ
An imprint of HarperCollins*Publishers* Ltd
1 London Bridge Street
London SE1 9GF

www.harpercollins.co.uk

HarperCollins*Publishers*
1st Floor, Watermarque Building, Ringsend Road
Dublin 4, Ireland

This edition 2021

1
First published in Great Britain by
HQ, an imprint of HarperCollins*Publishers* Ltd 2019

Copyright © Kerry Barnes 2019

Kerry Barnes asserts the moral right to be
identified as the author of this work.
A catalogue record for this book is
available from the British Library.

ISBN: 978-0-00-833649-3

This book is set in 10.7/15.5 pt. Sabon by Type-it AS, Norway

Printed and bound in Great Britain by
CPI Group (UK) Ltd, Melksham, SN12 6TR

For Terrie Taylor

You were an inspiration and I only hope you knew that.
God bless.

Chapter 1

As soon as the huge metal door that sealed off the hidden room was slammed shut, Torvic felt the muscles in his shoulders tighten and his jaw clench. He still couldn't feel his hands because the ropes were so tight that his circulation was cut off. As his bowels churned, he felt sick. He needed to shit but he had to stop himself. He was the Governor and could take on most things, but shitting himself and losing his dignity wasn't one of them.

He looked at his granddaughter Tiffany and wondered if he should just have let her lead a normal life instead of pulling her into his world. He stared at her head. It was tilted back, with sweat covering her brow, along with a blue tint that lined her lips. His eyes watered as he recalled that horrific moment when Zara made him choose either Tiffany's life or his son Alastair's. He wondered if he ever managed to escape this hellhole, he would be able to forget the torment of making the choice. The smell of his son's burning flesh still lingered inside the hangar and Tiffany's semiconscious moans still rang in his ears. To him, his granddaughter was still a kid, but Zara Ezra hadn't seen it that way.

He gritted his teeth when he thought of the hard-faced bitch.

She had to be the sickest-minded woman he'd ever met. He should have admired her, and yet his anger towards her over-ruled his rational mind. She'd said she would stoop to depths lower than the Governor – he himself – would ever dream of, and, by Christ, she had meant it. He really thought he'd had her fooled. He'd been the man they were hunting down – the Governor – and there he'd been, right under their noses all the time, pretending to be a dear old friend of her father's. He should have given her more credit. Yet, never in his wildest dreams would he have believed her to be as smart as her father. Izzy Ezra had been a genius. Not many could match his brains and power. But Torvic realized that his earlier assessment of Zara's ability had been completely wrong. For while her father had been a good teacher, she'd been an exceptional student.

There was no question that Zara had listened to Izzy and listened well. Torvic felt every nerve in his body come alive with fury because Zara had played him for a fool. Pretending she was in over her head, she'd acted like a vulnerable woman, lost in confusion. Zara was good, he had to give her that. All the time she'd confided in him, letting him believe she had concerns regarding the Lanigans' and the Regans' loyalty, she'd been dangerously plotting his capture. He should have sussed her out; he should have realized that Zara wouldn't suspect Mike Regan – the one man she loved – or his brother Eric for that matter. Torvic knew he'd been mugged off big time, and yet he had one last hope, which was that his new recruit was up to all she'd promised. However, he did have that nagging doubt as to whether she would be a match for Zara.

Tiffany was insensible, the terror over the last few hours having knocked the stuffing right out of her. Torvic wished he could just take away her fear. He looked at the shut door. 'Hurry up, woman, for fuck's sake,' he said to himself. A sudden vision shot through his mind, and, for a moment, he had to breathe deeply to hold back the vomit that was about to protrude from his mouth. He wondered if he'd actually been blindsided by all his previous success. Had he really gone down the path that had made him believe he was invincible?

Alastair sure as hell thought he had, but, yet again, his eldest son had been a psychopath, and up until the point that the flesh-eating acid had been poured over his head, he'd shown absolutely no emotion.

He looked back at Tiffany. No wonder she was so traumatized, seeing such a horrific scene. Not even Stephen King could have dreamed that one up. He shuddered and then felt his bowels rumble again.

Just as he thought there was no hope and that the woman had bottled out, the sudden heavy rumbling, as the door began to slide open, made his heart pound. He stared at the opening, willing it to be her and not Zara. His prayers were answered. There, standing like Catwoman, dressed in black jeans, a black jumper, and with her black hair tied back, stood his dark angel. She looked sleek – like Zara – and even her stance was similar, but she was a little rougher around the edges.

The woman looked behind her and then quickly nipped inside. Torvic's notion that maybe she was a match for Zara soon went out of the window when she nervously fumbled around in her oversized bag. Eventually, after digging around and pulling half of the contents out, she found what she was looking for – a knife. She quickly got to work cutting Torvic free.

As soon as his hands were in front of him, he ripped the tape from his mouth. 'You took ya fucking time, didn't ya?'

'I had to be sure they were all out of sight. Don't moan at me. I did what ya fucking wanted. Now, where's the rest of me dosh?' she demanded, as she began putting everything back into her bag, battling with a sudden gust of wind, which had blown some of her papers across the smoothly polished concrete floor.

Torvic was unravelling the rope from his feet. 'For fuck's sake, woman, cut her ties, will ya!'

Shaken by the bellowing from Torvic's mouth, she scooped up the remainder of her belongings and rushed to cut his granddaughter free. By the time she'd hacked through the rope, Torvic was on his feet.

He aggressively took over. 'Right. Take us to the car and I'll get you your fucking money. Help me with her, will ya! The girl's traumatized.'

'Cor, you've changed ya tune. You were all sweet words and roses last week. Now, you're like a bear with a sore head.'

Torvic was about to lay into her verbally but thought better of it. He didn't need any two-bit brass running and squealing to the Regans. 'Sorry, babe, it's just been a tough night.'

'You're fucking lucky I actually managed to open this fucking door or whatever the hell it is. It was only the fact that Zara forgot to put the remote in her pocket and it was on the worktop, or you would've been locked up for good and probably dead in a few hours.'

Torvic glared. 'Dear woman, they wouldn't have killed me. They think I have something they want.'

'Oh yeah, and what's that then?'

'A contact, a piece of information,' replied Torvic, with a sickly grin and an evil look of spite in his hooded eyes.

She stared for a moment. Was she looking at a reincarnation of the Devil? A man in his sixties, Torvic was dark and devious, and the way in which he lifted up Tiffany demonstrated that he was as strong as an ox.

* * *

Shelley Marwood sat on the hard wooden chair, nervously biting her nails. It should never have been this way, grovelling for her father's help. She wondered if the cold, uncomfortable chair was a deliberate ploy to make his clients tense or whether its purpose was to deter them from sitting there for hours and talking too much. *Was he getting a kick out of this?* she thought. Nevertheless, she had no choice – he was her only hope.

Colin Crawford, a man in his early seventies, still had an extreme air of authority about him. As a child, Shelley could never understand why people feared and respected him. Why they stuttered or shuffled nervously in his presence was beyond her. He was always so sweet, gentle, and kind to her – at least he had been at one time. But as he turned from gazing out at the urban landscape, she could tell from that grave look in his eyes what it felt like to fear him.

He clasped his perfectly manicured hands together in front of him. A thin smile formed, one that lifted his cold, grey eyes. 'So you want my help?'

She nodded fast. 'Yes. Please, Dad.'

He unclasped his hands, stood up, and walked back to the window and stared off into the myriad shapes of London.

She followed him with her eyes, holding her breath, and waiting for him just to tell her he would. The silence seemed to linger for so long, her palms were wet with sweat.

'You have a fucking nerve, Shelley. But you have front asking me, I'll give ya that. I like your balls.'

'Dad—'

He spun around, sharply stopping her from continuing. 'Don't you "dad" me. Dad is a term of endearment. The proper word is father. However, even that doesn't seem fitting, coming from your mouth.'

She swallowed hard and wanted to cry. He was a stranger at that moment. The man with the pearl-grey hair, chiselled cheekbones, and thin lips looked at her like she was a piece of shit. Longing for the expression he'd shown her in the past brought tears to her eyes.

'Shelley, don't put on the fake waterworks. It has the least effect on me.'

'Dad, *please*, it was such a long time ago …'

Colin narrowed his eyes. 'Yes, you are damn right there, and a lot has changed, like your dear mother dying without you showing your face, with not even a call. That poor woman died longing to hear your voice one more time. But you, ya selfish bitch, couldn't even be fucking bothered. So why should I do anything to help you, eh?'

The venom in his voice raised her anger. 'Because, *Father*, he's your fucking grandson.'

No sooner had the words left her mouth than she wished she hadn't said them. He was over to her in a flash. With one almighty flick of the back of his hand, she was knocked sideways. She clutched her mouth and felt her puffy lips sting.

With both knuckles now on his desk, his eyes bore into her. 'Grandson!' he yelled. 'You have no idea what you fucking did to us. You let us bond with the boy, and then you did the unthinkable. Not only did your sweet mother lose you, she lost her grandson too, and now you expect me to help him when I don't even know the boy.' He threw his hands in the air. 'Christ alive, you're one selfish bitch. D'ya know that?'

'Dad, doesn't this show you just how desperate I am? I know what I did was wrong, and I've had to live with it for over twenty years. I'm sorry. You have to believe me. I am so sorry.' She could force another tear, but he hated tears, never believing that they were real.

'Oh yeah, that's right. What you did *was* disgusting. Of all the fucking men on the planet, you shacked up with my enemy. Oh, and I bet he was having a right good flaming laugh. Well, Shelley, tell me this. Why ain't your fucking *husband* coughing up the goods, eh? Why ain't your darling Nicolas making arrangements? Past it now, is he? Washed up and dried out, is he?'

Shelley lowered her gaze in shame.

'Well?' he screamed.

'He's left me,' she whispered contritely.

Colin stared in disbelief. His daughter – this good-looking woman – had married Nicolas Marwood, a much older man. In fact, he was nearly the same age as himself. At forty-three, Shelley could easily pass for thirty-three. Her auburn hair, cut in a pixie style, and her round hazel eyes were fashionably attractive, and she'd not let her figure go to waste either.

'He's left you? *Why?*' he demanded.

She looked up, hoping to see some compassion on his face, but he just stared ominously at her with those cold, dark eyes.

'He was sniffing around a younger woman, took me credit card, and then he threw me out with just enough money to rent a gaff.'

'You're his wife. You're entitled to fucking half! Jesus, girl, you ain't that thick, surely to God, are ya?'

'No, Dad, I ain't that thick. But our money wasn't in any fucking bank accounts, was it? The house was in his brother's name, the cars were in his name, and the cash was hidden in places that only he knew about, so that's about the fucking strength of it.'

'I fucking knew this would happen. You can't even do up your shoelaces by yourself. For fuck's sake, that bastard took you away from me, and now he's left you hung out to dry and he's *still* having the last laugh.'

She wanted to defend Nicolas, but then she thought if she agreed with her father, he would be more inclined to help her.

'Yes, Dad, I reckon he is, but, as I said, I can't do fuck all about it.'

'Well, I can. Where's his brother live? I'll send him a visitor. I want that house in your name and—'

'Dad, I don't care about the money or the status. I just need you to help my son. And you're the only one who can sort this situation out. *Please!*'

'He got himself in this fucking mess. He's a stinking druggie.'

'No, I swear, he's not anymore,' she pleaded.

'Well, he's a bloody idiot, chucking shit down his neck. It only ends up one way – huge debts or being dead.'

'I know, I know, but please help me. You have contacts, so you can help him.' She watched his face, knowing the cogs were turning. She really wanted to be brave and suggest that it was probably his drugs that her son had been hooked on. She wasn't blind and knew that her father had his hand in the drug underworld. But she kept what she knew about her father's dealings to herself.

'Ya know what? I never had your husband put in a concrete boulder and stuck at the bottom of the river because you were his wife. End of. But now, I have no reason to hold back. You give me everything you have on that man, and I'll help your son.'

'Your *grandson*, Dad. He's your bleedin' flesh and blood too.'

'Don't push it, Shelley. Now go, and then come back when you have enough information for me to annihilate that son of a bitch.'

As Shelley got up from her chair, she faltered, unsure whether to attempt a hug; yet, again, he turned his back on her and looked out of the window once more.

Closing the door behind her, Shelley allowed a satisfied grin to creep across her face. She thought the meeting could've gone a lot worse. However, she'd put on her best acting skills and exaggerated the truth just enough to suck him. It had clearly worked.

* * *

Zara pushed back the white cotton sheet and was about to swing her legs around to clamber from the bed, when a heavy hand stopped her.

'No way is my future wife gonna slip outta the sheets without a kiss. We'll start as we mean to go on.'

9

Zara allowed a smile to lift her cheeks. It felt surreal, waking up in Mike's bed for the first time ever. The years of stubbornly playing with each other's emotions had now come to this. She was the boss, and yet, in their relationship, he would call the shots. She rolled into his open arms and snuggled her nose into his neck. 'You feel so good, Mikey.'

'And don't you forget it, my wife-to-be.'

'Er … I don't see a ring on this finger yet.' She laughed, holding up her right hand.

For a moment, Mike's heart felt heavy. She should have been holding up her left hand, but she couldn't, as there wasn't one.

'Well, today, we are gonna do something about that. You and I, my angel, are gonna pick the biggest, fattest diamond you fancy and show the world ya mine.'

'A bit controlling, wouldn't you say?'

Mike shuffled so that he was face-to-face with Zara. He blinked as he took in her natural beauty. Her skin glowed with the freshness of the morning.

'There is no man or woman alive that could control you, and you bloody well know it.'

She gently kissed his lips and then pulled away. 'No, Mikey, there isn't because outside of me and you, there's my business, and that's when I'm the boss. But inside this house and outside of work, I might just let you take control.' She winked. 'Er, well, every so often perhaps.'

'What, like this?' he replied, as he rolled on top of her and grabbed at her underwear, ripping her knickers away from her. She looked at the passion in his eyes and felt her heart race. She loved the way he was so animalistic in the bedroom, and yet she could be just the same. She snatched the back of his head and pulled him close, biting his bottom lip.

Disturbed by the phone ringing, Zara tried to pull away.

'Leave it, babe.'

'No, not today. We still have business to attend to.'

Mike rolled off and stared up at the ceiling. She was right. Torvic and his granddaughter, Tiffany, were still tied up in the secret room at the back of the hangar.

'Hello, what's up?' asked Zara, as soon as she answered the call.

'Fuck me, Zara, the hangar. Torvic and Tiffany have gone!' said Neil, her business partner.

Mike could tell from the shock on Zara's face that something was awry. He jumped up from the bed. 'What the hell's going on?'

Instantly, Zara sat upright. She put the phone on loudspeaker so that Mike could hear. 'You what? How can that be? The fucking room was locked. No one apart from us knows how to open it, and I have the … Oh shit, wait. Did I bring the remote with me? Hold on!' She turned to Mike. 'Where's my jacket?'

He bent down and picked up the padded jacket that had been thrown on the floor before they'd ripped each other's clothes off in the early hours.

She snatched it from him and searched the pockets. To her horror, they were empty. 'Oh no! Damn it, I must've fucking left the remote there!'

Mike shook his head and expelled air heavily from his mouth. 'Fuck me!'

For a moment, Zara looked at Mike and considered whether

he viewed her as an idiot, because, right now, she saw herself as exactly that. After all they'd achieved last night, she'd blown it completely by leaving behind the bloody remote device that opened up the back room.

Seriously agitated, Mike was running his hands through his hair and pacing the floor. 'It's all my fucking fault!'

Zara was puzzled and gave an exaggerated frown. 'How do you work that one out?'

His face dropped in shame. ''Cos if I hadn't distracted you so much before we left, you would've remembered the remote. Bloody hell, we were tired, *you* were tired. I should've let you finish up before I decided to propose and get all fucking soppy.' He sighed heavily.

'Mike, have a bloody day off, will ya? It wasn't *your* fault. You're right. It was a hell of a long night and shit happens. Now we need to get ourselves together.'

There was silence as all three, including Neil, who was still on the phone, tried to take it in.

'Neil, give me a minute. I'll call ya back. I need to get my head around this.'

She placed the phone back on the bedside table and turned to face Mike, who was now jumping into his jeans.

'What the fuck d'ya think's happened?'

Mike was white-faced and angry. 'I dunno, but we all need to meet up. I'll call the lads. If that bastard is on the loose, then whoever set him free has more clout than us. Fuck me, we don't even know who we're dealing with.'

Zara wrapped her silk robe around her naked body. She would have drooled over Mike in just his jeans and with his huge muscular chest on show, but not this morning. The fear of Torvic taking revenge shot through her like shards of glass. Her stomach churned when she thought of what she'd made Torvic do to his own son. The acid had burned the man's skin from his bones. *Jesus*, she thought, *what if he planned to do the same to anyone in her firm? Would she ever be able to forgive herself?*

Mike was now frantically trying to find his phone. His main concern was for Ricky, his son, who'd been recovering in hospital following Torvic's son's brutal attack on him. Ricky was supposed to be discharged at lunchtime.

Mike was sweating profusely. He couldn't let anything happen to Ricky – not now, when they had just been reunited. He'd lost contact with his son from the age of six, until meeting him unexpectedly in Maidstone Prison only months before their final release.

In all that time apart, both Ricky and his father believed each other to be dead, so now they had an unbreakable bond, and Mike was buggered if he was going to let Torvic get his hands on him now.

'Ring my phone, Zara. I can't fucking find the poxy thing.'

With her body shaking, she dialled his number; Mike pulled his phone from his back pocket.

Zara rolled her eyes. 'Babe, we need to calm down and think this through.'

Mike didn't answer her; he was calling the hospital. After a few minutes, he yelled, 'Aw, for Christ's sake, why don't they bloody pick up?'

'Mikey, seriously, you need to calm down. Call Ricky's mobile.'

Mike took a deep breath. She was right, of course. He really wasn't being clear-headed.

Ricky's phone rang twice before he answered. 'Dad, are you coming to pick me up? The doctor said I can go home in an hour's time. They're—'

'Son, listen to me. Stay put and I will get Staffie to pick you up. Do not, and I mean do not, leave that hospital with anyone other than him.'

'Dad, what's going on?'

'I ain't got time to explain. Please, just do as I ask.'

'Of course, Dad. No worries.'

Mike sighed with relief. 'Right, I'm gonna get the lads over here now and make a fucking watertight plan.'

Zara raised her brow. 'Er, no, we'll meet at my house. It's more secure. I have cameras.'

Mike was about to demand otherwise but he was aware she was in charge. It was agreed and that was that. He bit his lip and nodded.

Zara quickly pulled on her jeans, threw on a black jumper, and tied her hair back into a ponytail.

'Let's go. We'll call the others on the way.'

* * *

Once Zara had reached the entrance to her long drive, she pressed the fob clipped to her car visor and the ornate metal gates opened. She drove slowly, surveying the land on either side of the drive, looking for anything that was out of place. The early morning dark clouds made the house in the distance appear eerie. It was dauntingly large and resembled a castle – just how her father had designed it. Paranoia wormed its way through her mind as she began thinking all sorts of crazy things. It wasn't surprising though, after the previous evening's events at the hangar. Knowing Torvic, he would seek retribution, so, in the cold light of day, anything was possible right now.

As she peered in the rear-view mirror, she could see two cars behind her. Fortunately, she recognized them as Willie Ritz's and Neil Lanigan's vehicles. Lou Baker was riding shotgun with Willie.

Willie and Lou stepped out of the car and made their way to Zara's Range Rover, where they climbed in.

Willie looked like Stig of the Dump, with his hair sticking up in all directions and his eyes heavy with brown rings.

Mike shook his head. 'State of you! Ya need to leave off that gear, mate. You look like death warmed up.'

'Thanks for the compliment. Anyway, what's the hold-up?' He winked and gave a cheeky grin.

Mike looked at Lou, who was the polar opposite of Willie. In his Hackett three-piece dark-blue suit and with his hair neatly cut and freshly shaven, he appeared groomed to perfection.

'We're not sure if Torvic or his men are already at the house.'

Unexpectedly, Willie sighed, climbed back out of the car, and marched on ahead.

'Oi, Willie, what the fuck are you doing, mate?' called out Mike, from the open passenger window.

Willie, in his long jacket and with his sleeves a tad too short, spun around. 'It's been pissing down all night. Wet mud will show any footprints.'

Zara stepped out of the car on hearing Willie's thoughts. She was followed by Mike and Lou.

'He has a point. I haven't had a chance to have the gardens around the house landscaped yet, so it's all just soil. If anyone's been up there, he'll know.'

They held back and watched as Willie wandered around, searching for clues to any intruders.

Lou laughed. 'Cor, blimey, he even *looks* like a Red Indian tracker. All he needs are a few feathers in his hair.'

As they watched, Neil Lanigan and his cousin Shamus approached the house. They got out of their car and joined them. 'What's happening?' asked Neil, in a less than confident tone.

Zara turned and gave Neil a soft smile. For the first time, she saw the look of a worried man on his face. 'Willie's just checking for footprints. We want to make sure no one's been up there.'

Neil shivered and pushed his hands deeper into his pockets.

His discomfort had Zara a little on edge. She didn't like to have men around her who were nervous unless of course they were on the other side of her wrath. Yet the Lanigans were her trusted business partners, and even when she was held prisoner for five years by her brother Ismail and the Segals, Guy and Benjamin, they still kept her going concern in order, splitting every penny earned completely down the middle. She flicked her eyes to Shamus, who was now puffing furiously on a cigarette. As much as they were big, muscly Irishmen, both had soft faces with large, round, boyish eyes.

Shamus was patting his cousin's back. 'I didn't have a good feeling about this. Remember, I said to you last night, what if we are being fecking watched?'

Neil nodded. 'Aye, yer did that.'

Still blaming herself for the cock-up, Zara felt sick. She looked from Mike and Lou, then back to Neil and Shamus. There was a marked difference in the men. Mike, Lou, and Willie were ready for battle; she could see in their eyes that they weren't so afraid. On the other hand, Neil and Shamus looked like two rabbits caught in car headlights. She would have to make a plan that wouldn't include the Lanigans – not this time – for she couldn't afford any more mistakes, and their terrified expressions told her they would be more of a hindrance than a help.

Willie, with his crooked smile, held up his thumbs. 'No fuckers 'ave been 'ere.'

Lou laughed. 'Well done, Sitting Bull.'

As Zara entered the house, she paused and listened. Her nerves were on end. She just couldn't help but feel freaked out. It was all well and good having Torvic and his evil family tied up and tortured for information, but it was another thing knowing he was out there somewhere with multifarious plans for her firm and Mike's. The revenge on her would be horrific, and the others who were involved last night wouldn't be able to sleep comfortably either – that was a given.

Mike gripped her shoulders and whispered in her ear, 'You're safe with me. Go on, babe.'

She continued on and into her father's study where the monitor for the CCTV cameras sat on the desk.

She quickly tapped the buttons to rewind the footage and watched to see if anyone had been on the property in the last twelve hours. All she could see were leaves floating in the air and the bows of the trees bending in the wind. No one, it seemed, had been near or by. She felt her tense shoulders relax.

Glancing out of the window, she saw another car heading up the drive. Her eyes widened for a moment before she realized it was Mike's brother Eric driving, and he had Lance with him. He was the man her father called 'The Machine', who she only recently discovered was called Lance Ryder and not Torvic. It took a while before her heart began to stop beating so fast. She left the monitor and went over to the bar. 'Brandy anyone?' she asked, as she turned to look at the five seated men.

They all nodded. It was still early, yet, under the circumstances, no one objected, and they gratefully accepted the drink offered.

The loud knock at the door had Mike on his feet. 'I'll let 'em in.'

Eric's appearance was in direct contrast to Lance's. Much like Lou, he was clean-shaven and smartly dressed in a neatly pressed shirt and suit trousers. Lance, on the other hand, looked dishevelled, although his expression never gave anything away. He always wore a severe poker face. His long, thick, dark hair lay on his shoulders in messy waves, and his brooding eyes were almost unblinking.

Once everyone was seated, Zara took her position behind her father's desk. Neil and Shamus sat to her right, while Mike, Willie, and Lou sat to her left. Lance and Eric took seats across the desk.

'So, tell us exactly what you found, Neil.'

Her sudden change in tone brought everyone to focus on this slim, tall woman with the copper-coloured eyes. Her slender neck and tight jawline gave her an almost regal aspect.

Lance was intrigued more by the intensity of her personality, which seemed to radiate charisma. It reminded him of one of his female commanding officers over in Afghanistan on his last tour of duty, years ago now. She was similarly built and a real firebrand when the mood took her – which was often.

He hadn't known Zara for very long. Yet last night, he'd watched her command her army with a cold, stern heart. He was dumbfounded by how the man they called the Governor – the head honcho behind the new drug Flakka – had been right under the noses of him and the special operations team.

It was Zara who had managed to capture the monster. Her shrewdness and detailed planning would have put the Army to shame. Yet there was something more than that which had fascinated him. It was her ability to act so coolly and almost mind-read Torvic. How she'd sussed him out and then pieced everything together was sheer genius.

'We got to the airfield and I said to Shamus that the back wall of the hangar looked ajar. So, as we drove nearer, we could see that it was actually wide open,' said Neil.

Zara nodded. 'But the hostages had gone, so there was no sign that they'd been killed, was there?'

Neil shook his head. 'No. The chairs we had them tied to were where we left them, but the ropes had been cut and left on the floor. There was no blood or mess anywhere. They'd simply vanished.'

Zara tilted her head to the side. 'Was there a note left or anything or—?'

Shamus interrupted. 'No. Nothing. The place was as clean as a whistle. We had a good look around before calling you, but, honestly, it was as if the SAS had done a search and rescue.'

Zara looked at Lance. 'Any thoughts?'

Lance glared around the room with his dark penetrating

eyes. There was not a smidgen of niceness about him. She appreciated his composed demeanour and his straight-talking. Her father was right about him: his skills and strengths were to be respected. Ex-military, he was a lone wolf now, working for whoever paid the highest. Her father, of course, could afford the very best, and so, back then, Lance's abilities had caught his attention.

'I think we know who's behind it. It's this Barak Segal guy. That Torvic fella gave you his name under extreme duress, so we should turn our attentions to him.'

Eric sat almost shoulder to shoulder with Lance; both were heavily built men. He cleared his throat to say something but immediately looked at his brother. He didn't want to be shot down in flames for speaking out of turn, which was a habit he made all too often in Mike's company. Yet, surprisingly, Mike nodded for Eric to talk.

'Me, if I were Torvic, after last night, I'd be too shit-scared to try and take revenge. We all saw how terrified he was of his granddaughter getting hurt.'

Zara shook her head. 'No, Eric, he would do what I would and that's to get Tiffany far away, out of reach, and *then* come for us. And he knows we have a substantial united strength. He will take us down one by one. Probably, he'll start with our families, our closest loved ones, because he'll want to see us in pain. He'll want us to be begging for forgiveness, like he was.'

As she looked around, she could see the fear in their eyes. All of the men in the room now, no matter how big, hard, and ruthless they were, still felt the ultimate fear deep inside for their kids or their women getting hurt.

Willie was fidgeting and rubbing his hands down the front of his trousers.

Mike rolled his eyes. 'Mate, ya need to stop using cocaine. We have to keep our heads straight.'

Willie looked up and raised his brow. 'Don't you worry about me. I'm clear-headed, coked-up or not!'

Mike was taken aback; Willie never got shirty, not with him anyway.

Zara sensed the tension and put up her hand.

'Right, listen up. For now, we need to get the kids away, and when I say away, I mean out of the country.' Her father always sent her away when things got too hot. 'What about Poppy and Brooke, Lance?'

He nodded. 'Well, I think you're right. Arty and Liam seem to have sparked up a friendship with my girls, so I'd feel better if they all stayed together.'

With Ricky on his mind, Mike got up from his seat. 'I'm gonna check that Staffie's with Ricky. Lance, can you organize flights? Lou, you call the missus and arrange for your lot to go today.'

Zara knew only too well that until their families were safe, the men wouldn't be able to get down to serious business. She had to take control and make decisions but what could she really plan? It had taken the police force, the special operations team, and the toughest criminals to hunt the man down, and it was more by luck than good judgement that she'd managed to suss out who he was. He was, after all, right under her nose. Now he was missing, and she knew deep down that it would take more than their combined skills to find the fucker again. Also very worrying was who had been watching them. If it was Barak's men, or even Barak himself, she would sacrifice her own life if it meant she could metaphorically get her hands on him and kill him.

She stared off into the garden as the men made the requisite calls. Her mind was now on how she would hunt down Torvic.

Once they regrouped, Zara tried to temper everyone's anxieties. They needed to stay dispassionate.

'Right, we don't know a lot, except for the fact that if we were being watched, and I suspect we were, then it was by either Torvic's men or this Barak guy. And, more importantly, they couldn't have had the force to intervene or they would've done so. They wouldn't know that we would hold Torvic hostage, would they? Not even I knew that at the time until Torvic told us he was working for Barak. So, that much we do know.'

Neil nodded. 'Look, we're all safe for the moment, we're all here and accounted for, so I reckon you're right. They didn't have the manpower to take over last night.'

Zara suddenly went white. 'Shit! Joshua! I haven't called him.'

She quickly pulled out her phone and made the call; yet it went straight to voicemail. Her mouth felt dry. Her cousin had been the first one to leave last night. She tried again but there was still no answer. Then she scrolled down to find his landline number. His wife would know if he had got home safely or not. Zara felt sick and filled with guilt because Joshua was only called in to help her. He didn't live her way of life anymore. He was a sweet, gentle man who now lived for his children.

The phone rang and rang until, finally, Bella answered in a flustered voice. 'Hello, Josh?'

'No, Bella, it's me, Zara. I take it Josh hasn't arrived home?'

There was a long pause. 'Er, no, Zara, I was hoping he was still with you. I've waited up most of the night, but I've heard nothing. His phone just goes to voicemail. Oh my God, Zara, do you think he's okay?'

The terrifying thought drained the blood from Zara's face. She swallowed hard before she was able to speak. 'I'm sure he's fine,' she lied. 'Listen, don't worry. He had a few errands. I was just calling to see if he'd finished, that's all.' She hoped she sounded convincing.

'Okay, Zara. Please tell him to call me, once you hear from him. I'm so concerned because he always answers his phone.'

'Oh, it's probably run out of battery.'

'Maybe,' came the deflated voice.

'I'll call, Bella. Goodbye.'

The men all stared open-mouthed, waiting for some explanation.

'Josh didn't go home, and he ain't the type to go off without telling Bella. They've got him. I'm fucking sure, but if they …'

Her anger was rising, and she could feel her heart beating relentlessly. The notion that her sweet cousin was being tortured or mercilessly killed at the hands of Torvic was hard to bear.

'I swear to God, I'll shred every fucking piece of skin from the man's bones if he …'

Mike gave her hand a squeeze. 'Hey, listen, we don't know what's gone on yet. Please, Zara, babe …'

Not wanting to crumple, Zara stiffened. 'I'm fine, Mike. I think we need to establish first whether it was Barak or just some of Torvic's druggies in his firm. Once the kids are out of the country, we need to check out all the places from where that shit drug Flakka was sold. Let's find out what's going on.'

She looked at Neil. 'Look, no disrespect, but I want you to go back to Ireland with Shamus. Torvic will want to pick us off, one by one. I need you away …' She tried to find the right words that wouldn't insult him.

'No!' he said, sharply, before lowering his tone. 'I'm your equal business partner, so this fight is just as much mine. Shamus and I will check out your restaurants. Torvic and his gang of druggies may not start with the families. He could try to destroy your businesses first.'

Zara nodded. She knew he had a valid point, which made her realize that her knowledge of Torvic's sick acts probably only scratched the surface.

'Fine, but never alone.' She shot a look at Shamus, who nodded in agreement.

Chapter 2

Arty washed his face and combed his hair. He then searched Lance's bathroom for some hair gel. Liam stood in the doorway. 'Fuck me, mate, this is serious shit. Me ol' man sounded right worried.'

Arty looked at his reflection in the mirror once more and turned to face Liam. 'I dunno what I'm gonna do, Liam. I ain't even got a toothbrush, let alone a change of clothes. And Spain, I hate mainland Spain. They could've booked flights to Ibiza.'

Liam shook his head. 'Arty, mate, you can buy as much fairy fart smellies and Hugo Boss T-shirts as ya like, once we get there. We gotta take this seriously, right? I ain't never heard me dad talk like that before.'

Arty chewed the inside of his lip. 'All right, mate. How are the girls doing?'

A cheeky grin slithered its way across his face. 'Poppy's using me as a crutch, which I kinda like. I can't believe the bird likes me. I mean ...' He pushed Arty away from the mirror and pointed. 'Look at that face. Who the fuck would fancy that, eh?'

Arty put his arm around Liam. 'You ain't so bad, Liam, mate. Stop doubting yaself.'

Liam looked Arty up and down. 'Aw, come on, Art. You look like you've stepped outta an action-packed movie, but me, well, I've stepped outta a fucking horror film.'

Arty laughed. 'See, bro, I may have the looks, but you have the humour.'

Liam looked again at his long, bent nose and skinny, lanky body. 'Yeah, I guess I gotta have something, eh, 'cos that Poppy is one stunner and she likes me.'

Arty ruffled Liam's hair. 'Nothing to do with ya big dick, then?'

Liam giggled. 'Nah, she ain't met that yet. That's gonna be a bonus.'

* * *

Poppy stared down at her cornflakes. 'Brooke, it's all exciting and fun, but, in reality, this is so alien to us. What the hell do we know about this way of life, and why is Lance so determined to keep us safe? He's not even really related to us.'

Brooke, her twin sister, reached across the table and grabbed her hand. 'You are the clever one. I thought you would have worked it out by now.'

Poppy looked up and frowned. 'Worked what out?'

Brooke moved a loose long blonde strand from her face. 'I think Lance is actually our real father.'

Poppy nearly choked on her cereal. 'That's absurd.'

'No, it's not. Listen. While you were in the hospital, and I was here, Lance said don't go poking around. Well, I took a leaf out of your book and became the Secret Squirrel. I did have a good snoop and ...' She got up from her seat and wandered over to a cabinet.

'What are you doing?' asked Poppy.

Brooke removed an album from the top drawer. 'Look!' she said, returning to her seat and opening the first page. She pointed to a picture of a woman.

Poppy pulled the album closer, to get a better view, and suddenly gasped. 'Who the hell is that? Oh, my word, she looks just like us. I mean, she could be our mother. Let's face it, we look nothing like our mother, do we? And we certainly look nothing like Alastair.'

'No, exactly. I looked at the other photos, and there are some with Lance and her. I think she's his sister, which means that we could be his family.'

Poppy leaned back on her chair. 'Oh, I don't know. Maybe it's wishful thinking. Perhaps we are just scrabbling around for answers. I mean, our mother is hardly the motherly type, and as for Alastair, he isn't really the ideal parent, and both you and I came to the same conclusion. So perhaps we are purely fantasizing.'

Brooke was adamant. 'No, Poppy, of course it's possible. Think about it. Kendall was only a year old when we were born. Kendall was Lance's daughter, although Mother did insist we all have the same surname. So who's to say we weren't his as well. Anyway, when he comes home, I am going to ask him outright ...'

Poppy sighed. 'Brooke, stop a minute. Do you really want Lance to be our father? I mean, what difference will it make now? We are grown women.'

'He came into the bedroom last night and must have

assumed we were asleep. He removed my glasses and put them on the side. I would quite like to have a real father who cares, even when I'm fifty years old. It would be kind of nice, don't you think?'

Poppy looked at her twin sister's sweet, childlike expression and felt sorry for her. The poor girl had been to hell and back. The rape must have been horrendous, so she could see why Brooke would want a strong man to make her feel safe and loved.

'Yes, Brooke, you're right. But I think, from the sound of things, we have more pressing issues, like understanding why we need to leave the bloody *country*. Lance has gone to the house to collect our passports. It's all happening rather too fast for me to get my head around it all.'

Brooke placed the album back inside the drawer and joined her sister. 'We will have Arty and Liam with us.'

Poppy smiled. 'I guess that's a bonus, then.'

By the time Lance arrived back home, he looked worried and had no time for any girlie dramas. He pushed the door open and marched into the dining room, ready to act like a sergeant major and kickstart the girls into gear.

'Right, this is what's going to happen. Firstly—'

Brooke stopped him in his tracks. She rose from her chair and stood in front of him, with her hands up, signifying that she had something to say.

He tilted his head and took a breath. Poppy noticed how his stern features softened as soon as Brooke was in his face. It was at that moment she wondered if Brooke was right about them being related.

'Lance, may I ask you something very personal?' said Brooke, in her sweetest voice.

Lance appeared to blush slightly, and a gentle smile crept across his face. 'Um, like what?'

The huge serious-minded man seemed to have shifted personalities, which made Poppy want to laugh.

Brooke stepped back. 'I know you said not to be nosey, but I did find an album …' She paused, waiting for a reaction. *Either he will go ballistic or remain with that soft expression*, she thought.

Luckily for her, he chose the latter option. She took a deep breath, glanced back at her sister, and then asked outright, 'Lance, are you our father?'

Poppy looked down, embarrassed, wishing the floor would swallow her up.

However, Brooke stared directly into his eyes. It was most unlike her. She was the shy one – normally.

His huge, broad shoulders relaxed, and he took a seat at the table. 'Only a DNA can confirm it either way.'

'I can sense a "but" in there, Lance,' said Brooke, eager for him to continue, as she too sat down at the table.

He looked from one girl to the other. 'You could be. I believe your mother lied about your due dates, and you both look so much like my sister. She had the same eyes, and I've no need to tell you that, if you've been looking through the album.'

Brooke looked at Poppy's gaping mouth and grasped her sister's hand. This was so unbelievable.

'So, what will all this mean, Lance? I mean, like, between us?'

Lance unexpectedly grabbed her hand. 'I don't know, Brooke, but what I do know is this. I lost Kendall, although she actually wasn't my own flesh and blood. I discovered that eventually. But I loved her all the same. I hate to say this, but your mother wasn't as sweet and innocent as she made out. And, by the way, I heard she's been arrested for running you down, Poppy. Nevertheless, I need you two as far away as possible because something pretty serious has happened. I don't want you both in the way. Luckily, I managed to find your passports.'

Brooke knew he had changed the subject deliberately, but like a dog with a bone, she pressed him again. 'Lance, please, before we go, what do you want to do? I mean, a DNA or ...?'

Lance smiled and shook his head. 'The truth is ...'

Poppy suddenly noticed his little finger was bent. Her heart raced as she looked at her own and then at Brooke's. They all had the same condition. Without rationalizing it first, she blurted out, 'Lance, you *are* our father. I know that now for a fact.'

Lance frowned. 'How?'

Poppy slid her trembling hand across the table and tapped his crooked finger. 'Look! We have the same condition. It's hereditary, so I think we can safely say that you're our father.'

Brooke was suddenly beaming with excitement. 'Oh my God, you're our dad, our real dad, then!'

Totally out of the blue, Brooke leaped from her seat and flung her arms around his neck. 'I knew it, I just knew it.' Her excitement brought tears to her eyes.

It suddenly hit Lance that it was one thing saying they were his daughters, but it was quite another dealing with the emotion and now the responsibility. However, he was unexpectedly gripped by a warm feeling – a new sensation. His years of combat had made him cold and heartless, but the look on his girls' faces stirred another emotion.

Out of character, he turned to Poppy and held out his arms for her to do the same. She hesitated at first, but once those huge arms pulled her into his chest, she also felt a great comfort.

The revelations and reactions from the trio were halted as Arty and Liam entered the room. Arty looked a little uncomfortable, almost sheepish, since Lance was such a big, stern man, and his expression gave nothing away.

'My dad called. I think we're going to Spain … all of us.'

Lance straightened up and nodded. 'Yeah, that's right. We just need you guys to be away until we get something sorted out. I know, Arty, that it's not your responsibility to look out for my girls but …'

'Lance, we will anyway, take my word. We'll look after them.'

Liam pushed his way into the room. 'Yeah, mate, we'll take care of 'em.' Then he looked over at Poppy and winked.

Lance rolled his eyes. 'Christ, you're so much like your father, Liam. What I mean is, make sure no harm comes to them.'

Liam was nodding as if his head would fall off. 'I know what you mean, Lance. But I ain't what you think. I wouldn't take advantage, would I, Arty? I ain't like that.'

'He's right, Lance. We've been brought up to be respectful.'

'Sorry, lads. Yeah, I know your fathers, and I know if you're half the men they are, then my girls are in safe hands.'

A car horn sounded.

'Willie's here already. Right, lads, you go with him, and I'll take the girls. We'll meet you at the airport in an hour.'

Liam wasted no time in kissing Poppy on the forehead, and Arty kissed Brooke on the cheek.

Once they were out of sight, Lance turned to his daughters. 'So I guess they will look after you then? Do I detect more than a friendship going on?'

Poppy blushed. 'No, Lan … I mean, do we call you … I mean, can we call you Dad?'

Lance squeezed her shoulder. 'Baby, you can call me whatever you like, but Dad sounds good.'

She blushed again. 'Dad, we are just friends, for now. They are good men. I feel safe with them.'

He chuckled. 'A bit different, I guess, from your mother's friends.'

Brooke laughed. 'Worlds apart, Dad. But you know what? I hated Mother's way of life. It was so stilted and cold, and as for Alastair, well, he was like a passing shadow. I always wondered why he wasn't like my friends' fathers. Still, I am sure he won't miss us.'

Lance gave a fake smile. Inside, he was reliving the moment when the acid was poured over Alastair and the painful, ugly way in which he was killed. How was he going to explain what had happened to him?

'Come on. Let's get going, girls. We can't waste any more time.'

* * *

Willie drove more rationally than usual. He didn't want to attract any attention. Arriving at Arty's house, he instructed him to grab his passport and not fanny around. They would be given enough money to buy a wardrobe of clothes once they reached Spain. Arty did as he was told and was back in the car in record time.

As they approached his ex-wife's house, Willie was so intent on getting the lads to the airport that he wasn't aware of a black BMW parked across the street. Inside, a man wearing a dark hoodie was watching them.

The thought of the previous night's events still trickled through Willie's brain. If Torvic were to capture any one of the lads, there would be carnage. He had to keep his mind on track. He'd never before felt fear, and now it was beating him over the head and causing waves of nausea to engulf his body.

Liam was his mini-me, the be-all and end-all of his life. As he watched his son skip towards the car with his hair messily blowing in the wind, his heart ached. If only Liam had taken on his mother's looks instead of being cursed with his own features. Still, there was something very lovable about Liam, and the firm all had a soft spot for him.

The excitement had the lads chatting for England; however, Willie remained quiet. If the boys knew why they had to get away, he wondered if they would be so up for it. He decided he would discuss the seriousness of the present situation when they reached the airport. He just had to find the right words that would instil vigilance yet not frighten them. He wasn't the best with words; that was Lou Baker's job or Mike Regan's, for that matter. He tended to be a little reckless and never thought before he spoke, but he realized that today would be different. His worry was so intense that he'd even ditched his cocaine pouch. There would be no more drugs until this was over. He had to be clear-headed because too much was at stake for any flippancy.

Gatwick was busy, and a sudden downpour had everyone busily crossing the road as if a tsunami had hit them. The rumble of people and cars had Willie distracted, and so he was still unaware that the black BMW, which had been parked outside his home and had then been tailing them throughout the whole journey, was now parked two cars away from his own.

Arty and Liam were still babbling on about the two girls, oblivious to the concerned expression on Willie's face. Always the joker or the butt of jokes, Willie was silent. With very little time left before departure, Willie turned to Liam and Arty and shepherded them over to a quiet area. He needed to have a serious conversation with them about the events surrounding Ricky's injuries and the death of the twins' sister Kendall, now that Torvic had managed to escape from the secret room in the hangar. He knew what he was about to tell the boys wouldn't go down well. It didn't. The look on Liam's and Arty's faces spoke volumes.

Checking their passports were in order, they followed Willie into the departure entrance. Willie marched ahead, looking for Staffie and Ricky. He didn't bother with the long conveyor belt ride, wanting to be in front and not have to squeeze past people. Arty and Liam had to keep hurrying to catch up. Once they were by section C of the check-in counters, they spotted Ricky, and both rushed over to embrace their friend.

Ricky looked surprisingly well for someone who had been near to death after the horrendous beating he'd taken. He still looked a tad pale, but, other than that, his large, round, grey eyes were sparkling.

Liam hugged him. 'So, are we gonna have a blast, kiddo?'

Ricky gave him a weary smile. 'Good to see ya, Liam, but, I dunno. Dad sounded pretty serious. Do you know what's going on?'

Not wanting to alarm Ricky, Liam shook his head. 'Nah, only that we're off to Spain with Poppy and Brooke.'

Ricky had met Poppy in the hospital, after she'd been mown down by her mother. He frowned. 'Poppy *and* Brooke?' He looked at Arty.

'Yeah, mate. Brooke's Poppy's twin sister. It's a long story, but, anyway, they're coming with us.'

* * *

Staffie pulled Willie to one side, making sure they were out of earshot. 'I don't like this, Willie. I wish I'd never got involved.'

Willie ran his long, thin fingers through his hair. 'Well, we are, buddy, so let's just get on with it. 'Ave ya seen Lance yet?'

Staffie shook his head. 'Nah, I ain't, but I spoke with Terrence. He's made all the arrangements. The kids can stay at one of his villas. He'll have them picked up at the airport, and he's got some serious tools if needs must.'

Willie grinned. 'Nice one, 'cos if that Torvic turns up, they'll have to fucking shoot the cunt. He's like the man that never dies, and I don't like it, Staff. I ain't afraid to say it, but we're in over our fucking heads. That bastard is on the loose, and so that means he has one hell of an advantage.'

Willie suddenly spotted Lance and the girls. Poppy was being helped along by her father. Not only was her leg still badly bruised, but she needed an arm to lean on. 'Oh, shit me. Will they let her on the plane like that?'

Staffie sighed. 'Oh Christ, that's all we fucking well need.'

Willie hurried over and pulled Lance to one side while the lads wasted no time in fussing over the girls.

'Lance, mate, they won't let her on the plane without a doctor's note.'

Lance grinned. 'Well, my girls are one step ahead. Clever little things they are, they did a mock-up doctor's note on the phone, an e-mail or something. Anyway, don't worry, they'll be on that plane.'

Once they were ready to go through passport control, Staffie handed Arty one of his bank cards. 'Don't rinse the fucker.'

Arty laughed. 'Thanks, Pops, but ya know I will.'

Staffie looked his handsome son up and down. He was proud of his boy. He was a fearless lad with good looks, yet he had a heart of gold when it came down to it.

Willie was still on edge when he placed an arm around Liam's shoulders. 'Listen, my boy. Don't talk to anyone. You make sure at all times the security alarms are switched on in Terrence's villa, got me? If ya think anyone's watching ya, you call Terrence right away. And ya know me number. You look after yaself and call me every fucking day.'

Liam didn't like the look on his dad's face. He knew that this was probably the first time in his life that his father was genuinely shitting himself.

'Dad, don't worry. I'll be careful, I promise.'

'Good lad, and listen, boy. I love ya, yeah?'

Liam frowned. He knew his father loved him, but he'd never heard his father actually say those words.

'Hey, Dad, we'll be fine, and I love ya too, ya silly ol' git.'

Staffie was giving Arty strict instructions as to what to do if Torvic turned up. He described the man and then finished by saying, 'Don't fuck about, Arty. If the bastard turns up, kill him. We'll sort out the mess afterwards.'

Arty raised his brows. 'Fuck me, Dad! What? You want me to *actually* kill him?'

Staffie felt the tears in his eyes well up. 'I'd never tell you to kill anyone, but for your sake and theirs, you won't have a choice. The man is evil. I mean, really fucking evil.'

Arty stared into his father's eyes and knew then that whoever they were running from had the power to take out the firm.

'Dad, are you gonna be all right?'

Staffie laughed. 'Son, I'm always all right. I might be reaching me sell-by date but I ain't there yet.'

Poppy and Brooke hugged their father. 'It's so sad that we have only just met you and now we're going away,' said Brooke, teary-eyed.

Lance kissed her cheek. 'It's not forever, babe, and take this,' he said, as he pulled a fat wad of notes from his inside jacket pocket.

Poppy's eyes widened. She had never seen so much money. 'Oh, we couldn't possibly. That's so much.'

Lance then kissed Poppy's cheek, which made her blush. 'Poppy, spend it on what you like, but just make sure you two stay together and with the lads. Never go off on your own.'

Both girls nodded, each wanting to know more, but they knew that this was not the right time or place.

* * *

As the youngsters said their final goodbyes, the man in the dark hoodie watched from a distance and made a call. He turned his face away so that Willie couldn't see him. He whispered

37

down the phone, 'The flight leaves in one hour.' He reeled off the flight number and then ended the call. He took one last look to make sure they were definitely going to check in, and then, as he watched Arty hand over his passport, he scurried away. His job was done.

Chapter 3

Neil and Shamus left Zara alone in the office with Mike while they made coffee in the kitchen. It still fascinated Shamus as to how Zara could bear to be in this house. Putting aside the fact that it was her childhood home, it still became her prison for five years. His eyes shot to the floor on the far right, and he wondered if that was the actual entrance to the room downstairs where her brother held her captive. Just as Neil poured the last cup, Shamus had a thought.

Without helping Neil, he went back to the office. 'Zara, your brother. Wouldn't he know about Barak?'

Zara looked up and frowned. 'Ismail is a sap. He would know fuck all. Barak wouldn't trust him with any sort of significant information. I spent five years listening to him being ridiculed by Guy and his son Benjamin. Nah, he wouldn't know a thing.' She stared at Shamus, her mind going over something.

'What, Zara, what are yer thinking?' asked Shamus.

She turned to Mike. 'Guy and Benjamin are inside. They won't let me visit them, that's a dead cert. But there are other ways to get blood out of a stone.'

Mike grinned devilishly. 'Yeah, some of me oldest pals in Brixton Prison specialize in that. I'll make a call to Boomer.'

Zara looked back at Shamus and winked. 'One way or another, I'll need to find out what they're up to.'

Mike scrolled down his phone, looking for Boomer's number. The man was inside for a multitude of crimes and wasn't getting out anytime soon. He'd been inside for years and had everything he needed, including his own phone.

'Boomer, it's me, Mikey Regan. How ya doing, mate?'

The deep, gruff voice replied, 'Not as good as you, ya lucky fucker, getting out on parole.' He laughed. 'Really, mate, I'm as sweet as a nut, and you?'

Mike's face lit up. He liked Boomer. The nickname was given to him because when he re-enacted a fight, along with the air punches, he would also make the sounds. The loudest and most common one was 'Boom!'

'I need a favour, mate.'

'Well, spit it out, Mikey boy. I'm a very busy man, as ya know.'

Mike laughed. 'Guy Segal, the old Jew, and his son Benjamin. I need some information out of those bastards. I wanna know if Guy's brother Barak Segal is alive or dead, and what his plans are. I also need to know if the man is in the country.'

'Right, mate, I think I know who you mean, but tell me more.'

Mike went over the past, making sure that Boomer knew everything, including the circumstances leading to Benjamin Segal cutting off Zara's hand and how he and Guy had kept her a prisoner for five years.

'So, are ya up for it, Boomer?'

'For sure. No worries, lad. I'll have that info for ya. Call me in a couple of hours. I don't wanna waste me minutes. Oh, and do us a favour, will ya? Me ol' girl needs some dosh. Could ya whack her over a couple of hundred?'

'I'll pop over five grand. How's that suit, bud?'

The thick, gruff voice seemed to soften, and Mike detected an emotional tone. 'Aah, Mikey, you are a real gent, ya know that? Call me later and give my regards to ya father. The man saw me missus all right for me. He's a good 'un is ol' Arthur.'

'Cheers, Boomer. I'll bell ya later. Watch yaself.'

* * *

Trenton Smith leaned against the metal doorframe, rolling his last lot of tobacco. 'All right, Boomer? Any chance of a baccy loan? I'm clean out, mate,' he asked, as he peered into Boomer's cell.

Boomer grinned and nodded. Trenton knew then that there was something evil on the man's mind. He straightened up, and for a second, he wished he hadn't asked. Boomer was a man in his sixties but had more standing in prison than anyone else. He ran the wing, had the screws eating out of his hand, and was the only man who could sleep without his door wedged tight. Any drugs – even tobacco or hooch – going around the prison were generally dealt with through Boomer. Anyone looking at the two of them would never have thought that little Boomer was more reckless and tougher than Trenton. However, as much as Trenton was a tall, muscular man, with quick movements, no one was as fast as Boomer.

'Go on, Boomer, let's 'ave it, then. What ya got on ya mind?'

Boomer stood up and beckoned Trenton in. 'Close the door.'

41

As Trenton did as he was told, Boomer offered him a seat on the bunk.

'There are two geezers in here, Benjamin Segal and his ol' man Guy Segal. Two Jewish men. I need information from them. They may squeal like pigs, or they may need a little coaxing.'

Trenton nodded. 'I know who you mean. That Benjamin is the fat, ugly ginger fella that follows his ol' man around like a lost lamb.'

'Yeah, that's him. So, are you up for getting me what I want?' asked Boomer, with a raised eyebrow.

Trenton took a deep breath. 'Got any puff to go with that baccy?'

'Crafty fucker, you. Yeah, go on, then.' Boomer laughed as he pulled two pouches from under his mattress. 'Take them. And listen. Those Segals are cruel bastards. They cut off the hand of Mikey Regan's bird and kept her captive for five years.'

Trenton's eyes nearly popped out of his head. 'You're joking, ain't ya?'

Boomer dramatically shook his head. 'Nope. So listen. This mission is for Mike Regan. He wants a few answers out of those two, and if it means getting nasty, and you feel the need to put the pressure on them, you'll 'ave Mikey's blessing. They're gonna end up dead anyway.'

Trenton moved his long fringe away from his eyes, and then he rubbed his beard. 'The Hells Angels' way it is, then.'

'Good lad. Now then, after exercise, I'll give you instructions, and you'll need to memorize the questions because that's the most important bit. We want answers before they end up in the prison mortuary.'

Trenton smirked, showing his black teeth. 'I'm surprised they made it to prison, with Mike Regan gunning for them.'

'Don't you worry about that. His bird wanted them locked up. Ya know, so they could have a taste of what she went through, but now she and Mikey want them done away with.'

* * *

Guy and Benjamin had a cell next door to each other. They'd managed to pay a screw to organize it, yet they couldn't afford the amount it would cost for protection. Both were quiet and had tried to keep themselves to themselves. Outside prison, they had power through their wealth and influence, mainly in the Jewish community, but inside Brixton Prison they were sitting ducks.

Every day they worried that the Regans, or Zara Ezra, for that matter, had paid someone off to do away with them. In fact, Guy strongly believed his days were numbered and it led to him coming out in a permanent rash. Benjamin, as big as he was, was really just a fat pussy. He only had clout on the outside because he had men behind him. Those same men ran a mile to avoid the looming trouble when he and his father got nicked. They were all well aware of the Regans' and Zara Ezra's reputations and were shit-scared of any repercussions.

After exercise was over, Trenton and his two sidekicks, brothers Wasp and Zane King, met up on the landing. Each brother had a glass shard tightly bound to a stick.

'Tooled up?' asked Trenton.

Wasp, a small, chubby, bearded man, with only one tooth in his head, nodded and looked down at his hand. 'Yep, I ain't

43

used this in a while, but she's still as sharp as the day I made her.'

Trenton then looked at Zane. 'And you?'

Zane didn't answer. He just nodded and chewed on his gum.

As they made their way along the landing, a senior officer gave them the once-over. He didn't like to see the three characters together. They were devious, and, worse, dangerous. Yet, as he was spying Trenton, Boomer was clocking him, and he instantly called out, 'Oi, Gov, can I have a word?'

Senior Officer Gladding recognized the deep growl coming out of Boomer's mouth and spun around. He liked the wing to run smoothly. Any hiccups from Boomer, and the inmates would all be on lockdown, and then the nightmares would begin. 'All right, Kitson?'

Boomer leaned against the wall and waited for Gladding to approach; he wanted him distracted.

'I've got this bit o' skirt coming up on a visit. Any chance you could organize a family visit? Ya know, in one of those private family rooms?'

Gladding sighed and felt a little uncomfortable. He hated saying no to Kitson, but the lifers were only allowed one family visit per year, and he'd already had his quota. 'I'll see what I can do, but I can't promise, 'cos you've already had yours this year, and we don't want to draw attention. The number one governor is clamping down on special treatments and keeping a close eye.'

Boomer quickly peered over the officer's shoulder to see Trenton slip into Guy Segal's cell and Wasp and Zane slide into Benjamin's.

'Fuck me, I thought that would be easy, a man of your

power and status.' He gave his twisted grin and watched as the officer squirmed. 'Aw, all right, mate. Look, don't worry. I tell ya what. Can ya get me some of that hair gel, so that I can at least look the part when she turns up?'

At last, Gladding relaxed his shoulders. 'Yeah, sure, I can get some for you.'

He was about to walk away when Boomer stopped him. 'So, how's your son getting on with the new football team?' he asked, knowing that once Gladding started boasting about his son, he would talk forever. The question worked, and Gladding pushed back his shoulders with pride and gave Boomer a rundown on how brilliant his son was at scoring two goals for the new team. Inside, Boomer was laughing because Gladding's son was only eight years old and anyone listening would assume he was playing against Manchester United.

* * *

As Trenton entered the old man's cell, he quickly closed the door, causing Guy to jump and turn around. 'What the hell are you doing?' His voice sounded firm, yet it didn't suit his Wee Willie Winkie appearance.

Trenton held up his bare hands. 'Just a word, mate.'

Guy's thinning hair and long white beard were kept well groomed, and Trenton noticed that on closer inspection, the man was quite solidly built with a look that was pretty much daring.

'And what word would that be?' asked Guy, bitterly.

'Cor, you're cocky for an ol' dead man walking, ain't ya?'

Guy's jaw shot forward in a temper. 'Just ask your fucking questions and leave me in peace.'

Trenton stepped forward. 'Barak, your brother. What's he up to?'

Guy's frown deepened as he twisted his head. 'Barak's dead!'

'Fucking liar, he's in Poland. Now, I was polite, and I asked you nicely, but *now*, I won't be so polite, so what the fuck is Barak up to?'

Guy's face dramatically paled, and his eyes widened. 'I am telling you the truth. He's dead. I went to his fucking funeral.'

'Mikey Regan says you're one evil cunt. And your son's no better. He had his bird's hand chopped off. You're a right slimy bastard, so I don't believe ya, and no one cares what happens to you either fucking way!' Suddenly, he pulled his tool from his back pocket and held it up. At the same time, he showed his heavily stained teeth and chuckled. 'Now then, I think I'll let me blade ask the fucking questions.'

Guy backed away, his body trembling. 'I promise you, he's dead. I swear I was there when they lowered him into the grave. Please …'

Trenton was fast, and in one fluid movement, he slashed his jagged knife across Guy's face. Guy clutched the loose flaps of skin and was about to scream when Trenton grabbed him and threw him on the bed, plunging the weapon into his stomach. With his hand over Guy's mouth, he glared into his eyes. 'Now, you, ya 'orrible prick, will tell me where this brother of yours is and what he's up to, or you, pal, will fucking bleed to death.'

Guy could feel the dull pain and knew he was in trouble.

Without any help, it was true he would bleed out. He stared back, trying to think of what to say, but the fear of death was consuming him. He just couldn't put his thoughts into any logical order. Then he heard the muffled screams from next door. His son. They had got his son. His eyes filled with tears. It was over. He knew one day the Regans would have him and his son killed, but he didn't think it would have anything to do with his brother.

'Now, I'll remove my hand, and you're gonna tell me everything you know about Barak, and if I'm satisfied, then I'll press that emergency button. If not, I'll plunge you again. Got it?'

With beads of sweat covering his brows and a sickening feeling as though he was underwater, Guy could only nod.

Trenton pulled his hand away. 'Talk!'

The thick blood was covering his sweatshirt and pooling on the bed. Guy knew he didn't have long.

'Please, believe me. He really is dead. He was buried at Golders Green Jewish Cemetery … on Hoop Lane, two years ago … through old age.'

Trenton stared at the old man. He was obviously telling the truth. He then watched as the man took his last breath. He was dead. Trenton looked down at himself. Luckily, he didn't have blood on him. He cleaned the knife in the sink, washed his hands, and crept away. The landing was quiet. As he clocked Gladding still chatting to Boomer, he slipped into the next cell. Wasp and Zane had gone over the top.

'Lads, clean up and let's go.'

Zane was covered in blood and Wasp was standing with his tool dripping in claret. Benjamin was on the floor with so many puncture wounds, it looked as if the Apaches had used him for target practice.

'I hope you got what I wanted before ya killed him? What did he say?'

Wasp lisped through his toothless mouth. 'His uncle's dead … buried in London. He died a couple of years ago.'

As Zane ran the taps and cleaned himself, Wasp rifled through Benjamin's locker, stealing all his chocolate bars.

'No wonder the fucker was so fat. He must've spent all his canteen money on sweets. The dirty git stinks, so he ain't been spending it on smellies. Cor, and I thought those Jews were kinda pure. Ya know, religious an' all.'

'Come on, lads, let's go. The coast is clear. You, Zane, ditch ya sweatshirt. It's covered in claret.'

As they left the cell, Trenton took one last glance at what looked like a beached whale. The man was one ugly bastard in life, and he didn't look any better in death.

* * *

Mike took the call. 'Any news, mate?'

Zara stood up and waited anxiously while Neil and Shamus remained seated. She tried to gauge Mike's expression, but, as always, he was composed and just listened.

'Okay, thanks, mate. I owe ya one. And I'll have that five grand sent to your ol' lady tonight. Cheers. Stay safe.'

Mike ended the call and sighed. 'Well, they questioned Guy and Benjamin separately. Both said that Barak was dead. He died two years ago, and he's buried in Golders Green Jewish Cemetery.'

Zara gritted her teeth. 'They're lying. Did your men use force? I mean, did—'

Mike interrupted, slightly annoyed. 'Zara, of course they did. Jesus, they ain't gonna have a nice chat over a cup of tea, are they?' He took a deep breath and sighed. 'They knifed 'em. In fact, both of 'em are now brown bread.'

Neil grinned. 'Fecking good job as well.' He turned to Zara. 'Listen. You knew them better than us. Would they take information to the grave or would they sing like canaries?'

Zara nodded. 'Yeah, they were weak men, especially Benjamin. He would grass anyone to save his own arse.' She shuddered when she pictured him. It was that satisfied grin on the man's face as her hand was severed from her wrist. She contemplated whether she would ever get over that moment.

It was Mike who recognized her troubled expression. He followed her eyes as she looked down at her prosthetic hand. In that second, he wanted to comfort her, but he wouldn't because this was business and she had to be in charge.

'Just to be sure, I want the cemetery checked out. Then, we'll know. But right now, we have to assume they were telling the truth, which means that someone else broke Torvic and Tiffany out of the hangar, and I, for one, am baffled,' said Zara.

Shamus slowly rocked back and forth on his chair; he was tired and worried. 'That Torvic has someone who has the guts to take us on, and by letting that bastard loose, he, whoever he is, has just got himself heavily involved. Who would have the balls?'

Zara picked up her phone and dialled her cousin's number, praying that he would answer. Yet, once again, it went over to answerphone. 'They have got Josh. I can feel it. He would never ignore my calls, ever.' She left the room, not wanting to show how upset she was.

Neil got up to follow, but Mike grabbed his arm. 'Leave her, mate. She needs a moment.'

Neil had worked with Zara for five years while Mike was inside. They had a bond like a brother and sister connection, and he didn't want Mike to think otherwise, so he stepped back. 'Yeah, mate, you're right.'

He paused. 'Mike, I love Zara, but not how you might think, yer know. She's like me sister, that's all.'

Mike patted Neil's shoulder. 'You don't have to explain it to me. I know you looked after my girl, and if there was anything between ya, it would 'ave happened when I was in the nick.' He laughed.

Neil lowered his head. 'Good. I've always wanted you to know that.'

'Some things don't need explaining,' replied Mike.

It was so apparent to Neil why Zara was in love with Mike. He was firm and projected a persona that commanded attention. Just his gravelly voice and intimidating glare made anyone want to listen. Yet with Zara, there was a slight softness when he spoke, and his eyes were shining when he looked at her. Neil would have wanted Zara for himself, but he knew there was only one man she'd ever loved and that was Mike Regan.

Zara came back into the room. 'I want to go to the hangar to see if there are any clues.'

Shamus shook his head. 'I checked. It was as clean as a whistle.'

'I'm sure you did, but I just want to go back. I know the hangar like the back of my hand. If anything is out of place, I'll know.'

Mike shrugged. 'It's your call, babe.'

Just as she was about to speak, her phone rang. It was Bella. Quickly, she took the call and held her breath.

'Zara, the hospital's just called.'

With the blood draining from her face, she asked, 'Is he hurt? Or ...'

'No, well, yeah, he is, but the stupid man didn't eat after he took his insulin, and I guess working late or whatever ... Anyway, he forgot, and so he went into a hypo and crashed the car. The doctor reckons he'll be okay, but he's got a few broken ribs, concussion, and no doubt the DVLA will take his licence away this time.'

Zara chuckled in relief. 'Thank God.'

'What do you mean, Zara? He's in bloody hospital!'

'Sorry, Bella. I just mean, thank God he's alive.'

'Well, yes, but, it's still not a laughing matter.'

Brought to task, Zara cleared her throat. 'No, sorry, it's not, but listen. Don't worry about him not being able to drive. I'll organize a driver for you.'

'Zara, please, I'm begging you. Don't pull my Josh into your circle. I know what you're about, but your cousin is ... well, he's a gentle man. I ... we ... just want a normal life.'

Zara fully understood. 'Don't worry, I promise I won't pull him in again, rest assured. Now, listen. This is serious, Bella. I want you to take the kids and go on holiday, yeah? I'll make sure Josh is okay.'

Zara sensed the hesitation in Bella's voice.

'You mean it, don't you, Zara? This isn't a request, is it?'

'No, love, it's not. Just go today. I'll transfer money into your account, but just go now.'

Bella's voice sounded sincere. 'I will, but promise me you'll make sure my husband's safe?'

'He's my only remaining flesh and blood who I can call family, so you have my word.'

Chapter 4

Poppy and Brooke sat on either side of Liam on the plane, while Arty sat with Ricky. Arty didn't want Ricky to feel like a gooseberry. 'D'ya reckon you're gonna be all right? I mean, there ain't no chance of your brain going funny again, is there? 'Cos ya did give us a right royal fucking shock.'

Ricky crossed his eyes and put on a funny face, making Arty laugh.

'No, Art. They fixed me up. I'm as right as rain. I just can't take another blow to the head for a while. I've got a plate behind my ear, and they sorted out all that water on me brain, so I'm ready for the sun.'

Arty stared at the last of Ricky's yellow bruises and wondered how he could be so upbeat. He'd been in a chemical coma after the vicious beating. The doctors were reluctant to say he would survive, and yet, here he was, with his round girlie eyes and his prominent dimples, smiling back at him.

'You're a lot like your father, ya know that?'

Ricky beamed. 'So everyone says, and if I am, then I'll be proud of meself. I'm so glad I found me dad and you guys. It's like I was never away all those years. I've still got a lot to learn, though.'

Arty guessed what he was on about. 'Ricky, you just take your time and let me and Liam take the lead. Any grief, and you get behind us, yeah? Because, right now, something's going on. I've never heard me ol' man so shit-scared for me. Neither has Liam for that matter. His dad's face was so serious. The situation is tense but it's nothing me and Liam can't handle.'

Ricky nodded and looked across at Liam. Chuckling away, he said, 'He's in his element, ain't he?'

Arty laughed along. 'Like a pig in shit. That Poppy really likes him, ya know. I think she's a bit of a geek, and they say opposites attract.'

Ricky thought about Zara and his father. 'Yeah, that's supposed to be the way, but I worry that Zara and me dad are too alike.'

'You really like Zara, don't ya?'

Ricky blushed. 'Yeah, I do. She's ace, ya know.' He held up his wrist. 'She gave me this gold bracelet with BRAVE engraved on it ... I wish she'd been my mum, instead of Jackie.'

Arty noticed a sadness creeping over Ricky's face. 'Was she really as wicked as they said she was?'

With a deep breath, Ricky replied, 'The truth is, Arty, me ol' man only knows part of it. If he knew the full extent of what she put me through, he would kill her. Not that her death would be on me conscience, but the risk of me dad going back to prison would. I fucking hate her.'

Arty didn't press for details. He could tell that whatever it was that Ricky had endured it had been cruel at the very least, and the expression on Ricky's face suddenly changed from a soft, sweet, schoolboy look to one of Mike Regan's in a rage. Those piercing pearl-grey eyes dulled, and his brows knitted together.

'Well, let's try and treat this as a bit of a break. We'll soak up the rays, have a dip in the pool, and shop.'

Ricky laughed. 'Shopping? What are ya? A girl?'

Arty screwed his nose up. 'And so, Ricky, me ol' son, are you gonna wash out ya smalls every day, then?'

Ricky rolled his eyes. 'Point taken, mate.'

As the plane changed its course, the boys knew that they were not far away from their destination. Arty glanced over at his friend and realized what the problem was. Ricky was worried about the impending descent and the effect this would have on his ears. Ricky had discussed this with Arty on the flight, telling him that as they descended there would be a corresponding change in air pressure that would send sharp pains around his tender scars where the doctors had operated on his brain to stop the bleeds.

By one o'clock in the afternoon, the aircraft began its descent. Arty panicked as he watched the agony on Ricky's face. He pulled him close and covered his friend's hands with his own, trying to help with the pain. Ricky was sweating profusely, and Arty was attempting to comfort him.

'Suck on these sweets.' He handed Ricky a few sherbet lemons. 'See, I said we'd take care of you. Fuck me, I should 'ave been a nurse.'

Wasting no time, Ricky began sucking on the sweets until he felt his ears pop and the pressure begin to release. The colour then came back to his cheeks. 'Christ, I thought for a minute I was going to have another haemorrhage.'

'Don't say that. Jesus, you had me sweating for a minute.'

As the plane landed, Arty looked for his passport and phone in among the safety leaflets and magazines stuffed in the pouch of the seat in front of him. Then his attention was diverted to two men roughly the same age as himself, who were making disparaging remarks regarding Liam and the two girls. At first, he thought he had misheard, until one of the cheeky bastards laughed.

'Cor, I bet he thought all his Christmases had come at once, sitting between two lookers.'

The other young man, now in on the joke, replied, 'No, mate. I bet the girls thought all their Halloweens had come at once.'

Arty looked over at Liam who must have just caught the end of their joke. Instead of looking ready for a punch-up, he actually appeared hurt. Clocking Liam's gutted expression instantly had Arty gunning for the opinionated bastards. He watched the passengers all shuffling, ready to get their bags together, and then he noticed Ricky's bottle of water still in the pouch. He smiled to himself, retrieved the full bottle, and unscrewed the lid. As the two men fiddled with the overhead lockers, Arty tapped one on the shoulder. 'Is that my bag, mate?' he asked. As the guy turned to face him, he stared him straight in the eyes and poured the contents of the bottle down the front of his trousers. Arty stepped back. With a voice a little louder than necessary, he said, 'Er, mate, you should've used the toilets. A bit too old to piss yaself, ain't ya?'

The young man glared and then looked down at his light-coloured chinos. Sure enough, it did look like he'd wet himself. Then he spotted the bottle in Arty's hand. 'Why, you fucking shit!'

Ricky and Liam were now laughing very loudly, and they were joined by Poppy and Brooke. The furious man looked across at the group and decided it was best to keep his mouth shut.

Poppy leaned into Liam, feeling sorry for him, and kissed him on the cheek. 'Will you help me up, Liam?' she asked, in her sweetest voice.

Liam looked over at the angry man and grinned. ''Course I will, my babe.' Then he returned the kiss. Inside, he was elated. His pretty bird had gone out of her way to make a public show of affection for him and he felt a million dollars. Not many women would have done that: most would have edged away.

Brooke, however, was impressed with how Arty had managed the situation, and a sense of excitement ran through her. She wasn't used to men who could handle themselves. All the boys that she'd dated in the past were proper geeks and would run away from any confrontation.

As Liam helped Poppy, and Arty did likewise with Ricky, they made their way through the terminal. Once they were outside, Liam spotted Terrence.

Terrence, a tall man, dressed in beige linen trousers and a white casual shirt, was leaning against a Bentley stretch limo. He looked fit and well, with a tan that set off his white hair and blue eyes. In his late sixties now, Terrence had once worked for Arthur Regan, Mike and Eric's father. He was only a kid back then but soon got in with the firm and joined them on two heists that made him a mint. They called him Terrence The Skid because he could handle any vehicle and was their top getaway driver. He was fearless behind the wheel of a car and could easily outrun the police, having done it many a time. He wisely invested his money in property and prudently made friends with the local Spanish mayor. Now with two restaurants and a nightclub to his name, Terrence was going straight, except for the fact that he took a significant cut in any drugs that were sold on his premises.

As soon as he saw Arty and Liam, he pushed himself away from the car and walked over with his arms outstretched to hug the boys. Arty was first to embrace the man, followed by Liam, and then Terrence turned to look at Ricky. Arty knew that once Terrence clapped eyes on him, he would get emotional.

Ricky grinned as his vague memories of Terrence came flooding back like a film. Visions of Terrence teaching him to dive, when he was six years old, flashed through his mind.

'Fuck me, 'ave I missed you. Come 'ere and give ya Uncle Skid a hug.'

Ricky fell into his arms and allowed the man to hold him for more than the customary two seconds for a greeting embrace.

Arty and Liam smiled at each other as they both noticed the tears welling up.

'Look at ya! I would've recognized you anywhere. You're like ya grandfarver was back in the day. It's good to have you back, my boy.'

Ricky's cheeks glowed. 'And it's good to see you too, Uncle Skid.'

'Terrence, I need to get some clobber, mate. We didn't have time to pack,' said Arty, itching to get some new clothes.

'Arty, just get in the motor, will ya? We can't hang about, fella. I've been given strict instructions to get you to a safe villa. It's me new drum that not a single soul knows about, including me missus.'

Poppy and Brooke were now smiling. They both knew that

this was another world. Of course, they'd watched the gorgeous tough guy Vinnie Jones in *Lock, Stock and Two Smoking Barrels* – but that was pure theatre! The way this man and Ricky's dad and his friends spoke and acted, though, with their flash cars and their serious demeanour and urgency, was altogether a different ballgame. And it was cool.

The excitement of seeing Ricky again had caused Terrence to take his eye off the ball. He didn't notice the unsuspecting tatty car following them. Even as he weaved about along the winding roads into the mountains, he still didn't see the red Ford Focus that allowed other cars to get in front.

The Ford Focus followed the Bentley for about fifteen miles and still showed no signs of catching it before the limo shot up a private drive. The driver slowed down and glanced across to the right to see a gated entrance and the gates closing automatically. Retrieving a phone from the passenger seat, he took a snapshot before driving away.

'Now, lads. I've everything you need except a housekeeper, so I'm afraid you're gonna have to clean up ya own shit, yeah? The fridge is loaded with food, the pool's clean, and the bar's stocked. You two lovely ladies, you have the top floor. The windows 'ave shutters you can lock, and, lads, I've three hand-guns with your names on 'em. One other thing. I know gin is all the rage these days, so I've twenty different Vera Lynns, all ready for ya in the drinks cabinet. I can't say fairer than that!'

Poppy's and Brooke's eyes were on stalks. Vinnie Jones had nothing on Skid. Poppy loved his outfit. And, of course, she couldn't help but spot the gold Rolex and the mirrored sunglasses – *did all gangsters wear these?* she mused. Then she thought about what he had just said. *Handguns.*

Terrence spotted Poppy's reaction as he peered into the rear-view mirror. He could see she looked nervous, but he didn't know why. 'All right, back there, Poppy?'

The lads went quiet, waiting for her response.

'Er, what's the matter?' asked Terrence.

'Um, Poppy and Brooke, well they … Ya see, it's like this, Terrence …' Arty was at a loss for words. He didn't really know how to explain that the girls weren't from their world.

Ricky took over. 'Uncle Skid, the girls don't really know what's going on. It was only a few days ago that they were at uni. Their muvver's an MP. It's kinda complicated.'

Terrence stopped the car directly outside the impressive-looking villa. He twisted himself around to face the look of shock on both the girls' faces. 'Jesus. Listen, girls. All I can say is, you'll need to learn fast. Uni students, eh? Well, if ya both have brains, the lads'll 'ave to teach ya stuff that you ain't ever had to learn before.'

Poppy then smiled and nodded. 'Look, we'll be okay, I am sure.' She chuckled. 'Is there anywhere we can do some target practice? Mind you, I have to say, we have been clay pigeon shooting, and Brooke is first class, aren't you Brooke?'

Brooke beamed. 'Oh, yes. So, loading and handling a gun for a different sport isn't alien to me.'

Terrence almost roared with laughter at that remark, but he didn't want to embarrass who he now believed to be two very middle-class young girls … and pretty to boot. Instead, he allowed his smile to reach his eyes. 'Good on ya. Maybe you can teach Liam, then, 'cos you ain't a shit-hot shot, are ya, Liam? D'ya remember, you nearly shot me cat last year? Poor ol' Lucky ain't never been the same.'

Liam couldn't help laughing at that wisecrack, and he was joined by Arty and Ricky, who were doubled over, which instantly broke the worried tension.

They stepped out of the car and followed Terrence into the villa. Brooke marvelled at the inside. The entrance hall, which was wall-to-wall marble, led into a massive lounge, which boasted an enormous fireplace surrounded by sofas. Just off the lounge was a dining area with eight fashionable white leather chairs set around a long oak dining table. Although this was impressive, it was the huge bifold doors opening up to an amazing view of the mountains beyond that stunned the girls. Brooke had only seen something like this on TV while watching the *X Factor* contestants performing at one of the judge's houses.

Terrence led the way back to the entrance hall and into an enormous room leading off to the right. ''Ere's the kitchen. It's all stocked up. There's the cooker, and, well, you lot can suss out the rest.'

Poppy and Brooke were looking at each other in astonishment. They'd never been inside such a plush villa. They knew one chapter of their lives was over. The suffocation of living with their mother, Rebecca, and their so-called father, Alastair, they thought had come to an end. Now they were being drawn into a new world – a very different world – they really didn't know how they felt about it. It had all happened so quickly.

Brooke had been preoccupied, obsessed even, with her own problems. The rape incident had affected her very badly, and it had only been a few days ago that she'd agreed even to leave her bed, never mind the house.

Poppy, for her part, had been busy revising for end of term

exams, her life focused on herself. But something had made her think more about Brooke. They had both lost their stepsister, Kendall, and maybe it was for that reason they'd suddenly become close. The fact that their own mother had consistently lied to them regarding who their real father was only made them realize that they'd been living in a fake family. How their lives could have flipped on their heads in just a few days was mind-blowing. Meeting Ricky, for example, in the hospital, after her mother had mown her down in a hit-and-run, only to discover he was Kendall's boyfriend, proved how strange life could be. And while Kendall had been killed in the horrific assault, he'd been beaten near to death.

Nevertheless, they were here now, and excitedly she bit her lip, thinking about Liam. In such a short time, he had become her rock.

Terrence came back through the lounge and unlocked the door to the outside. The warm air instantly hit them, a stark contrast to the air conditioning inside.

'Wow,' said Brooke, as she spied the infinity pool. 'That is beautiful.'

Arty and Liam looked at her and smiled. This was just the norm for them. They often spent their holidays with the firm in Spain, and Mikey's villa was in the same league, so they were used to no less.

Poppy and Brooke, though, had only ever been on package holidays where everyone fought for a sunlounger around the pool.

'Lads, come through to the bar. I need to get you geared up,' he said, as he looked at Poppy and Brooke, who were still soaking in the surroundings. 'I didn't get a chance to organize flak jackets, but I'll bring 'em tomorrow.'

The girls strolled back into the villa, and Ricky, ever the gentleman, decided he would escort them upstairs to their rooms.

Liam and Arty followed Terrence into the games room, which was more of a lads' room, comprising a full-size snooker table, a poker table, and a well-stocked bar, with a huge curved TV screen set up on the wall.

'Cor, Terrence, this is the mutt's nuts, mate.'

Terrence nodded. 'I had it put in for when your farvers come over for a break, so don't you youngsters go and have wild parties and fuck it up, will ya?'

Arty laughed. 'Terrence, have ya seen those two girls? The wildest they'll ever get up to is a glass of Pimm's over a game of Scrabble.'

'I see one has a bruised face. She looks as though she's been in a car crash!'

Liam exchanged glances with Arty. Terrence looked on, wondering if he was witnessing a private exchange, until Arty realized that his dad's mate hadn't been briefed on every event over in England.

Accordingly, he said, 'Unfortunately, you ain't far wrong, mate. Ricky met Poppy in hospital when he was recovering from the attack. Ya knew about that, right?'

Terrence looked at them both, all traces of humour now over. 'No, not that. Mike told me a lot about what's been goin' on, and, quite frankly, I just couldn't believe it at first. What he didn't mention, though, was the business with the girls. He just said that they were with you and would I treat them like I would you lads.'

'Well, Poppy and Brooke's muvver is the local MP.

She's a dodgy prat. Anyway, she ran Poppy down, probably by mistake, 'cos it was dark, but she didn't stop, so it was a fucking hit-and-run. I think she's now on remand, but I don't know if the girls know that.' Arty noticed Terrence's face, which was poised for more information.

'The twins, Brooke and Poppy, had a stepsister called Kendall. She was Lance Ryder's daughter, who was killed during the attack on Ricky,' said Arty, eager to fill in the missing details.

'About the twins. Who is their father?'

'Well, funny you should ask. They thought their ol' man was Alastair, the son of this Torvic bloke. But they only just found out their real dad is Lance Ryder.'

'Mike told me about this Alastair bloke. Do the girls know he's dead?' Terrence suddenly lowered his voice.

'No, but from what I can gather, they weren't that close to him. In fact, they weren't close to their muvver either. Kendall's dad, this Lance bloke, is looking out for them now,' said Liam, who had remained quiet up until this point.

'Fucking hell. There's a lot of coincidences,' said Terrence, with a deep frown.

'No, not really. The only fluke was Ricky dating Kendall. The blokes who attacked Kendall were after Ricky because he's Mike's son, but they killed Kendall. The sick twist is that not only did that bastard Alastair play a hand in killing his own stepdaughter but he fucking raped her first,' said Liam.

'The dirty fucker! Right, I'd better show you the gun collection.'

Terrence then walked over to the cabinet and unlocked it. As the door was opened, Arty grinned. 'Cor, fucking tasty, mate.'

Ricky appeared in the doorway and made his way over to see what they were looking at. 'I told the girls to check out the upstairs. Ya don't mind, Uncle Skid, do ya?'

'No, lad, not in the least. Right, now you're all here, those three guns there are loaded. I'm supposed to have them separate from the ammo, but I didn't see the point. Anyway, don't get drinking and start playing silly buggers, 'cos I don't wanna have to explain how the fuck any of ya got shot.'

Arty patted his shoulder. 'Terrence, in case you ain't noticed, we're all grown men now.'

Terrence raised his brow. 'Yeah, is that right? Well, you're still kiddies to me. Okay, in that drawer, there are two small handguns for the girls. Now, look on those walls. See those red buttons? If ya press them, make sure no one is near the windows or the doors, 'cos you may well lose a foot. The minute you press any of the panic buttons, those metal shutters come down, and trust me, they're fucking heavy and they hit the floor like shit off a shovel.'

As confident and self-assured as Arty was, he suddenly felt uncomfortable. 'Terrence, tell me, mate. How serious is this business back home? We were given a quick briefing at the airport, but, I mean all this.' He pointed to the gun cabinet. 'What's going on?'

Terrence leaned against the bar. 'Sit down, lads. Ya wanna brandy?'

Liam nodded. 'Yeah, sounds as though we're gonna need one.'

As soon as the tumblers were placed in the boys' hands, Terrence took a deep breath. 'Okay, there ain't been many times when Mikey Regan calls me in a right two and eight, so when he does, I pay attention. All you really need to know is that some geezer called Torvic, a dangerous fucker by all accounts, was held captive by Zara Ezra and Mikey, while they tried to get information out of him. Ya know, "the Mikey way". Anyway—'

'Hold it, Terrence. What do ya mean by "the Mikey way"?' interjected Ricky.

Liam put a hand on Ricky's shoulder. 'Oh, trust me, buddy, you'll live and learn, now you're part of the firm.'

As Ricky turned to face him, Liam winked. 'Our pops take no shit.'

Ricky thought back to the brief spell he'd spent in prison when he'd been reunited with his father, and how he had put the fear of God into people. 'Yeah, Liam, I ain't really surprised.'

Terrence was relieved that the boys' fathers hadn't kept them wrapped in cotton wool. Clearly, they were following in the footsteps of their fathers and grandfathers before them. But he didn't know what they knew and what they didn't. Although he and Mikey spoke on the phone occasionally, they never spoke about business. That was a no-no in their line of work. Fucking GCHQ and all that listening bollocks was apparently being extended from listening in on known espionage and terror related set-ups to any nefarious activity that was making serious money and denying the government of valuable revenue.

'Well, this Torvic bloke was set up by Zara and Mike. Torvic's sons got murdered, and his precious granddaughter was threatened. The deal was that Torvic would lead them to a man called Barak Segal in exchange for Torvic's granddaughter's life. Anyway, Zara and Mike had 'em locked up overnight only to find that the bastard and his granddaughter had escaped by the morning. This Torvic geezer is on the loose, and, apparently, from what Mikey told me, he's one sick fucker who will come for one or each of you, out of revenge.'

'Why did they kill the man's sons?'

Arty tutted. 'For fuck's sake, Ricky, they would've had their reasons, wouldn't they?'

'I know that, but I wanna know why.'

Terrence poured them all another drink. 'Because, Ricky, and Liam has just confirmed this, one of his sons was responsible for your beating ... and another thing,' he pointed his finger upwards to where the girls were, 'he was supposedly their father ... a bloke called Alastair. It's all a bit of a mess. Torvic was importing a drug called Flakka into the whole of South-East London and had gangs of druggies doing his dirty work. But the bastard was killing and hurting innocent people. His son, Alastair, also killed his own stepdaughter by forcing that Flakka shit down her throat before he raped—'

'Kendall?' interrupted Ricky, horrified by what his uncle was telling them.

Terrence had been gauging the effect his news was having on the lads and particularly on Ricky. 'Yeah, sorry, son. She was ya girlfriend, weren't she?'

Ricky looked away, tears forming, and he suddenly felt very light-headed. He took deep breaths, as suggested by his nurse Constance at the hospital, whenever he experienced a flashback where he was subjected to that savage beating in Kendall's flat. He got up from the bar stool and walked around in circles, processing this news, while Terrence, Arty, and Liam spoke quietly, trying to give Ricky some private time.

Terrence knew this would be difficult for Mikey's son. In truth, he hadn't wanted to get involved in all of this mess, but he owed Mikey big time for all the work the big man had given him, and, of course, for the rewards he was now blessed with. He needed to be there for the lad, and he would be.

Five minutes later, Ricky was back, sitting at the bar. His mind made up now, he said, 'Evil cunts! Ya best show me how to use one of these guns, because if this geezer shows his face, I'll blow the fucker's head off!'

Arty and Liam had never seen Ricky get angry. But then, Ricky was a relatively new face, as an adult, anyway.

Ricky had just started school when Jackie, his mother, had taken him from Mike's home, ostensibly to escape to Spain and to safety, following a war that had just taken place between the Regans and both the Harman and Segal families. Jackie, though, didn't go to Spain. She used all the money she had siphoned from Mike to buy a house in Cambridgeshire, intending to shack up with Scottie Harman. But her illicit involvement with one of the Harmans was a step too far for Mike. Knowing what Mike would do if he caught her, she scarpered off to Ireland, back to her roots, to live in a caravan. No one knew where Ricky was until fate decreed that both Ricky and Mike would be reunited in HMP Maidstone.

The handsome, cheeky chappie with an innocent smile had transcended into someone far more frightening. Now his look of rage was identical to Mike's. Even Terrence spotted it.

'Cor, you're your father's son all right. It's like watching Mikey all over again.'

'So, are you gonna show me how to fire that thing?'

Arty got up and pulled Ricky away. 'Listen. They'll find this Torvic fella, so slow yaself down. Let's get settled in and then we can have a little target practice, but first, mate, you need to get rid of that anger, 'cos no one learned anything when their mind's on revenge.'

By the time Terrence had given them the complete rundown and left the villa, they were ready for the pool except they had no swimming gear, only their underwear. The situation was so bizarre to the girls that they were done with being so ladylike and self-conscious. The boys were in the pool in just their boxers, which was okay by them. Arty thought, though, that the girls might be a little embarrassed going into the pool wearing only a bra and knickers. But Poppy and Brooke didn't need asking twice: they stripped off and joined them in a flash.

Enjoying the attention, the girls played around in the infinity pool. Meanwhile, the lads still had the looming threat firmly on their minds and kept ever vigilant. And they had to be even more so now that Poppy and Brooke were with them because they had lived somewhat privileged and sheltered lives, and so they wouldn't really have a clue how serious this situation was. But their fathers had made it clear that if Torvic showed up, then there was to be no messing about: they were instructed to shoot to kill. It was the first time ever that they'd been told to kill anyone, so they weren't going to take any chances. It was the day they had to grow up – to step into their fathers' shoes and to take no prisoners.

Chapter 5

Once Mike had been informed that the boys were safe, he knew he would be able to relax a bit. Staffie and Willie continued to make calls, trying to track down Torvic and anyone linked to him. Shamus and Neil had their men covering the restaurants. They would probably be places that Torvic would likely go to find them. Mike, though, hoped his firm would be one step ahead.

By nightfall, there was no news on Torvic's or his granddaughter's whereabouts. There was damn all left to do but sleep. Zara and Mike returned to Mike's house where they tried to rest, but it proved to be an impossible task. Any noise caused them to sit bolt upright. Zara slept very little anyway: she was tossing and turning, thoughts of what she'd done to Torvic's sons firmly on her mind.

* * *

It was seven o'clock in the morning when Zara arrived at the hangar, which had now been the focus of two macabre episodes in the last decade or so: the demise of some of the Harman family, and, most recently, the deaths of Torvic's sons.

She shivered as her eyes fell on the two chairs taking centre stage in the secret back room. There, on the floor, lay the abandoned ropes that had been cut by the mystery person coming to the rescue of Torvic and his granddaughter. Bizarrely, everything else had been left untouched. Even the remote device remained on the worktop.

Shamus stood by her side, his jacket lapels turned up, shielding him from the cold breeze that encircled the large open area. He had his hands in his pockets, and his shoulders were slumped. 'See what I mean, Zara? It's as if they've just vanished. I don't like it one bit.'

Zara looked over at Mike who was wandering around the room. 'Someone must have been hiding back there in the bushes with a pair of binoculars and watching the whole fucking drama. All I can say is they couldn't have been strong-armed because they waited for us to leave before they came to set Torvic free. Which means one of two things: either he had already planned to have someone there that night, believing that I wouldn't kill him, or one of our own men went back. Me, I think he was one step ahead of us.'

Neil shook his head. 'I don't get it, Zara. How could he have been so cocksure you wouldn't kill him?'

Zara slowly and deliberately turned to face Neil. 'Because he's fucking clever, that's why. He threw me a line that I would go for, and, stupidly, I took the bait – hook, line, and sinker. He knew I needed information and putting out that Barak was the main supplier was a clever ploy on his part. He shrewdly guessed that name would have me determined for a meeting. He knew about the past; the bastard knows everything, including how to fucking play me. Jesus, how could I have been so gullible? Of course it's not Barak who supplied him with the drugs. He threw that in there to secure his own life. The man knows too much about me. How the hell he does is a mystery, but the fact is, he does. But I have to hand it to him. He employed the oldest trick in the book. Give your interrogator something that sounds convincing and they'll buy it. Well, it worked, didn't it?' She shook her head and sighed. 'Okay, now we know that Barak is not behind this, we'd better put out a few feelers and find out as much as we can about this Torvic bloke.'

She paused as she watched Mike's eyes focus on one of the kitchenette cabinets. Ignoring her, he squatted on his haunches and placed his cheek on the cold concrete floor.

'What are you doing, Mikey?'

Still ignoring her, he tried to stretch his arm under one of the units that was attached to the back wall. He groaned as he reached further. Then, suddenly, he was on his feet, holding a piece of paper. 'Zara, your hangar, as you once told Staffie, is always as clean as a surgeon's scalpel, so what's this?' He unfolded the tatty piece of paper as Neil, Zara, and Shamus hurried over to see for themselves. The note was partially printed and in the corner was part of an address. At first, they all looked dumbstruck: no one recognized it for a moment.

'It may have just blown in with the wind. The back room's been open to the elements,' said Shamus.

But then, Zara looked at Mike's face. He was staring as if what he was seeing meant something.

'Mike?'

He snapped out of his gaze and slowly turned to face her. 'I've seen this before, but … no, there must be some mistake. I, er …'

'Mike, spit it out! What's going on?' demanded Zara.

He scratched his head. 'This is mental. When Jackie was at mine, I tipped her bag out. She told me that on one of her court summonses there was an address of the Flakka supplier. It was Number Three, Sycamore Cottage. To me, this looks like the start of that address. And look at the corner of this paper. It has a reference number and serial numbers. That's an official letter, like a court summons.'

Zara stepped back and screwed her face up. 'Aw, come on, Mike. This has to be a coincidence. I mean, Jackie, your fucking ex-wife, in cahoots with Torvic? Give me a break. The bird's a tent short of a circus, as thick as pig shit, and twice as stupid. No way!'

As Mike stared at the paper, he tried to remember if it was the same one he'd read at his home at the time of finalizing the divorce with his wife.

'Zara, this is no coincidence. Who writes down addresses in pen these days? In fact, who uses a pen? Nah, this was in her bag, I'm telling ya.'

Stunned by the find, Zara paced the floor. She pulled a packet of cigarettes from her pocket, removed the cellophane with her teeth, and, after lighting up, she puffed away like a steam train.

'I'm going to fucking kill her,' Mike said. 'Doesn't the stupid bitch realize what she's done? My Ricky could be in fucking danger because of her. Right, I'm going to Essex, and I'm gonna burn her fucking caravan down, with the ugly prat in it!'

'No! Don't be so reckless. That piece of paper may not confirm she was the one who released Torvic and Tiffany. For all we know, he may have been in her company, and, in some way, that piece of paper ended up with him.'

Mike stood with his hands on his hips and gave her a defiant glare. 'Give over, Zara. It's more likely that he's given her a stash of money, and we all know she'll do anything for cash. I ain't gonna stand here and leave her be. I've had enough. She's been the fucking thorn in my side for years now. It ends today.'

'Mikey Regan, you might just find yourself back in the same position you were thirteen fucking years ago, with you inside and no help to anyone ...' She paused, allowing the words to filter. 'Listen. Torvic was one step ahead of the game, but we have something now. We have Jackie. We ain't going in like escaped maniacs, we're gonna plan this out and find a way to get to Torvic. Jackie can wait. There'll be plenty of time later to deal with her.'

Mike rolled his eyes and bit his lip. Zara was right, of course, so he had to control his urge to let rip.

* * *

As the Spanish sun dipped beneath the horizon and the cold crept in, Arty went inside. He decided to make a fire. It would give them all something to focus on and they could enjoy time snuggling up on the sumptuous sofas with the big screen on. It was essential, he reasoned, for them to keep their minds firmly on doing things. Otherwise, too much time spent on reflection would bring all their worries to the fore. Poppy and Brooke were fun to be around, the three lads were tight, and all five of them seemed to gel effortlessly.

The screeches and laughing simmered down as they slowly wandered inside. Poppy and Brooke were both huddled in the entrance hall, shivering inside their towels. Their eyes lit up when they spotted see-through bags of what looked like tracksuits, T-shirts, and jumpers. Arty was prodding the logs, stopping them from sliding off the grate.

'All right, girls. We should be warm pretty soon unless you want the heating on as well.'

Poppy looked tired. The pool was great for the recovery of her leg injury, but she still hadn't really had enough time to recuperate from her ordeal.

Brooke, however, was still lively and wandered over to the bags. 'Arty, are these for us?'

Arty was still kneeling on the floor, attending to the fire, but he looked over to see what Brooke was referring to. 'Oh, yeah. Terrence stopped by. He dropped off some clobber. He doesn't want us to leave the villa unless it's an emergency.'

Brooke was trying to see what exactly was in the bags; it wasn't every day she was given new clothes.

'Can I have a look? I need to get something warm and clean on.'

Poppy sat shivering close to the fire. 'Y-e-ss, me-e to-o.'

With the go-ahead, Brooke began opening the bags. To her delight, they were crammed with designer clothing, with authentic labels, no less. Two fleece-lined Nike tracksuits in pastel shades caught her eye and instantly she looked at the size. They were spot-on. 'Here, Poppy, this will warm you up. They're lovely, so soft, and, Poppy, they're Nike. Wow, I love them. Do you think we could keep them?' she asked excitedly.

Arty stood up and helped Brooke to carry the bags into the lounge. 'Of course, babe. I don't think they'll look much cop on Terrence.'

Brooke giggled and blushed, and then turned to her sister, who, by now, had blue lips and was covered in goose bumps. 'Hey, are you okay?'

Poppy nodded. 'I've just got too cold, I think. Maybe I over-did it a bit.'

Brooke quickly got her sister to her feet. 'Come into the other room, get out of those wet bits, and I'll help you get dressed. You will warm up soon enough.'

While the girls left to get changed in the games room, Liam and Ricky came into the lounge, still laughing. Both looked like drowned rats. 'Where are the girls?' asked Ricky, clearly concerned for them.

'Getting changed, I believe. Oh, yeah, there are tracksuits for you two. Terrence dropped them off. We ain't to leave the villa, apparently. He brought us some big steaks an' all, so we can have a right good feast up.' He stepped back away from the huge TV screen and fiddled with the remote. 'There we go, lads. A warm fire, a good film, and you, Liam, ya think ya some kinda naked chef, so you can cook us all dinner!'

Liam rubbed his hands together, beaming. 'Yep, ol' Gordon Ramsay has nothing on me.'

Ricky laughed and shook his head. He enjoyed Liam's sunny personality. He was always so upbeat and funny. In fact, he laughed at everything, including himself, sadly.

As they all sat around the fire, drinking beers, Liam, the joker, dressed in just an apron, came into the lounge hold-ing a frying pan. 'So, how d'ya like ya steaks?'

They all fell about laughing as he turned around to show his bare backside. Poppy winked and laughed along. 'If I could get to my feet quick enough, I think I'd slap that arse of yours.'

Her sudden change to a cockney accent made everyone roar, including Liam, who was loving the attention, especially from, as he saw her, the prettiest girl in Spain.

Ricky threw him a tracksuit. 'Get dressed, or the sight of your two cheeks will put me off me steak.'

Liam dodged the tracksuit as it flew past him and landed in the kitchen. Laughing away, he returned to cook the steaks.

Poppy had stopped shivering and was now curled up sipping her beer, while Arty flicked through the TV channels.

Ricky laid his head back and closed his eyes. With tiredness sweeping over him, perhaps he too had overdone the playtime in the pool.

Brooke chatted away to Arty about the best Marvel movie she'd watched, which impressed Arty because he had a liking for the same film.

After a few minutes, Arty called out to Liam, 'Oi, chef, are you fucking milking that cow or cooking it? I want mine rare, mate.' He chuckled, but there was only silence.

Suddenly, the room went quiet. Ricky opened his eyes and held his breath. Brooke looked at Poppy with tremendous fear on her face. Arty silently got up and put his finger to his mouth, telling the others to be quiet. He backed away from the lounge, hurried to the games room, and returned with a gun in his hand. 'Liam!'

Ricky was now on his feet and behind Arty as they crept towards the kitchen. As they reached the door, Arty cocked the gun and peered in, but the kitchen was empty. The frying pan was sizzling away, but the tracksuit was on the floor, and Liam was gone.

'What the fuck?'

The side door slammed shut. Arty ran across the marble floor and ripped the door open. Outside, there was no sign of movement, and the air was still, with no obvious sound whatsoever. And no lights could be seen. It was baffling. Liam had seemingly vanished into thin air.

'Liam!' screamed Arty.

Ricky ran back to the lounge to check the girls were still there. 'Liam's gone. Stay there. Don't move.'

Poppy grabbed Brooke's hands, and, instantly, they both held each other. This was so terrifying, like one of those slasher movies.

Ricky ran into the games room and pulled one of the shotguns from its case. He then dashed to the pool, where, immediately, the floodlights came on, lighting up the complete back area. 'Liam!' he screamed. But all he could hear was an echo of his own voice.

Arty ran from the side of the villa around to the back where Ricky was standing, now totally flummoxed.

'Christ, what if they've got him? I mean, how the fuck did it happen?' asked Arty, whose face was deathly white.

'Are the two cars still there? Maybe he left to go to the shop to get other stuff for dinner.'

Arty shook his head and peered at the innocent expression on Ricky's face. 'The cars are both there, and he wouldn't go out in just that fucking stupid apron. Ricky, someone's got to him. Oh, Jesus Christ, they've got him ...' He suddenly ripped at his hair and tears filled his eyes. 'Oh no, no, no!' he cried.

Ricky could feel his mate's pain as Arty slumped to the floor, banging his fist like a silverback gorilla.

'Wait, Arty. We don't know for sure. Come on back inside. Let's think.'

Arty allowed Ricky to pull him to his feet as he sniffed back a tear. 'Christ, Ricky, if they have him, it's my fault. I said he should cook dinner. Fuck. If only I was in the kitchen, not Liam.'

Ricky put his arm around Arty's shoulder. 'Listen, we need to think straight, right? Call his phone.'

Arty snapped out of his grief and worry and started to head back inside the villa. He looked at the girls, who had now come outside to see what was going on.

Poppy was as white as a sheet, too afraid to actually know the truth. Brooke could tell it was serious by the look in Arty's eyes. 'Someone's taken him, haven't they, Arty?'

Arty was too upset to reply. His deflated expression spoke volumes about what he felt inside. He shrugged his shoulders, avoiding her look of concern.

Ricky knew that Arty was going down the road of resignation and needed geeing up to get his act together. 'Arty, call his number, will ya?'

As soon as Arty dialled the number, a phone began ringing in the kitchen. Liam had gone. They all looked at each other as if an ominous entity had entered the room. 'He never went anywhere without his phone.'

'Call Terrence.'

Arty did as Ricky ordered, letting him take the lead. He was in too much of a state to focus properly.

'Terrence, Liam's gone. I mean, one minute he was cooking dinner, and then the next, he just vanished. The side door was open, the cars are still here. He ain't even got clothes on, and his phone's still on the side.'

There was silence as all three stared at Arty's expression,

praying that Terrence would have some answers, yet the pause was very long.

They couldn't hear what Terrence was saying, but they got the impression that whatever it was it had knocked the stuffing right out of him.

'Yeah, will do, mate,' was all Arty said before he finished the call. 'He's coming to get us now. He told us to close the shutters. He'll ring when he's outside.'

Poppy felt her breathing quicken. It was instantly noticed by Brooke. 'Pops, it's okay. Take deep breaths. Slowly does it,' she said, as she gripped Poppy's shoulders.

'Hey, is she having a panic attack? Because, to be honest, girls, we really need to pull ourselves together.'

Ricky's tone was gentle, but, nevertheless, the point was a good one. In a flash, he ran up the stairs and snapped into action, and within a few seconds, all the shutters were hitting the floor like guillotines. The only light in the lounge was coming from the fire and the TV.

Brooke decided she needed to join in because sitting around huddled in a terrified state wouldn't help them one bit. She turned on the lights and went into the kitchen to ensure the shutters were down. Then she noticed on the floor, just abutting the kitchen unit nearest the doorframe, there was a syringe.

'Arty, come here!' she yelled.

'What is it?' asked Arty, as he rushed into the kitchen, looking anxious.

She bent down and carefully held the syringe by her fingertips. She showed it to Arty. 'I think someone has taken Liam, unless Terrence is a drug user.'

Arty carefully took hold of the syringe and placed it on the granite worktop. He stared for a moment as Brooke looked at his expression of fear – pure fear. Visions of Liam being drugged and taken to a warehouse, naked, and strapped to a torture table, gave Arty a foul taste of bitterness in his mouth.

'Are you okay, Arty? What do you think this means?'

Arty wasn't about to divulge his inner terrors, and so, gently, he shook his head. 'This could mean anything, but, listen. Let's just stay put in the lounge and wait for Terrence.'

They didn't have to wait long before he called – he was outside.

By now, Ricky had similar thoughts to Arty, once he'd been told what was found in the kitchen; however, Ricky wasn't afraid. He was angry. This was a serious piss-take.

Terrence parked his car in between the two others. His men wasted no time in jumping out from their cars and scouring the perimeter. Terrence bundled the four youngsters into his Bentley and stood for a moment like a bodyguard. After all, as far as he was concerned, he had precious cargo to get to safety.

Once they were away from the villa, Terrence asked them to relay every bit of information before he would make that all-important call. He knew that it would turn Mike's firm entirely upside down.

And he also knew it would set off a chain of events that would probably lead to a devastating outcome.

* * *

Zara decided it was best if they all returned to her father's house. She couldn't devise a plan alone as she needed their input on how they should move forward.

Mike phoned Eric and told him to go to their parents' place and make sure they were ready to move out for a while. Mike knew what his father was like: it would take more than the threat of Torvic, the Russian, to have him running scared.

Eric reluctantly agreed to go, as he felt excluded from the decision-making, and he wasn't happy about that. As usual, he reasoned, big brother Mikey was playing the role of top dog while he – barely ten months younger, for Christ's sake – was the puppy once again. It was a fucking nightmare. He felt out of it, quite naturally, and it wasn't as if this was the first time either. However, he wasn't going down the road of another confrontation. This was serious business, and if he was being truthful, he really was best out of the way.

Sitting behind the desk, Zara looked at the men in front of her. They were all tired, and as much as she wanted to reel off a plan, in her mind, she had nothing that would ease their concerns or even get them motivated.

Mike's phone rang. It was a distraction that Zara welcomed.

'What? Go on. I wanna know everything,' said Mike brusquely to the caller, as the others remained silent.

Zara noticed right away that Mike not only looked deeply troubled, but his eyes were intently focused on Willie. Her skin became covered in goose bumps.

Suddenly, Willie clocked that out of all the people in the room, Mike was looking at him.

With wide, frightened eyes he jumped up. 'What the fuck's 'appened?'

Mike ended the call and stepped towards Willie, preparing for an embrace. Yet, Mike's sombre smile filled with grief and sorrow made Willie jump back.

'What, Mikey? What's 'appened? Just tell me, will ya!'

'Willie, mate, I'm so sorry …'

Willie's eyes darted around Mike's face. 'Nah, nah, not my boy, no way. He ain't part of this. Fuck me, he's …'

Mike leaned forward to reach out to Willie, to hold him before the man went nuts. But, to his surprise, Willie suddenly slammed his hand into Mike's shoulder.

'Get the fuck away from me! This ain't my war, or my boy's fight. It's yours, Mike, and …' He spun round and glared with spite at Zara. 'And yours!' He stared defiantly, looking Zara up and down. 'Ya see, don't ya? This is *your* fault! Why *my* boy, eh?'

'Willie, please,' said Mike, desperately trying to comfort or even calm a situation that could easily turn nasty. 'Look, we don't know what's 'appened yet.'

'Well, has he been shot or stabbed? What the fuck's going on? Tell me! Now!' he bellowed, as his eyes turned red with rage.

Stupidly, Zara thought that being a woman, she could intervene and somehow calm Willie down, but the moment she was a mere foot away, he viciously flung his arms about and knocked her prosthetic hand. The clanging sound made everyone jolt and prepare themselves for the backlash; either Zara would lose it or Mike would.

Willie's actions shook him into sanity. Instantly focused, he looked from Zara to Mike, expecting a nasty repercussion.

But Mike held his hand out, still intent on comforting Willie. He knew he was the only man in the room who would know precisely how Willie felt.

'Willie, don't assume he's dead. One minute he was in

the kitchen, preparing a meal for them all, and the next, he vanished. Someone has taken him, but …'

He looked at Zara and then back at Willie. 'But Terrence thinks he was drugged and taken away. Now, before you start jumping to conclusions, right, we don't know he's dead.'

Willie could hear Mike's words but they just wouldn't register. All he could see was his son being cruelly murdered.

'Get fucking real, Mike. Look what we did to that cunt Torvic. Jesus, it was sick.' He glared again at Zara. 'What you made him do to his own son, it was obscene. And you reckon the bastard won't do that to mine? What … are you lot fucking delusional?'

Zara felt physically sick because she knew no amount of talking would ever stop Willie from thinking the worst. After all, in his position, she'd feel exactly the same. 'I don't think it's Torvic's style—'

She didn't get to finish. Suddenly, Willie was in her face. 'Style? Style? What the fuck would you really know? 'Cos if you knew so much, he wouldn't have fucking escaped, would he? And he wouldn't now be torturing my boy!'

It was Lance who brought Willie back to thinking rationally. 'Look, let's not get ahead of ourselves. Torvic hasn't got your son because he couldn't have got to Spain and set this up all in a matter of hours. The kids were rushed out of the country. He would've had to second-guess everything. So, there's no way Torvic's involved. I don't believe it was him.'

Willie kicked the chair out of the way, ran his trembling hands through his hair, and then punched the wall. No one said a word as they watched the man collapse to his knees with cries that would set off a pack of wolves.

Mike hurried to his side and flung his arms around the man, holding him close. 'Come on, mate, try and stay with us. We all feel your pain. Ya know I do, what with all that happened to Ricky. You were all there for me, and we'll all be there for you too. We don't know what's happened yet, but I swear to God, we'll do everything to find out. And one more thing: there'll be fucking murders *when* we find the fuckers who have done this to one of our own.'

Willie's chest heaved in and out as the sobs choked the life out of him. But slowly, after he'd calmed down, those words of Mike's resonated with him. They were all family. Ever since their school days, it had been all for one and one for all. It had served them well in the past. He earnestly prayed it would do so now.

Zara could only watch on, helpless. This was turning into her worst nightmare.

* * *

It was early evening when Shelley parked outside her father's office. The rush-hour traffic was at its height, and she couldn't find a parking space for love nor money. In her frustration, she pulled into a reserved parking bay and climbed out of her car, slamming the door shut. The wind was fierce and almost knocked her sideways, forcing her to regain her composure.

Just as she was about to lock the door, a jumped-up traffic warden called after her, 'Sorry, but you can't park there!'

Raging, Shelley spun around to face him. 'Go fuck yaself!' she hollered back, to the disgust of some passers-by.

'Madam, those spaces are paid for and—'

'Aw, fuck off. It's my father's building and his parking slots, so mind ya own business.'

The traffic warden looked at the windscreen of her car and grinned. 'Well, that might be so, but you don't have a pass on show, so that means you can't park here.'

Shelley didn't have time to argue. She took a deep breath and was about to walk away, but the traffic warden wasn't having any of it.

'Madam, I said you can't park here. You'll have to move.'

Inhaling through her nose, she tried to hold in her anger, but she was on edge and had been for days.

'I said, go fuck yourself!'

Suddenly, the tall glass doors to the building opened and out stepped Glen Maitland, the security guard, a long-legged black man with a cold, expressionless face. He held up his hand. 'It's okay. She has a pass!'

'Not on the windscreen she hasn't, and—'

Before the traffic warden could finish, the security guard pulled a card from his pocket and waved it in front of the man's nose. 'Yes, she does!'

Glen turned and sneered at Shelley. 'He's waiting for you. Give me your keys.'

Shelley wondered if all of her father's staff hated her, but then her mind cast back to her son, and, instantly, she went into one of her couldn't-give-a-shit moods. She slapped the keys into Glen's hand and made her way into the building and took the lift to the top floor.

As usual, her father was dressed impeccably. Anyone who found themselves in this building facing him would only assume he was a successful financier. Underneath the sleek facade was a razor-sharp businessman, with a keen eye for illegal gains. She had admired him as a kid. Then, as a teenager, she'd understood why he was so well off and why he had men kissing his feet. His game had initially been counterfeit money. He'd set up factories all over the country. So good were his copies that it had caused mayhem back in the eighties, severely affecting the banking system. He knew when to call it a day, though, and by the time he was loaded, he reinvested some of the money into property. He had the local MPs and councillors in his back pocket and managed to secure run-down warehouses and disused factories, turning them into luxury apartments for the Russians to purchase as an investment.

Shelley paused for a moment, wondering what mood her father was in. He was seated and staring at a computer screen. She hated it when he didn't acknowledge her right away; it was one of his trademark management tricks to show those he allowed into his working space had to pay homage to him. It made her think that perhaps that was why she'd run into the arms of his enemy. The thought sickened her because her father was worth a fortune, and since she was the only child, she should eventually inherit the lot. But that wouldn't be the case now: he'd made that crystal clear.

'Any news, Dad?' she asked, in her softest tone.

'Yes, your brother-in-law will be assigning the house to you.' His wicked smirk etched its way across his face, and it turned her stomach. She knew what he'd done. It was another one of his euphemisms: Mack would have been tied up and forced to sign the paperwork.

'I meant, did you make arrangements for Lucas?'

Colin looked away from the computer and sighed. 'Yes!' he spat, as his skin tightened around his jaw. Shelley hated that look: she knew it was controlled anger.

Yet, right now, she wasn't concerned. 'Oh, Dad, thank you. Oh my God, I've been so worried. I feel like …'

'Shut it!' he yelled, which made her recoil. 'I ain't doing it for *you*. I'm doing it because it's what ya dear ol' mother would've wanted. You were right to fuck off with that bastard husband of yours, 'cos you two are cut from the same mouldy cloth. You're as useless as he is, and as for your son, he fucking got himself into this mess!'

'Dad, you would've done it for me when I was a teenager, wouldn't you?'

Colin stared straight through her. 'I've bailed your arse outta shit many a time. Having men beaten or buried, I did it to protect your name, when, really, you were nothing but a slut, using my reputation to swan around like you fucking owned the place. I paid your debts, I gave you everything, but you still went off with that bastard. See, that's where me and you are worlds apart. I know which side my bread's buttered. You've been brainwashed by your estranged husband for so long, you're not my girl anymore, you're still his.'

The pulse in her neck felt like a jackhammer, and she wondered if he was actually right. But then the vision of her son came into her head, and she didn't care what her father thought of her, as long as she got what she wanted.

'About Lucas. How long will it take, Dad?'

'It's happening tonight. And I'll tell you this much. This has cost me a fucking shitload of money, so once it's done and dusted, I don't ever want to see your face again. And when

Lucas is sorted, please don't think for one minute that by sending your son to butter me up, it will in any way change things. It won't. He's off limits, as you are. Have I made myself clear?'

'Dad, he's a lovely boy. You really should get to know him.'

The flash of anger in her father's face made her eyes widen.

'Listen to me, and fucking listen good. I don't want no fucking needy kid of yours knocking at my door! Got it?'

With a firm nod, Shelley got up to leave. 'Yeah sure, Dad. Message received. Is there anything I can do?'

He shook his head. 'No. I've everyone and everything in place. I don't want you interfering, or you'll fuck things up, and I ain't going to jail for you, so you stay well away. My private jet will be leaving tonight for Spain, with Lucas on it.'

'Oh shit! You're flying him out of the country, then?'

'Yeah, tonight, so keep away. I have my people on the case, and they know what they're doing. I'll have your ticket ready at the airport. You fly separately, though. Understood?'

'Yeah, sure, but why Spain?'

Colin flared his nostrils in a temper. 'Shelley, either you want my help, or you don't. If you have the right bloke, then he is in fucking Alicante. Your dipshit of a son is just lucky I have contacts in Spain to sort out this problem. Now shut up with the fucking questions and piss off.'

She had a million things to ask, but she knew it was her call to leave.

Colin watched as his daughter, dressed in her tight-fitting black tube dress and her short cream leather jacket, toddled out of his office like some Barbie doll on drugs.

He sighed and took out a small bottle of Scotch from his side drawer. It was hard to believe that his daughter, the former love of his life, was now like a looming dark shadow, gnawing away at his conscience. He'd planned to go completely straight and leave all his criminal days behind him, yet Shelley bursting once more into his life was sending him right back to the past where he'd done anything to get to the top. Now he was at his peak, he was annoyed that she'd put him in this position.

All he could do was to thank his lucky stars that he knew many people who owed him, and now he had to call in every single favour. He shuddered; pouring another drink, he gritted his back teeth.

* * *

Amanda Wells, Colin's personal assistant, had the door to her office partially open, hoping to earwig on his conversation with Shelley. She'd heard Colin on the phone the day before and knew that his daughter was expected around mid-morning. Knowing Colin's history with Shelley, Amanda felt uneasy that he was even entertaining his daughter. 'Gold-digger,' she mumbled, under her breath, as she heard the clip-clop of Shelley's stiletto shoes recede along the corridor.

* * *

As soon as Shelley stepped outside, where the blustery, cold wind whipped around her bare legs, she felt as though a sudden dark veil of guilt and sadness covered her mind. She did miss her father, if she was being honest with herself, and now there was just him alone, she wondered if he was happy. Would he have still been the same man if she'd not gone down the path she had? It was too late now though – or was it?

Once he met Lucas, he would see that the boy was just like him, his grandfather. Maybe Lucas was not as handsome, but he was tall and smart-looking, with the same chiselled face, except his nose was longer and his eyes were piercing blue. Yet she saw her father in him and hoped her father would too.

Chapter 6

Jackie sat nervously in her caravan as she watched Torvic pace the floor. He tutted and moved her belongings out of his way, using his forefinger and thumb as if he might catch some disease.

He growled, with his eyes glaring at her. 'I gave you enough money as security to get a decent car and follow the bitch and keep a lookout. Yet you fucking turn up in your shitty jeep with gaffer tape and an engine, which, in another twenty miles, would have given up the fucking ghost. Bloody hell, woman, how fucking stupid are you? The fumes blacked out the village. Talk about leaving a fucking trail. Ya nearly gassed half of Kent.'

With each sharp word, she blinked. 'Look, Mr Torvic, you didn't give me any time to get a decent motor. One minute, you were at my door, putting on the bleedin' charm, and the next, I was hiding in the fucking bushes with a bloody pair of binoculars watching ...' She paused and looked away, reliving the horrific scene. 'Well, let's just say, I didn't expect to be caught up ... in this shit.'

Her last words faltered as she recalled the moment Torvic poured that acid over the bloke's head. Her ex-husband, Mike, who she'd lived with over thirteen years ago, had a reputation, and that was no secret. But she'd never seen him in action, and as for Zara, she shuddered, because a while ago, she'd fronted the woman out and got swiped across the face with a blade for her trouble. Never in her wildest dreams would she have ever believed her life would've turned out in the way it had.

Nausea made her mouth fill with saliva. It was all very well in the past giving Mikey some verbal stick because she believed then, deep down, he wouldn't have hurt her. After all, she was the mother of his precious Ricky. Now, though, after what she'd witnessed in that hangar, she was having second thoughts. Equally, she was stuck in her poxy caravan with some nutter and his granddaughter, who was in and out of consciousness. She swallowed the rising puke and took a deep breath.

'Right, listen to me very carefully. I need to sort something out. This is the last place that Mike or that bitch Zara will think of coming to. So I need you to take care of Tiffany for an hour or so, and I *mean* take care of her. You'll get the rest of your money, all in good time, but, for now, guard that kid with your life!'

Jackie looked over at Tiffany who was slumped on the sofa. She leered at her in annoyance. *Kid?* Was he having a laugh or what? She was a woman. End of. She stared at Tiffany more intently, noticing the gold chain around her neck and the expensive-looking watch on her wrist. *Yes, those would keep her in Grey Goose for a couple of months*, she thought.

Torvic snatched her car keys, shook his head, and exited, without even closing the door behind him.

'Fucking pig,' she grumbled, under her breath. Then, she

94

turned back to Tiffany, who suddenly appeared to be coming round. Her eyes blinked, and she tried to sit up.

'Where am I?'

With flushed cheeks, Jackie excitedly jumped to her feet. 'Aah, it's all right, babe. Your grandfarver's gone to get some 'elp. He said to give you something.'

Tiffany's long dark hair was matted, and her usually pretty, made-up eyes were smudged as if she'd been on the piss all night.

Jackie pulled open the drawers, like a frantic burglar, until she found the box of sleeping tablets. Pouring four in the palm of her hand, she shoved them under Tiffany's nose.

'Take these. You'll feel so much better. Ya grandfarver said to take 'em. He'll be back soon.' Jackie tried to sound soft and motherly, but it really wasn't in her nature. Still, she would give it her best shot.

'Go on, babe. You've been through one 'ell of an ordeal. This'll take the edge off.'

She gave the tablets to Tiffany and went over to the rotten, dirty sink where she grabbed a glass that had congealed milk at the bottom, swirled it under the tap, and then filled it with fresh water.

Tiffany was still slightly wobbly and didn't notice the tiny milk particles floating on the top. She threw the tablets to the back of her throat, groggily took the glass, and swallowed the contents. The cold water seemed to help: it livened her up. Suddenly, her expression was different: cold and dark.

'Who the fuck are you?'

Jackie stepped back and frowned. 'Ya grandfarver asked for my help. He's just popped out.'

Tiffany had a teenager's attitude, but her level of violence was that of a grown mental maniac at times; it was a trait which made Torvic thoroughly proud.

'What am I doing in this shithole? Fucking 'ell, don't tell me that Pops has been banging a skank like you? Jesus!'

Seriously insulted, Jackie retorted, 'Oi, ya cheeky little cow. If it weren't for me, you would still be inside that room pissing in ya knickers.'

'Oh, shut up. Who d'ya think you are?'

'Me, love? More like who the fuck d'ya think *you* are! I rescued you, ya ungrateful bitch. I should've left you and ya grandfarver in the hands of Mike Regan and his lot.'

Jackie snatched the glass out of Tiffany's hand and threw it in the sink, mumbling under her breath, 'Ya fucking nasty cow.'

'But I don't get it. So who are you?' Tiffany persisted, thoroughly disgusted with her surroundings.

Jackie turned around to find the girl with her nose in the air and wiping her hands down her trousers.

Leaning against the sink, Jackie curled her lip. 'Ya Pops, or whatever the fuck he's called, asked for my help. Now, if you ain't happy sitting in my caravan, you can just as easily do one. There's the fucking door.'

They locked eyes, each sussing the other out, until a sudden wave of tiredness gripped Tiffany. The visions of last night avalanched through her mind. It had been like seeing her dad and uncle thrown into a shark tank with buckled bars while a great white circled before them, ruthlessly devouring its prey. The fight had been relentless, harsh, cold, and – yes – very one-sided. She felt sick but swallowed hard to control the feeling of nausea.

Tiffany's mind once again began to switch off as the shock was back with a vengeance, except, this time, it was laced with an overdose of the sleeping tablets that stopped her from fighting the state of unconsciousness. She nestled her head against the worn, threadbare sofa and closed her eyes before she was out for the count.

Jackie continued to stare until she was sure the girl was out of it. Then, quickly, she kneeled next to Tiffany, hooked her index finger just under the gold chain and eased it from under the girl's top. It was a long, thick belcher chain with a gold horseshoe and three sizable diamonds set into it. Jackie's eyes widened as she guessed the value. And the charm being a horseshoe as well was such a bonus, she could sell it on to most of the gypsies on the site. Carefully, she unclipped the clasp and slowly pulled it from the girl's neck.

Tiffany was gently snoring.

As Jackie kneeled down on the floor, she carefully lifted the girl's arm, twisting her wrist slightly to see the safety catch on the watch. Still, Tiffany didn't move, and Jackie got to work, removing the gold watch while thinking of the perfect buyer. The watch slid off easily, and as Jackie held it close to her face, she could see the gold hallmark. Her grin cruised across her face until it revealed her stained teeth.

With the watch and necklace in her hand, she looked around her caravan. For the first time in such a long time, she saw it for what it really was – a tin shell, filled with bleak belongings, reminding her of who she now was and where she had come from. The mould on the walls was from when she'd been too drunk to worry about the condensation. The ripped, stained sofas and faded curtains had once been immaculate and admired by the other gypsies. In fact, the women on the site used to marvel at her caravan, even drool over it, wishing they had the same. Yet now she was left with fuck all – just a filthy, rotten, and stinking mess. Holding the solid gold pieces in her hand, admiring their clean, classy quality, only served to emphasize just how disgusting her place and her belongings actually were.

After slipping the chain over her neck and fastening the flash gold watch to her wrist, Jackie's eyes flicked to Tiffany sprawled out on the sofa. The girl's hair, although somewhat matted, still shone like the wings of a blackbird. Her skin was smooth and fresh and everything about the young woman looked clean and untouched. At one time, she'd been the same, before having Ricky and messing with her face and her body. It was before she believed the grass was greener on the other side. Slumping down into the only armchair, she suddenly felt sick from an eerie feeling of reality. What the hell was she doing, and, more importantly, why had she done all those terrible things? And what had she been looking for? Everything around her now didn't depict a better life, that was for sure. The drink, the drugs, and even selling herself to anyone, literally anyone, was for what? Nothing, that was what.

She reached across the small coffee table that was piled high with shit: ashtrays, court summonses, her decree absolute, empty bottles of vodka, and dirty glasses. Everything in this room was a reflection on how she had conducted her life. The ripped stomach and sore throats from too much drinking, the sour milk to ease the burning, the endless smoking, and the charge sheets for the number of times she'd been arrested for theft – all were testament to a life that had been to live for the moment.

Snatching the cigarettes, she sparked up the end of one and inhaled deeply, as she peered over at the girl once more. Tiffany certainly reminded her of her former self. Her eyes returned to the table, and she stared at the envelope containing the money that Torvic had given her. She pondered over how he'd been so sure she would have it in her to rescue him. Maybe he was well informed on how much she hated Zara and Mike, but did she really hate them? Zara maybe, but Mike, she wasn't so sure. He'd left her with nothing after she'd signed the divorce papers, but she'd stolen a lot of money from him in the past.

As if someone had turned a light on, she felt a sudden overwhelming sense of loyalty – to Mike. She placed the remains of the partially lit cigarette on the ashtray and gripped the envelope containing the money. Her heart was beating fast, mainly through fear, but it was laced with excitement. With her thoughts so fixed on getting away and running to Mike – to the only man who had cared for her, even if it had been many years ago – she didn't bother to check to see if Tiffany was okay. She opened the door, and through force of habit, she locked it behind her. Since she had nothing on her mind now except how she would wangle this situation in her favour, she knew she needed to think of a way that would look as though she'd planned to help Mike.

Over the years, the decking around her caravan had sunk into the ground, and she jolted her back as she slipped on the wooden surface that was wet from a recent heavy rainstorm. Holding in her urge to curse, she straightened herself and headed for the car park while looking around for curtain twitchers or nosey bastards as she called her neighbours. A few yards away, on a small gravel area, was where the gypsy residents parked their vehicles. One of them, the tattiest, was Tatum's. She knew he was still inside Maidstone Prison. He'd always kept his keys just inside the driver's wheel. It was a habit of his. She hoped the car would start after a year of standing idle. Glancing around one more time, she crouched down onto the ground and felt around the tyre. Sure enough, the keys were there. Quietly, she unlocked the car.

After she climbed in, she put the key in the ignition and listened to the noisy exhaust; it was just another reminder that this car had once been the envy of the site. But now, it was an old rust bucket, and, what was worse, it didn't even belong to her anymore. She'd sold it to Tatum. All she had to her name was the car that Torvic had shot off in and her poxy caravan. Still, Tatum's car was her only way of escaping the madness with Torvic and perhaps into the open arms of Mike, although she would have to work on that part.

The car jolted and shuddered as it warmed up, the engine backfired, and then she tore away, across the gravel towards a gap in the hedge that led to the narrow lane.

* * *

The cigarette rolled away from the overfilled ashtray and landed on the pile of court summonses and police charge sheets, causing the gentle flame, that, within seconds, climbed to great heights. The book on the table that Jackie had wanted to read, one of several from her dated collection, caught alight and fuelled the fire that was now threatening to engulf everything in its way. Tumbling to the floor, the book fell apart, and the flames licked the pages, resulting in them floating towards the low ceiling and catching alight the spiderwebs and trapped dust. The fire instantly latched onto the peeling ceiling wallpaper. Like a circle of fire, ready for a circus act, the fierce flames rose and grew in intensity, filling the room with deadly smoke and devouring everything in their path.

Tiffany coughed and tried to breathe, but as her eyes opened to the horror, panic set in. In desperation, she gasped for oxygen, but all that filled her burning lungs were toxic fumes. With her T-shirt now covering her mouth, she scrambled along the floor towards the door, but as she tried to turn the handle and push her way out, she found her only exit was locked. With the smoke now burning her eyes and her throat, she tried frantically again, but it was no use. She bashed and banged and clawed at the door, desperate to get away from the smoke, the heat, and the naked flames. But it was impossible: the harder she tried, the harder it was to breathe. On all fours, she coughed and struggled, the smoke and the flames consuming any oxygen in her body and the heat blistering her skin. She couldn't breathe. She couldn't escape. She knew she was about to die.

* * *

The car choked and spluttered, causing Jackie to curse. Boom!

'Fuck! What was that?'

Jackie slammed on the brakes. The sound was behind her, yet it was so loud, she could feel the vibration. In her rear-view mirror, she could see the red flames just visible above the hedgerows. Perhaps the lads had burned out another car. Maybe she should get them to take her old banger away and burn it out for the insurance money when Torvic brought it back. Then she remembered she didn't have insurance anyway.

Just as she approached the end of the lane to turn right, she saw a flash-looking motor; it was heading towards her, and as soon as it was close enough, she recognized the driver. It was Torvic. Her heart rate increased, and her palms instantly became wet, making gripping the steering wheel so much harder. She couldn't hang around though; she needed to get away. Torvic wasn't like Mike. He had no scruples, and she'd got the sense that he could easily get rid of her. And did he really intend to pay her the rest of the money? She thought not. She also wondered if she would ever see her car again.

As Torvic slowed down to turn left, she shot out and put her foot down. The force of the turn made her swerve, yet she wasn't going to stop now. She had to get away. As soon as she'd straightened the car, she looked again in the mirror, and her heart rate slowed down. With a deep breath, she sighed. He'd obviously gone straight to the caravan. Perhaps he hadn't recognized her in Tatum's car. For after all, it was dark.

* * *

The sound of a fire engine from the distance suddenly had Torvic feeling unusually on edge. Then he saw the flames towering above the bushes, and his heart was in his mouth. The dreaded thought that the woman speeding away from the site might have been Jackie charged through his mind. If that was her, why was she leaving? He'd given her precise instructions to look after his granddaughter. Putting his foot down, he left a trail of dust behind him. As soon as he reached the gravel car parking area and saw the caravan ablaze, his head felt like it was on fire. His breathing increased, and panic gripped him hard around the throat. He rushed from the car and ran towards the towering inferno, where he was met by two men.

'Slow down, mate. That thing could explode,' said one of them, grabbing Torvic's arm.

Torvic tried to shrug the man off. 'My granddaughter might be inside that fucking caravan!'

The old man, dressed in just his jeans and a black vest, let him go, but as soon as Torvic tried to get near the caravan, the intensity of the heat forced him back. With his hands over his eyes, he tried again, but it was no use. The structure was a ball of flames. No one would have survived in there. His granddaughter, if she was inside, would be a fragile bunch of charred bones.

'Noooo!' he screamed, at the top of his voice.

But his desperate cries of pain were drowned out by the fire engine's sirens. The two older men dragged the helpless, crumpled man away from the heat.

Two firemen were making their way to the blaze with a hose and pushing people aside. A well-built firefighter approached Torvic and helped him to his feet.

'Is this your caravan, sir?'

With his face covered in beads of sweat and his hairline singed, Torvic shook his head.

'No, but I think my granddaughter is in there. Please ...'

The firefighter looked back at the red glowing ball, and suddenly, like a sardine can, the walls peeled back, revealing nothing standing of any recognizable shape. Torvic felt his legs buckle and allowed the man to lower him gently to the ground.

'Sir, we'll have a paramedic here soon!'

'You what? Fucking hell, no one could have … Oh my God! No one would've survived that fire. What use is a fucking paramedic?'

A sad smile inched its way across the large firefighter's face. 'I'm sorry, sir. I meant for you.'

As Torvic looked up at the man, he glared with dark, menacing eyes, from which the firefighter recoiled in surprise. If looks could kill.

As fit as a man in his twenties, Torvic, now in his advanced years, still managed very easily to jump to his feet and lean into the firefighter's personal space, and growl, 'Just tell me if my granddaughter *was* in that fucking fire!'

The firefighter stepped away from the demonic eyes of the evil-looking gentleman. He'd been used to aiding desperate relatives who were helpless to save a loved one from a fire, but never in his career had the anger been aimed at him; he could almost taste the fury emanating from the man. Then he wondered if this was no ordinary citizen and he'd just walked into some dangerous feud, because, right now, the guy was saying someone would be held accountable.

'I'll talk with the other firefighters and the police.' His manner changed, became more assertive, to demonstrate he was in charge. 'What is your granddaughter's name? And you think she could be inside?'

Torvic twisted his head. 'Just fucking find out if there's a body in there, will you?' He stepped away and ran his hands down the back of his neck. His whole body shook with an overwhelming sense of grief mixed with rage – an intense feeling that he was hard-pressed to hold down. If his granddaughter *was* in that caravan, then he would take the Regans, the Lanigans, and that bitch Zara to the fire of hell and make them see what the Devil was really capable of.

It didn't take long before the fire was out and for the occupants of every caravan to form a crowd, just to be nosey. None of them cared if that towering ball of fire was Jackie's cremation; it would just be another month's worth of gossip for them. The police arrived and pushed the crowd back; they tried to cordon off the area so that the special investigation unit could have access before the scene was tampered with. Normally, Torvic would have shielded his face and made a swift exit but not today. Today, he'd lost any concerns for his liberty; he had to know if Tiffany was in that fire.

The body of bustling firefighters and police suddenly stepped aside as four special fire investigators made their way through. The tall firefighter who had spoken with Torvic then talked to the police officers.

They nodded and made their way over to Torvic. Phil, the older one of the two, gently tapped his arm.

'Sir, could you help us, here? The firefighter said you suspect a young woman was inside that caravan.'

As Torvic turned to face Phil, his eyes were red and angry. 'Yes,' he hissed, 'my granddaughter. Now, I want to know if anyone can fucking tell me if she was in that fire!'

Like the firefighter, Phil was taken aback. 'Er, sir, we are investigating that now. Please would you come with me? I do believe the ambulance is on its way. Let's get you checked over and I'll organize a cup of tea for you.'

Torvic frowned at the officer. 'Tea? I don't want fucking

tea or checking over. I'm fine. Just talk to me when you know if there was a body in that caravan!'

The firefighters continued to spray the surrounding areas, soaking the neighbouring caravans, in case sparks led to the fire spreading. Jackie's caravan was now a black skeleton. The gasps and mumblings from the crowd pricked Torvic's ears.

He pushed his way through to look for himself. And, shockingly, there as clear as day were the charred remains of a body. The sight was sickening, and even the toughest of the gypsies had to turn away. One threw up on the spot. The police and the firefighters tried to push the crowd back, but they were reluctant to go until they'd seen the evidence for themselves. Two teenagers even pulled out their phones and started to film the devastation, zooming in on the burned body. No doubt that video would go viral.

Phil tried to urge the older man away. 'Sir, come with me.'

'Get ya fucking hands off me!'

'Please, sir, we need to clear the area, to do our job, and to get you your answers. You said you think your granddaughter was inside. Are you sure?'

Torvic didn't answer. His eyes were glued to the horrific sight of the blackened, hairless body with the unrecognizable face. In his mind, he was trying to interpret the shape as anything other than a body, but it was so clearly the remains of one. A thought occurred to him that if it was his Tiffany, then he would see the heavy gold chain around her neck or the gold watch on her wrist, but there was nothing that resembled those, only blackened remains. Suddenly, he glared as a firefighter went up to the body, blocking his view. Torvic, though, wanted to have a closer look, but he was held back by another firefighter.

Torvic blinked and came out of his trance. His eyes diverted to the fire investigators who were kneeling down by what had once been the door. They were spraying something over the areas where the handle and the lock were. Then the penny dropped. He knew they were checking to see if the door was in the locked position. Torvic shrugged the man off him and then focused on the bright-red fire blanket that covered who he assumed was his granddaughter. Now the pieces suddenly fitted together. She had been at the door, frightened out of her life, and the fucking thing had been locked. Jackie had locked her in. He suddenly had a hopeful thought. Perhaps Tiffany had locked Jackie in. Yes, that must be it. Tiffany had locked her in.

As he turned to storm away, Phil clutched his arm again. 'Sir, we need to ask you a few questions.'

Torvic shook his head, shrugged the officer off, and marched towards his car.

Just as Phil was about to call after the scary old guy, a big-bellied gypsy accosted him. He came so close, Phil could smell the garlic from his breath.

'I know who was in that caravan. Her name's Jackie Menaces. She probably got pissed and set the van alight, mate.'

Phil stepped back to get a clearer look at the man who was in his face. 'Do you know the woman? Only ...' – he pointed to the wild man who was about to get into his car – 'that gentleman wanted to know if it was his granddaughter in the caravan.'

Torvic stopped in his tracks and turned to face them.

The chubby traveller, with a toothless grin, shook his head. 'Nah, it was Jackie. I saw her through the window earlier.'

'Was anyone else with her?' asked Phil.

'Nah, I only saw her walking around in her caravan. She's a pisshead. She likes a good drink, that one.'

'Are you sure no one else was with her?'

The toothless gypsy nodded his head. 'I tell ya, it was Jackie Menaces in that van. Ask me missus. She saw her an' all. We were coming back from feeding the horses, and as we walked past her van, me ol' gal, said, "Look at her. She's got a glass of vodka in her hand already."'

'Are you positive it was Jackie Menaces, though?'

'Cor, yeah. 'Course I's sure. I ain't blind. We all knows Jax. She's the local slut.'

Phil frowned. 'And how do you know it was vodka she was drinking?'

The gypsy laughed. ''Cos that's what she always drinks – morning, noon, and night.'

'And your name, sir?'

'Jericho. Me missus is Mena. That's her, over there.'

Phil nodded and gingerly stepped towards the large woman, who was clearly shaken up. Her face was pale, and her eyes were turned down at the sides, red-rimmed and glazed over.

'Your husband said you saw Jackie Menaces in the caravan before the fire. Is that correct? And is there anything else you can remember?'

Mena swallowed hard and wiped the sweat from her top lip. 'All I saw through Jackie's window – she don't have nets up, see – was her standing with a large glass tumbler in her hand. It was clear liquid. The gal never drinks water, so I guessed it was vodka.' Her voice cracked. 'She has a son, little Richard Menaces. Sorry, I mean Ricky Regan.'

Torvic had heard enough. The police were now busy taking notes, and so it was his call to leave.

Cora, Tatum's wife, heard Mena talking to the policeman and decided to join in. She edged her way over and stood side by side with Mena. 'Yeah, that's right. The bitch told us the boy was called Richard Menaces, but it was all a pack o' lies. The boy got released early from prison, probably living with his real farver, no doubt. He's some geezer called Mike Regan.'

Phil pulled a notebook and pen from his pocket. 'Mike Regan, did you say?'

Cora nodded. 'Yeah. He was in the nick an' all. Me husband reckons he's a bit of a gangster or summat.'

'So, then, did this Mike Regan hold a grudge or …?'

With a smug smile on her face, Cora put in her two pennies' worth. 'She had loads of enemies, that skanky bitch. She was always conning people, selling gear … even her own arse. She lied about her boy, and from what me ol' man says, Mike Regan thought his boy was dead until he met the kid in the nick.'

Phil smiled and nodded. 'Thank you. Um …'

'Cora. Me name's Cora. I live in that van over there.' She pointed to the caravan, two behind the remains of Jackie's.

'I'll call by and get a statement from both of you, if you don't mind.'

* * *

An hour later, Phil had left the site, on his way back to the station to write up his report. He decided to put in a call to Detective Inspector Lowry. 'Mike Regan. Does that name mean anything to you?'

Lowry was just about to tuck into a burger when he answered the phone. 'Yes, it does. Why?'

'Gov, his ex-wife's van has been burned to the ground. There's a body inside. It may be her. It could be murder, Gov, because the door was locked, and so whoever was inside couldn't escape.'

'Okay, Phil, leave it with me. I'll pay him a visit.'

'Gov, do you think he may have torched it, revenge and all?'

'No, Phil, it's not his style, but, Phil, leave Regan out of this. He's … Let's just say he's helping us with our inquiries.'

Lowry wiped the tomato sauce from around his mouth and let out a heavy sigh. Releasing Mike Regan and his firm early in return for cleaning the streets of the Flakka drug was questionable at every turn and not a decision he'd agreed with at the time. As far as he was aware, the firm had found the gang leader, the man they referred to as the Governor, and that was the end of it. The team were told not to ask questions, and, sure as hell, he wanted the least bit of involvement as possible. His superior, the Police Commissioner Conrad Stoneham, was on leave, and it was a good job too since it wasn't looking good for him at the moment. For Stoneham's sister, the MP, had been arrested for failing to stop at an accident, and, right now, with the Commissioner's face plastered across every newspaper, he was right to take time off. Having Regan brought in for questioning was something he really didn't relish, but it might have to be done. He would put it off though until Stoneham returned. The Commissioner could take the stick if Regan had killed his ex-wife. He himself wanted nothing to do with it.

'Damn you, Stoneham. You should've let sleeping dogs lie,' he mumbled to himself.

Chapter 7

Roaring along the lane, Torvic suddenly braked; his car and his mind were running out of control. A recollection stabbed him hard, bringing his hopes down to earth like a bloody great boulder crushing him. What if he was wrong and it was Jackie leaving the site in a hurry? If she had double-crossed him – murdered his granddaughter – then, no doubt, she would be heading for Mike's drum. 'Bitch!' he yelled, as he banged the steering wheel. 'The fucking bitch!' Anger and frustration burned the back of his throat as his eyes stung with bitter tears.

He had no time to plan his next move. All he could think of was to go in like a bat out of hell and shoot every last one of the Regans and then carve up Zara like a Sunday roast. Jackie, though, if she was alive, would suffer a different fate. He would take extra delight in consuming her to ashes. He would first douse her in petrol and then watch her burn alive. No one hurt his Tiffany and lived to tell the tale.

* * *

Jackie felt relief as she approached Mike's house. She had looked a hundred times in her rear-view mirror to check that Torvic wasn't chasing her.

She went over and over in her head how she would approach Mike. What was her excuse for rescuing Torvic? How would it look to Mike? Yet she had the granddaughter locked in her own caravan, and she'd passed Torvic on his way back. She could hand Mike the keys with a smile on her face and say, 'All yours.' She would look the hero, except for the fact that she'd rescued Torvic and his granddaughter in the first place. So how was she going to overcome that little issue?

Slowing down as she approached Mike's drive, her palms felt clammy, and her heart was suddenly racing. Fuck! What was she thinking? Who was the lesser of two evils? Mike hadn't physically hurt her, even though she'd stolen his money and taken Ricky away from him. She still had one thing over him, though: she was Ricky's mother. So many questions kept popping up in her mind, she had to stop the car and take a deep breath. Out of the blue, another thought materialized. What if she told him that she'd had no choice? What if she said that if she hadn't rescued Torvic, he would have instructed one of his men to have Ricky killed – *their* beloved Ricky?

The gates were closed, and so she had to ring the buzzer set into the wall. There was no answer. She buzzed again and waited, pulling her tatty old coat tighter around her as if by a miracle it could protect her from the cold. Staring up at the house, she noticed that there were no lights on, and as it was still quite dark, they almost certainly would be if he was there. A final press of the intercom had her worried. If Mike wasn't at home and she didn't find him soon, then it would be over because Torvic would no doubt come gunning for her. She swallowed hard when she realized that no amount of buzzing would make Mike miraculously appear.

Returning to her car, she locked herself in. Chewing her fingernails down to the quick, she winced as the sores stung. There was only one thing left to do and that was to go to his parents' place, Arthur and Gloria's. She shuddered, knowing full well that they would look at her with utter disgust and probably send her packing – with a swift kick up the arse as well, if Gloria had her way. All she could hope for was that Mike would be there.

* * *

Torvic knew exactly where both Mike and Eric lived. He drove like a madman to his lock-up, a dirty old garage at the end of his dead mother's garden. It was an unsuspecting place, which was overgrown with weeds and ivy. He'd kept the house going and used it as a safety net; it was his hideout when needed. Inside the garage, he kept his tools, his weapons, including an arsenal of guns, a few hand grenades, and his collection of butcher's knives. He put on the single centre light and wasted no time in scooping up the firearms and carrying them to the boot of his car. Luckily, the lane that ran the length of the back of the houses onto the main street was hardly ever used. Most of the residents were elderly pensioners who didn't own a car. Once his boot was full, he slammed it shut and zoomed away.

In his mind, he imagined shooting the Regan brothers down like tin soldiers. So what if he went to jail; he really didn't care anymore, as long as he killed them all – every last one of them.

Eric checked the back door was bolted shut. 'Dad, listen. You have to keep this door locked, right?'

Arthur gave a grin that said he was up to something.

'What?' asked Eric, concerned that his father wasn't taking the situation regarding his own safety seriously enough.

With that, Arthur pulled a gun from the back of his trousers.

'Jesus, Dad, this Torvic geezer ain't like any old-school fucking gangster. He's on a whole different level. He won't talk and give you time to pull your bloody gun out. He'll come in like a tornado.'

Arthur stopped grinning and studied the worried look on his son's face. 'Son, you and your brother have run the firm for years after me, but I ain't past it, ya know.'

Eric stood with his hands on his hips, shaking his head. 'This ain't *like* old times, Dad. I told you: this Torvic has no scruples. You can forget that he won't hurt women and children. He'll throw acid in Muvver's face as soon as he looks at her. You don't understand. The guy's a complete arsehole.'

Arthur dropped his shoulders and sat heavily in the armchair. 'All right, Son. So what's going on now?'

Eric was about to reply, but he stopped when he spotted his mother standing there in the doorway, her face almost grey with worry.

'Carry on, Eric. I think I've as much right to know as ya farver.'

Eric sighed as he looked at his mother. In her designer dress, she wouldn't look out of place in *The Lady*. He'd never seen her during the day without a hint of make-up and her hair immaculately styled.

'Mum, listen. There's this geezer called Torvic that we had locked up, and trust me, when I say he's one cruel, evil bastard. He's now on the loose. Mike and Zara sent the youngsters to Spain, and now Liam's gone missing.' He stopped when he saw his mother drop the towel and throw her hands to her mouth in horror.

'Jesus, little Liam. Oh my God.'

'Well, we don't know for sure if it was Torvic that snatched him, because as soon as we found out he'd escaped, we flew the youngsters over to Terrence's villa. It would take a lot for this Torvic bloke to get on a plane and manage to kidnap Liam as well. However, we all need to be really vigilant. It might be worth you two going away for a bit. Why don't ya? Don't tell anyone. Just grab a few bits and get on a plane or nip down to the coast.'

Gloria, still in shock, looked at Arthur. 'Well, don't just sit there like a gormless git! If our Mikey wants us away, then let's just go and give him less to worry about.'

Eric bit his lip. It had always been the same. She had invariably referred to Mikey as the voice of reason. Why couldn't she just do as *he* said and respect *his* wishes for once? It was as if Mikey was the only person she wouldn't see upset, hurt, or stressed. Still, this wasn't the time to be arguing about that now.

'All right, Glor. Pack a bag – not a fucking large suitcase – and throw me in some strides and a few tops. We can go to the Lake District.'

With her mouth open and her eyes bulging, she glared at Arthur.

'Well, get a move on, girl! You've frigging well moaned for

years that you wanted to go there. It beats me why, though. It's a fucking damp, dreary place, full of sheep and hills. I bet ya can't even get Sky up there.'

'To be honest, Arthur, I couldn't give a shit right now. I won't enjoy it, not while I'm worrying about the family, and as for poor little Liam, love his heart, I'm absolutely heartbroken. My God, what his mother's—'

'Glor, get a wiggle on, will ya!'

Gloria didn't wait about: she hurtled off up the stairs to begin the packing.

'Dad, be safe, yeah? We don't know what his next move is.'

Arthur rose from his chair and straightened his jumper. 'You just keep me and ya mother informed. I wanna know that you lot are okay and won't take any chances. We've been through enough in our family to last a lifetime.'

Eric hugged his father and quickly left. He had work to do, to try and track down the so-called Governor before Torvic found *him*. He knew damn well that he would be first on Torvic's hit list.

* * *

Gloria was heavy-handed, forcing the clothes into the small suitcase. Her heart was thumping as her inner anger was bubbling. She only wished she was twenty years younger – she would have hunted this Torvic bloke down herself.

Just as she was imagining what she would do to him, there was a bang at the front door. She stopped zipping up the case and bolted down the stairs, only to find Arthur, at the side of the door, trying to see through the small hallway window who was outside.

She tutted as she pushed past him. 'Who is it?' she bellowed.

'Er, it's me, Jackie. Is, er … is Mike there? I need to speak to him urgently.'

Arthur placed the gun back into his belt and sighed. Tensions were high, but what he didn't expect to see was Gloria rip open the door, pull her fist back, and crack Jackie full-on on the chin.

Jackie was just as surprised as Arthur. She faltered, wobbled, and stepped back, clutching her face.

'You good-for-nuffin fucking whore! How dare you come here looking for my boy! You almost destroyed all of us, with your lying and fucking cheating, and as for poor Ricky, ya fucking trollop, I …' She stopped to take a deep breath.

Arthur grabbed Gloria around the waist before she launched another attack.

'What the hell are you doing 'ere, Jackie?' asked Arthur, in a calm and yet firm voice.

'I need to see Mikey. I've some information for him.'

As Arthur stupidly let go of his wife to invite Jackie in, Gloria threw herself again at Jackie, snatching a large clump of her hair and pulling her to the ground. She clawed and punched at Jackie's face until Arthur eventually managed to pull her off.

'You evil scumbag! Just fuck off! If you've something for Mikey, I've something for you …' But Arthur's grip was too tight for her to have another go.

Jackie was horrified and totally unprepared for that vicious attack, especially from a woman old enough to be her mother. Yet she shouldn't have been surprised; she was Mikey's mother, and her past record was enough to remind everyone that when it came to her son and grandson, she took no shit.

Arthur was still struggling to hold Gloria. She wriggled and tried to yank herself away, almost turning her cardigan top inside out and ripping the seams of her freshly ironed dress.

'You'd better piss off, Jackie, because the minute I let her go, she'll take your fucking face off.'

'Arthur, get the fuck off me! I wanna smash the life outta that tramp, after all she's put us through!' screamed Gloria. It took all of Arthur's considerable strength to hold her back. He knew the minute he released her, she wouldn't stop. She was like a feral cat, hissing and spitting.

'You fucking scrubber. I'll kill ya, fucking kill ya … Let me go, Arthur!'

Jackie clutched at her cut and swollen face and felt the pain. As her eyes fell to the path, she saw clumps of her hair strewn everywhere. Yet it was the punch on the chin and the other one to her nose that had her reeling. Everything seemed foggy as if she'd just smoked a joint. Luckily, she still had enough awareness to know that it was time to run. Blinking back the tears in her eyes, she turned and scurried away. Usually, she would've given anyone a right mouthful back, but she was knocked sideways, and she knew in her heart that if Arthur hadn't been there, Gloria would've hurt her badly, if not killed her.

As soon as she was safe in the confines of her car, she took several deep breaths to calm her heart, which was pummelling at a rate of knots. Her hands were shaking as she tried to insert the key into the ignition, but the more she panicked, the harder it was until, finally, she stopped and took more deep breaths before she was able to drive away.

Tears now streamed down her face. What the hell had she

got herself into? Where should she go now? She drove aimlessly, trying to think of a safe haven. Just as her heart began to slow down, the news came on the radio. All she heard was the newscaster saying 'Merrywell Lane has been closed off due to a serious incident at a travellers' site where a body has been found after firefighters fought to put out a blaze. The incident is being treated as suspicious.'

Gasping out loud, Jackie momentarily swerved, sending the car careering towards the other side of the road. 'Jesus, no!' Torvic's face and thoughts of what he would do to her, if she'd been responsible for a blaze that had destroyed her caravan and burned alive his precious granddaughter, tore through her mind like a rogue tornado. She mentally recapped how it could have happened, praying that it wasn't her trailer, because she remembered locking the bloody door. Tiffany would have probably been off her nut on the pills that she'd rammed down her throat. If that was the case, Torvic would be after her; he would kill her and no doubt set *her* alight.

* * *

Staffie had made scores of calls to every man he knew who either owed him or Mike a favour or who would be up for earning a few quid. Mike had put up a two hundred grand bounty on Torvic's head.

Neil and Shamus called their men and had them stationed at all of Zara's restaurants – on standby – if Torvic showed his face.

Lou Baker was sent to scour the surrounding areas of all the firm's homes.

And Eric had been dispatched to make arrangements for their relatives to pack up and get out. He wasn't too impressed, though, with the fact that he wasn't in on the discussions; he was only called if there were updates regarding Liam going missing.

Lance took the next plane to Spain to join Terrence. They couldn't be 100 per cent sure that Torvic wasn't the man who'd taken Liam or whether one of his men had. Lance's fear was for his girls. Although he was the most equipped to track down Torvic, he'd failed the first time around, and so the best place for him was to join forces with Terrence. He had his own contacts in Spain and would use them to find out what had happened to Liam.

Zara poured Willie another brandy. 'Here, Willie, drink this, mate. We'll find him.'

Sitting crouched over the desk, his face soaked in tears and hidden by his long straggly hair, he peered up and stared at Zara, almost looking through her. As his forehead puckered and his chin trembled, another tear tumbled down his cheeks. 'Why my boy, eh? Why him?' he quietly probed.

That desolate tone in Willie's voice brought an immediate response. Zara kneeled beside him and stroked his back, only too aware that he could easily push her away again. 'Willie, I don't know what to say, except you know we'll do everything—'

Unexpectedly, he spun around to face her, holding his arms out to hug her. She gripped him tight, feeling every muscle in his body convulsing as the uncontrollable sobs overpowered him. The moment was heartfelt, and she couldn't help but cry with him.

Willie's cries stopped Mike from making the next call. He watched as his best friend was broken, and he knew how that felt. His arms fell by his side, and he sighed heavily. His past feelings of desolation and grief all came flooding back. The only thing to do was to take over from Zara and hold his mate. Grasping him, as if his arms would somehow protect Willie from the pain, he wanted to cry as well, but, instead, the two of them just rocked each other, united in grief.

As Zara straightened up, she listened to Staffie. His words were getting harsher as he called all their known associates. 'Staff!' she called.

Staffie had his back to her, and as he turned around, she noticed the anger in his eyes. 'Make that bounty a million.'

Staffie held his hand over the phone. 'Ya what? A million?'

She nodded. 'It's only fucking money, but it will get the bastards crawling out of the woodwork to help.'

Staffie nodded and continued with his conversation. 'Mate, we're just upping the amount to a million for Torvic's head on a fucking pole.'

Willie pulled away from Mike, his eyes wide, as he looked at Zara with incredulity. 'Did ya say *a million*?'

Zara nodded with a sad smile. 'I'll pay whatever it takes to get your son back. It's all my fault ...' Her words faltered as the guilt and shame from the consequences of her earlier actions hit home. She struggled not to burst into tears again.

Willie jumped up and grabbed her by the shoulders. 'Now, you just forget what I said before. 'Course it ain't your fault. I was just ... Well, you know, babe. I never meant to blame anyone. We're all in it together. I could've walked away … I just can't fucking get my shit together, though. I should get over to Spain. It's all the not knowing that's killing me.'

Mike felt drained with worry, and the overthinking was bringing him down. His phone rang, which made everyone stop what they were doing and stare at Mike, as he held the phone in his hand. 'No caller ID.'

'It's Torvic, I bet. Answer it!' she urged him.

'Yeah?' he said coldly to the caller.

'Mr Regan, it's Lowry from the nick. Listen, where are you?'

Mike looked at Zara and shook his head. 'Why d'ya wanna know where I am, Lowry?'

The detective had taken himself off to an interview room, away from prying ears. 'Mr Regan, just tell me you're nowhere near Essex and haven't been there over the past twenty-four hours.'

'Essex? No, why? Lowry, what the fuck's going on?'

'I've some bad news. Jackie Menaces is your ex-wife, I believe.'

'Yeah, but what about her?'

'Her caravan was burned to the ground, and we believe it's her body that was locked inside. The investigation team haven't confirmed it's hers yet, but the neighbours reckon they saw her just before the fire started.'

Mike paused, giving himself time to get his thoughts together, while Zara and Willie looked on, anxiously holding their breath.

'Jesus, do you have any idea who did it?'

Lowry cleared his throat. 'Well, that's why I called. I was hoping you could help us … Er, Mr Regan, it wasn't you, was it?'

'What!' he screeched. 'No, it fucking weren't. She's me boy's mother. What the fuck d'ya take me for? I ain't that sick, mate.'

'No, I didn't think so, but I just had to ask ... Do you have any idea who might have done this?'

'None, Lowry, but she's pissed a lot of people off. Christ, I don't have anything to do with the bitch. I ain't got a clue who she was involved with, but it sure as hell wasn't me that did it.'

'Do us a favour, Mr Regan. Give me some kind of proof that it wasn't you, then I'll get the force off your back.'

Mike held his hand over the phone and relayed the conversation to Zara. 'So how can I prove it wasn't me?'

Zara looked at the clock on the wall. 'Ask him what time it happened.'

Mike removed his hand. 'Lowry, when did all this happen?'

'About an hour ago.'

'Right, mate, can you do this FaceTime thingy? I can show you where I am, and there is no way I would be here from Jackie's in an hour. It would take at least an hour and a half with no traffic.'

Lowry wanted to laugh at Mike's terminology. 'Yeah, go for it. I'll call ya back.'

Mike ended the call. 'We're gonna FaceTime.'

Lowry called back and could see Regan. 'Sorry about this, Mr Regan. It's just I need to eliminate you as your name obviously came up.'

Zara took the phone and showed Lowry the CCTV footage of the time Mike arrived at her house. It was clear that he couldn't have been in two places at once.

'Thank you,' said Lowry, as he smiled to himself.

Mike then looked at the screen and could see Lowry's

chubby red face, with a slither of mayonnaise still present at the corners of his mouth.

'Will that be all, Lowry?'

'Yeah. Listen, I don't know if you've heard, but the Police Commissioner is off on leave for a while, so I've taken over for a bit. Is there any news to report back?'

Mike gave a sigh. 'Nah, but I'll keep ya up to date. Cheers, mate. Bye.'

He returned his phone to the back pocket of his Levi's and puffed out a large mouthful of air. 'So that tells me one thing, Willie. Torvic can't be in two places at once either. If he burned that caravan down an hour ago, he wasn't in Spain. And, believe me, if it was Jackie that broke him out of the hangar, then he would do away with her. She has too much of a gob on her – or perhaps I should say *had*?'

Zara was still trying to absorb the news. She tilted her head and frowned.

'Mikey, I know you hated her for what she did to you and Ricky, but, Christ, she's been burned alive. Ain't you bothered … even a bit, or has it not sunk in yet?'

Staffie and Willie had the same surprised expression as they waited for Mike's response.

'Don't fucking look at me like that. I ain't being heartless. It's just that I've far more serious shit to sort out now. Like your boy, Willie. So that gives us some hope regarding Liam. If Torvic is still here, then Liam may have just gone AWOL or … fuck knows where the kid is.'

Within a second, the phone rang again. This time, it was Arthur. Mike rolled his eyes, thinking that Eric hadn't convinced his father to leave the house. 'All right, Dad?'

'No. Ya mother's just lost the fucking plot. She's still ranting and raging. We were all ready to bloody go when Jackie turned up. Ya mother's gone and—'

Mike broke in. 'You what? Did you say Jackie?'

'Yes! Bloody Jackie. Well, anyway, ya mother's just gone and ripped half the girl's hair out, and now she's fuming because I held her back. I thought she was gonna claw me *own* face an' all! Fucking hell!'

'Are you *sure*? I mean, did you actually see Jackie?'

'Son! I may be older than you but I ain't fucking senile! Yes, *Jackie*! Whether she's recognizable now, though, is another matter. Ya mother's just battered her.'

Mike rubbed his forehead, trying to digest the information. 'What did she want?'

'I dunno. She said she had some information for you, but ya mother never let her get the rest of the words out. She propelled Jackie off the doorstep, dragged the girl to the ground, and mauled her ...' His annoyed tone changed to a giggle. 'I tell you, an alley cat has nothing on ya mother!'

Mike's face remained serious, his mind on the ramifications of what Lowry had been telling him. So, while on any other occasion he would have laughed, he was in no mood to do so now.

'Dad, just get Mum in the car and go, will ya? I'll explain later. I just don't have time now.'

Mike returned the phone to his pocket as he looked over at Zara.

She was pacing the floor, deep in thought. Then something hit her. All the jigsaw pieces that had been tumbling about in her mind were now joining as one.

'You know what's happened, don't ya? It ain't Jackie that's been burned in that fire. I bet you it's Torvic's granddaughter, and I wouldn't be surprised if Jackie went to your parents to find you and tell you what she'd done. So the question we need to ask ourselves is what does Jackie know? You need to track her down and get the answers, PDQ.'

Chapter 8

Liam tried to open his eyes, but the bright white light above his head made it impossible for him. Still partially sedated, he tried again, but his eyelids felt as though he was carrying boulders. Trying to move his arm, he panicked; he couldn't move at all because he was strapped down. The fear forced the adrenaline around his body and made him want to puke. As soon as he was able to force his eyes open and fight against the bright light, he thought he'd then be able to see where he was. But he couldn't work it out because he was still blinded by the glare. His throat was sore and extremely dry. It was the smell that hit him; it was a clean, antiseptic odour, one that he recognized, but, for the life of him, he couldn't fathom where from.

'Help!' he tried to scream, but the sound that left his mouth was a muffled croak.

Suddenly, he heard voices and saw shadows. There was more than one person in the room.

'Knock him out!' came a stern, cold, and yet well-spoken voice.

'No!' Liam shouted, as he tried to struggle free. Thoughts of torture ripped through his mind and images of being strapped down and mutilated – his limbs cut one by one – made him want to scream. 'Oh God, no!' he cried. Silence. The room became fuzzy, and a warm feeling enveloped him. However, he did manage to catch the last few words.

'I am not happy about this at all, though,' said the man with the stern voice.

'You are in debt. Now, if you don't do this, it will be you who's on that table, and we won't use anaesthetic. Besides, a million in the bank will set you right up,' replied a deeper, harsh voice.

So terrified by what he'd just heard, Liam craved sleep. Within a few seconds, his wish was granted: he was out cold.

* * *

With Mike on his way to see Jackie's mother, Gilly, and Staffie taking Willie to the airport, Zara found herself alone. She had pushed Mike to go, insisting she was safe. She had the CCTV that would show any intruders, and her own arsenal. She allowed herself a wry smile. She was an expert in so many defensive disciplines, so she knew she could hold her own against all comers.

Their considerable resources weren't infinite. Because both her firm and Mike's had to track down Liam and get to the bottom of this frightening mess, they didn't have time to fuss over her safety, which she was pleased about. Her guilt over the whole situation ran deep.

She checked the CCTV monitors and watched as Mike's car, followed by Staffie's, hurtled along the drive and through the entrance. She then pressed the lock button and observed the large, heavy gates automatically close behind them.

Suddenly, the room became deathly quiet except for the ticking of her father's grandfather clock. She ran her hand across her chest, feeling her bulletproof vest, and then fingered the gun just inside her belt.

If Torvic knocked at her door or even peered through a window, she wouldn't attempt to reason with the man – she would blow his brains out. As her stomach churned, she experienced a hot flush that left her with a nauseous feeling. But without the distraction of Mike, she knew she would be more clear-headed.

Looking away from the monitors, she allowed her eyes to fall on the empty brandy glasses. Then she looked at the bottle of her father's special Courvoisier Reserve. Her mind cast back to the day that Torvic mentioned how proud her father was of his vintage spirits and how she assumed he was a dear and close friend of Izzy's. Something niggled her. She, of course, discovered later that Torvic wasn't a friend at all but was in fact Izzy's enemy, so how did he know about her father's specialized knowledge of liquor? In truth, she assumed there were a few little details that he would only have known had they been friends. Her eyes then glanced around the room. Unless he could actually have seen inside this office, and, more to the point, could hear her conversations, there was no way he could have known.

She racked her brains, trawling through small snippets of conversation from the past. Her mind went back to all the meetings she'd had with him up to the present. Something then clicked. She remembered that there were moments when he would say to her, 'From what you told me, Zara.'

But, she recalled, she hadn't told him very much – at least

not about Izzy's tastes and views on life – and yet he seemed to know an awful lot about her father.

Damn! Why had she trusted a complete stranger, all because he'd said he was her father's close friend? And now a particular conversation did come back to her. Torvic – Victor, he'd said his name was – had brought her back from her father's jewellery business in his taxi. There'd been a fight earlier. She'd had to sort out two thugs who'd tried to rob her and 'Victor' had got her through the police checkpoint by telling the officer she'd just come out of an operation at King's College Hospital. She'd even admitted to Torvic what she'd done to one of her attackers. His kindness had sweet-talked her in, and when they'd reached her home, she'd offered him a coffee, and they'd spent quite a while chatting about her life since Izzy's death. It was then he'd said to her: 'You trusted me a little too soon. I'd be careful who you trust.'

And she'd laughed and replied, 'Oh, Victor, believe me, I'm not silly. The reason I trust you is because I know my father must have been friends with you since only his closest buddies ever came to the house.'

He'd appeared to know so much about Izzy that she'd had no reason to think otherwise. He'd played her for who she was at the time: a woman clinging to a part of her father's past.

Her mind began unravelling how Torvic knew about her relationships and other aspects of her life. Torvic had got into her mind and used small pieces of information to blindside her. He was certainly the arch manipulator. He'd known far too much about the Regans, about how to play Mike and Eric off against her, and yet, up until last night, she'd been just that one step ahead. A cold shiver ran up her spine; her palms became wet with sweat and pins and needles tingled her arms.

So if Torvic couldn't see inside her mind, perhaps he could see inside this room, her father's office? But how could he? As her eyes glided back to the small antique bar and then to the opposite side of the room, she noticed the grandfather clock. *Hmm.* If he had installed a camera, then he would have been privy to so much. He would know about the hidden compartments where her father had kept the deeds, the bank accounts, and anything of substantial value. But if that was the case, why hadn't he cleaned her out?

She tried to retrace where she'd been over the last few weeks. Had the meetings taken place in her office or in the dining room? Had Torvic planted a device before her father's death or afterwards? Her nerves ran ragged as she tried to remember everything.

Then she recalled the ledger with the phone number in it. She had been in her father's office when she'd pulled the book from the drawer and saw a telephone number rubbed out. She remembered using a pencil to rub lightly over the indented phone number. All this, Torvic could have seen, if he'd installed a camera. But certainly, if he had, he would never have agreed to meet her at the hangar. Chewing her lip, she tried to recall where she'd made the phone calls to everyone after she'd discovered who Torvic or the so-called Governor actually was. She'd made those arrangements for his capture via phone. But where had she been at the time? Retracing her steps, she recollected that she was upstairs in her bedroom, searching for her bulletproof vest.

If her theory was right, then, it wasn't a camera but a listening device; they were more common years ago. She went over to the grandfather clock and stared at the large gold face, at the heavy weights, and then, slowly, she opened the glass front and gently ran her fingers up inside the rim of the wooden frame. As she reached the top, she felt a small metal object. Bending her knees, she looked under and then up and saw what it was: it looked to be a very old covert listening device but still in good condition. So there was no camera then. The bastard would only have heard what was said inside her father's office. She straightened up and smiled. This meant that Torvic needed a receiver to listen to any conversations. As she turned the old device around in her hand, it all made sense. This was planted when her father was alive. Torvic, the sly bastard, had concealed it to bring her father down. She grinned, knowing that it would have taken a lot more than some stupid bug to get one over on Izzy.

As she planned her next move, she peered once more at the monitors, and a sudden ugly feeling crept into her bones. The CCTV was installed by two men who Torvic had recommended. Shit! Perhaps he did have a way of seeing what she saw herself after all. She would have to disconnect the set-up.

The simplest way was to turn the system off. No sooner had she pulled the plug than the outside sensor lights went out. She swallowed hard. That wasn't supposed to happen. And surely it wasn't a coincidence. She shook her head to knock out the overwhelming feeling of paranoia. Unexpectedly, a few seconds later, the inside lights stopped working. *Had someone manually turned them off?* she wondered. With the curtains drawn, she found herself in total darkness. The only sound was her own breath as she fiercely inhaled.

Her hand gripped her gun as she sank slowly behind the desk. The sudden darkness and the idea that Torvic had escaped and was in the house, hunting her down, was more terrifying than the day she realized her hand had been chopped off. Deep down, she was aware that Torvic was capable of far more than just cutting her hand off – he would brutally torture her first. She closed her eyes and tried to visualize her father's office, mentally scanning the room. There was no way he could tell that she was in here. All the curtains were closed, and she could realistically be in any other room. She listened, holding her breath for any creak or footstep. Heightening her senses, she tried to listen to the sound of anyone else's breathing or even to feel a brisk movement of air. It was so quiet that she wondered if it was just a case of the electrics packing up. Turning the CCTV off may have caused some issue along the way.

Stretching her arm, her fingers searched along the top of the desk for her mobile phone. Unable to speak, she could at least text. Just as she was about to message Mike, the battery died. Now she really did feel exposed. Her body trembled, and she knew she had to get a grip of herself and think things through.

The sudden loud rap at the front door made Zara jump. She remained motionless until the knocking became erratic. Her first thoughts were that it was Torvic, but then she rationalized it. If he'd pulled the plug on the electrics, why would he be knocking at her door? Surely, he would find a way in, if he wasn't already.

She listened and waited. Then a woman's shrill voice screamed out, 'Zara, Mikey, please open the door. I need to talk to you. Please, help me!'

Zara recognized the screech that was spiked with a hoarse growl. It belonged to Jackie. Zara froze, listening. Had Torvic used Jackie again but this time as his way in? But if Jackie was the person who'd helped Torvic to escape, why would she be begging for her help or Mike's? The knocking was now relentless, and the panic in Jackie's voice seemed too genuine to be an act. Zara felt for her gun again and decided to make a move. Stepping to the side of the door, with her weapon in her hand, she still managed to release the catch, despite her disability, so that the door was actually opened slightly. The final bang from Jackie's fists pushed the door fully open, and she stumbled forward just enough to find Zara's gun aimed at her head.

Not realizing the cold object was a shooter, Jackie continued in. Zara, in one quick movement, used her foot to slam the door shut. Glaring at Jackie, she remained silent, holding the cocked gun.

Jackie was actually relieved that she was inside but that was soon tempered by the determined and dangerous glint in Zara's eyes. Instantly, she held her hands up. 'Er, listen, please. Please, Zara, don't shoot. I've, er … I've fucked up, yeah. I need to speak to Mikey. It's this bloke called Torvic. He's gonna kill me.'

As soon as Zara heard the name Torvic in connection with Mike, she guessed that Jackie was in some way in league with Torvic, and she concluded that the man had given Jackie her address. That could be the only explanation for Jackie knowing where she lived. Zara had a clear measure of Jackie. Every part of her body was shaking, her face was white, and her lips were dry and thin. Jackie was telling the truth.

At that moment, the sudden sound of a generator, and the light in the entrance hall coming on, made Jackie jump out of her skin. As they stared at each other, Zara saw the woman for who she really was – a prideless, pathetic creature, who had made stupid decisions in her life and who was now grasping at straws to survive. Zara had always hated her, for two reasons. First, because she was the woman who'd married Mike and had a surviving son, and second, she'd been so cruel to Ricky and destroyed a part of Mike that would never be healed.

Yet Zara felt a sense of superiority; it was a feeling she'd never thought she'd experience outside her firm at least. They were probably of a similar age, but her mirror told her that she looked younger. Jackie was wrinkled, her skin was uneven, and the small scars, pitted in her cheeks, clearly showed that she hadn't looked after herself. The dark-stained teeth and the thin lines around her mouth made it obvious she was a smoker – a heavy smoker. The woman had fought – the scars confirmed that. Holes where her earrings had once been, the misshapen eyebrow, and, of course, the other thin scar that ran from her mouth up and under her nose, from the day Zara had swiped Jackie with her blade, were all signs of a hard existence. But it wasn't the physical appearance: it was the defeated expression and the slumped shoulders that illustrated to Zara that Jackie's life had run its course.

'You're taking a chance coming here—'

'Yeah, I know. He'll probably follow me and kill us both!'

Zara scoffed. 'No, Jackie. You took a chance because *I* will kill you.'

'No, listen please, Zara. Yeah, I know you hate me. Fuck me, I've got the scar to prove it. But I had no choice. This bloke, Torvic, he made me … Oh, I mean—'

'Shut it, Jackie. Just shut the fuck up. You'll answer my questions, or I won't hesitate to blow your head off.'

Jackie bit her lip and glared at the gun aimed at her chest. She nodded, wide-eyed.

'Where's Torvic now?'

'I dunno, honestly I don't. But I do know this: he's gonna kill me.'

'Why?'

Jackie swallowed hard as if she was ready to puke. 'I heard on the radio that there was a fire at my caravan site. I think it was my van, but the thing is, I shut Torvic's granddaughter in there. I must've left a fag burning, 'cos, apparently, the caravan was burned to the ground.'

So I was right. It was Jackie who broke Torvic out of the hangar, thought Zara. But was Jackie really that stupid, jumping out of the frying pan into the fire? Zara, now shocked, lowered her gun.

'Are you fucking kidding me?'

Jackie didn't move except to shake her head.

'So why come *here*? I mean, didn't ya think for one minute that *I'd* kill ya, because we know it was you who let that monster out of the hangar. You are one thick bitch, d'ya know that?'

Jackie was too consumed with what Torvic might do to her if he found her to try and deny anything.

'Come on, tell me. Why are you so sure I won't kill ya?'

'Well, as much as I know you and Mikey hate me, and you have every reason to, ya never did anything other than scar me face when you could've done so much more. Like you once said, you could've cut me throat.'

'No, Jackie. I said *next time* I would slice your neck.'

Zara noticed the fresh bruises on Jackie's face. 'Who did those?' She rudely pointed.

'Gloria. I went to hers, and she fucking laid right into me.'

Zara smirked. 'Yeah, I'm not surprised. But the question is, what am I gonna do with you now?'

With her head tilted to the side, Jackie asked, 'What d'ya mean? I just wanted to talk with Mike, explain what happened and stuff.'

Zara laughed. 'Well, darlin', he ain't here. It's just me and me gun, so, like I said, I'm now going to have to decide what to do with ya, ain't I?'

The cold, menacing expression on Zara's face told Jackie that she'd made an enormous blunder. But it was a case of better the devil you know than the devil you don't.

'Er, please can I use your loo?'

'No.'

'What? Come on, Zara, I'm bursting. I'll piss meself.'

With a stony face, Zara said, 'Fuck if I care.'

'Please, look, woman to woman ...'

'But, Jackie, you ain't a woman, are ya? You're a creature, a lowlife – a slimy, ugly bloodsucker.'

Zara's insults sent a rush of blood to Jackie's face, and she forgot about the gun in Zara's hand. Lashing out, she cried, 'You've no idea what I've been through. You'd never understand—'

'What you've been through?' screamed Zara, making Jackie jump. 'I'll show you what I've been through. Move on.' She waved the gun, pointing to a passage leading off from the hallway.

Jackie walked down the passageway, thinking how spooky the place was.

Zara suddenly demanded that she stop.

Jackie looked to the room on her right and couldn't see

inside because of the pitch-black darkness in this part of the house.

'Go in!'

Jackie didn't argue, all the while the gun was pressed against her back.

Zara was confident that Torvic wasn't in the house or he would have made an appearance by now. And she was even more convinced that Jackie was here of her own accord. She needed all the lights back on and assumed that turning the CCTV off had, somehow, turned the electric off as well. But once again she thought, *what a clever man her father had been to have some emergency lighting installed*. Clearly, the system was designed to come on after a set time if the lighting stopped functioning for whatever reason.

'Stand there.' Zara pointed to the other side of the desk in her office.

Without taking her eyes off Jackie, Zara placed the gun down and switched the CCTV back on. As predicted, the lights lit up the room.

Jackie, in a rush of madness, instantly reached for the gun, but she was beaten to it by Zara, who, in a split second, smashed the metal shooter across Jackie's face, sending her toppling backwards on her arse.

'Aah, you cunt!' she said, between gritted teeth. Her hands flew to her mouth, and her tongue felt the broken tooth. She spat it out, along with a mouthful of blood.

'Bad move, Jackie. I thought you'd have learned by now that you'll never win a fight against me.'

Jackie wiped her mouth with the back of her hand. 'Well, you can't blame a girl for trying.'

Zara grinned malevolently. 'That's true. Now, bitch, you're going to have a taste of what my life was like first-hand. Move!'

Jackie was taken back along the passageway to the basement entrance. A staircase led down to another long corridor, and at the end, she saw what looked like one room secured with a metal barred door.

'Go in!'

Jackie hesitated. 'Are you fucking serious? That's like a ...'

'Prison? Yeah, it was mine for five fucking years. Go inside.'

Jackie knew she'd no choice. But what she was walking into had to be better than facing Torvic. Perhaps it would be a sanctuary, at least for the moment.

Chapter 9

Once Jackie was safely locked behind bars, Zara charged up her phone enough to call Mike right away to give him the heads-up on Jackie's movements, secure in the fact that Torvic couldn't hear her conversations outside the office.

'I'm on my way. I wanna grill that whore like a barbecued trout. Don't let her move.'

'I've no intentions of letting her out, unless it's in a wooden box.'

Mike sensed the harsh and meaningful tone in Zara's voice and grinned to himself. Jackie had definitely met her match with the most important woman in his life.

It wasn't long before Mike returned, along with Lou. He left his car parked directly outside the front entrance and marched into the house quickly, acknowledging Zara, before he made his way down the staircase to the basement suite.

Lou followed the big man behind. He winked at Zara as if to say, 'We'll get blood out of *this* stone.'

Zara locked the front door and joined them; she wanted to see for herself how Mike was with his ex. Did he still hold some affection for Jackie? He'd always demonstrated how much he hated her, but would he be different if Jackie was in such a vulnerable position? Zara knew that she would only be able to tell once she'd seen him face-to-face with her.

He aggressively pulled the door open and glared at Jackie, who was sitting on the bed, sheepishly wringing her hands.

'You're gonna tell me fucking everything, right now. No bullshit, Jackie. I want the fucking truth or I'll dismiss the idea completely that you're Ricky's muvver.'

Realizing that resistance was futile, Jackie merely nodded.

'Did you burn the caravan down with Tiffany, Torvic's granddaughter, inside?'

'Yeah, I did, but not intentionally. I gave her some sleeping tablets and then locked her in to come and find you, to tell ya what I'd done.'

'Was it you who let Torvic out of the hangar?'

'Yeah, but he threatened to kill Ricky if I didn't do as he said.'

Unexpectedly, Mike lunged forward. With one hand, he tightly gripped Jackie's throat and lifted her off her feet. 'You fucking liar! You let that cunt out 'cos he offered you money. Ain't that right?'

Coughing and choking, she nodded, her face bright red.

Mike dropped her instantly.

'Please … I'm … I'm sorry. I didn't realize,' she said, as she got her breath back. 'I mean, once I did, I came to find you, I swear. I even went to ya ol' girl's place.'

'Where did Torvic go if you were left alone with Tiffany?'

'I dunno, I swear. He just said he had to go out and would be back. I knew I'd fucked up, and so I locked her in and left. I passed him a little while after. He was driving towards the site, but I don't think he knew it was me. He carried on driving, but if he knows now, then he'll be after me. Mikey, please. You have to help me. He'll kill me.'

Mike laughed. 'Of course he'll kill ya, and not just you but all of us, you stupid tart.'

He turned to face Lou. 'Call Willie and let him know that Torvic ain't in Spain.'

Lou pulled out his phone but then frowned. 'Mike, what if Torvic's got someone else he knows who's been told to kidnap Liam, and what if—?'

Zara interrupted. 'No. How would he know the kids are in Spain? Something else is going down. I don't believe now that Liam's disappearance is anything to do with Torvic.'

Jackie's life had been like a cat's – she'd escaped death so many times – and she sensed an opportunity to save one of her nine lives again today. She felt her input could help Mike – perhaps he'd see her as an asset. *It was worth a shot*, she thought.

'Torvic didn't call anyone; he didn't have a phone. I drove him straight to me caravan. That was a good two hours' drive, and then he paced the van for fucking ages. When he left, he wasn't gone that long – maybe an hour or three. He never mentioned Liam, though, only you, Zara. Oh, yeah, he also mentioned what he was going to do to you, Mike.'

Mike gave her a cold stare. 'Oh yeah, and what was that then, eh?'

'He said, "I'll make Regan suffer." That's what he said.'

Zara shook her head. 'Jesus, you are one thick prat! I bet you never grasped the significance of what he meant, did ya? *How* d'ya think he'll make us suffer, eh? By hurting the family, the kids, that's how, you idiot.'

Mike and Zara could tell that Jackie was nonplussed, knowing that she was too selfish to entertain that threat because she couldn't think of anyone other than herself. To her, an intimidatory remark like that would wash right over her head.

Lou, who stood watching quietly, suddenly spoke up. 'Look, the problem we have is that Torvic has one over us. He knows more about us than we know about him.'

'No shit, Sherlock,' replied Mike, exasperated by his friend's input.

'Nah, wait, Mike, before you shout me down.'

With raised eyebrows, Mike glared. It was unusual for Lou to be so upfront with him, the boss, yet if Lou spoke out, which was rare, then everyone tended to listen because the man chose his words carefully unless he was in a bantering mood with Willie.

'Look, what do we know about the man except for the fact that we've killed his two sons and now his most precious procession? Tiffany has been burned alive. He'll be fucking raging, and that means he won't be *compos mentis*. Trust me, he won't have all his ducks in a row, and that makes him weak. Who will he call, 'cos we have his phone, don't we?'

Zara suddenly hurried back to the office and rifled through her bag. There inside a black case was Torvic's mobile. She could have kicked herself for not doing this earlier, and yet with Liam going missing, it had knocked them all out of kilter.

She rushed back to find Mike still interrogating Jackie. 'Mike, we have all his contacts on here.'

'Don't look at me. I can't even use me own. You, Lou, you're better at technology than me. See what you can find. Tell his associates that we have a present for him.' Mike looked at Jackie and grinned.

'Oh no, please, Mike. He'll fucking torture me ...'

'I know, I know, babe, but shit happens, eh?'

'You bastards! You fucking cruel bastards!'

'Me cruel? Huh, that's a joke. You put Ricky's life at risk helping Torvic escape, because even your pea-sized brain should've worked out that he'd be gunning for Ricky, just to torture me.'

Jackie knew then that she couldn't get anything past Mike. He could see right through her. He always had and always would. She racked her brains, thinking of something that would save her now. And, for once in her life, she found herself able to think clearly, probably because her life was on the line.

'Wait! I know. He did make a call. He used my phone,' she said, quickly, hoping her little plan would work.

'Where is it?' demanded Mike.

To his surprise, she pulled it from her back pocket, along with her car keys. Snatching them both from her, Mike glanced at Zara and frowned.

Zara felt awkward because it should have been the first thing she ought to have checked. She didn't respond with an excuse, merely glaring back, almost daring Mike to show her up in front of Jackie.

To her delight, Mike's frown turned into a smile. 'It's your call, Boss. What shall we do now?'

Zara watched the confused expression on Jackie's face, and, for a moment, she drank it in, feeling good about herself.

'Why didn't you just call Mike?'

Jackie rolled her eyes. ''Cos I don't have his number, do I?'

'I'm gonna check the number on her phone against Torvic's, to see if there's a name.'

Mike winked. 'Sounds like a plan. Right, come on. Let's leave the scum locked up for now.'

* * *

Jackie looked to the floor; it was her attempt at pretending to appear shameful. As soon as Zara bolted the door shut, Jackie looked up and smiled. She may have had the jitters about Torvic, but she'd learned a lot from hearing all of his ramblings. She hoped she could be successful in taking a leaf out of his book. Next up, she surveyed her surroundings. With relief, she spotted a bathroom and went inside to have a pee.

* * *

Zara wasted no time in tapping the number into Torvic's phone, relieved he didn't have a password. A name came up instantly as 'Eric'. She stared, aghast, and showed the screen to Mike.

'No way! It must be another Eric. That call wasn't to my brother, surely? I mean, he helped us capture Torvic. Well, at least he was there. If he was pally with the bastard, then he would've tipped him off.'

Zara scrolled down her own contacts list. Sure enough, it was definitely Eric's number.

'Mike, your brother didn't know what I was up to. I just asked him to meet me at the hangar. Lance took over at that point, so Eric wasn't prewarned that I was setting up Torvic.'

Mike ran his hands through his hair; it was a habit of his when he was stressed about something. 'No, there's some mistake. I don't get it. Eric was working with Lance... No, I'm sorry. No way would Eric do this. I know we had our differences, but, Christ, he knows how evil Torvic is. It's not in Eric's DNA to go against his family.'

'Okay, then, so why would Torvic call Eric?'

Mike wanted to defend Eric because the thought that he could be wrapped up with Torvic in any way was unthinkable. Zara's question irritated him: after all, Eric was his brother, his own flesh and blood.

After a moment of thought, Mike said, 'To find out where he was, to track us down, I s'pose. I really dunno.'

'That's it, Mike. Exactly. We don't fucking know, so we'd best find out.'

Zara dialled Eric's number on Torvic's phone and let it ring. There was no answer. 'Mike, call your brother from your phone.'

Mike, now agitated, did as Zara asked. Within two rings, Eric answered.

'All right, Bro? Any news?' Eric sounded very upbeat.

Mike paused while he placed him on loudspeaker. 'No, Eric, not yet. Did you get Mum and Dad off okay?'

'Yeah, they're going to the Lake District or somewhere like that. Have you heard from Terrence yet? Did he take the youngsters to a safe place?'

Mike's eyes narrowed. 'No, I haven't heard anything. Where are you?'

'Er, me? I'm just on me way home to grab a few bits. Where are you? I can meet up in an hour or so, if ya like?'

'I'm going to the lock-up,' replied Mike, in a monotone voice.

'What for? Is Zara with you?'

Mike looked at Zara, his eyes wide and his face taut. She knew he was struggling to keep his voice on an even keel. 'Yeah, she is.'

'Good.' His voice sounded worried. 'I think Torvic will go for her, ya know. Keep her safe, and I'll meet you there. Is there anything else you need me to do, Mike?'

'Nah, just meet us there. My house ain't a safe place to be right now, and we need to organize a plan to take that bastard down.'

Zara nodded, encouraging Mike to make his efforts sound convincing.

'Righto, mate. See ya there.'

As Mike ended the call, he shook his head. 'I dunno. He wanted to know a lot, especially about where the kids and you were, but he didn't sound anything other than genuine.'

Lou sparked up the end of his cigarette and blew a large plume of smoke into the air. 'Well, we'll soon find out, Mike. So, let's get off and meet 'im there.'

The lock-up and events from the past made Mike shudder. The place was his torture chamber; it was full of memories he wanted to forget. Yet, it was the first place that came to him. But could he really torture answers out of his own brother?

A nervous sweat peppered his brow as he thought about the past and what he may have to do now. Eric had always been by his side, passing the tools or being the lookout. He thought back to the old days, when they were just two brothers, close in age, and similar too in appearance and moral values. Shit! Had that bond between them really snapped? The tears in his eyes welled up when he recalled the conversation in the hangar after they'd captured Torvic. Eric apologized to him and Zara for his behaviour and he seemed so genuine. He couldn't blame his brother for loving Zara, as that was just an emotion, but to side with Torvic? That was another matter. He knew that as much as he was a family man, he was also a ruthless bastard and meeting Eric face-to-face would be a test as to how merciless he could really be.

'Let's get going. Lou, you follow me in Jackie's car. It'll be the heap of junk parked on the lane near the entrance. If that Torvic turns up here, he won't have reason to believe that she's down in the basement.'

'I'll wait here, Mike, with Jackie, just in case,' said Zara.

Pulling Zara into his arms, he hugged her tight. 'I would rather you were somewhere safe. I don't want that bastard getting his hands on you.'

'Mike, listen. I'm safe here. I'll wait in the basement. There's only one way in, and if he chooses to walk down those stairs, I'll blow his ugly head off.'

Mike pulled away and looked at her face. Those eyes that drew him in formed a lump that lodged in his throat. 'Please, babe, make sure you kill him. Don't ask questions, just shoot him.'

'I will. And I promise you, I'll be careful. You be careful as well because this has to be a set-up.'

'I know the lock-up and its location better than anyone. I'll be one step ahead, and if Eric is behind this, then I *will* kill him.'

Zara watched as the sadness crept over Mike's face. She knew that it would be the hardest thing for him to do – to murder his own brother.

* * *

Shelley looked out of her hotel window at the building site all around her and tutted. Her father could have booked her into a five-star place. 'Fucking dump,' she mumbled under her breath. She sat on the bed with the sulks and tutted as the mattress sank beneath her. 'Fucking skinflint.'

Just as she was unpacking, a knock at the door pulled her head out of the suitcase. 'Who is it!' she snapped.

'Colin.' The voice was strong and brusque.

Surprised, she opened the door. 'Oh, I didn't think you were coming to Spain.'

He gazed around the sparse room, straightened his cufflinks, and sighed. 'I'm putting a lot on the line for this. I mean a fucking lot, and I wanted to be here myself in case anything goes wrong.' His eyes nervously twitched, which often happened when he was angry or uptight.

'You said you would get the best. I mean, is my son in danger?'

Colin waved his hands in dismissal. 'Not your son, you bloody fool. I mean my fucking liberty or my life.'

'So, he's okay, is he? I mean, I haven't heard a word, no calls, nothing.'

Colin swept his hands across his neatly combed back hair and stretched his neck. 'You're not the least bit interested in what happens next, are ya? As long as your precious son is okay!'

'Dad, come on. Of course I am. I do care, you know.'

He waved his hands more furiously this time. 'No, you don't, and please stop insulting my intelligence because I can

150

see right through you like a sheet of glass. Anyway' – he tutted – 'it's all sorted.'

'And no repercussions, Dad? I mean, no one will link him to any of this, will they?'

Colin shook his head. 'No, nor to me. Everything has been carefully planned and executed my end, but, mark my words, Shelley. If anything *does* come back to bite me on the arse, then it will only have come from you or your son, so be warned. Any comebacks and I won't worry which one of you was responsible. I'll have both graves dug and both of you done away with.'

Shelley's eyes nearly popped out of her head. She couldn't imagine her father ever making a threat like that to her, his only daughter – his only child.

'I swear, I'll not breathe a word. Neither will Lucas. He ain't the type to go around shouting his mouth off. You would like him. He's a lot like you.'

'What? First, no, I wouldn't like him. Second, no, he's not like me. And third, he'd better fucking not shout his mouth off. Once this is all over, he must act like nothing has happened, or, I promise you, I'll kill him myself.'

With his chin jutting forward and the twitch in his eyes even more prominent, Shelley knew she needed to shut up or pacify him. However, when her father was angry, it would take a double dose of an elephant tranquillizer to calm him down.

'Thanks for the room, Dad. I appreciate it,' she said, trying to soften him.

'Oh yeah? Don't act like you're grateful.' He looked around. 'This is a shit pit, no mistake, but, funnily enough, it's one of my shit pits that by next year will be a five-star hotel.'

Shelley listened, imagining herself being part of all this. Her husband was loaded but his wealth was nothing compared to her father, and she bit her lip in frustration. How long would her father live? Would there ever be enough time to get back into his good books? Probably not, she decided.

'You know, Dad, Spain would be good for Lucas and me. We could start a new life, leave the past behind. Perhaps—'

She didn't get the rest of the words out of her mouth before he snapped at her with a high-pitched laugh. 'Don't even go there. Like I said, I can see right through you. As if I would ever let you anywhere near my business. I may not be on this earth for long, but one thing is for sure: none of my fortune will be left to you. You'll not receive a stinking bean. Got it, Shelley?'

'I don't want your money. I want my father back, that's all.' She tried to sound hurt but even that was hard, and yes, he was right: she couldn't pull the wool over his eyes.

'Yeah, 'course you do. Well, it ain't fucking happening. I'll call you in the morning when everything is done and dusted. Then, you can see your precious son. And, by the way, he isn't anything like me, so cut out the crap.'

'What? You've actually seen him?'

Colin scoffed. 'Yeah, I did. What an ugly bastard he is and all.'

Those words set her teeth on edge; she'd heard them too many times. 'Well, that's as may be, but, like I said, he *is* a lot like you.'

Colin examined himself in the mirror directly above the bed, smoothed his hair again, looked at his daughter, and winked. 'Yeah, right, sure he is. Anyway, you'll get a call when it's time to leave. You won't see me ever again.'

As the door slammed shut, she sat back on the bed, and in frustration, she punched her fists into the mattress. 'You bastard!'

* * *

Liam coughed and tried to swallow, but he couldn't. Something was stopping him. His eyes once again felt as though he had lead weights pressing on his lids. He could hear voices that started off as mumblings, but then, as his awareness came back, he recognized the sounds. One was from a woman; her voice was soft, and the other was from a man, which resembled that of a schoolteacher – posh and sharp.

A sudden panic ripped through him as his recollection returned. He tried again to move his arms, but they were still clamped to the bed. The smell was distinctive, and then he remembered his mother in the kitchen overdoing the bleach and the disinfectant. He could hear rhythmic bleeping sounds and the whoosh of a pump. However, he couldn't fathom where he was or what the hell was going on.

Then the pain hit him. From his chest down, he was hurting; it was a burning, a deep, agonizing ache. For a moment, he thought his captors had cut him in half, and, in a flash, he began to sweat. He tried to scream out in fear, but something in his throat was stopping him. His eyes opened, and the bright light that was there before had now gone; it was just a vast silver dish-like structure, hanging above his head. The room was dim. He expected to find himself in some empty run-down warehouse or lock-up, but the plastered walls and the small room suggested otherwise. Closing his eyes again, as the waves of tiredness washed over him, he heard that sharp voice again.

'Leave him. He'll bleed out eventually.'

Christ, what's happening to me? What the hell are they doing? Liam fretted to himself.

Once the door slammed shut, he could hear another voice inside the room. It was the woman's again.

'Dear God. Please, help me.'

It wasn't a cry for help that came from her. She was praying.

Liam opened his eyes and looked straight at her. Dressed in green scrubs, with just her sweet round face showing, Liam realized that she was either a surgeon or a nurse. Their eyes locked, and for a moment, he saw the shock and panic written across her face.

She gasped. 'Oh shit, this wasn't supposed to happen.'

She quickly looked at the door and then back at Liam.

'Oh my God.' Her eyes darted around the room, desperately searching for something.

Liam watched as she scrambled to the other side of the bed and fiddled with his arm. He looked down and saw a cannula. She was injecting him with something. Her eyes displayed terror.

'I can't do this.'

Liam wondered who she was talking to.

'God, if you're listening, please help me. I can't let him die.'

Those words were bittersweet; he was going to die anyway, but this nurse, whoever she was, was attempting to save his life. A sudden feeling of comfort softened his muscles and relaxed his terrified thoughts. His eyes were heavy again, but he was still awake. The nurse untied his arm, and in one swift movement, she pushed him onto his side. Then the pain hit him. Whatever the nurse was doing, it felt like hell on earth.

He tried to scream, and yet nothing but a muffled groan came from his mouth.

'Please, please be quiet. You must.'

For a second, the pain subsided, and she was face-to-face with him. Slowly, she removed the tube that had been put into his throat, and whispered, 'Please don't scream or they will kill you. Please.' Her eyes turned down at the sides, and a crinkle across her nose showed she was afraid.

He wanted to gag, and started to panic, but she spoke again. 'Please don't move. I need to sew you up. I know it will hurt, but, trust me, I will get you out of here. Just do as I say.'

Liam swallowed hard, feeling the freedom and yet also the dry soreness at the back of his throat. He nodded, his eyes glistening. The nurse stroked his cheek as a tear left her eye and trickled down her face.

He could feel her pushing and poking around. Everything from amputation to experimental surgery ran through Liam's mind, but he was too weak to fight; he had to put his trust in the nurse.

The stinging and burning wore him out. Desperate to cry, as every nerve was on fire, he bit his bottom lip, making it bleed. Tears filled his pillow; and no matter how much he tried to hold them back, his eyes just constantly filled with water. The pain was unbearable and all he wanted was his dad. It was as if he was a six-year-old kid again. He'd had appendicitis and his dad was there hugging him as he cried with the pain. He had been so afraid of the operation but his father's words of comfort seemed to have made everything okay at the time. Not this time, though. He was powerless, completely at the mercy of this young woman, who, it appeared, was rooting for him.

It seemed like hours before the nurse finished. Exhausted and in agony, relief came when she finally stopped and turned him over onto his back. She'd been crying too; he could see the red rings around her pretty green eyes.

A rustling outside the room forced the nurse to act quickly. She pulled a sheet over his entire body. 'Be quiet and don't move,' she whispered, as the door swung open.

Now, he heard a different voice, an older man's, with a cold, calculated tone. 'What are you doing, Nurse?'

'I was clearing everything away, as you asked.'

'Is he dead?'

'Yes, a minute ago.'

'Are you sure?'

'Yes, absolutely. His heart stopped.'

'Take him to the incineration unit. He is expected.'

'Yes, Sir,' she replied with confidence.

Liam desperately wanted to be sick, but he held his breath for all it was worth.

As soon as the door slammed shut, the nurse peeled back the sheet. 'Listen. I have to get you out of here. Okay?'

Liam nodded and took a deep, painful breath. 'Please, tell me what's happened to me.'

'Not now. Just be quiet.'

Liam knew he had to do as instructed; she was the only person right now on his side.

The nurse unstrapped his other arm, covered him back over, and just as she was about to wheel him out of the room, the door opened again. Liam heard a different voice.

'Kirsten, you will have to take over from me next door. I need to make some calls. I will take the body to incineration.'

Dread washed over her, like a tidal wave.

'No, I can't. I think I have come down with a fever. My hands won't stop shaking, and I feel so sick.'

'Pull yourself together. I need to call home and ...'

'Your girlfriend?' asked Kirsten to her nurse colleague.

'You what?' he replied.

'I know what you're up to, Grayson. You make up to me, but I've seen you with Nurse Halloway. What would your wife think, I wonder? Anyway, I feel ill. I can't afford to make a mistake, and I know I will, if I go in there now. Like I said, I feel rough.'

Liam could sense the tension in the room, but, lying still, he held his breath.

'You breathe a word, Kirsten, and I will ...'

'Grayson, please go back in there and leave me to be sick in peace. I won't tell your wife.'

The door slammed shut, and Liam breathed deeply, in relief.

'Prick,' she said, under her breath, which gave Liam a great sense of relief, knowing that she was still in the room.

He heard the door open again and this time he was on the move. He had no idea where he was. It was quiet with just the sound of the trolley wheels as they trundled along. A sudden left turn and he could feel the speed pick up. The nurse had used the gurney to push through a set of double doors. The noise echoed. Faster she ran until Liam could feel every lump and bump. Underneath the white sheet, he could see the light and feel the change in the air temperature. They were outside.

When she removed the sheet from his face, he saw the clear blue sky. As he turned his head to the side, he saw the building half-buried into the steep rock face. The front was freshly bricked with glass doors, and a silver sign reflected the sun – Dash Plastic Surgery Clinic.

He craned his neck to look behind and saw the double doors from where he'd come. It was the delivery entrance. Christ, what had they done to him? To the left of him was a tall brick wall.

Wasting no time and breathing hard from pushing the gurney along the winding drive, Kirsten stopped for a rest behind the wall.

'I need to get you away from here to a hospital. Wait here. Don't try to move. I'll be back in a minute.'

Liam trembled. He tried to move a little, but the pain was excruciating. He closed his eyes to the bright sunlight and prayed she would be able to pull this off without being caught. Every time he thought of a furnace, he felt nauseous. The minute seemed to stretch to hours as he lay there fraught with fear.

As soon as she returned, he relaxed a little and started to breathe more easily. Her voice was like a lullaby, a comfort blanket. 'I need to get you dressed.'

She said it with great urgency. He was willing to do whatever she asked as long as she was saving his life. She proved to be a dab hand. First, she popped a sweatshirt over his head and pulled his arms through. Then, she put on some tracksuit bottoms, lifting his rear like she was dressing a baby. As Liam moved his arm, he wanted to laugh; maybe it was a reaction to overwhelming fear, but the sight of a bright-pink tracksuit was bizarre. The red cherry logo on the front might even have made him smile if he wasn't in so much pain.

'Sorry about the outfit. It's all I have.'

Liam winked. At that moment, Kirsten's heart melted. Guilt covered her like an invisible veil; how the hell could she have done this to such a sweet lad. Ugly he may be, but just that wink transformed his looks. He was charming enough. She was amazed at how he responded when most men would have been screaming in pain.

She popped a baseball hat on his head, put on sunglasses to cover his eyes, and quickly shoved a note in his tracksuit bottoms.

'This is going to be so hard, but please try to walk with me. I will bear most of your weight, but I have to get you just down the road. If I park outside the clinic, the camera will see us. At the moment, love, we are out of view.'

'I'll do me best.'

Kirsten noticed that Liam was staring at her; in fact, he couldn't take his eyes off her. She knew then that his survival right now was all down to her. As she tried to sit him up, he yelled, 'Aah, fuck, it hurts.'

'I know it's going to be tough, but it will be far worse if we don't get away, like now.'

Those words made Liam go into flight mode; he bit back the pain, placed an arm around her shoulders, and slid from the gurney onto his feet. At first, as his legs took his weight, he buckled, but Kirsten held him upright.

'Come on, you can do this,' she said, encouraging him.

With a deep breath, he held back the screams that wanted to escape and staggered along with her. Every step he took was like a knife thrust in his side, but he soldiered on until they were standing by a dusty red car. She opened the back door and helped him inside. Once the door was shut, he lay down, and for a moment, he lost consciousness.

He finally came to as Kirsten began tugging him to get him into a sitting position to help him out of the car. Dazed and light-headed, he allowed her to help him to his feet. She turned him around and seated him in a wheelchair.

He could hear the panic rising in her voice, as she said, 'Please, love, stay with me. Come on, you can do this. Stay with … Oh my God! Not now! Please don't die!'

As the light began to fade, it looked to Kirsten that her patient had too.

Liam tried to hold onto the feeling of her hands gently stroking his cheek, but the world was closing in, as his body lost its fight to survive.

Chapter 10

As soon as Eric turned the key in the lock and pushed his way in, he knew something was wrong. The musty odour of sweat and stale air hit him. Being a man who took pride in his appearance and who was forever bathing and splashing copious amounts of aftershave on his body, he was sensitive to his own home smelling of nothing less than rose, honeysuckle, and jasmine.

As if his world had turned into slow motion, he heard the distinctive sound of a gun being cocked and felt the breath from the man he feared most. He froze – too afraid to look to his left.

'Now you're fucked,' came the unmistakable voice.

Unable to move, Eric stared ahead, waiting for the bullet, and hoped it would be quick.

Torvic, however, wasn't going to let him off that easily – not in a million years. One bullet through the head wasn't punishment enough; that wasn't sweet revenge, and it wasn't going to happen.

'You, of all the motherfucking bastards, double-crossed me. If I ever made a bad mistake, it was trusting you, ya cunt,' growled Torvic, through clenched teeth.

Eric was defenceless. There were no words or excuses he could even attempt to use to get himself out of the deep crap he was now in.

'How could I have been so blinded, unless, of course, you had a sudden change of heart? What was it, eh? Was it Zara's soft words of forgiveness, or her masterly skills in manipulation perhaps?' He paused. 'Come on, then! Tell me!' he screamed, making Eric jump.

Eric turned to face Torvic. He had just locked eyes with the Devil. With a bristly stubble and brown rings shadowing his eyes, Torvic appeared incensed. Eric could see the tiredness in his face, but there was an unmistakable rage written across it, and he guessed that the man was only able to keep going on adrenaline alone.

If he made an attempt to attack him, then Torvic would shoot him on the spot. It would then be over. There would be no torture. But the problem was his brain just wouldn't function as he thought it should. He was looking desperately around the room, hoping for some kind of miracle to extract him from this nightmare scenario. But he couldn't fucking move! His legs seemed almost paralysed as if they were glued to the floor. He then realized that his survival instincts were telling him not to risk a bullet and to wait for events to unfold, however unpleasant those would be. His impulses were trying to keep him alive. So, no way was he going to do anything rash. And he certainly wasn't going to beg and plead or even cry out with some feeble excuse. He was a Regan, for Christ's sake. He did have *some* pride!

'It was nothing to do with Zara.'

A sickly giggle, like a girl's voice, left Torvic's lips. 'Oh, come on, Eric. You're obsessed with the woman.' He laughed again. 'I can see why, though. She would put all you men to shame. You're a joke, really. You're pathetic. A woman having so much power, I'm surprised one of you hasn't done her in already.'

Eric smirked and looked the dishevelled man up and down. 'You never did, though, Torvic, did ya? And you had plenty of chances, alone in her home with her. But the thing is, you didn't, and that makes you as pathetic as us.'

Torvic flared his nostrils and grimaced. 'Shut up!'

Eric smiled sarcastically.

'The truth hurts, eh, Torvic?'

'I said, shut the fuck up!'

They remained with their eyes not budging from each other.

'You could've had it all, Eric – the money, a partnership, any bit of skirt you fancied – but you switched sides, and that intrigues me. So why did ya do it?'

Eric protruded his lower lip and raised his eyebrows. 'You were deluded, and for a man that could outsmart the Filth – even the special operations team – you somehow never questioned me.'

As Torvic's breathing increased, Eric sensed he was hitting a nerve and winding the man up. Under normal circumstances, anyone wielding a gun becomes extremely dangerous when anger builds. However, Eric knew that Torvic wouldn't kill him cleanly, not when he was so irate. He knew so much about the man – more than anyone else did, in fact.

He watched the man falter and considered how the hell he was still standing. He had to give Torvic some credit. He'd been awake now for forty-eight hours. He'd seen his sons tortured and murdered and watched his granddaughter's expression of horror as a bottle of acid was held ready to pour all over her head to burn her face off.

In that moment, Torvic could almost read his mind. Eric was upright, fresh as a daisy, with not even a crease in his shirt. But what was so galling was Eric's body language. The lack of nervousness made Torvic angry.

'Move!' Torvic demanded.

Eric stepped forward, towards the lounge.

'Go in and sit down. We're going to have a talk: you, me, and my gun.'

Eric then realized that he'd been proved correct: Torvic was tired. With himself sitting down, it meant that Torvic would do likewise and take the weight off his weary bones. And the man was weary, that was for sure. A far cry from the person he'd met a year ago. A genius at manipulation, he had the gift of the gab and the presence to pull it off.

Eric, although nervous, was revelling inside. He wondered how long it would be before Torvic would show himself as the old man he indeed was. How many hours would it take to strip back the layers until he could be exposed for his age and vulnerability?

Staying awake when the mind and the body were desperate for sleep, was a colossal ask of anyone – not least a man in his sixties. That act in itself, although self-inflicted, was an act of torture. All Torvic's negative thoughts, all the personal slights to his reputation, gnawed away at him as they pierced his brain, like a thousand needles, consuming vital energy.

Torvic realized that he must stay focused and remain one step ahead of Eric. It was tough going when he knew he was suffering from bouts of delusion brought on by exhaustion and drugs. Using every last bit of stamina, he tried to remain standing, poised and in control, and not appear like the madman who Eric very probably thought he was. But a wave of tiredness forced him to sit down.

'Tell me one thing, Eric. What made you change your mind? I can make your death quick … but you need to tell me.'

Eric now felt he could breathe a little easier. He had a hold over Torvic. He had something Torvic wanted – answers – and he knew the man was desperate for them. Whatever was going through the man's crazy brain, Eric was going to use Torvic's need to have him confess in order to stall the bastard long enough in the hope that he would eventually let his guard down.

'What I'm gonna tell you is a story, Torvic.'

Angered by the calm, confident tone in Eric's voice, Torvic growled, 'Cut the crap. Get to the last line of the chapter. I wanna know why you switched sides.'

'Well, it won't make sense unless I start from the beginning.'

'What the fuck is this? Fucking *Listen with Mother*? I don't think so … Just spit it out.'

Eric loosened his tie and leaned forward with his elbows on his knees. 'Like I said, it won't make sense otherwise.'

As Torvic, in a fit of fury, jumped up from his seat, Eric clocked him stumble. The man was drained.

'Start fucking talking, Eric, or I'll make your demise a little nastier and more painful and unbearable than any others I've had the pleasure of finishing off.'

Eric took a deep breath. 'It's all about leapfrog. Not that I see myself as a fucking frog but—'

'For fuck's sake! Get on with it!' Torvic bellowed, as he paced the floor.

'Ya know, me brother was always top dog. Everyone listened to him. Me mum, me dad, the lads, and Zara. She, I guess, was the final nail in the coffin. I wanted her. For years I loved that woman, and there was Mike, with all his charisma, his take-no-shit attitude, whisking her off, right under my nose.'

Torvic sighed and sat down again.

'You wouldn't understand though, would you, because you've never loved anyone, have ya? Not even your own flesh and blood. Well, apart from your granddaughter, that is.'

'Just get on with it or I'll finish your story with a fucking bullet.'

'Anyway, Zara turned her nose up at me and went running into Mike's arms. That was like a sword in my heart. Mike had won again.'

'Sounds to me like a jealous brother,' mocked Torvic.

Eric curled his lip. 'Yeah, ya got that right. I had every reason to be.'

He looked over at Torvic, who still appeared on edge, but at least he was sitting quite comfortably in the cushioned chair. It was the one that he himself always seemed to doze off in.

'I fucked off when Mike got banged up. Everyone was running around trying to find Ricky. I knew where he was, though. I sussed that out early doors, but I kept me mouth shut. So, Torvic, you might think you're the Devil, but I can be too. Anyway, there was nothing left for me. Zara then disappeared, and so I fucked off. I wanted to mould myself into the complete opposite of Mike the gangster, the hard bastard, the villain. I couldn't be him, or even live in his shadow anymore, so I tried to go straight. I started a business in Spain growing food – specialist food – such as snails and mushrooms.'

Torvic had switched off. He fumbled around in his pocket, still holding the gun in the other hand.

Eric watched as Torvic pulled out a small clear bag containing a white powder. He decided to stop talking and glared as Torvic poured some of it onto the back of his hand and coarsely snort every last bit.

'Christ, you're hooked on that shit as well, ain't ya? You, Torvic, have gone down in my estimation.'

Torvic wiped his nose, using his jacket sleeves. 'Don't be a prick, Eric. This ain't Flakka. It's the best cocaine money can buy. I wouldn't stoop that low.'

Eric nodded. He might have known. But what was interesting was the fact that by snorting a livener, Torvic was exposing his weakness – he was flagging. Eric would play him for all it was worth. For such a long time, everyone had assumed that he was the slower brother, the weaker son, the less appealing friend. They should never have done that. Not even Torvic, the man who had everyone shitting hot bricks.

'Now, Eric, get back to telling me why you double-crossed me before I get bored with your fairy stories and plant a bullet right between your eyeballs.'

'Oh, Torvic, you won't be bored. In fact, I think you'll want to order in pizza and popcorn and make a night of it.'

'Your face will look like pizza unless you get to the point.' Torvic had livened up; at this point, he was extremely dangerous. He was cocaine-fuelled and angry: both were a recipe for recklessness.

'So, I was in Spain, and to be frank, I was bored

shitless. I couldn't go straight. I had to have a purpose. Shit, me brother was fucking right again. So, I came back to England. I decided to lie low for a bit. I kept away from the manor, but I kept me ear to the ground. Funny, because I was hoping that I would be the man that would find Zara. You know, to be her knight in shining armour. I dreamed that she'd fall into my arms, and we could start something special. And it might have happened. But, fate played its hand. Almost as soon as I rescued Zara, Mike had found Ricky, and it was all one big soppy reunion. Mike proposed, and that was it. I didn't get a second look.'

'Aw, my heart bleeds.' Torvic smiled. 'Now, get the fuck on with it!'

'Why do you have such a desire to know the reason I double-crossed you? Tell me that first, Torvic.'

With his eyes staring at the top of Eric's head, Torvic appeared to be lost in space. He wondered, maybe somewhere in his subconscious, if he blamed his father, the man who left his mother, only to return when he was a teenager to rob him blind. He'd come back into his life and for two days he'd convinced him that he would be there by his side. He'd offered him a stake in his own business that he was setting up in Bristol. They would earn a fortune, and he would be an equal partner, with the one man he loved and desperately wanted back in his life. However, the bastard took all his savings, promising he would send word when the business was fully up and running. Of course, it never happened. He did a runner, and all he heard, years after, was that his father had died on the streets from alcoholism. Not long after receiving the news, his mother then also passed away. He vowed after that never to trust a living soul. He changed and became the master at double-crossing. His father had taught him that much – believe no one and get out of life as much as you can because everyone is out for themselves.

His mind drifted, back to Izzy, the man he could never beat, the only crook who would be just the one step ahead. Now, all that was left was Izzy's daughter, Zara, and he would take everything from her as payback for all the shit Izzy had put him through. Eric's question still circled his mind: *why* did he have to know the reason for Eric double-crossing him? Perhaps the answer was because he never understood why his own father did it. He was looking for one answer and he thought that Eric could give it to him.

'I helped you, Eric. I set you up in business. I trusted you with my contacts, and you delivered. There were no fucking issues. I don't remember fucking you over. But you fucked me over. Why?'

Eric was grinning inside, just seeing the crumpled expression on Torvic's face as if he genuinely was hurt.

'Yeah, Torvic, you did take me on, but let's be honest here. You used me for what and who I knew, so it wasn't as if you picked me up off the streets and put me in a palace. It was a two-way deal. I gave you names and places, and you went in and took over the cocaine business.'

Wiping the sweat away from his brow, Torvic licked his dry lips.

Eric was watching intently, calculating the man's present state. Clearly, he was dehydrated.

'Yeah, and you were paid well. So, come on then,' he

bellowed, 'why did ya blindside me?' In frustration, he leaped up from his chair again.

Eric could see Torvic's eyes flickering from side to side, the sweat running down his face, and his cheeks glowing red. He was sure the man was going to have a heart attack at any minute, and he would watch that with pleasure, but he didn't expect the man to lurch himself forward and ram the gun into his mouth. The action was so fast and aggressive that his head was forced to the back of the chair, the barrel smashing his front teeth in. How the force hadn't caused Torvic's finger to pull the trigger was beyond him, but now he was in agony. His lips were split open, and he gagged on the barrel of the gun. Torvic was wild-eyed as the cocaine reached its full impact.

Fuck, thought Eric. He'd underestimated Torvic by playing it cool and taking his time while stringing out a story that had pushed the man to his very limits. Now he had to change tactics and fast.

As Torvic removed the gun, Eric clamped his hand over his bloodied mouth, feeling the broken teeth like tiny pebbles in his hands. The raw nerves sent excruciating pain up through his head, making his eyes water. Yet he needed to talk. He had to get the man back onside. He wasn't cut out for torture. He may have dished it out in the past, but he'd never been on the receiving end of it, and if this was what it felt like to have teeth pulled out, he would rather die.

'Okay, Torvic, let me speak.'

Torvic flared his nostrils and glared. 'Go on but make it quick. I'm fucking done with you.'

'Yeah, I fucked you over, like I was saying.' He winced as the cool air hit his bare nerves. He ran his tongue over the remains of his teeth and swallowed hard. 'Right. Back to leapfrog. By that I mean I lean on a man to jump to the next best thing. Lance Ryder approached me. He sucked me in over a few brandies. I guess I was pissed, but what he offered me sounded pretty attractive. It was a position in the special operations team. I'd still be a civvy but I'd have a hell of a lot of clout. And as an ex-villain, I'd be held in high regard. That's all I've ever wanted, in my entire life. I've wanted respect. To be seen as *someone*. I was never held in any fucking regard working with you, Mike, or any other fucker. All I had to do was to track down the man behind the gangs. It was so easy yet it was clever because I could drag it out, you see. I earned money from you *and* the special ops team. No one knew what the fuck I was doing. Then Mike got out, and I realized that my big brother and Zara were all after the same person – *you*. So, I was left with tough choices to make, but you, Torvic, made it such a fucking walk in the park.'

Eric stopped and smiled. It was a slow, sadistic smile, which spread across his bloodied mouth, making Torvic jolt. It was a look that Torvic had never seen before – a cruel smirk, perhaps similar to his own mirror image.

He tilted his head to the side. 'But you still haven't explained why you blindsided me?'

'As much as I've hated the bond between Ricky and Mike, I detested more what you did to that boy. You hurt Ricky – that's something you should never have done. You were double-crossing me all along, pretending that it was me who was taking over Zara's restaurants and running the gangs. It wasn't me though that was going to inherit half the business. It was Alastair, your psycho son. I have to hand it to you, Torvic, you were bloody clever, mate. Swapping the cocaine business for Flakka, you built an empire. I was supposed to be a part of it but that would never have happened, would it? Because you use everyone, and I mean everyone.' He stopped and took a deep breath, before shaking his head. 'You even used your granddaughter to help convince Zara, but …' – he huffed and scoffed – 'Zara was too clever for you. You underestimated the woman, and now you want answers from me. Well, now you have 'em, Torvic. I might be a cunt, but you are the fucking Devil's cunt.'

Torvic sat back down and smiled. 'Well, thank you, Eric. I just wanted to know, that's all. It wasn't me who battered Mike's son, though. Just to confirm what you should know from the hangar set-up, it really *was* Dez Weller and Alastair.'

'Yeah, you mean the evil bastard raised by you and *your* teachings, don't ya? That makes you just as much to blame.'

'Eric, you surprise me. I really thought you were a heartless bastard, but somewhere, in that chest of yours, there is at least a heart.' He shook his head. 'It's a shame. I'd hoped the reason was something more dramatic. Perhaps a better offer from a more powerful man who you defected to, but, no, you did so all because of a kid, a stupid kid at that, who got bashed up.'

'No, not any stupid kid, Torvic. He's *my* kid. He's *my* son!'

Torvic stared, his eyes on stalks. 'What?' He couldn't believe his luck. 'I take it, dear Mikey has no fucking clue, then?' He didn't need an answer: the resigned look on Eric's face said it all. The new knowledge gave a boost to his mood and a fiendish chuckle left his mouth.

'Well, well, well. I can't wait to see the look on big Mike Regan's smug fucking face when he hears that his son – his precious boy – ain't even his, and, worse, he's *yours*!' With that, Torvic threw his head back and roared with laughter.

Eric looked up to see Torvic's red face beaming with excitement. Then, as if a new thought had ripped through Torvic's mind, his face returned to its demonic, cold glare.

'I can't be bothered to play games with you, Eric. You've given me enough satisfaction today, just knowing I've something on Mike that'll destroy the man. Like you said, you had a choice to make, but your choice has just got you killed.'

Eric heard the bang before the bullet hit him.

Torvic pulled out his cigarettes and lit the end of one, puffing senselessly. His hands were shaking, and his mouth was still very dry. He needed a drink. Perhaps he'd overdone it with the cocaine and shot Eric too soon. What a waste. He could have dug deeper for answers, to reel the others in. The excitement of Eric's disclosure had made him act recklessly. But now? Now, he needed to get his own act together before he fucked up anything else.

His mind drifted back to his granddaughter. Perhaps it was Jackie who was dead in that caravan. The gypsies were sure it was her. Where would Tiffany have gone, though? He'd trained her well, so all he had to do was imagine how she would think. He suddenly had a sinking feeling in the pit of his stomach. He had to find her before Zara, Mike, or any other person in that firm got to her first.

Just as he gulped down some cold water, Eric's phone rang. He paused and listened. It was coming from Eric's trouser pocket. Quickly, he placed the long glass on the side and grappled inside Eric's pocket until he found the phone. Unexpectedly, the man's dead weight fell on top of him. He cursed. Sliding out from underneath Eric, he then staggered upright and grabbed him beneath his armpits, hauling him up into a sitting position. Picking up the phone, a name flashed on the screen: it was Mike fucking Regan. *This should be fun*, he thought. He pressed the accept call button and listened.

'Eric, where the fuck are you?'

'Well, if it ain't the brother, Mr Fucking Regan.'

Torvic could almost taste the panic as he heard Mike's breathing suddenly change.

'Put my underhanded bastard of a brother on the phone,' Mike bellowed.

Torvic blinked. What did he just say? He paused before he spoke, his brain trying to process why Mike would call Eric an underhanded bastard. *Did Mike know that Eric had once worked for him before he defected to the other side?* he wondered.

'He's busy. I bet your arsehole's gone now, Regan, eh? Never thought I'd escape, did ya? You believed you were on top. Well, how does it feel now?'

'You're nothing, Torvic. Why don't you come and meet me face-to-face and then let's see who's chickenshit, 'cos, old man, it ain't fucking me.'

A surge of anger ripped through Torvic like an electric storm, setting all his nerves on edge. 'Meet you? Nah, I'm gonna make you sweat, and as I take out every member of your family, one by one, trust me, I won't make their demise sweet. It will be bitter and painful. And, just so you know, I've one down already and what a pleasure it gave me too.'

Without a thought as to who it was who Torvic had murdered, and assuming too much, Mike carelessly screamed down the phone, 'You murdered Liam, you sick bastard, didn't ya?'

Not knowing who Liam even was, Torvic replied, 'Yeah, that's right, and another one of your lot will be next.'

'When Willie gets to you, I swear to God, you'll wish you'd taken Alastair's place, 'cos that man will keep you alive and torture you every fucking day.'

Torvic grinned. So Liam was Willie's son, then, and the chink in the firm's armour would be their boys. He'd not known their names, except for Ricky. Hesitating before he blurted out what he knew about Ricky, Torvic thought quickly. It made sense for now for Mike to believe he was still the boy's father until he could see the crippled look on his face when he told him otherwise. 'Your boy will be the next to go, mark my words, Regan.'

'Yeah, is that fucking right? Well, you'll have to get through me first, and I'll annihilate you, you can be sure on that score.'

Mike's hands were sweating as he gripped the phone, trying hard to keep it to his ear instead of launching it across the lock-up floor. 'Put Eric on. I want to personally tell him what I have in store for him an' all.'

Torvic called out, 'Eric.' He paused. 'He's in the bathroom, getting cleaned up. I'll tell him you called, though.' Before he ended the call, he gave a sickly chuckle.

* * *

Mike's nostrils flared as he looked at Lou. 'Would you believe it, eh? Me own brother in cahoots with Torvic.' His eyes scanned the lock-up. 'And to think the last time we were here we were fighting the world together.'

Lou nodded his head and sighed. 'I think the good ol' days are long gone, mate.'

* * *

Zara dragged a chair along the corridor and sat outside the barred door while Jackie nervously sat on the bed. Her hands were under her backside, her knees bobbing up and down, as she chewed the side of her lip.

'Horrible in that place, ain't it? I was stuck inside there for five years,' said Zara.

'Well, at least it was comfortable and you got food. Me, I had fuck all. I did what I had to do to survive, so I would've traded places.'

Zara shook her head. 'You, Jackie, are totally deluded. You had it all: Mike, Ricky, wealth, but you chose to fuck off, steal the money, and make a new life for yourself. You weren't kidnapped and held against your will. You had the world at your feet, but you were just too stupid to see it, letting your fanny rule your brain.'

Jackie could see the gun resting on Zara's lap and guessed she wasn't going to get shot anytime soon. For, like any woman, Zara would be curious about her and Mike's relationship. It was her chance to make Zara feel as worthless as she did right now. 'It wasn't that, Zara. I had to leave. I just couldn't handle all the pampering. Mike wanted sex every minute of the day. Smothered with love, it suffocated me, ya know what I mean?'

Those words would have ripped through Zara like a hot knife through butter, but not today. She smiled.

'Yes, I know what you mean, Jackie, but I guess I can handle that. You couldn't.'

Jackie glared; she hadn't expected that reaction. She thought Zara would be heartbroken.

'I bet it's hard for you, having my cast-off, eh?'

Zara remained calm. She could see exactly what Jackie was doing; it was like a teenager at the school disco provoking a catfight. Yet somehow this was fun. 'You forget, Jackie, I had Mike first, so it was you who had the cast-off. Married or not, I could've had Mike back at any time. And you know it, Jackie, don't you? You never ever really had that man's heart because it always belonged to me and it always will.'

Jackie screwed her face up in a temper. 'Yeah, well, whatever, Zara, he ain't my fucking type. You're welcome to him.'

'Tell me this, Jackie. If you left for no other reason than he was suffocating you with love, why would you keep Ricky from him? You left everyone completely in the dark. That family searched for years for that boy. Why?'

Jackie hopped off the bed and walked to the bars so that she could look directly into Zara's eyes and give her the biggest smirk of her life. 'Not everyone, Zara.'

'What?'

'Someone from that family knew exactly where he was,' replied Jackie, with a condescending snigger.

'Liar!'

Slowly and deliberately, Jackie shook her head. 'Oh yes they did.'

It was now Zara's turn to look worried.

Jackie could almost see the cogs whirring as Zara absorbed the shocking news. Savouring the discomfort on Zara's face, Jackie watched her gloomy eyes and gave her another mocking half-smile.

But Zara wasn't stupid. She tightened her face, raising a well-defined eyebrow. 'Ya know the trouble is, Jackie, whether you are telling me the truth or not, you have a reputation for telling lies, and so that's where your little story is consigned to – in the bullshit pile.'

Jackie curled her lip. 'No, seriously, there was one of the Regan family who knew where Ricky was all along.'

Zara shrugged her shoulders, demonstrating she didn't give a shit.

'What, don't you want to know?' asked Jackie.

'No, Jackie, not really. It doesn't affect me in any way. In fact, I couldn't give two fucks, to be honest.'

'But …'

Zara jumped to her feet and faced Jackie square on. 'But what, Jackie? But fucking what?'

'I thought you'd want to know.'

'What, so you can play another game of pulling that family apart? I wouldn't give you the satisfaction.'

Frustrated with Zara's nonchalant demeanour, Jackie tightened her lip. 'Well, Mikey will want to know, and I'm gonna tell him.'

'Good. You do that. I'm sure the sentence will end up with something like *in exchange for …*'

'No, he's a right to know. And I don't want nuffin for the information.'

Zara laughed. 'You mean, then, you want something.'

'What?' asked Jackie, with her nose crinkled in confusion.

'If you don't want *nuffin* it means you want *something*. Think about what you just said, or shall I get out the crayons and a colouring book?'

'Cor, you really think you're better than me, don't ya?'

'Yeah, I do. In fact, I don't think, Jackie, I know I am. You are a scummy piece of dog shit, who cares for no one but herself. No one believes a word that comes out of your mouth.'

Jackie moved away from the bars and sat back down on the bed. 'Eric, he knew. I saw him one day, hiding behind the hedgerows along from my caravan. I thought, any minute now, I would have that bastard smashing through my door and taking Ricky. He never did, though. One minute he was there and the next he was gone. So there, and I don't want money for it. That bit of information comes free.'

Jackie glared again, waiting for a reaction, but Zara was silent and motionless, with not even a blink from her cold eyes.

'Er ... did you hear me?'

Zara nodded. Slowly, curling her top lip, she smirked. 'Yeah ... funny, because even if I did believe that story, it still wouldn't shock me. So, it wouldn't be the big revelation that you'd hoped for. You won't get a reaction out of me.'

Jackie was fuming. She'd never managed to rein in her temper and this time was no exception. She lashed out without thinking. 'Yeah, well, that may not fucking shock you, but this will, ya cocky cow. Ricky ain't even Mike's. Eric is Ricky's *real* father!'

No sooner were the words out of her mouth than Jackie froze. She then stood up with flushed cheeks and wide eyes. Her reaction was the most honest thing she'd ever demonstrated.

Zara believed there and then that Jackie had actually told the truth for once in her miserable life.

They both stared at each other, wondering what the hell to do next.

'And what do you propose to tell Mike?'

'Well, er … the truth. Eric was there when Mike wasn't. He shouldn't have put me second best to every other fucker, like the firm and his bleedin' muvver and farver. Eric cared, though. He was there for me, always caressing me cheek and telling me how beautiful I was.'

Zara could tell from Jackie's tone that this wasn't fighting talk: this was her real story – it was nothing short of the truth.

Zara nodded for her to go on.

'I thought he really loved me. He always seemed to pop up when I was at my lowest point. He even told me that Mike was mad to have dated you, and he told me what I already knew: that Mike would always love you. When Mike wasn't around, we …' She paused and looked at the floor.

Zara wondered if Jackie actually felt ashamed of herself. She knew Jackie wasn't lying because it was exactly what Eric had done to her. He appeared when Mike was busy, stroking her cheek and hinting that Mike was up to no good. 'So, are you really going to tell Mike and cripple him and Ricky?'

'You, Mike, and his family all looked down on me. You treated me like scum. Well, I'm a lot like you, Zara, and I want to have my moment too … my little bit of revenge.'

'Revenge! For fucking what? They did no wrong. It was all about you.'

Jackie gave Zara a sneering glance. 'Whatever, Zara, I'll still have the last laugh.'

'How much do you want, Jackie, to keep your trap shut?'

Jackie laughed. 'You really do love him, don't ya?'

Zara didn't answer.

'I don't want money, bitch. If you want me to keep schtum, then you walk away, and I *mean* away – for good. Get out of Mike's life – and Ricky's – and fuck off. If you don't, then I'll tell him the truth.'

'I could shut you up for good, Jackie. I haven't got to leave Mike. One bullet and it will all be over.'

It was Jackie's turn to play the trump card. 'But you won't. Firstly, because the police will be crawling over this gaff, and, secondly, you wouldn't hurt Ricky. He loves me, that kid does.'

It was those last few words that had such a hollow ring to them. Zara knew Ricky didn't love his mother at all; he'd told her as much.

'The police won't be crawling over this place because firstly, you thick prat, they may well believe you're dead, burned to death, and secondly, by the time they discover it's Tiffany's body, I'll have yours dismembered and sent to various parts of the country. And, let's be honest, who's going to make a fuss about your disappearance? You have no one, and why? Because you fucked everyone over in your life who actually cared for you. You brought it all on yourself, Jackie.'

'Ricky cares, and you wouldn't hurt him, would you?'

Zara raised her brow. 'Cares? Seriously, are you really that deluded? You fucking traumatized the kid. In fact, you left him mute with scars all over his body and you fucking think he *cares*? He doesn't!'

Jackie seethed as she glared at Zara, but her anger was laced with fear because behind Zara's elegant exterior and cold eyes lay a very formidable and dangerous woman.

She changed the subject. 'I don't even know what Mike sees in you anyway.'

'No, you wouldn't, because you don't possess the level of emotional intelligence *to* understand. But he does love me, and I love him too, with all my fucking being, and so when my loved ones get threatened or hurt, I will step in the way.'

Jackie watched as Zara stood with her feet evenly apart and held the gun pointed at her head. The bronze-coloured eyes darkened over as if she was staring at a target. Her whole body – like a stone statue – made Jackie uneasy.

'Look, okay, then. I won't say a word. I promise, hand on heart.'

Her eyes widened in utter disbelief as Zara slowly cocked the gun.

'No, please, Zara. Don't do it! I swear, I won't ever mention it again. Oh, Jesus, don't shoot. I lied okay, I lied. It's not true. I was just being a cunt. O' course Ricky *is* Mike's boy.'

She held her hands in front of her, shaking all over. Her eyes partly closed, waiting for that bang – the sound that would be the last thing she would ever hear again.

The second that Zara lowered the gun, Jackie felt she could breathe more easily.

'Christ, seriously, I thought you were gonna pull that fucking trigger.' Out of breath, through fear, she went on, 'Oh my God, I thought that was it. You fucking scared the shit outta me. Right, I promise you, I'll never say another word about Ricky.'

Zara smiled. 'I know you won't. Bye-bye, Jackie.'

Bang! The sound echoed along the stone corridor as Zara stared at the clean shot that passed right through Jackie's head. The body lay flat out on the bed, and the only sound was the drip-drip as her blood made its way like a stream onto the floor. 'No, Jackie, you won't say another word. Not ever.'

She knew she could never trust Jackie because the truth was out there. It couldn't be a made-up story because the details of Eric's advances were all too familiar. The difference was though, she was stronger and resisted them, while Jackie, however, was weak, shallow, and selfish.

* * *

An hour later, the banging on the front door pulled Zara out of her introspection. She guessed it was Mike. The three hard knocks followed by two more were his signature method of letting her know it was him. She dragged herself from the chair and took one further look at the dead woman. Slowly, she climbed the stairs, her mind going over what she would say. How the hell could she justify her actions? She couldn't tell him the truth or else killing Jackie would have been pointless.

As soon as she pulled the door open, in marched Mike. 'Fuck me, Zara, I've been trying to call you. I've been outta my mind with worry.'

'Oh shit. Sorry, I was downstairs. I left the phone on charge up here.'

'Well, listen. You ain't gonna believe this one. I called Eric but Torvic answered the phone. We were right. My stinking two-faced brother is working with him. Jesus, I should've known. Fucking hell. I keep racking my brains, trying to think of everything I told Eric. What does that bastard know that he could possibly share with Torvic? And I reckon Torvic did kill …' He stopped and grabbed Zara's shoulder. 'Hey, you look as white as a ghost. Is everything all right, babe?'

Zara slowly nodded. 'Yeah, it's all good, love.'

'You must be shattered, babe. Look. Lou's gone to a hotel to get some kip, Staffie's gone to his uncle's place, and the others are all safe. Well, as safe as can be, that is. We need to get out of here, get away, get our thoughts in order.'

Zara was still thinking about Jackie.

'Zara, are you listening to me?'

She looked into his eyes and wondered if he would still have the same level of compassion if she told him she'd just killed his ex-wife, the mother of his son.

'Babe, listen to me. We can't stay here, so let's grab a few bits and go.'

Zara nodded and headed up the main staircase. There was nothing more she could do if Mike went down to the basement; she would just have to pray he didn't.

Her heart seemed to beat outside her chest as she dragged a holdall from the wardrobe and began throwing the clothes into it, while listening to every creak and sound, wondering if he'd pay Jackie a visit. The only sound, however, was the zip as she closed the bag. Just as she was about to leave the bedroom, her eyes fell on the cabinet that held the bulletproof vests. She'd left hers at Mike's. Without hesitation, she opened the cabinet and pressed the button that released the hidden unit. There, sure enough, tucked inside, was her father's. With no time to try it on, she laid it over her bag and swiftly made her way back down the stairs.

Mike was peeking through the curtains. 'It's all clear, babe. Come on, let's get going.'

She snatched her phone and followed him outside. Once they were in the car and heading away from the house, she relaxed her breathing.

'So, Mike, what happened? How do you know for sure that Eric's working with Torvic?'

'Because Torvic answered the phone.' He paused. 'I'm gutted. It was definitely Torvic, ya know, who killed Liam. That poor fucking kid. I dunno how I'm gonna break it to Willie.' He let out a deep sigh.

'It doesn't make sense. If he was with Eric, and your brother was here in this country, then how did he manage to kill Liam? Liam was in Spain.'

'That's what I'm still trying to work out. I dunno how much Eric knows and what he could've possibly told Torvic. The man may well have people in Spain. Eric knows Spain like the back of his hand, and he knows Terrence. It wouldn't take a lot to track down the kids, would it? I wish I'd never sent them there. Well, Willie will be landing soon, so at least the kids will have the protection of those two.'

As they approached the main junction and stopped at the red light, Mike suddenly said, 'Shit! Jackie! We fucking left her behind.'

Zara knew she didn't need to lie. 'Well, she's not going anywhere. She's in the basement.'

The lights turned green. 'Oh fuck! Hang on. I'll do a U-turn.'

'No, leave her, Mike. The place is locked up. She's comfortable enough down there. Christ, I stayed there for five years and I survived.'

Mike continued on. 'I just can't get my head around me brother. Why the fuck would he do that to us? Poor Liam, he's fucking – was – fucking innocent in all of this shit.'

Chapter 11

As soon as Willie walked through the front door of Terrence's home and saw the stricken expression on Arty's face, he held out his arms. Arty fell into them and sobbed. 'I loved him, like a brother.'

Willie held him tight. 'I know, boy, I know, and when I get my hands on whoever took him, I swear I'll make sure they have the worst death in the history of fucking torture.'

Arty sniffed back the tears and wiped his face. 'And I'll pass you the fucking tools.'

Through an expression drenched in pain, Willie suddenly grinned. 'You are so much like ya farver. He was always the tool passer. Me, I guess I was the carver, Mike was the mechanic, and Lou, well, Lou was the voice of reason.'

Arty nodded and decided to change the subject. 'The girls are in the lounge. They're a bit anxious, especially Poppy. She really liked Liam. As for Ricky, he's not well. I think it's all too much, so he's resting upstairs. Terrence is calling the quack in, just to make sure he's okay, ya know.'

'Good, so I s'pose I'd best introduce meself.'

Willie followed Arty into the lounge where the two girls and Terrence were sitting. Poppy was curled in a ball asleep, resting her head on Brooke's lap. As Brooke looked up, she put her finger over her lips and mouthed the words 'Let her sleep'.

Terrence quickly rose to his feet and hugged Willie and then led him into the kitchen. 'I dunno what to say, mate. I had that villa secured. And I mean better than Fort Knox. I just dunno what happened.'

He noticed how exhausted Willie appeared. His pupils were mere pinpricks and his face was grey. 'I'll make a bite to eat and then you can go and have a bit o' shut-eye. You look like ya need it, mate.'

Willie waved his hand. 'Nah, I'm fine. I'll comb every inch of Spain to find my boy ...' He faltered and coughed to stop himself from crying.

'Yeah, okay, but you ain't gonna think straight without sleep. Come on, mate. Have a lie down before you fall down. You ain't gonna be any use finding your boy if you're—'

'He's dead, Terrence, I know he is, but I need to find his body. I have to know what happened to him before I can rest. I won't rest until I know. It'll eat me up alive.'

Terrence patted Willie's shoulder. 'I know, mate, I know.'

'I've always been a bit of a twat at times. Ya know, being reckless, mad, a coke-head, but ya know what? I was always in control around my boy. I loved him, more than life itself. I would die for that kid ... Why couldn't it have been me? Why him, eh ...?' He broke off, too choked to speak.

'Come on, get some rest.'

With his slow steps and slouched shoulders, Willie followed Terrence up the stairs to the back bedroom that faced the pool. 'We'll find him, Willie. One way or another, we'll find him.'

'Where's Lance? I thought he was here already?'

'He was. He checked on the girls and then left. Apparently, he has contacts over here. He's gonna do a bit of digging. The man's a big fucker. I don't know much about him, but, I tell ya this, I wouldn't wanna cross him.'

Willie lay down on the bed. 'He was Special Forces. I like the geezer. He's straight up, he is, and if he does get a lead, he won't fuck around with the police or shit, he'll be right on 'em.'

Terrence watched as Willie fought to keep his eyes open. The second he was asleep, Terrence crept back down the stairs. He didn't have kids of his own, but the one thing he did know was how tight the firm was and how much the men loved their boys. He checked the front door was locked again. He couldn't risk losing Ricky or Arty or even the girls for that matter. Whoever this Torvic was, he had really put the wind up Mike's firm. Terrence had never in his life, even as a young lad, seen Willie look so worried. The circumstances had sparked a definite change in the man.

As the sky darkened, Terrence called two of his men to guard his house; he needed to sleep himself and wanted the place watched. The whole situation had put the fear of God into him, and he wasn't easily spooked.

* * *

Zara lay in the bath of their hotel suite. She stared up at the ceiling, going over in her mind how she would explain Jackie's murder to Mike. Whichever way she looked at it, Mike wouldn't forgive her. He may have disliked Jackie, and for very good reasons, but it wasn't her place to put a bullet in his ex-wife's head. The water was turning cold, and she knew she had to get out and face Mike with some kind of explanation. Climbing out and wrapping the white hotel bathrobe around her, she dried her face, rubbed her wet hair, and entered the bedroom.

Mike was lying on his side scrolling through messages on his phone. He stopped and looked up with that glint in his eyes. She knew exactly what he was thinking, but it wasn't her intention to look seductive; in fact, she felt quite the opposite of sexy right now – she just felt sick.

He patted the bed and rolled onto his back. 'Come here, me darling.'

'Mike, listen. With everything that's going on, I'm not in the mood.' She smiled. 'It's not you, it's this fucking situation.'

Mike sat up. 'No worries, babe. I've been thinking an' all. About Jackie.'

Zara's eyes widened. 'Er … what about her?'

'I hate to say it, but if Torvic breaks into your house, he'll kill her, ya know.'

Zara was still afraid that Mike would go straight over to the house. Her heart was pummelling, but she hoped she looked in control of herself. She swallowed hard but said as calmly as she could, 'So what do you want to do about it?'

He lay back again with his hands under his head. 'Nothing.' He looked into Zara's eyes. 'You don't think badly of me, do ya?'

Zara blinked and looked away. 'No, I don't. I guess she really did put you and Ricky through a lot, huh?'

'To hell and back. I would've taken her with us, kept her safe, ya know, but …' He sighed heavily. 'She sided with Torvic. She put her own son at risk again. I don't know who I hate more – Torvic or Jackie. Nah, fuck it. If he murders her, I won't shed a tear. I'll probably dance on her grave.'

At long last, Zara felt her shoulders relax, and she breathed out slowly with relief. That was the answer she wanted to hear; it was there from Mike's own mouth. Whoever found her dead, Torvic would be blamed. It stood to reason because Jackie was running for her life away from the man. So, at least now, Mike would never know the truth about his son.

'You really do detest the woman, don't ya?'

Mike pulled Zara onto the bed and gently kissed her lips. 'You, Zara, are the only woman I've ever loved.'

'No, I don't mean for you to compare us. I mean, does she really deserve to die?' She had to know what he truly felt, to lessen the guilt that was gnawing away at her.

'There's only so much you can forgive a person for. There's a lot you don't know about Jackie and how bloody wicked that woman is. When I look back and try to think of anything good about her, I just hit a blank. Some people are born bad, and she is one of them. When I saw the scars on Ricky's leg and back, when I first met up with him in stir, after all those years apart, I couldn't believe it. They are fucking horrendous. My boy endured nearly thirteen years of hell with her. And not only that, but she has treated her own mother, dear ol' Gilly, like utter shit.'

He stopped and lowered his eyes.

'What's the matter, Mike?' asked Zara, as she noticed his face crumpling. She lifted his chin to find his eyes full of tears. 'What's up? Please tell me.'

He blinked and gave her a sorrowful smile. 'Sorry,' he said, wiping his eyes. When he relived those sad memories, it tore him apart. The truth was that it was not only Jackie who was the root of the problem here. He knew his criminal lifestyle was also partly to blame.

'What else did she do, Mike?' asked Zara, knowing that Mike never cried, so whatever he was thinking about, it must be bad.

'She hated Ricky. I didn't want to admit it at first because what mother hates their own kid? But when I look back, she was a cruel cunt. When Ricky was eighteen months old, we had a nanny. Well, I employed one because I was too afraid to leave Jackie alone with him. She didn't pay the baby the attention she should have. You know, she'd let him cry, wouldn't change the nappies. One day, it was in the summer, the nanny was off for the week, looking after her mother. I had a meeting with your father, I think it was. Anyway, I told Jackie I would be out all day, but as it happens, I was back home by three o'clock ...' His voice cracked, and he coughed.

Zara could see that whatever it was he was about to tell her, it would hurt him deeply.

'Well, she didn't hear me come in. I stood at the French doors looking out into the garden, and there she was, pissed with two of her mates, who were also blind drunk, dancing around the pool. It was so fucking hot that day, the hottest day of the year, I think. I remember panicking, 'cos I couldn't see Ricky. I flew through those doors, and one of her mates tried to grab me to get me to dance. I pushed her off and glared at Jackie.'

Zara leaned over and took Mike's hand. It was as if he was falling apart in front of her eyes.

'Well, her face said it all. She was so spiteful, she said, "There's me ol' man, ol' misery guts."'

Zara moved across the bed and held Mike in her arms. Just then, she cursed not having two hands to comfort him.

'Then I saw my baby, and I could've drowned all three of those women. He was stuck in a playpen. Not only was his face shiny with sweat, but his body was red raw. The poor little fella had nowhere to go to get out of the sun. By the time I'd given him a drink and cooled him down, he had sunstroke and blisters all over his forehead and shoulders. He was only a baby. He could've died out there.'

Zara put her hand to her mouth in horror. She thought about her own baby, little Michael, who had sadly died due to a heart condition. She would have given anything for him to live, and now she truly understood why Mike hated Jackie. The ill-treatment of Ricky had obviously started at an early age and had then been continuous.

'So, I don't care if Torvic kills her. I was tempted, many a time.'

* * *

Staffie stopped outside his uncle's house and gazed at the flash pad. It was one of Brentwood's finest. The property was made secure with steel gates. The island in the middle of the drive had a fancy mermaid fountain that lit up, spouting water five feet high. He smiled to himself. His mother always said her brother was a flash bastard. Apparently, ever since he could talk, he'd always wanted the best.

Although he loved his uncles, they weren't business associates. On no account would they mix in the same circles, and they never called upon each other for backup. Family they may be, but only in the sense that they met up at weddings, funerals, and christenings, and that was about it. However, this day was different. No one associated the Staffords with the Marwoods. Nicolas and his brother Mack were a few years younger than his mother and drifted away from the family once they'd turned eighteen and seventeen respectively. Staffie wouldn't class himself as close, but there was always that unspoken promise, and it was this: if the shit really hits the fan, they could call upon each other.

Teddy, Staffie's father, had never liked Nicolas. He found him too much of a sly bastard, so he said. And so, when Ted worked with Arthur Regan back in the sixties, Nicolas and Mack, who were a few years younger, made sure they didn't have any dealings that remotely encroached on the Regans' turf. They tended to carry out their business in Essex. Their wars were mainly with a firm over in North London.

Staffie got out of the car and unlocked the gate and then hopped back in to drive around on the gravel driveway to the front door to be greeted by lights coming on from all angles. At this time of year, it reminded him of Santa's grotto. Staffie chuckled; Nicolas really was a gaudy git.

As Nicolas answered the doorbell, Staffie was greeted by an overweight, red-faced man with blinding-white gnashers. He was wearing a bright-green Lacoste T-shirt, which stretched tightly across his beer belly, and faded jeans that were more fitting for a younger man. 'Well, this is a fucking turn-up for the books, boy. Come on in.'

Staffie wiped his feet as soon as he noticed the white carpet.

'Come into the lounge, Staffie. D'ya wanna glass of bubbly? I've just popped a cork.'

Staffie followed his uncle along the hallway, with its over-sized gold mirror and mirrored glass units, into the main living area. Flash wasn't the word. It was so over the top that Staffie wanted to laugh again. A huge crushed velvet corner suite dominated the room. More mirrors, this time in the bar area, reminded him of a nightclub, and the black-and-white photos of Nicolas, posing in just a white shirt and black slacks, made him appear to anyone visiting as if his uncle was a celebrity.

Nicolas swaggered over to the bar and poured a generous glass of champagne. He passed the flute of bubbly to Staffie and then took a seat. 'Take the weight off, mate.' He gestured to Staffie. 'So, what's going on? It ain't like you to want to lay ya head down at my gaff. Trouble brewing, is it?'

Staffie placed his glass on a coaster on the large, square coffee table and sat back down. 'Yeah, there's an issue. Some geezer is on the warpath, and he's one dangerous fucker, so I was hoping that until the bastard is found, I could crash at yours.'

'Yeah, yeah, no worries, mate. So, who is this geezer? Do I know him?'

Staffie shook his head. 'I doubt it. Up until a couple of days ago, we didn't even know him, not by his correct name. Now we do. His name's Torvic.'

Nicolas screwed up his chubby red face. 'Nah, I can't say I've heard of him … and he must be pretty bad, 'cos I've never known your tidy firm to back off from anyone. Still, that's not my business.'

Staffie didn't like his undertone. He bit his lip to stop himself from saying something that he might later regret. His priority was to stay safe, and this gaff was ideal for his purpose.

'What about your boy? How's he doing? I ain't seen him since he was what? Gotta be thirteen years old at the time.'

Staffie smiled, and his whole face lit up. 'Arty? Yeah, he's a diamond. He's got a good head on his shoulders, and he's a looker an' all.'

Nicolas laughed, his face reddening even more. 'He must take after his muvver then.'

Staffie joined in. 'Yeah, thank fuck. No, he's doing all right. How come you never had any kids, Nicolas?'

'Me? Oh, Jesus, no way. Shitty nappies and whining? Fuck that.'

Staffie looked around the lounge. 'You've done well for yaself, though. I guess not having kids saw you okay?'

Nicolas sipped his champagne. 'I haven't kids of me own, but my Shelley's boy, I sort of treat like he's mine, well, when I have the time. She's brought him up, really. He's a spoilt little fucker. Whatever he wants, she gives him. Still, as long as she keeps him from under me feet, I ain't complaining.'

Staffie frowned. 'Where is Shelley? I ain't seen her in years. I've never met her boy.'

Nicolas laughed again. 'You ain't missed much. Me and Shell, we do our own thing these days. The truth is, I fucked her off.'

Staffie raised his brow and looked Nicolas over. He guessed that his uncle had moved on to a new bit of skirt. 'Oh yeah? Who is she, then?'

'Some kid, really. Honey, her name is. Anyway, I ain't getting any younger, mate, so I'm living it up. I've got the pad to meself and a quick how's ya farver when I want it.'

'Shelley wasn't that old. Christ, she was younger than

me. We all hung about together many moons ago. She was, if I remember, a good-looking woman. She had a mouth on her, but she was pretty,' said Staffie.

'A mouth on her? Yeah, you're right there. And she's still stubborn. But, yeah, she was a stunner, that's for sure, and, back in the day, I fucking loved the cow. She loved me an' all.' Nicolas smiled as if he remembered something. 'It was only supposed to be a bit o' fun behind her farver's back, 'cos, ya know, me and him, we hated each other. But the silly cow caused a right war when she told him she was seeing me. He fucking disowned her, so I had to marry the bitch and sort of take on that kid of hers.'

Staffie was feeling comfortable talking with his uncle. It was strange because years before, in his twenties, he'd feared Nicolas. At the time, he'd been regarded as the big man with a lot of influence, but things had changed. He knew he, himself, had grown up and matured, whereas Nicolas obviously had turned into a kid, reliving his youth.

'So, who's the kid's farver, then?'

Nicolas sighed. 'Who knows? She never told me her little secret. I reckon he could've been one of many. Ol' Shelley was a dark horse, ya know. Anyway, enough about her. D'ya fancy a bit o' grub?'

Staffie nodded. 'Sounds good, mate.'

As soon as Nicolas headed for the kitchen, Staffie relaxed his shoulders. He was washed out and just needed a bed. But he doubted he'd get much sleep tonight: Nicolas was such a chatterbox. He really didn't feel like sitting up 'til all hours, chewing the fat with his uncle, but it was a case of needs must.

When Nicolas returned, with a round of bacon sandwiches, Staffie was asleep on the sofa. Nicolas smiled to himself. As much as Staffie was his sister's son, he was still a man with a reputation and decent contacts. One day, he could call in this favour.

* * *

Torvic was completely wired; he'd finished his pouch of cocaine and was now pacing the floor. Eric's corpse was changing by the hour, and the more he stared at the man's open eyes, the more freaked out he became.

Yet this was the safest place to be. Who would've looked for him sitting in the lounge at Mike's brother's? He let out a childish giggle and jerked his head. His nerves were all on edge, making his body twitch unnecessarily. Eric's face was now a purple colour, and his lips were dark. He'd seen many a dead man in his time, mainly at his hands, but this was different.

It was quiet, eerie, and the vision was fucking with his head. Again, the image of that burned body as firefighters doused the fire came into his mind. He tried to shake his head to rid himself of the scene. No, it couldn't have been Tiffany. She would've left the caravan. If Jackie had any ideas of hurting his granddaughter, then she would've been given a good run for her money. His Tiffany would've beaten the living shit out of Jackie. And that woman in the car couldn't have been Jackie – no way. She'd told him she only had one car.

He suddenly became desperate to have that notion confirmed. He couldn't handle believing for a second that the virtually cremated body was his precious Tiffany. He glanced at Eric; for a moment, he couldn't take his eyes away. He jerked. Did Eric just wink at him? Surely not. The man was dead. With a bullet through his head, he couldn't wink. Torvic swallowed hard but his eyes remained glued to the expression on the corpse. He had to blink because he was convinced that Eric winked again. Beads of sweat covered his forehead, and he felt sick and faint.

Slumped on the chair opposite, he tried to take deep breaths, but the vomit idled there, ready to come up. His mind went blank. He just couldn't figure out what the hell to do next. How would he know who was in that caravan? Christ, he couldn't imagine what he would do if that body was Tiffany's. Immediately, his heart began to beat rapidly and his breathing became fast. He jolted again but then swooned. *That's it*, he thought, *I need another line*. As he pulled the pouch from his pocket, he discovered it was empty. He fumbled nervously inside the other pocket and freaked out when he saw that that one was too. He'd consumed two grams in an hour. Shit!

He looked at the clock. It was five p.m. What? Where had the time gone? He'd been awake for three days and nights now, or was it four? His mind was in turmoil, and, for the life of him, he couldn't rationalize any thoughts. This was all Zara's fault. She should never have been left with so much power. Izzy should just have let Ismail, the son, take over; he could've worked with him – the gullible prick.

He had to concentrate and deal with one thing at a time. Focusing on what to do with Zara was his number one priority, and since she was calling the shots, he would take her out of the picture first.

As Torvic started up his car, he paused before driving away. His breathing increased again as he was consumed by fear, and adrenaline surged around his body. This wasn't him at all; he was brave, daring, and flagrant. He wasn't a pussy.

After a few deep breaths, he pulled away and drove towards Zara's house. For a moment, he had to stop because he'd completely lost his bearings. Twitching, he lowered the window to take in the fresh air. The heater inside the car was drying out his eyes, and he had to blink furiously to be able to see the road ahead. Then, the heavens opened, and the windscreen wipers screeched as they fought to clear the glass. It appeared that anything, whether it was a high-pitched sound or a single raindrop landing on his car, felt like a hammer blow to his head. The journey seemed to take forever, but, finally, he was on the lane that led to her mansion. The vampire house on the hill, that's how he saw it, and probably everyone else did too. With no plan in place, he worked on his instincts, although in his present state, they left a lot to be desired. He drove straight on past her drive and turned into the farmer's lane just a mile up the road. A few yards further on, the private road changed to a track surrounded by woodland. He parked up and looked about him. As he did, the car engine died. He questioned if he was going mad, so he tried to start the vehicle again. Nothing. Then he realized that he'd run out of petrol. 'Fuck, fuck!'

Confident that his car couldn't be seen, he leaped out and opened the boot. As he stared at his arsenal, his eyes widened, and he punched the lid of the boot in frustration. There, in all their glory, were his prize guns, but there was not a single fucking box of bullets. In his rush to get back to the caravan, he'd forgotten to grab them. He gave a deep sigh and slammed the boot shut. He still had his handgun though.

Traipsing through the wooded area, he slipped and slid on the wet, muddy soil and cursed as he continued on. Half a mile further, he came to a clearing. There, in front of him, he could see the mansion in all its sinister glory. He knew where the cameras were placed and the areas that would be undetected. He grinned to himself. The silly bitch had been too naive, having entrusted him with the job of overseeing the installation of a CCTV system all around the property. So he marched ahead, confident that no one inside the house would see him approaching. As he neared the garage to the side of the house, he strained his eyes looking through the murky window. Next to Zara's car there was a black BMW 7 series, Stephan's pride and joy. The bastards had not only killed both his boys – making him murder one of his own in the process – but they'd had the audacity to take his son's car as well. His anger and frustration were climbing to new heights, and he imagined killing Zara, cutting off her limbs one by one, and enjoying the sound of her blood-curdling screams.

Creeping into the garage, he checked to see if Stephan's car keys were left in the ignition. He could use the vehicle to get away. Damn! They weren't there. He stared at the cold mansion, watching for any signs of life – even a tiny flash of light or condensed air from the central heating vent perhaps. There was nothing. He struggled to stand upright after being crouched down for so long. That's when he realized he was weak. Clutching his gun felt as though he was holding a dumb-bell. He desperately needed a livener to clear his messy head and to give him the strength he needed to take on Zara Ezra, the bitch from hell. That was if she was inside the house.

He made his way over to the back entrance. Like a door from *The Secret Garden*, it was partially hidden by a brick wall that was covered in rambling ivy. He turned the handle, but, as expected, it was locked. The leaded window was his only option, and with the butt of his gun, he tapped the small pane of glass. It broke, leaving a sharp triangle in the lead strip, so he tapped it again. Then he listened for any sign that he'd been discovered. Nada. His reckless impatience made him smash the rest. Quickly, he poked his hand inside and felt for the bolt. He pulled it across and then tried to push the door open. It was locked. Now, his frustration was sending him screwy. He pulled the gun from his pocket and fired one round at the lock. 'That should have her running, the tramp!'

The lock exploded, and he was able to force himself in. Still holding the gun in front of him, he walked through the small passageway and peered into the kitchen to find it empty. Slowly, he crept towards the office, listening for every creak. His senses were on high alert, but all that could be heard was the grandfather clock: tick-tock, tick-tock. It irritated him and hastened his steps.

He drifted from room to room, but so far, the house was unoccupied. Once he reached the final bedroom, he stopped dead still and stared. This was the room, all those years ago, where he'd stood in this very same spot and watched the most beautiful woman. She'd lain there sick; he'd loved her with all his heart, but she was Izzy's wife. Izzy, the bastard, had betrayed him, had cleaned him out, ruined his business, and chased him out of the country.

The one person who Izzy had loved apart from his daughter was his wife; she was the elegant brunette with rosebud lips and skin like double cream. He could still see her face and then the fear that emerged from her gentle eyes when she realized he was there by her bed, pouring the poison down her throat. He'd wondered that day if he would ever forgive himself for hurting her; however, his hatred towards Izzy was an overriding emotion more powerful than anything else.

Now, looking at the very bed, it seemed as though it was only yesterday he was here. The deep burgundy throws, the heavy wooden four-poster frame, and those huge plump cushions, which had supported Isabel's frail body partially upright, were a vision of the past. Now, however, that image stood out so clearly at the forefront of his mind. He stared longer, as if he could see her there – her delicate white cotton nightdress, her long, thin, feminine fingers – for she had been just perfect. And yet, she'd never been his to keep. The tick-tock sounds brought him out of his daydream, and the torrent of a thousand thoughts began again eating away at his sanity.

Just that small piece of satisfaction that Zara may have fled because she feared him brought a wicked smile to his evil-looking face.

Once he returned to the office, he made his way over to the grandfather clock. He hated that clock. As he opened the front compartment, he felt for the device that he'd planted years ago. It was no longer there. Still, it had only been a useful tool to hear conversations taking place inside the office. Zara's father would have been proud of that little spying device. Anything outside the room could not be heard. But the CCTV system he'd recently had installed for her was great if he wanted to see who was coming and going to the property. The installation engineers had connected an app to his phone so that he could see precisely what Zara would see. However, it wouldn't serve him well anymore because Zara had his phone. His eyes scanned Izzy's old desk and *voila*! There were his son's car keys.

Wandering around aimlessly, winding himself up, a sudden thought crossed his mind. The basement. He'd never been down there, but he was aware, after his first encounter with Zara – when he'd given her a lift from the Old Kent Road to this miserable place – of her imprisonment there at the hands of Ismail and the Segals. As he walked along the hallway and past the kitchen, he could see a door to the left. Although to any unsuspecting visitor it resembled a cupboard, it was far more than that. Izzy's architectural brain had conjured up a clever secret entrance to some stairs that led down to a suite of rooms deep below the main house.

He pulled the door open and peered at a wooden staircase. Listening to the silence, he slowly crept down until he could see a long stone corridor. At the end was a room that was made secure with a reinforced steel frame and heavy-duty metal bars. He wondered for a moment if Zara was inside there, hiding, and waiting to exact further revenge. Prudently, he held his gun pointed forward, knowing that just one shot to the head would be enough to kill her. As he reached the entrance, he noticed a chair abutting the door. She couldn't be inside, he figured. But who would've pushed the chair against the door? It seemed odd as the bars allowed for easy viewing inside the cell.

At first, he saw what looked like a classy bedroom, with cabinets and a wall-mounted TV, but then, as his eyes scanned the room, he stiffened. On the bed lay a woman. She was on her back with her arms spreadeagled, and on the floor he noticed a pool of blood. He guessed the person couldn't be Zara because this woman had two hands. And yet, from where he was standing, he couldn't quite see who it was. Quickly, he climbed onto the chair and peered down. The shock of seeing who the person was caused him to lose his balance, resulting in the chair flying across the room. Gripping at the bars as he fell, he tore two fingernails and smashed his knee on the stone floor. There he remained, his breathing coming in fierce gasps, and the ensuing rage sending his body into convulsions. 'Noooo!' he yelled, at the top of his voice. It was Jackie, which could only mean that the body in that fire must have been that of his granddaughter. 'Noooo! Oh my God! Oh my God!'

He retched three times before the contents of his stomach were empty. Leaning against the metal bars, his head a mess, he cried like he'd never done before. The image of the grotesque burned body wouldn't leave his mind; it swirled around like a never-ending carousel. Smashing his head back and forth against the bars didn't achieve anything more than cause physical pain, and yet it was nothing compared to the mental torment he now endured.

Someone would pay. He looked at his gun and suddenly realized there were no bullets left in his magazine. 'Damn!' he screamed as he smashed the gun on the floor. He needed at least four bullets for Zara, Mike, Ricky, and one for himself. There was no way anyone would take him alive.

Yet he couldn't go back to his mother's house for his ammo – someone might be watching. He wiped his tired eyes and snotty nose, before taking a deep breath. *Somewhere in this bloody great Devil's castle, there would be a loaded gun, surely?* he thought.

Chapter 12

Zara awoke to find Mike sitting upright on the edge of the bed. He was looking at a phone. She lifted her head and rested it on her hand. 'What are you doing, Mikey?'

He turned around and gave her a gentle smile. 'I'm going through Torvic's phone to see if I can recognize any of the numbers.'

Zara pulled herself up and covered her naked body with the white sheet. 'Let me see if I can.'

He handed her the phone and kissed her cheek. 'I'll order some room service. I've texted Mum and Dad. They seem to be okay. They're staying in some cottage out in the sticks. Dad reckons Mum wants to move to a farm.'

Zara smiled. She began to scroll through the contacts list, but then her expression changed, her forehead now crinkled as she tilted her head to the side.

'What is it, love?' Mike said, with the hotel receiver in his hand.

Slowly turning her head to him, a look of concern was clearly evident on her face. 'This is Ismail's number. Well, at least it used to be. Why the fuck would Torvic have had my brother's number?'

Mike frowned as he put the receiver down. 'You have to be kidding me! Your brother in bed with Torvic? That makes no sense.'

She glared at the number again. 'Well, it's definitely his.'

Her eyes narrowed as she tried to think back to a time or a place that would have connected Torvic with Ismail. Guy Segal had had her locked away to take over her business. Ismail had demanded she must be kept alive, even though the slimy shit was controlled by Guy Segal. So where did Torvic fit into all of this? She searched her mind for any clues but could think of nothing to explain the connection.

'Well, Zara, your brother was one underhanded son of a bitch. Perhaps he'd planned at some stage to double-cross the Segals by working with Torvic, but that all blew up in his face, and he didn't do it. And, let's be honest here, not many people knew about you. Who knew you were kept locked away, and, apart from us, who else knew you'd been freed? Ismail is on remand, and the incident wasn't broadcast on the news. It's odd, though, because Torvic turned up when you went to your father's jeweller's place. I don't think he found you by chance. I reckon the bastard had been following you all the time, waiting for the right moment, like when you were at your most vulnerable after the fight with that Lennon geezer.'

Hearing that made Zara's stomach churn. 'Of course! Why didn't I think of it? For five years that jeweller's had been more or less empty. So, then, it follows that Torvic wouldn't have been hovering around for all that time. He would have assumed that someone else had bought it and left it vacant. He wouldn't have known I was back on the streets unless, that is, someone had told him. So, the question is who?'

Mike sighed. 'Well, it's either my brother or yours who informed Torvic.'

Zara got up from the bed and pulled the towelling robe around herself. 'Eric?'

Mike looked uneasy. 'To tell ya the truth, he's been on my mind, and as much as he's been a bastard, something about him doesn't add up. Torvic had Eric's phone, and initially, I assumed my brother was with him, but when I woke up this morning, I had a dark feeling.'

Standing face-to-face with Mike, she gripped his left arm. 'You think Torvic's killed him, don't ya?'

He nodded. 'I know Eric. If he was with Torvic, he would've answered his phone or shouted out something, but ...' – he pulled away and sat on the bed – 'I think he's dead.' Looking up, he said, 'I'm gonna go to his house, see if he's been home. I've called him twenty times this morning and he ain't answering. Something stinks.'

'Then I'll come with you.'

He shook his head. 'Please, Zara, stay here. Be safe, and then at least I won't have you on my mind.'

She stood in between his legs and placed her hand around his head, pulling him to her stomach. 'I love you, Mikey Regan. Promise me you'll be careful. I can't face losing you.'

He undid her robe and kissed her navel. 'I'll be careful, 'course I will. Just stay here.'

'And Ismail?' she asked.

'I can get blood out of a stone, but it's your call, Zara. He's your brother.'

Zara pulled away and walked to the window. She opened the lock and flung the window as wide as it would go.

Mike watched her. For years he'd loved her. After all the shit they'd both been through, they should now be looking to the future, planning a wedding and enjoying life. He blinked away the moisture in his eyes and swallowed the emotion trapped in his throat. He would never admit it to anyone, but he was terrified, not for himself but for Zara and Ricky. A man like Torvic would be true to his word – of that, he was dead certain. Gazing at the contours of her neat, slim figure, he felt the urge to pull her back to bed and keep her wrapped in his arms, safe and secure. But she wasn't the type to want to be smothered with a safety blanket; perhaps that was part of the reason he loved her so much. A cold shiver ran up his spine; he had to kill Torvic or he would never rest.

As Zara leaned her head out of the window, he suddenly realized what she was doing. 'I thought you'd given up.'

Ensuring the smoke went out of the window, to prevent activating the smoke alarm, she replied, 'This? It's just a figment of your imagination.'

He smiled to himself but was quickly drawn back to reality. 'So, your brother, then?'

She took another long drag. 'Yes, I know. It's just, he's still my brother.'

She tried to picture Ismail's face when he'd watched her when she was behind those bars. Her main feeling then had been one of hatred, but that was because she'd been trapped and helpless. Then she visualized his face when her hand had been severed and the look of terror when he'd realized what Tracey Harman and Benjamin Segal had done. He was so shocked and had screamed, 'No!' So, she concluded, for all his underhanded moves, she had seen by his reaction that he'd never known they were going to go that far. Perhaps inside, despite her knowing he was weak and he'd played dirty in order to take her place as head of the family, he still felt something for her.

She spun around and faced Mike. 'Can you get your men on the inside to give him a message without hurting him?'

Mike rolled his eyes. 'Zara, after everything, I don't believe a few words from you will get him to spew out the information we need.'

She smiled. 'You may be right, but you don't know how my brother's mind works. With him, it's always been about power. He's never had it, not really, so you need to imagine that if he thinks he can gain it now, he may just talk.'

'Okay, then. We'll do it your way. What's the message?'

'It's this: I underestimated you, Little Bean. You still owe me, but now I need your help to take down the Regans.'

Mike raised his eyebrows, clearly surprised but nevertheless impressed once again by Zara's cunning mind. 'Clever, Zara, very clever. But how do we know Torvic hasn't been in touch?'

Zara grinned. 'Torvic wouldn't be interested in Ismail anymore. He would've used the little snitch, so I can't see how he would need him now. Torvic would've already bled him dry.'

'Okay, I'll call my man and tell him there are to be no threats or violence, just a gentle word. And you'll know if Ismail buys into it, if he calls you. I'll give my man your number, and then we'll know, yeah? Or, if he decides *not* to play ball and calls Torvic ...' – he smiled and held up the phone – 'well, babe, we have his phone.'

She nodded deliberately, still in thought. 'Right, then. Call your man.'

'Yeah, okay. Er … "Little Bean"? What's that all about?'

'He'll know the message is from me. I called him that when we were young. It's an affectionate term. I used to say, "One day, Little Bean, you'll grow into a stalk where you can reach the clouds and be whoever you want to be."'

She took one last drag and watched the cigarette butt fall from the window to the ground.

Mike stared at her. 'You loved him, didn't ya?'

She remained fixated on the fag butt and sighed heavily. 'Yeah, I did. I helped bring him up after our mother died. I guess I babied him too. But I was just looking out for him. You know, fighting his battles, beating up the kids at school if they bullied him, and stuff like that. That's why I was so gutted when he turned on me.'

'I'll make that call, babe.'

* * *

The sound in the distance was soothing. It was like a gentle melody, a feeling of being wrapped in warmth, which was so comforting. Then, suddenly, it became real and not at all dreamlike. The voice was louder, and now the surrounding muffled tones became very real.

Liam opened his eyes to another bright room; only, this time, he wasn't looking up at a circular silver light. He experienced a rush of memories; it was like a team of galloping horses that shot through his mind. The operation, the nurse who rescued him, the pain – it sent him into a panic. He instantly lifted his hands to feel if they were free, and as he did, he saw the cannula in his arm.

The sweet melodic voice came from the nurse, who tried to calm him by gently lowering his arms.

'Hey, it's okay. You're in a hospital bed, so you're safe.'

As he met her eyes, he lowered his arms and relaxed. She looked to be about thirty years old and she was dressed in a starched uniform. Her Spanish accent was comforting and reassuring.

'You came in here very poorly. We have tried to find out who you are. What's your name?'

Liam stared, trying to recollect and then process the most recent events of what had happened to him. But they were all a blur. All he knew was that one minute he was cooking steaks, and then the next, he was grabbed from behind. At some point, he remembered, he'd woken up in excruciating pain, with a harsh man's voice telling the nurse basically to let him die. He then recalled the nurse running along, pushing him out of the hospital or clinic, or whatever the fuck that place was. He couldn't trust anyone. Feeling so confused, all he wanted was his dad.

'Please, can I use the phone?'

The nurse moved the patient's hair from his eyes. 'Of course, er …'

Liam knew she was fishing for a name, but until he'd spoken with his father, he was going to stay schtum. 'Please, I need to make a call. Please help me.'

The nurse looked behind her towards the glass cubicle door.

Liam followed her eyeline and noticed two doctors standing outside. He didn't recognize either of them. 'Where am I?'

'You are in the Hospital General de Alicante. Do you know what happened to you?'

'Please, just get me a phone or I will walk to one myself.'

'Okay, I will get one for you. Please try not to move for the moment. We had to give you a blood transfusion and antibiotics. We also had to do an emergency operation to stop the internal bleeding.' She waited for a reaction, but the young man didn't respond. She tried again. 'We checked your blood against the live donor register, but there seems to be no patient on that list with your blood type or description. We had to inform the authorities, so someone will come soon to ask you questions.'

Liam narrowed his eyes, totally oblivious as to what the hell she was on about. 'What? Police?'

'Don't worry for now. I'll return shortly.'

Liam stared through the window at the doctor who appeared to be doing likewise. He sensed that the look wasn't friendly. Was he getting paranoid now? But then, he had so many questions. His first one was obvious enough: who did what to him?

He continued to watch as the doctor slipped into his room and closed the door behind him. He was a tall, heavily built man with silver streaks at the sides of his dark-brown hair. He guessed the man was in his late fifties. His body language was very self-assured, and, in a way, it reminded him of his dad. He could scare the shit out of anyone, if the need was there, and this guy appeared to be no different.

Liam expected all hospital doctors to have some kind of sympathetic bedside manner, but this situation was definitely not normal.

The doctor didn't smile or speak; instead, he gave Liam an odd look before he pulled a syringe from his pocket.

To any unsuspecting person, Liam may have looked like a bit of an oaf, but that was not the case. On the contrary, Liam could be a clever and hard fucker when he'd the mind to be. But what concerned him was the fact that the doctor was approaching with a hypodermic needle in his hand. And with no gentle words of explanation from the man, the circumstances seemed sinister, to say the least.

Liam felt his adrenaline surging; unlike before, he didn't feel pain, and, at that moment, he wondered just how much strength he had in him.

'Er, what ya doing, mate?' asked Liam, as he tried to sit himself up.

'I am topping up your antibiotics.'

Instantly, Liam recognized the man's harsh and lord-like tone. It was the same person who'd said, 'Leave him. He'll bleed out eventually.'

As the doctor grabbed his arm, Liam pulled it away. However, the doctor seized it again, this time holding it firmly. He was about to insert the needle into Liam's vein, when Liam, who was left-handed, swung his fist and caught the doctor clean on the chin, knocking him backwards.

'Get the fuck off me, you!'

In horror, the doctor looked around to see if anyone was witnessing the altercation before he went in to grab Liam again. But he was stunned with the young lad's ability to use such force to push him away.

'I said, get off me!'

'Look, you need this, so stop fighting, young man.'

Liam realized that although he was still groggy, he had to stop the doctor. Shaking his head to try to stay awake, he knew he had to prevent that needle from going in his arm. 'I hate fucking needles, so fuck off!'

The doctor then grinned. 'Aah, okay. Is that why you hit me?'

Liam was now pushing his way up the bed and glaring at the man with a cold stare. 'Yes, of course. Why else? Look, please, mate, er, I mean, Doc. Don't put that needle in my arm.'

The doctor backed off. 'So, do you know what happened to you?'

Liam shook his head. 'No, not a clue. One minute, I was cooking steaks, then, the next, I woke up in here. Do you want to tell me what happened, Doctor? I mean, did I collapse or something?' he asked, as he kept his eyes glued to the man, biding his time before the nurse returned with the phone.

'Well, no. We are not quite sure. You have been operated on, though—' He didn't finish.

The door swung open and in walked the nurse with a beaming smile. That was until she saw the doctor. 'Oh, sorry, Dr Bourne. I didn't realize you were doing the rounds today.'

'I was just talking to your patient, Nurse.' He smiled – almost bowed – as he made his way from the room.

The nurse gave an exaggerated frown and waited until the door was closed behind him. She looked quickly at her patient. 'The hospital phones are all in use, so I have brought my own mobile. You can use it.' She pulled out the phone from her pocket and handed it to Liam. 'Can you manage, or shall I dial the number for you?'

Liam felt safe in her presence and wanted to laugh out loud. He could definitely handle dialling a few numbers if he could almost manage to knock that doctor off his feet. 'Yeah, I can do it, no problem, and thank ya, sweetheart. Er, what's ya name?'

Charmed by his choice of words, his very distinctive accent, and the way he winked, his unattractive appearance suddenly became quite becoming. 'It's Melissa.' She didn't attempt to ask his name again and assumed he would tell her in his own good time.

Before he dialled the number, he looked up. 'Do ya mind, babe, if I make this a private call?'

Melissa felt herself blush. 'Sorry. Yes, of course. I will be right outside.'

* * *

Arty, Poppy, and Brooke sat around the large oval table in the open-plan dining kitchen area. Hardly a word was spoken between them. The shock of the situation had taken hold. Terrence was cooking breakfast, at a loss as to what he could do to help, when Lance came through the front door.

The noise made Poppy almost jump out of her skin, but as soon as she saw who it was, she struggled to her feet, the tears streaming down her face. Although she hadn't known for long that Lance was her real father, in that short space of time, she felt as though he was her saviour, and as soon as he noticed her tear-stained face, he hurried over and put his arms around her.

'Listen. You're safe here, okay? Nothing's gonna happen. I won't fucking let it.' He helped her to sit back down, before taking a seat himself.

'How did you get on, Lance? You look shattered, mate.'

'Yeah, not so bad. Have you got a coffee with my name on it?'

'Coming up,' replied Terrence.

'I met up with a pal of mine. He's ex-Army and he works with Interpol. We checked out a few high-profile men who owe him a few favours, but, so far, we haven't any leads. Torvic couldn't have done this alone, if it was him. But not a single soul has heard of the name. How's Willie doing?'

Terrence poured the freshly brewed coffee and placed it under Lance's nose. 'He's still sleeping. I threw a couple of tablets in his drink last night. He looked fucked, to be honest. He needs to sleep to get a clear head, or, knowing Willie, he'll go through fucking Alicante like a tornado.'

Lance looked around. 'And Ricky?'

Terrence's face looked serious. 'He's not well. I'm calling the doctor out to see him.'

Lance nodded. 'Oh, speak of the Devil!'

There, looking like a zombie – with dull and lifeless eyes and his hair poking in all directions – stood Willie. His five o'clock shadow was now a scruffy mess, which added to his scary features.

Arty jumped up. 'Take a seat, Willie. Get some grub inside ya.'

Willie offered a partial smile and sat down heavily at the table. He looked around at everyone before remarking to Poppy, 'So you're the girl my boy liked then?'

Poppy wiped another tear and nodded. 'Well, I liked him, Mr Ritz. I mean, he'd been so kind to me ...'

She stopped and another tear escaped. 'Sorry,' she said, snivelling. 'I hadn't known him very long, but he was the nicest man I'd ever had the pleasure of meeting, and we had been planning to date ...'

Willie leaned across and rubbed her hand. 'At least he had you. I know my boy. He would've been so chuffed, babe, to be dating a beauty like you.'

His kind words made more tears plummet. But they weren't just for herself. Everyone was talking about Liam in the past tense. She could scream in frustration at not knowing for sure whether her boyfriend was actually dead.

Terrence placed a coffee on the table for Willie. 'Get that down your Gregory Peck.'

Just as Willie took a sip of the strong coffee, his phone buzzed in his pocket, followed by a ringtone that under normal circumstances would have made everyone laugh – it was 'Friggin' in the Riggin'' by the Sex Pistols.

He stared hard at the number but he didn't recognize it. 'Who's this?' he demanded, in a curt tone.

'Dad, it's *me*!'

Everyone stared and didn't move a muscle when they saw Willie's shocked expression. The blood completely drained from his face as he swallowed hard.

'Liam? Fuck! Where are you, boy? What's happened?'

'Dad, tell Terrence to get me out of here. I'm in Alicante's general hospital, but he has to come quick. There's a doctor here. He's gonna kill me. I dunno what the fuck's happened but tell Terrence to hurry up. I ain't got much time left.'

'Boy, I'm in Spain with Tel. I'm coming. Stay on the bleedin' phone.' He jumped up from his seat. 'Tel, we need to get to the hospital, like now. Our Liam's there. Liam, we're coming now, boy. Where did ya say you are?'

'Dad, I'm in Alicante's general hospital in a private room. There's a nurse here. I'm using her phone. She's called Melissa. But listen. There's a doctor, right, and he did something to me. I ain't got a clue what, but, anyway, another nurse helped me get out of where they'd taken me, and I've ended up here. But this doctor was the one at the other place. I know it for a fact. I recognized his voice. I know he wants to kill me. Hurry up, for fuck's sake, will ya!'

Terrence was out of the villa and starting up the car before Willie had left the kitchen. Willie didn't even have a chance to shut his door before they pulled away.

'Liam, stay on the phone, right? What can you see around ya?'

Liam looked through the internal window and across the corridor he noticed a sign. He squinted his eyes to focus. 'I think I'm on Saint Philomena Ward or some wing, but I dunno. It's all in Spanish.'

'We're on our way. Jesus, I thought you were dead. Who took ya? Was it Torvic?'

'I've no idea, Dad. One minute I was in the kitchen. I think I went to put some rubbish out, and then I had a hand over me mouth. That's all I remember, but when I woke up … Hang on a minute. Dad, the nurse is coming.'

Melissa popped her head into the room. 'Are you okay? Can I come in?'

Liam nodded. 'Dad, how long will you be?'

Willie's phone was on loudspeaker so that Terrence could hear. 'We're three minutes away, Liam,' called Terrence.

Like shit off a shovel, Terrence's car reached 120 miles per hour and was flying along the main road. 'Two minutes!' he called out again.

'I've got to go, Dad. It's the nurse's phone, I'm using.'

'No, boy. Stay on the phone. I thought I'd lost ya. I ain't fucking losing you again.'

Liam held his hand over the mouthpiece. 'Melissa, listen. Me dad's on his way, right? Please stay with me. Don't let anyone in. It's really important.'

Melissa knew instantly that this young lad wasn't messing around. Whatever had happened to him, he was terrified. She stepped inside and leaned her back against the door. 'Okay, er …' She really wanted to know his name, now everything had changed. She knew he was worried about someone in the hospital and her main concern was Dr Bourne. She'd never liked him and felt that he was power mad. He was always swanning around like he owned the place.

'It's Liam. Just don't let anyone in.'

'I won't,' she replied anxiously.

'Dad, I'm all right. Just hurry up, yeah?'

'We're 'ere. Oh fuck, Tel's nearly hit a bleeding ambulance.'

Liam heard the car door slam and the sound of his father running.

'Melissa, I need you to tell me dad where I am.'

She ran over to his bed and took the phone. 'Sir, it's the Saint Philomena Ward. Go into the entrance, take the lift to the fourth floor, and come right up. We're in the third room on the right.'

'Got it, love. Put me boy on, and thanks.'

Just as Melissa handed back the phone to Liam, the door opened. It was Dr Bourne. 'Aah, Nurse, you are needed in Room Two. I want to check on our patient.'

Melissa didn't move; instead, she stood by Liam's bed and glared at the doctor.

'Nurse, you are needed in Room Two.' As his eyes fixed firmly on Liam, he noticed the phone to his ear.

'Sorry, but you are not allowed phones on the ward.'

Those words confirmed that Dr Bourne was up to something. Melissa's stomach flipped over, and the most frightening thoughts crossed her mind. No way should this be happening here. It was the kind of thing you might read about in a thriller. She had an agile mind and could think quickly on her feet. 'Sorry, Dr Bourne, it's the police on the phone. The patient is just explaining what has happened to him. I think they're on their way.'

The doctor's eyes were almost on stalks, confirming that he was indeed up to something that had nothing to do with a patient's normal day-to-day care. But he'd also inadvertently communicated to Liam and Melissa through his body language that he was in some way negatively involved in his patient's condition. Melissa mentally questioned his intentions to uphold the Hippocratic Oath.

'The police have asked me to stay with him until they arrive so could you ask Nurse Trudy to see to the patient in Room Two, please?'

Liam could hear heavy footsteps approaching the room. He knew that at any moment his father would be through the door like a rocket. Right on cue, the door was flung open and there, looking like a six-foot character from the living dead, and completely out of breath, stood his father.

Dr Bourne stepped back, totally surprised at the man's aggressive demeanour. *Surely, he wasn't from the police*, he thought.

'Dad!'

Willie gently moved the nurse aside and wrapped his arms around Liam and hugged him. Willie's body was moving up and down as the sobs that had seemingly been trapped inside him for days now flooded his face.

Melissa rubbed Willie's back and looked back to find that Dr Bourne had evidently slipped away.

'Dad, you're squashing me.'

Willie pulled back and stroked his son's cheek. 'Jesus, Liam, we thought you were dead. I just can't fucking believe it. You're here, you're ...' He turned to the nurse. 'Is he all right? Can I take him with me?'

She looked behind her again. 'Look, sir, I have no idea what's been going on, but ...' She took a deep breath and gave Liam a sympathetic look. 'Your son came to us unconscious with a scar that, to be honest, is shocking. We had to operate right away to stop internal bleeding from the nephrectomy he'd had.'

Willie frowned. 'What's a nepher whatsit?'

'His kidney was removed, sir. Did you not know?'

Willie's ruddy complexion changed instantaneously as he gripped the bed to stop himself from collapsing on the floor.

'Sir, did you not know? Was this operation not planned?'

'No, 'course it wasn't. What the fuck! Why did someone take his kidney? I mean, what the hell *for*?'

Melissa looked at all of them in turn, her lips trembling at the consequences of what she'd just witnessed since coming on shift. 'I think we need to call the police.'

Willie nodded. 'Jesus!'

'No!' said Liam. 'No, don't do that. Please.'

Melissa was taken aback. 'But this is a crime, a grave crime.'

Liam nodded. 'I know it is, love, but I also know who was responsible, and there's no way the police will believe me. I can't prove it.'

'I'm taking him out of here,' said Willie firmly, expecting the nurse to protest. But she didn't; instead, she nibbled on her bottom lip, in deep thought.

'He is still very poorly, you know. He's been through a lot. In fact, we did have to resuscitate him, but he's now on fluids and antibiotics and a few other standard medications such as—'

Before she could finish, the door opened. It was Terrence.

'Tel, go and get a wheelchair, mate,' demanded Willie. He looked at the nurse. 'Do us a massive favour, babe. Can ya get his medication or whatever? I swear to God, I'll see you all right over this. We owe ya a massive debt for 'elping our Liam, and we won't forget ya. Please, you have to help us, yeah?'

Without giving it another thought, she nodded and gave him a pretty smile. It was the look on Liam's face, and the fear in his voice, that had finally confirmed to her that Dr Bourne had something to do with this. And the young man was right. A well-respected consultant like Bourne would have the police tied up in knots. It was too unbelievable to take seriously, but she knew differently; she was a psychiatric nurse before she became a renal nurse, and so she knew that Liam wasn't mad. But Bourne's behaviour was most unusual. These people were right to get the youngster out of the hospital as quickly as possible.

Immediately, she pulled the pink tracksuit from the bedside

cabinet and handed it to Willie. 'Here are the clothes your son came in. Get him dressed. I'll be back with the meds,' she ordered, now taking control.

Willie looked at the girlie tracksuit and then at Liam. 'Is this yours, Son?'

Liam nodded. 'Yeah. Well, no, well, it's all I have.' His mind went back to the nurse who risked her life by helping him to escape. Although a little fuzzy, he suddenly remembered the note. 'Dad, you have to check the pocket. The nurse who saved me, she may be in trouble. She took me from this clinic, somewhere in Alicante, and drove me here.'

Willie could see the panic spreading across his son's face. 'Don't you worry, Son. Leave it to me.' He took the note from the pocket and saw a phone number.

While they waited for the nurse to return, Willie called the number. The phone rang three times until a soft-spoken Englishwoman answered.

'Er, listen, love, are you okay? I mean, I know you helped save my son.'

'Is he alive?' asked the nurse.

Willie sensed the apprehension in her voice. 'Yes, love, but we need answers. Is it possible for me to meet you?'

'No, please, I need to leave Spain. They will come for me and—'

'No, wait, I can 'elp ya,' said Willie quickly.

'Sorry, I have to go. I don't have time. Please, look after the boy. I will be safe. I must leave now. Goodbye.'

The phone went dead.

'Is she okay, Dad?'

Willie nodded. 'Yeah, she said she's leaving the country.

I'll call her again later. Now, don't worry. We just need to get *you* outta here.'

* * *

Ismail sat in his cell; it was a single unit. He had his knees pulled up to rest a book. He wasn't reading it; he just stared at the words. Dark thoughts kept whirling around in his head, wondering when he would be next to be murdered.

The description of Guy's and Benjamin's deaths haunted him. It could only have been orchestrated by one person: his sister. What was he thinking, trying to take her on? Still, now it was only a matter of time, and he knew he would be next.

His cell was the last one on the landing, so when he heard footsteps outside, he took a deep breath and closed his eyes. He didn't want to see the weapon that would be used or the man who would kill him. Even if he screamed, no one would come, no one would care. Squeezing his eyes shut, he listened. Whoever was outside was now in his cell. He could hear their breathing as they sniffed the air.

'I have a message for you,' came the rough voice.

Ismail expected the message to be a knife across his throat, but there was nothing.

'Listen up. Zara said this: "Little Bean, call me. I need you to help me to take out the Regans …" She also said this: "You owe me."'

Ismail opened his eyes and found himself staring at a thick-set man who was observing dispassionately his shaking hands, clutching the book. The inmate stood with his feet apart and a cocky grin on his face. ''Ere's her number. Call her!' He threw the scrap of paper at Ismail and left.

After expelling a lungful of air, Ismail tried to calm his racing heartbeat before he could go over what the man had said. He looked at the number on the piece of paper and tried to get his thoughts in order. She'd said she wanted to take out the Regans. It didn't make sense. How could he help? He was inside. Who did he know who could help her? And, more unbelievable, why would Zara even want to take out the Regans? Mike Regan was the only man she truly loved. It didn't add up, and yet the message was definitely from her because she was the sole person who called him 'Little Bean'. The tall, well-built, grizzly bear of a man could easily have plunged him with a knife, but he hadn't. He then realized that his sister could also have made that happen.

He looked once more at the number and tried to memorize it. His sister would have done it in a nanosecond, but he couldn't. He had to recite it five times before it was fixed in his head. Not that it mattered, though: he could take the note with him to the phone. A habit of his was constantly proving to himself that he was better than his sister. He gritted his back teeth. He shouldn't be torturing himself this way. He knew that one day he would stop competing – it would be the day he would die. After screwing up the piece of paper, he threw it in the bin.

* * *

Despite expecting a call from Ismail on either Zara's phone or Torvic's, when his own phone rang, it still made Mike jump. He looked at the number; it was Willie's.

'Are you okay, bud?' he asked, in a sympathetic tone, his heart beating a little less quickly now.

Willie's voice was so loud that even Zara, who was across the room, heard it.

'I've got me boy back! I've got him, Mike. He's here with me right now!'

Mike leaped from the bed. 'Fuck me, Willie. How is he? What happened? Is he all right?'

'Yeah, yeah, well, not 100 per cent, but he's alive. Some cunt's removed his fucking kidney, though!'

Mike frowned and screwed his face up. Zara hurried over as Mike put Willie on loudspeaker.

'Sorry, mate, what the fuck did you just say?'

'Yeah, some bastard's operated on him and taken out his kidney. I swear to God, I'm going to be operating on someone meself, without anaesthetic, when I get me hands on whoever did it. I'm taking him back to Terrence's place. Liam's sick, but I'll get him sorted.' Willie was out of breath with excitement and anger. His emotions, though, were bittersweet. 'Oh my God, I can't get me head around it all … But, he's okay. Jesus, thank God!'

Mike's whole body turned limp with relief. His eyes filled with plump tears. 'Can I hear his voice?'

Liam was now tired and semiconscious, but he managed to answer. 'I'm all right, Mikey …'

'Aah, boy, you had us so worried …' He choked on a sob trapped in his throat. 'If I could wrap you lads in fucking cotton wool, I would.'

Even in his dopey state, Liam still managed to crack a joke. 'Yeah, we'd look like three tampons.'

Torvic's phone rang. Mike froze.

'I love you, boy. Listen, I need to go. I'll bell you later, yeah?'

'No worries, Mikey.'

Mike ended the call and looked at Zara, who was now holding Torvic's phone in her hand. 'There's no caller ID. It could be the nick. If it is, I bet it's Ismail, the dirty bastard.'

Mike suddenly smiled. 'Hand me the phone.'

'No, I'll answer it.'

Mike nodded, urging her to continue before the phone rang off.

'Well, hello, Little Bean. I thought as much. You really underestimated me, didn't you?'

There was a long pause as Ismail's mouth suddenly dried up. He'd made the wrong decision – again. How the hell was his sister answering Torvic's phone, unless she was working with him or she'd killed him? Realization stabbed him in the throat as he tried to think through either of those two possibilities.

'Yes, I should imagine, Ismail, that you're now in a state of confusion. How does my sister have Torvic's phone, hmm? Yes, I can hear your fast breathing, Ismail. I suspect you are now shitting hot bricks, ain't ya? Your tiny mind is frantically trying to work it out, and I bet, Ismail, you're wondering what to do next. Am I right?'

The silence continued from his end. He could put the phone down and deny calling. After all, it would come up with caller ID unknown. There was the answer. *Just put the phone down, Ismail*, a voice was saying to him.

Zara stared at the screen as her brother rang off. 'Now he *will* be bloody scared and far more likely to answer my questions.'

'Yes, you're right. Shall I make another call, Zara? This time he needs to be taught a lesson. You were fair. Ya gave him a chance, didn't ya? But he must know now that that move will have consequences. So, let's not delude him.'

'You know what? A part of me actually believed he would call, out of a sense of sibling love. But I guess I was wrong. Do what you have to, Mikey. I'm done with him. For now, we can celebrate Willie's news. I'm so pleased, I feel like crying with relief.'

Mike pulled her close to him and sat her on his lap. 'Yeah, the best news ever about Liam.' He sighed. 'But as for your decision to give up on Ismail, I know how painful that was. I wouldn't wish that on anyone … well, except Torvic. Now, let me make that call.'

Zara gave Mike a full-on, lingering kiss and then hopped up from his lap. 'Go for it, babe.'

Chapter 13

Pacing the floor of his cell, Ismail was sweating buckets. He'd royally fucked up and knew damn well that she wouldn't forgive him now. 'Damn!' He punched the wall, which hurt, and then he rested his forehead against the cold bricks, allowing the tears to roll down his face. He had to think quickly before he was set upon, and he knew that it wouldn't be long. Wiping his eyes, he decided to head for the recreational area on the ground floor. Surely, he reasoned, no one would harm him in public view. He would just have to make sure he was surrounded by people. Either that or go to his personal officer. But, what could he say to him? No threat had actually been made – yet.

Just as he was about to leave his cell, a huge prisoner, as large as a bear, appeared in the doorway. His name was Joel, an ex-boxer from Hackney. If he hadn't murdered his trainer for doing him out of ten grand, he could quite conceivably have become cruiserweight champion of Great Britain.

Ismail couldn't have squeezed past the man even if he'd wanted to because he took up the whole doorframe. He looked a throwback to the Neanderthal age with his flat nose, thick forehead, and black hairs covering his huge hands. And that vacant expression – he looked like the lights were on but no one was at home.

Ismail stood rooted to the spot, absolutely terrified. This was it – game over. His heart beat furiously, and his palms were dripping. How the hell would he talk his way out of this? By Christ, though, he would if he could. But the size of the man's fists told him that one punch to his head and he wouldn't wake up in a normal state, if he even woke up at all.

'Sit!' came the harsh voice from the muscular monster.

Ismail retreated and instantly sat on the bed.

'Right, this is what's gonna 'appen. I'll ask the questions. You will answer truthfully. Ya see, some of the questions, I already know the answers to, so, any lies, and, well, let me see ...' he said, as he looked Ismail over and grinned. 'You already look like a rat who was dragged through the cat flap, so finishing you off won't take much effort.'

Ismail could feel and hear his teeth literally chattering. That was a first: he'd never been so shit-scared in all his life. He nodded and swallowed hard.

'Good. So, this should be a piece of piss. Question one. How do you know Torvic?'

Ismail flicked his eyes to the right and paused. 'Er, well ...'

The crack to the side of the head was so fast, Ismail didn't see it coming, but he certainly felt it, as his head hit the metal bedstead. He tried to sit up straight to compose himself, but that thump had left his ears ringing, and stomach acid began to rise to the back of his throat. Glancing up at the man, he saw absolutely no expression. His interrogator looked impassively at him, like a cobra, just biding his time to strike again. An ice-cold shiver ran down Ismail's spine. He felt he was an inch away from death.

'I can tell when someone's gonna lie. Ya see, I may look a thick bugger to someone like you, who was born with a silver spoon in ya mouth, by the looks of ya, but I've studied psychology and body language, so, let's try again, shall we? And, my friend – a warning. That was just a little slap, so the next time you lie to me or try to lie to me, I'll knock you into the wall so hard that your ugly face will be on back to fucking front. And if that don't work' – Joel bent down and lifted his tracksuit bottoms to reveal a knife tied to his leg – 'I'll cut ya tongue out, and you'll have to write the answers on a piece of paper. Got it, 'ave ya?'

Ismail nodded.

'Good boy. So, let's try again. How do you know Torvic?'

'He offered me a partnership in his business for information about my father.'

'Right, now you listen to me. I don't want the fucking basics. I want every last detail. Got me?'

Ismail licked his dry lips as he wrung out his sweaty palms. 'He wanted the names of all my father's suppliers and buyers and the details of the restaurants, the clubs, and the arcades. And he also wanted to know where my sister, Zara, was. So, I told him she was down in the basement of my late father's house. Torvic paid me every time I gave him information about her. But I couldn't tell him everything about the business because I couldn't find out where my father kept his ledger, so I told him only what I knew.'

'Where does Torvic live?'

Ismail hesitated. It cost him dearly. The next

moment, a lightning blow knocked two of his teeth clean out of his mouth. The blood tasted vile, and this time he didn't just feel sick, he threw up on the floor. Gasping for air, he stuttered, 'N-n-o-o, okay, pl-please, I'll tell you. I-I just needed time to remember his address, I swear.'

'One, two …'

'I don't know the number, but it's on Church Road, a red front door, a detached house in Sundridge in Kent.'

'No, not that address. He has another one,' said Joel. He'd been told that there were possibly other addresses.

Ismail blinked and wiped his bloody mouth. 'Please, wait. I'm trying to remember. There is another place he goes to. I followed him once. Er, it's in Crockenhill. There's a row of cottages with a back entrance and a garage with a green door. Fuck, fuck.' Ismail was now panicking so much, his brain couldn't process anything anymore. 'I'm really trying to remember. Please …'

Joel held off, knowing that the man was desperately trying to recall what he knew. And he was fully aware that if he whacked him again then he may not get any more information.

'Tylers Green is the place. Yeah, that's it. I don't know the number, but the garage door is green. It's the only one in use. It's down an alleyway behind the house.'

His eyes squinted, expecting another smack, but Joel merely grinned, showing his chipped tooth. 'You do know that I can snap you in half if I suspect you're lying? It may not be today. It could be tomorrow or even next week,' taunted Joel.

Ismail nodded. 'I swear, I'm telling the truth.'

'One more question … for now, that is. What were Torvic's plans for Zara and the Regans?'

With a deep frown, Ismail said, 'Zara? What do you mean?'

'Is he intending to kill her?'

'Kill her?' asked Ismail, now very surprised.

'Fuck me, is there an echo in 'ere? Yes, Ismail. Is Torvic likely to kill her?'

'No, not at all. He wouldn't, never. He loves her.'

Joel was on the point of raising his hand again, but Ismail pre-empted his move.

'That's why she was kept alive for all those years, because he wanted it that way. I stopped Guy Segal from ending her life, or she would've been dead within a month.' He knew he had to spill the beans or he was a dead man. In any case, he reasoned, who cared if he grassed up anyone now. The money, which he'd accumulated from working for Torvic, meant nothing if he ended up murdered or he was left in jail to rot. 'He paid me to convince Guy and Benjamin to keep her alive. I would've let her die myself, but I didn't.'

All the time Ismail was talking, Joel was becoming more and more interested in what he was hearing. He had plenty of time while in prison to satisfy his intellect, which just seemed to grow exponentially, the more he read. He had already taken an Open University BA (Honours) degree in Criminology and Psychology and was in his second year of a master's. He loved questioning anything put to him, and he had an analytical mind, which perhaps stemmed from his boxing days, so all the things that Ismail was telling him were giving him pause for thought.

First up, what would Zara do with the information he'd extracted from this slimy jerk-off? He'd already asked the questions given to him by Mike, but now something else was intriguing him.

'In what way did he love her?'

'He wanted her for himself.' Ismail smirked, innocently.

Now Joel was even more captivated. In fact, he was morbidly curious. 'Why?'

'Because she was the image of our mother, and he wanted her, but my father beat him to it. So, now he wants my sister.'

Joel flared his nostrils and protruded his jaw. The thought that Ismail would let some old fella go after his sister made him livid because he had a sister and no way would he allow anyone to touch a hair on her head and live. 'The sick bastard.'

'No, I don't mean he wants her like that. I mean—'

Joel was too sickened to let Ismail finish his sentence. 'You're a real weasel, ain't ya? You'd sell out anyone if it meant you could earn a few quid. Ya know what they said? They told me at first not to hurt you but just keep you in check and get information that they requested. But, later, they changed their minds. And it's a good thing an' all, now I know what you're about. But, to be honest, it wouldn't have mattered anyway. Ya see, me, I have me own rules and a mind that is me own. Sometimes, I can see things that others can't: it's called wisdom. As I see it, you're taking up oxygen that really you ain't entitled to. I'm gonna go and make a call, but watch ya back, Ismail, 'cos … well, just 'cos.' He winked, grinned, and left.

Ismail tried to relax his shoulders before taking a deep breath, allowing his head to fall back against the brick wall. He didn't know what was worse – a quick death here and now, or forever looking over his shoulders and constantly fighting his worst nightmares.

* * *

As the front door opened, Lance was on his feet, gun in hand. As soon as the others realized it was Willie and Liam, they rushed to help.

Poppy suddenly became alive.

'Liam, oh my goodness,' she cried, as she bent over the wheelchair and cupped his pale face. 'What happened to you? I was so ... Oh my ... Well, at least you're safe.'

She looked at Willie, who was fascinated by how much this pretty young woman fussed over his son. He was no fool; although he adored Liam, he was also aware that Liam wasn't at the top of the list in the looks department, rather like himself.

Liam gave her a cheeky grin. 'Poppy, babe, I'm fine. I'm just a kidney short of a full mixed grill.'

She chuckled at his humour, along with everyone else.

Lance looked at Willie and raised his brow, as if to ask what had happened, but Willie shook his head; he wasn't going to talk about it in front of the kids.

'Right, boy, let's get you into bed and have a read of all these tablets before I give you an overdose.' He held up a large bag and then shook it. It sounded like a baby's rattle.

'Oh, I can do that, Mr Ritz. I'm quite good with medicine. I studied it for a while before beginning my media course,' said Poppy, eager to help.

Willie ruffled her hair. He wasn't used to young women, only boys.

'Well, there you go. He's all yours, Nurse Nightingale. Arty, help me get him up the stairs and into bed, will ya?'

Arty was still pale, the shock of the last few days having affected his appetite, and the lack of food making him feel listless and frightened for his mate.

'Ya gave us a right shock, Liam, ya little fucker.' He sighed.

Liam grinned. 'Not as much as me, Art. Jesus, they were gonna throw me into an incinerator. I was fucking shitting meself.' He turned to Poppy. 'Mind you, I gave the doctor a left hook, the cheeky bastard. He was gonna inject me to finish me off.'

Arty then laughed, but mainly through relief. 'Well, you can't kill the living dead, now can ya?'

Liam was on the point of laughing but he was in too much pain.

'Fuck off, Arty. You're gonna burst me stitches.'

Arty grabbed Liam's hand and squeezed it.

'It's good to have you back, mate. I missed having someone to take the piss out of.'

'All right, but no steak and kidney pie jokes.'

The commotion downstairs brought Ricky out of his doze and he moved into a sitting position. His headache had cleared, and he felt so much better. The laughter he heard was uplifting. There hadn't even been a chuckle over the last few days. Slowly, he got to his feet and steadied himself to make his way downstairs, but as soon as he reached the landing, he froze momentarily, as he saw Willie and Arty carrying someone in a pink tracksuit up the stairs. *This couldn't be happening, right*? he thought. But when he blinked twice, he realized that this was no apparition but one of his best mates there in front of him.

'Liam, oh my God. You *ain't* dead, then! What the fuck 'appened?'

Liam, with his arms around both men's shoulders, smiled at Ricky.

'I'm all right, Ricky. I'm just a little lighter, that's all, mate.'

Ricky watched as suddenly Liam went very pale.

His body became a dead weight. Lance, who had followed the men up the stairs, knew then that Liam was fainting.

'Quick, Willie, get him on the bed.' Liam was rushed along the landing and gently lowered onto a bed in one of the many bedrooms in this oversized villa.

Ricky watched in horror, thinking the worst, but then Liam's eyes blinked and finally opened.

'I need a drink,' he muttered.

Poppy was just behind the men, holding the bag of tablets and a large glass of water. She ushered everyone away. Willie smiled as 'Miss Nightingale' lifted Liam's head and made him sip the drink. She removed three different tablets from the packets and popped them on his tongue. 'Swallow, Liam.'

He did as he was told, and then she took his hand and pinched the skin, much to everyone's curiosity.

'He's dehydrated. That's the problem,' she said to everyone. 'He needs more fluid. Liam, drink more, please.'

'Yes, nurse.' He winked in good humour, but the pallor of his skin gave everyone a fright.

Terrence phoned his private doctor to call in and check out Liam and Ricky. They'd both been through horrendous ordeals, and he knew it was really his responsibility to keep them safe and well.

Arty decided finally to spruce himself up, instead of staying in the same tracksuit, which was so unlike him. Lance, Willie, and Terrence sat around the oval table, while the girls rested in the lounge.

'So, what now?' asked Lance.

Willie raised his eyebrow and then gave him a sly grin.

'I would've thought that was obvious, me ol' mucker. I'm gonna find this fucking cockroach of a doctor and take his tonsils out via his arse.'

Calmly, Lance looked over at Willie, also with an enquiring eyebrow. 'How do you propose to do that? Do we know who this doctor is?'

'Yeah. He's called Dr Bourne, and he has his own fucking clinic where the bastard took my boy's body part and left him to die. Liam remembered the name of the clinic. He's sharp, that kid. What he lacks in looks he makes up for in brains.'

'Are you sure you wanna get your hands dirty? Because I have a few pals – ex-Army lads – who will be willing to lend a hand. They owe me. Not that I normally call in favours, but this time I will.'

Terrence waited for a response from Willie, although he knew what it would be.

'Kind of ya, Lance, but I wanna do the business meself. The bloke's taken a major liberty, and he's gonna pay. No one hurts my boy.' His face reddened as his eyes grew darker.

'So, when do you propose to do that?'

Willie glared over at Lance and then at Terrence. 'As soon as Liam is well enough to tell me everything. So far, he's told me all he remembers, but once he's rested, he might just remember more, 'cos I'm fucking sure it takes more than one doctor to operate. I wanna know who was involved and why. I mean, who takes someone's kidney, for fuck's sake? I've heard it's done in India or somewhere like that, but fucking *Alicante*? D'ya reckon this has anything to do with Torvic, like a warning, Mafia style?'

Lance got up from his chair.

'I can't see anyone removing a kidney as a threat. Maybe a finger or a hand, but a body organ? I've never heard of it. This is about something else.'

'Well, where the hell do we start?'

'Right, mate, I'll ask my contact to find out if this is a one-off or if there have been other incidences.'

Willie looked up, and his eyes glinted angrily. 'I don't want no authorities involved. This is fucking personal, so I wanna handle it my way.'

Lance nodded. 'Of course, mate. I can be discreet. It's what I'm good at.'

Willie decided to lighten the mood. He relaxed his shoulders and chuckled.

'Me and you, Lance, could be related, the way your Poppy and my boy seem to be into each other.'

'Cor, her mother would have fucking kittens, well, when she gets out of jail. That bitch – I can't believe Rebecca knocked her own daughter over and left her on the street as if nothing had happened. I hope she gets a real bashing inside. I mean, an MP with that conviction hanging over her head! She won't stand a chance in jail.'

* * *

Zara listened, along with Mike, to the very lengthy call from Joel.

'Anything else you wanna know, gov?' asked Joel.

'Not for now, mate, but cheers for all that. I appreciate it. Don't bash him up anymore. We may need further answers.

Oh, and keep a close eye on the little fucker. Make sure he doesn't use the phone. I don't want him warning Torvic or anyone who knows this man about our conversation.'

'Okay, chief. It's as good as done.'

The call ended, and Mike looked at Zara's wide eyes.

'D'ya think Ismail's lying?'

'That's a hard one because Ismail's so sly. I feel gutted that after everything, and I mean everything, I still gave him a get-out-of-jail-free card, and, even then, he was prepared to run to Torvic. Why my brother detests me, I don't know. With Izzy giving me control of the family's businesses, surely that couldn't have made my brother so hateful that he would want to see me dead, could it?'

'Jealousy is a powerful and evil emotion. It makes people do crazy things.'

'Ya know, those are almost the same words fucking Torvic used when Eric was sniffing around me. We have to find that bastard and quickly. I need to get back to business. Having him on the loose is restricting me, and I also hate having the feeling my arms are tied behind my back.'

Mike watched her expression turn cold. It was the dark charisma that always got him aroused, and only she possessed it. Right now, it made him want to pull her back onto the bed.

'I'm going to pay this other house of Torvic's a visit,' said Zara. 'I bet he's not there, but at least I can maybe get a sense of the man, so I can work out what makes the bastard tick.'

'Oh no, you're not. I'll go, and I bet he is there. His own place has been empty for a long time. I had me men keep a look-out. This other place with the green garage door must be an insignificant property, probably well hidden, and I'd also bet that no one knew about that one, not even the special operations team. Lance told me that they'd never been able to track him down. He was too damned clever.'

Zara twisted her head. 'So, of all people, how would Ismail know that?'

Mike grinned. 'Zara, you're the brains of the outfit. I thought you would've sussed that out.'

She screwed her nose up. 'No, I haven't got a clue.'

'Ismail managed to screw you over right under your nose. He sneaked about, listening in doorways, because he came across as so innocuous. I bet ya he followed Torvic not only to his main house but to this secret gaff too.'

'Hmm. Yeah, it's weird because he's such a skinny, almost fragile-looking man, who you just wouldn't think would know so much or have the gumption to find out anything useful.'

Mike stepped towards her, cupping her cheeks. 'Like your father always said, knowledge is power. So what he lacked in muscle, he made up for in sneakiness.'

Zara drank in Mike's pearl-grey eyes; in that moment, she just wished her life could be similar to most people's – relatively normal. Her mind tried to picture what a conventional existence might look like. Could she ever have a husband-and-wife life with Mike, a nine-to-five job, living in a three-bedroom semi with a Labrador and a holiday once a year in Benidorm?

The phone rang again, and her thoughts vanished as quickly as they'd emerged. With events overtaking themselves so rapidly at the moment – and unlikely to let up anytime soon, or, in all probability, in the future – she knew she would always live on the edge of her seat. Forget the life that most people led; it was one she would never have. This was who she was meant to be, and Izzy had created it for her.

Mike answered the call. It was Staffie. 'All right, mate?'

Staffie could hear his Uncle Nicolas upstairs somewhere, so he wandered around the lounge with his phone stuck to his ear.

'Yeah, not so bad, Mike. I crashed at me uncle's. I was so fucked. Anyway, what's the plan? What do we know?'

''Ave you just got up? Ain't you heard about Liam?'

'No, what's happened? Oh, please don't tell me he's been ...?' Staffie couldn't bear to say the word 'tortured'.

'No, he's been found. He's all right. But, apparently, some cunt's operated on him and taken out his kidney. I know it sounds mental, but he's alive. I realize I should've called you earlier, but we've been trying to suss out how to track down Torvic before he lets rip. And another thing: I believe Eric's with him, *unless* Eric's dead. Torvic answered Eric's phone a while ago. I'm very concerned, mate.'

Staffie was silent as the tears welled up. The relief that Liam was alive was enormous, and he tried to hold the crack in his voice. He didn't take in what else Mike had just said though.

'Are you there, Staff?'

'Er, yeah. I'm just fucking relieved, mate. I've been sick with worry over that lad. Jesus, who would've taken out his kidney? What the hell was that all about?' He paced the floor as he spoke and glanced at the photos of his uncle. *Flash bastard*, he thought. He always had his arm around someone famous: boxers, promoters, singers. Then his eyes fell to a picture in a silver frame. For a moment, he thought it was Liam. He snatched the picture and held it closer to his face and frowned.

Although the boy in the photo looked slightly older than Liam, he appeared to be so much like him, it was untrue.

'Yeah, we're taken aback as much as you. Willie and Lance have Terrence and his mob, so they're all right. Me and Zara are in a hotel for now ... Staff, are you still there? Staff?'

'Yeah, yeah ... I am.' he stuttered. 'Mike, I'll call you back, mate. I just need to do something.'

* * *

As soon as Staffie finished the call, he put the phone inside his jacket. Gripping the frame with both hands, he scrutinized the photo. He was so deep in thought, he didn't hear Nicolas enter the lounge.

'I thought ol' Shelley had taken all those bleedin' photos with her.'

Staffie turned to face him. 'Is this her son, then?'

'Yeah. Ugly fucker, ain't he?' Nicolas scoffed.

He'd really no time for the boy. He'd only been kind to him for Shelley's sake. Well, in actual fact, more for his own, because every time he'd treated her son to a few quid or a new bike, he'd been guaranteed a blow job. Lucas was her little blue-eyed boy although really his eyes were dark brown and very narrow, with a large nose that wouldn't put him in the running to be a model in any female mag. He would have liked to have been able to say that what the kid lacked in looks he made up for in intelligence or charisma, but he simply couldn't. The lad was an arrogant bastard, thick as shit, and spoiled beyond belief.

'And you've absolutely no idea who his father is?' queried Staffie, desperate to know.

'Nah, mate, she never let on.'

'Where's the boy now, then?'

Nicolas stood in a white bathrobe, a thick gold chain around his neck, and his hair – what was left of it – was still wet and swept back.

'Lucas? He went with Shelley. Tied to her fucking apron strings, that one. A shame, because if I'd had the chance, I could've moulded him into someone, but she took charge of the discipline. Ha! A joke, really. The boy hasn't had any. But why the curiosity?'

'Oh, I just thought he looked like someone, that's all. So where did they move to?'

Nicolas sniffed the air and his tone changed.

'Staffie, you may be me sister's boy, but what's this all about? 'Cos I know you, and you ain't one for sticking your hooter in other people's business, if ya know what I mean. So, what's the fucking interest?'

Staffie knew that Nicolas was right. He wasn't one for gossip. He didn't have the time or the energy.

'Sorry, Nicolas, it's just that he does look like one of me mate's boys. A dead ringer for him, if ya like.'

'Who?' asked Nicolas, now intrigued, as he reached down to the coffee table and retrieved a cigar.

'Me mate Willie Ritz's son, Liam.'

Nicolas lit the end and puffed away until a blue plume of smoke made a thin line and then rippled like waves to reach the ornate ceiling rose above his head. 'I know Willie ...' He paused, frowning. 'Shelley's son does look like him, but, to be brutal, I wouldn't have thought my ol' girl would 'ave gone with the likes of Willie Ritz. No disrespect, but he was never a babe magnet, was he? Let's be honest 'ere. Shelley, back then, was pretty hot.'

Staffie smiled at the thought. 'You'd be surprised how ol' Willie can get a bird in the sack. It blows my mind how he does it, but for some reason the women like him.'

Nicolas sat down in an armchair and continued to puff on his cigar. 'Hmm, well, I dunno, but, anyway, it's none of my business now. Before the bird upped and went, she took a shedload of my money and set up her own pad.'

Staffie remained gazing at the photo and shook his head. 'Yeah, my Arty's mother left years ago. I was just pleased that she didn't put a stop to me seeing me boy, though. She never took much, just a few grand, but I never married her, so she wasn't entitled to much. Although, I did see her all right and me boy, like.'

With a sneer on his face, Nicolas replied, 'Well, your ex ain't like my Shell. She rinsed me all right. Took fucking half. But then, I expected no less, to be honest. Hey-ho, shit happens. At least she's outta my life now.'

Still intrigued, Staffie asked, 'So, do you still see the boy?'

'Nah, not really. I did visit him in the hospital a little while ago, though. Poor fucker, he got into drugs and overdosed. It left him with fucked up organs or something.'

Suddenly, Staffie's face went grey, and it didn't go unnoticed by Nicolas.

'What's up, Staff? Are you ill?'

Staffie slowly shook his head and tried to swallow, but the shock left his mouth dry.

'Which organs?'

With a deep frown and his lips curled down, Nicolas studied

Staffie's face before he asked, 'Why? Look 'ere, what the fuck's going on?'

Staffie pondered over whether to tell his uncle the story.

'Which organs? Just tell me.'

'One of his livers, I think.'

'Nicolas, mate, we only have one bloody liver. Do ya mean *kidney*?'

With a shrug of his shoulders, Nicolas, clearly annoyed by this put-down, replied, 'I dunno. He was on some dialysis machine a while ago. Why?'

Staffie took himself over to the sofa, collecting his thoughts.

'We're family, Nicolas. Above all else, we're blood, yeah?'

Nicolas nodded patiently.

Staffie sat down heavily and sighed. 'Right. What I'm gonna tell ya stays with us. I don't want you getting on the dog and bone to Shelley or anyone else, 'cos there will be fucking trouble, and I mean *murders*. 'Ave ya got that?'

Nicolas's face tightened. 'You ain't threatening me, are ya, Staffie?'

With a deliberate tut, Staffie replied, 'No! I'm just saying, because this won't be my war, it will be Willie Ritz's, and, no doubt, with Mike Regan's backing.'

'All right, listen. I'm not sure I wanna know, mate. I ain't getting involved in any issues where that nutcase Mikey Regan's involved.'

'Okay, so just tell me. Where does Shelley live? And which hospital was Lucas in?'

With a measured glare, Nicolas replied, 'First, you ain't gonna hurt her, are ya?'

'No. It's for information purposes only.'

Pushing himself up from his seat, Nicolas reached down for the phone on the side table.

''Ere, her number's stored in there. I don't know her new address, but whatever it is that's going on, best ya watch ya step, 'cos you know who her father is, don't ya?'

'No.'

'Well, let me give you a bit o' background. His name's Colin Crawford. Me and him didn't see eye to eye, back in the day. Turf wars and stuff. Anyway, as I told you earlier, I wanted to get back at him, so I fucked his daughter, and then I married her.'

Staffie laughed out loud. 'Yeah, but fucking hell, that was a bit extreme, weren't it? And, yeah, I've heard of him, but that was years ago. He's got to be in his seventies now.'

'Yeah, and the reason you won't hear of him now is 'cos the man's gone international. He owns massive property development companies. You'd think he'd be taking it easy at his age, but I do know he'll still sniff out a deal if one is shoved under his nose. He supplies most of Ibiza with cocaine – and probably other countries – but the point I'm making is this: you hurt his daughter, and he'll come for ya, no question.'

The cogs were turning as Staffie began to add it all up. He may have been adding two and two and coming up with thirty-three, but somehow, and eerily, it all began to make sense now.

'Okay, I'll be upfront. Liam, Willie's son, was kidnapped by someone who took his kidney out.'

'What! Are you serious? I thought robbing body parts was only done in sci-fi films. I didn't think it really happened. Shit!'

Staffie leaned forward. 'So, now, can you see what I'm getting at?'

Nicolas lit the end of his cigar again after it had gone out. He decided to ask a question of his own.

'Are you sure that this Liam looks like Lucas?'

'100 per cent, mate. They're like two fucking peas in a pod.'

Nicolas felt a few beads of sweat tickle his brow, and he quickly wiped them away. 'Listen, Staffie, I've probably said too much. I don't wanna get involved. Can you keep me out of it? That Colin, he's left me alone for years ...'

Suddenly, he stood up. 'Jesus, I've just had a thought ...' He paced the floor with his hand to his forehead. 'Your Uncle Mack. I ain't heard from him in a while, right? Then our lawyer calls and says me brother's signed some paperwork regarding this house. I was too busy to deal with it at the time, but ...'

'Go on, Nicolas. What's on ya mind?'

'Well, this house. I put it in Mack's name. It was nothing to do with Shelley, 'cos she's had her dough. But, Jesus, if he's signed the fucking house over to her, then he would've only done it under duress. I bet that Colin was behind it. Ya see, Shelley hasn't spoken to her father in years, but I'm guessing she's gone running to him, now we're not together.'

Staffie frowned. 'Now, you've lost me.'

'Staffie, seriously, if you're suggesting that Liam's kidney was taken and given to Lucas, then, fuck me, she couldn't have orchestrated that on her own, could she? The tart can't wipe her own arse without a set of instructions. Her father, *he* would have the money, *and* the men. The bastard has friends in high places an' all. He's got MPs, lords, you name it. They're all crawling to him when they need help, like.'

Staffie shook his head in confusion. 'So? What's it got to do with Uncle Mack?'

'If that bitch went seeking help from her father, she would have to give him something in return, like me or me brother. Well, he's gone on the missing list, and now me lawyer's left some cryptic message about the deeds. Fuck, I'd better phone him and find out what's going on or going down.'

Staffie was only listening with half an ear. He'd just recalled something that Mike had said to him on the phone about Eric, and he also wanted to brief his boss about all this shit he'd just found out about.

'Nicolas, mate, I've gotta run. I need to meet up with Mikey and tell him what's happened. Fuck. That's two men he'll want to hunt down now.'

'No, don't go!' yelled Nicolas. 'Not yet! I may need your help too!'

Staffie sighed. 'I ain't being funny, Nicolas, but this ain't my mess.'

'Staff, he's your fucking *uncle*. I thought you'd show him some respect, even for your dear ol' muvver's sake.'

Scratching the back of his bald head, Staffie sighed again. 'All right, but you call Mack. I'll let Mike know, and then we'll go over to Mack's place and see what's happened. I bet he's just been very busy. Let's not panic.'

Nicolas was now dripping with sweat and pacing around in circles. He ended up having to wipe his forehead with the sleeve of his towelling bathrobe. 'Shit, if Colin has hurt Mack then he, or rather one of his henchmen, will come for me, that's a dead cert. The man's a mean, dangerous bastard, and I do believe he stayed away from me because I was with Shelley. But, if she *has* gone running to him, you can bet ya bottom dollar she's blackened my name to have her farver back onside.'

With his shoulders slumped and his breathing heavy, he continued to pace, flattening the cream carpet.

'Nicolas, just call Mack. If he doesn't answer this time, we'll have a drive around there, okay? Also, call your lawyer and find out what's going on with the deeds. He may tell you a bit more. Oh, and bring a tool.'

Nicolas's flushed face suddenly shrank.

As his uncle dialled his lawyer, Staffie could see the man was a nervous wreck. He left him alone to make the calls while he walked through the kitchen and out into the back garden. He needed fresh air and time to digest all the news.

Liam was safe but what a shock to hear he'd had one of his kidneys removed. Taking a deep breath, Staffie thought about the whole situation, and, for the first time in his life, he had regrets – big regrets. The last few years had been one nightmare after another, and what was it all for, besides money and power.

He'd always thought, since their early release from prison, he should find the man responsible for that evil drug. But it had been a bad idea. He would rather have served his time and been out in another year than be caught up in the war with this monster Torvic, and, as for Liam, it could have been his own son. When all was said and done, it was their boys who were inheriting their name, the Regan firm. Historically, that name had been handed down by Arthur Regan, his own father, and Willie's father, and now, their boys. History was repeating itself, but things had changed since Arthur's day. The gangs were different. They didn't care. There were no rules anymore: it was one big free-for-all. Now, as part of the firm, he was going to have to get involved in fighting the likes of Colin Crawford, and he knew that war would be a fucking tough one.

He looked at his phone for Mike's number, gritted his teeth, and pressed the dial button.

'Mike? Listen. I know who's behind this shit with Liam. It's Colin Crawford …' He waited for Mike to answer.

'What? Seriously? How the fuck did you suss *that* out?'

'Long story, but did Willie ever tell you he'd been with Shelley Crawford, as she was then, about twenty years ago?'

Mike sat down. He was in the hotel's reception, waiting for Zara to come out of the ladies' restroom before they set off to go out for something to eat. 'I dunno about that. He may 'ave, but I doubt it. Who'd wanna get involved with her when her father's Colin Crawford?'

'Well, Willie for one, because as you very well know, he's a reckless fucker, and since when would something like that stop him? Ya know what he's like. He don't think, does he?'

Mike thought that Staffie had a point. He had to agree because Willie, being Willie, would act first and then think afterwards about the consequences. Fleetingly, his mind went back to Leon Khouri's cottage where Willie was all set to smash his way in without any thought until he'd stopped him. His mind moved on to the conversation with his mate. 'He's always been the bleedin' same. So, what does all this mean, anyway?'

'Shelley has a son called Lucas. I swear to God, Mike, the kid's a dead ringer for Liam. Anyway, Nicolas told me he was in the hospital the last time he saw him. He was on dialysis.'

'Oh my God! Are ya sure? I mean, are ya 100 per cent sure?'

Staffie felt uneasy again and took another deep breath.

'Yeah, I am. Nicolas thinks that this Colin has done something to his brother. Nicolas gave up ownership of his house to Mack. It was a ploy to stop Shelley from claiming a share when they split up. Colin probably forced Mack to sign the house deeds over to him – as, by Nicolas's reckoning, Shelley wouldn't have had the brains to organize something as clever as that. Since she got with Nicolas, her father disowned her, but now they're separated, Nicolas thinks she's gone running to him for his help, which would make sense.'

Mike's astute mind went into gear immediately. He'd not had a university education. His father had seen to that. What he did have though, was savvy, balls, and a fearless attitude. The likes of Colin Crawford wouldn't put the wind up him, not in a million years. Stinking rich or not, Colin Crawford was still a man who bought his muscle. Mike, on the other hand, was no stranger to crime, and he didn't hide behind anyone. He would be the man leading the charge. His firm respected him because he was the first to get his hands dirty and also the last to clean up his own mess.

'Right, listen. Don't you worry about Colin Crawford, 'cos we can deal with him later. We need to find Torvic first,' said Mike, in a commanding tone, 'and me brother.'

'No,' hissed Staffie. 'I'm gonna help my uncle first. His brother's not answering the phone … He's family, so I'm gonna go over there and sort this mess out.' It was the first time that he'd ever said 'no' to Mike, and, in a way, he felt good about it.

'Okay, mate, of course. You stay safe, bud, and let me know that he's okay. Tell Nicolas we'll sort out Colin soon. He ain't on his own.'

Staffie suddenly felt guilty. Why he'd tried to lord it over

Mike, he couldn't explain. Mike wasn't a bad person. He should know. They'd been friends since primary school. Mike understood all about loyalty to family and close friends, and there was no doubt that if he asked Mike for help, his buddy would be there in a heartbeat. He wished he could say the same about Eric. Ever since Mike had been locked away, Eric had changed big time. He'd drifted away, acting dodgy – even sneaky – and now after Mike had allowed him back on the firm, there was still something about his brother that just didn't sit right. Mike might still feel through family loyalty that he needed to trust Eric, but Staffie wouldn't, and he thought he should actually front Mike about it when they next met up.

'Cheers. Mike, about Eric …'

'Yeah, I need to get to the bottom of that, 'cos he's either working with Torvic, or, as I said, he may be dead. But listen. You sort out your family, and we'll meet up later, yeah?'

'Yeah, Mike, no worries.'

Staffie realized that there was no point in discussing Eric any further. Both of them had so much on their minds.

The last few days had really affected him; he was still extremely tired, following the lock-up scenario with the Weller brothers, then the business at Zara's hangar, and now, to top it all, the emotion of believing Liam was dead and having to watch his own back over this evil bastard Torvic. It was more than most men could deal with. He straightened his shoulders and returned to the lounge to find Nicolas looking like death warmed up. 'What's the problem?'

'Me lawyer said the deeds have been signed over to Shelley and then signed by another lawyer – one of Colin's. The bastard's got to him. We need to get across to his place. I just hope to God they ain't killed him.'

* * *

As soon as Nicolas pulled up outside his brother's house, he sensed something was wrong. The curtains were drawn; his brother never pulled the curtains across. The cold air had a bitterness to it that forced Nicolas to pull his jacket tighter around him. The old Victorian house still had the original sash windows that let the cold air in. It was great in the summer but like an icebox in the winter. Mack had never bothered to sell up and get a classy drum like himself. He ploughed all his money into his place in the South of France. Nicolas stared at the central heating vent on the side of the building, hoping to see some activity, but there was nothing. Mack hated the cold; that system was always on if it was cold, and this morning, it was definitely brass monkey weather. His car's outside temperature gauge showed -6°C.

Staffie looked at his uncle's face. 'What's up?'

'He's either fucking dead or he's not here.'

Staffie didn't waste time asking why. He marched up the steps to the front door and banged hard.

Nicolas tried to look through any gaps in the curtains, but it was no use. 'Let's go round to the back.'

The back of the house was gated. A six-foot wrought-iron fence separated the front from the rear, but, luckily, Nicolas knew the code for the side gate. They hurried through and arrived at the double set of French windows and peered in. In frustration, Nicolas kicked at the glass, and the bottom pane cracked.

'Whoa! What are ya doing?' said Staffie, as he pulled his uncle back. 'Jesus! Talk about a bull in a china shop. Let me do it.'

Nicolas allowed Staffie to take charge, anxiously willing his brother to be alive somewhere inside that great cold monster of a house.

Staffie pulled his leg back and kicked the doorframe with so much force it immediately flew open.

'If I'm a bull, what the fuck are you, then? The bloody FBI?'

Pushing past Staffie, Nicolas went into the main part of the house where the dark, gloomy kitchen was. The sounds of the tap dripping and the clock ticking were all he could hear. Holding his breath, he crept along the hallway, with Staffie behind him holding his gun. As they reached the lounge, Nicolas switched on the light and gasped at the sight.

Staffie moved Nicolas aside to see for himself. It was at that point he realized that perhaps his uncle wasn't as hard as he would let on.

There, stripped naked and tied to a chair with wire, was his uncle. The rolls of fat looked like a lump of pork trussed up for the oven. His head was flopped forward, and his little finger was missing. The room was so cold that his uncle's skin had turned blue.

'Jesus!' yelled Nicolas, who was now crouching down and holding his brother's head in his hands.

Staffie kneeled next to Nicolas and tried to lift his uncle's head; it wasn't stiff, but his body was cold, although not corpse cold. Then he felt for a pulse; it was faint, but it was there.

'Look here, Nicolas, the poor bastard's still alive.'

Nicolas looked up and rose to his feet. 'What? Are you fucking sure?'

He needn't have bothered to ask: the groan coming from his brother confirmed it.

'Nicolas, get some wire cutters, will ya? And hurry up!'

Nicolas spun around. 'Shit, shit, think! Where would he keep his cutters? Oh, hang on.'

Staffie held his uncle's head, trying to assess the damage. The man's nose was shattered and blood dribbled from the bottom of his toothless gums. He looked what he was: fucked.

'It's all right, mate, stay with us. We'll get you out of here.'

Within a minute, Nicolas had returned, clearly out of breath and shaking to pieces. ''Ere! Use these, Staffie.'

Staffie took the cutters and began snipping at each taut wire. As they pinged apart, Nicolas helped his uncle to the floor.

Nicolas ran up the stairs and grabbed a duvet from the bed and dashed back down again to wrap it around his brother. 'Staffie, will ya get that fire on? He's freezing. I'll make us some hot tea. What else should we do?' He looked at Staffie with fear in his eyes.

Staffie decided he needed to take control. Although his Uncle Nicolas had been pretty handy in his younger days, what he'd seen today had really shocked him. Shocked them both, in fact. But he knew he would have to take charge of this mess. His uncle was in no fit state to make any decisions.

'You just make that tea and put some brandy in it along with a load of sugar. He'll be okay, Nicolas. Just concentrate on what you're doing.'

They both helped Mack onto the sofa, wrapping the duvet tighter around him. Staffie heard the central heating fire up, and he turned on the log-effect burner, which instantly threw out plenty of heat.

As Staffie checked over his uncle's injuries, Nicolas returned with a tray of tea and kitchen rolls as well as a bowl of warm water. ''Ere, lad, try and get him to drink this.'

Staffie held Mack's head and gently placed the cup to his lips, easing some of the liquid into his mouth. Mack sipped the tea with his eyes still closed. Some of it dribbled down his chin, but the tea was working. After patiently encouraging him to drink more, Mack blinked and then opened his eyes.

'Mack, it's me, Nicolas. You're all right, fella. We're 'ere, Staffie and me.'

The hoarse voice replied, 'No, I ain't all right. I need the hospital.'

Staffie gave Nicolas a worrying look. 'That will mean the Ol' Bill asking questions. It's up to you, but, me, I'd handle this meself, if I were you.'

Nicolas stood up and began pacing the room. He was struggling to get his brain in gear with all the emotion.

'Staffie, if it was Colin or his mob, they'll not be easy to take down. The man knows everyone, and I don't know a single soul that will go up against him.'

Mack groaned. 'I ain't gonna tell the Filth anything. Just call for an ambulance. I'm hurt bad.'

Staffie sighed. 'Right, then. Get on the blower, Nicolas. I don't think a couple of paracetamol will cut it. He's in a bad way.'

While Nicolas went into the entrance hall to call for an ambulance, Staffie stayed with his Uncle Mack.

'Was it this Colin geezer, by any chance?'

Mack nodded. 'And he's coming for me brother next. I tried to fight them off but ... they had shooters ...' His words trailed off before he passed out again.

Nicolas was just entering the lounge and heard the tail end of the conversation. He stared at his brother's wounds and shuddered. He was getting on in years now and didn't want any trouble. He certainly didn't need this kind of shit. He wanted to hang on to his looks, or at least preserve what he had left of them.

Staffie could read Nicolas's mind. 'Now you know he's coming for you, at least you can be prepared.'

'Prepared? I don't even own a gun anymore.'

Staffie pulled his own from his belt and slapped it in Nicolas's hand. 'You do now. Keep it. I have to go. There's a monster out there who is more fucking dangerous than Colin.'

'But, what about us, Staffie? I mean, what do I do now?'

Staffie was on his feet. 'Make sure Mack gets off to the hospital, okay? You go back to your house, and when Colin's men turn up, you call us. And then you tell them that Ted Stafford and Mike Regan will want a fucking word, and make sure Colin also knows that Willie Ritz will be coming for him, if we don't get to him first, that is.'

'Wait, Staffie. He ain't no two-bit gangster anymore. As I told you, the cunt's gone international. He deals with the fucking Russians and the Colombians. He's a multi-millionaire. Seriously, he won't give a shit about you or the Regans.'

Staffie stood with his hands on his hips and a cruel smirk formed across his face. 'He could be the Prince of Dubai, but that won't stop Willie Ritz. He's a reckless, ruthless bastard. He'll shoot his way through a fucking army to get to the man that hurt his boy.'

'But, Staffie, Colin has protection. He knows everyone who's anyone, and—'

Staffie stopped him, holding his hands up. 'Wait! So you reckon he literally knows *everyone*?'

Nicolas frowned, wondering where his nephew was going with this conversation. 'Yeah, why?'

'Well, he just might know the guy we're after. It's this Torvic geezer. We could strike a deal.'

'Ha ha!' replied Nicolas, in an exaggerated tone. 'Strike a deal? No way. Honestly, Staffie, son, you really don't know who you're up against.'

'Nicolas, you haven't got kids, have you? So you wouldn't understand. Willie won't care how powerful this Colin geezer is. He'll kill him. And Colin will be lucky if he just gets shot, 'cos Willie will torture him first and fucking laugh while he's doing it. You don't know him, Nicolas, or Mike Regan for that matter.'

Nicolas lowered his head. 'I just hope you get him before he hurts me or finishes off Mack.' He looked at his brother, whose mouth was still weeping with blood and pus. 'The sick bastard.'

'Nicolas, you'd better stay somewhere else then, mate. Go to a hotel and lie low, until we sort this shit out. All right?'

Nicolas nodded, looking a little less stressed now. 'Yeah, I'll stay safe, but keep me informed, will ya?'

Staffie nodded and was gone as soon as he heard the ambulance.

Chapter 14

Mike was already up and dressed when Zara woke up. 'What are you doing?'

Mike spun around and tightened his belt. 'I've called Eric a hundred times on his mobile. He ain't answering that or his landline. I've got an uneasy fucking feeling about that last call I made to Eric's house. Eric may well have been connected to Torvic, but I just have this gut instinct that maybe he was trying to take Torvic down himself. Me brother was always trying to prove himself but fucking things up along the bleedin' way too. I hate to say it, but I feel that Torvic's killed him.'

Zara put her hand to her mouth. 'You ain't the type to get all spiritual. Do ya really think Eric's dead?'

Slowly, he nodded. 'Yeah, I do, but there's only one way to find out. I'm going to his house.'

Zara sat upright. 'Okay, I'll get dressed and come with you.'

'No!'

'Mike, you ain't going alone. I *am* coming.'

He softened his voice. 'Babe, please stay here. This ain't about the business anymore, is it? I want you safe. Please, just do it for me, just this once. And I ain't going alone. Staffie's gonna meet me.'

'Mike, the longer that bastard is out there, the more chances he'll have to make a plan for himself. With Lance and Willie out there in Spain, we're thin on the ground. I'm going back to my house, to check on Jackie.'

'No!' he demanded again. 'I'll go there, okay, when I've been to Eric's place. Why don't you call Neil and his cousin to check out that address of Torvic's hideaway place your brother gave us?'

'Okay, no problem. I'll call them when you've left.' She tried to sound convincing, and it worked because Mike was still worrying over his brother.

Zara watched as Mike found his jacket. Her father had always instilled into her a simple mantra: make sure you are in control. But the problem was she felt that things were spinning *out* of control. What with Torvic on the loose, Willie on the warpath for some doctor weirdo, then hearing all about Torvic's infatuation with her – was the bastard serious? – and, finally, Staffie finding out that what had happened to Liam may be linked to Staffie's uncles, it was as if she'd thrown hand grenades up in the air and then been expected to catch them all at once before they exploded around her.

So, despite Mike's plea for her to stay at the hotel, that was not who she was. She needed to get back control – of her life and her business – before she could even think of a proper future with Mike and his family.

Once again, the rush to get out of that hangar plagued her mind. She'd been absurdly foolhardy after meticulously planning to set up that meeting with Torvic. So, the upshot was that as much as she wanted to do as Mike asked, she couldn't: it just wasn't in her make-up. She was the one who'd ultimately made the mistake of leaving that remote control behind in the hangar, and she sure as hell wasn't going to let her firm pick up the pieces for her cock-up. She would go to this secret hideout of Torvic's herself. First, though, she would have to go back home and pick up her other car, as Mike, no doubt, would be using her Mercedes.

* * *

Bluesy Watson rolled over and wanted to gag.

Lying next to her, with his arms above his head and stinking of stale sweat, was Striker. She'd been his go-to girl for as long as she could remember. Not that she wanted to muse over the idea that she'd been shagging the great fat lump for over twenty years, but he did pay her well.

'Morning, Bluesy,' he said coldly, just to let her know he was awake.

She tried to shuffle off the bed but was dragged back by her thong. Taking a deep breath, she quietly sighed. She knew what was coming and it would be him in twenty minutes if he pressed for his morning blow job. Still, that little chore would earn her a oner, so she gritted her teeth and turned around.

'Morning, Striker.'

It was a joke that he still preferred his nickname, even after all these years. Looking at the man now, with his rolls of fat and wheezy chest, she couldn't imagine that he'd earned that name from being so good at football. However, she was no spring chicken herself, being a little chubby around the waist, with a few deep lines under her hooded eyes. So, she was grateful, in some respects, that she still had Striker as her regular punter. Most of her customers had gone for a younger model, unless, of course, they liked a really experienced brass.

'Er, flash the cash, babe. You know the score.' He was good for cash; the man was fucking loaded.

Striker leaned over the bed to grab his trousers. With his bare arse in the air, he farted and didn't even excuse himself.

A moment later, Bluesy shook her head and took a deep breath; this was not going to be pleasant. However, with a hundred quid from last night's action and another ton this morning, she could pay her weekly rent. She had to suck it up and think of England or the Bahamas.

''Ere you go, girl, and make it good.'

Bluesy smiled sweetly, took the money, and shoved it in her bag.

Just as she was about to go down on him, his dog, Misty, started barking.

Striker sat up straight. 'Get dressed. Someone's outside.'

Instantly relieved, Bluesy, with the money in her bag, had an excuse to go. She watched the concern on Striker's face. 'Er, babe, shall I wait or …?' Yet, she already knew the answer.

'Nah, just fuck off now.'

She pulled her tube dress over her head, grabbed her shoes, bag, and jacket, and left the room.

Striker climbed into his trousers and followed her down the stairs.

Misty, a springer spaniel, was scratching at the back door.

'Go out the front,' he whispered, as he pushed her towards the hallway.

Bluesy didn't need to be told twice. She opened the door

and noticed her car covered in ice. 'Fuck it,' she grunted, as she forced the door open. Once inside, she put on her jacket and started the engine, glad to be leaving the fat old git.

Striker made his way to the kitchen and listened. It was quiet. His dog looked up at him and then sat down, waiting for her master to open the door.

'Jesus, you little fucker, I missed out on a blow job, all 'cos you wanted a piss.'

With a heavy sigh, Striker unlocked the door and let the dog out. Leaving the door ajar, he opened the large American-style fridge and retrieved eggs, bacon, and sausages, and then he turned the hob on.

'If I can't have a blow job, a fry-up's the next best thing,' he mumbled to himself.

Once he'd fried all the food, he buttered four slices of bread, made a large mug of tea, and sat himself down at the kitchen table, ready to get stuck in.

Smelling the food, Misty came charging back in, bringing with her an ice-cold gust of air.

'Now you're done. No more fucking barking.'

He watched the dog curl up in her bed and smiled to himself. He hated people, but he loved dogs. After he closed the door, he sat back down to enjoy his breakfast. Misty, however, was still grumbling under her breath.

Folding a piece of bread in half, he dipped it into the runny yolk, but before he'd a chance to take a bite, the back door flew open.

Striker dropped the bread and froze. Dressed in an old jumper and muddy jeans stood Torvic.

'Jesus, Torvic, I thought you were dead!' He peered closer

and sniffed the air. 'You stink, mate. What did you do? Fall into a petrol tank, did you?'

Torvic slammed the door shut and sat heavily in the chair opposite Striker.

'Fucking hell. Look at you, sitting there like nothing's wrong. Didn't you know I was captured by that fucking Zara Ezra and Mike Regan *and* his firm?'

'Oi, mush, don't you come barging into my house ranting, right! No! How would I fucking know that, eh? Anyway, looks like you've escaped.'

Torvic glared in annoyance, grinding his teeth.

'They fucking had me locked up in her hangar ...' He stopped and shook his head, unable to bring himself to say what had happened. It sickened him.

'And?' questioned Striker, as he wiped his mouth with a tea towel.

'They made me kill Alastair, and they killed Stephan. My Tiffany's dead an' all.'

'What? The fucking sick bastards ... Fuck, I'm sorry, mate.'

Striker looked over at Torvic and suddenly realized that the man's presence put himself at risk.

'Torvic, what are you doing 'ere? You need to leave. I don't want anyone sniffing around. And if the likes of Lance Ryder are involved, then that bastard will follow you right to my fucking doorstep.'

Looking nervous, Torvic shook his head. 'No one followed me, right? No one.'

Striker pushed his plate forward and leaned back on his chair. 'This ain't good. You can't come 'ere ever again, right? Now, what d'ya want? Money? A motor?'

'No, I need your help with something else.'

Striker wondered how the man could still string a sentence together; he looked as though he'd been dug up from the grave.

'What exactly?' He sighed.

'I'm gonna kill them all and I want that fucking monstrosity of a mansion of hers burned to the ground.'

Scrutinizing Torvic's lifeless expression, Striker replied, 'And why would you want to burn that house down?'

Torvic smirked so cruelly that even Striker cringed. He hated that evil glare because it reminded him that Torvic was such a dangerous, wicked man. Throughout their relationship, he'd always managed to have the upper hand over Torvic, but there were times when he felt his arsehole might go. Like now.

'Because I fucking well hate the place,' blurted Torvic, with loathing in his eyes.

Striker sighed, leaned back on his chair, and watched the man beating himself up with anger. He'd known Torvic for most of his life and was well aware of how reckless he could be. Now, though, things had changed, and Striker wasn't too happy that Torvic was bringing trouble to his own door. Torvic had definitely crossed the line.

Torvic snatched the cup of tea directly in front of him and gulped it back as if he had a raging thirst. Striker watched the man's hands shake. He was obviously exhausted and weak.

'Don't look at me like that. You have no idea what I've been through. I can still smell the burning flesh from my little Tiffany's body. It was all charred and ...' He choked back the words as he said, 'It was like a roasted pig.'

Immediately, the contents of last night's dinner rose to

Striker's throat. He pushed his chair away and ran to the downstairs toilet where he expelled the vomit like a tidal wave.

Ignoring Striker's departure, Torvic tapped his forefinger rhythmically on the table like a metronome as he thought about the last few hours' work. Then he looked at the contents of Striker's breakfast and pulled the plate to him and began devouring it like a starving animal. By the time Striker had returned, the plate was almost empty, and Torvic's face was slightly pink.

Striker didn't know if he should feel disgusted or impressed. More pressing was what to do now. He had to think of something quickly before Lance Ryder, the bloody ninja, came knocking.

'Tell me, Striker, do you have any idea what they actually did to my boys and me?'

Striker was swallowing another wave of sickness. He knew that what was coming next would have him throwing up again because that look on Torvic's face said it was an unthinkable act.

'No,' he replied, hesitantly.

'They tied us all up, and then they killed Stephan in front of me. They held acid over my granddaughter's head and then...' – the words stuck in his throat – 'they made me pour acid over Alastair's head. I was forced to watch as he screamed and screamed until he died.'

'Jesus!' It was all Striker could say as he visualized the horrific scene. Then he remembered what Torvic had done in the past. One victim stuck in his mind: Sonya Richards. The poor innocent woman had been left with no face after Torvic's granddaughter had poured acid over her. He didn't smile or show any reaction, but, inside, he was thinking, *what goes around comes around.*

'So, you're determined to take revenge, I take it?'

'Of course I fucking am! They killed my Tiffany. I have no family, and I don't care if I live or die anymore. I want them dead.' He took a deep breath. 'And just so you know, all my contacts are backing away. I made a call to my top man, who did give me a piece of advice, and that was to leave the country. Me, fucking me, leave the country? Not a fucking chance! Well, the Regans and that bitch Zara Ezra will not run *me* out of this country. Her fucking father may have done that years ago, but Zara won't do it, not this time. Even a million-pound bounty on my head will not have me running for the hills, I'll tell you that much.'

Striker's eyes widened. 'A million-pound bounty? Are you having a laugh?'

Torvic leaned forward. 'Don't get any fucking ideas, Striker, because I have too much on you. One word from me and you'll be gone from this life faster than you can blow your fucking nose. But I know what you're all about, you greedy fucker. So, *I'll* give you a million if you help me take them out.'

Striker shook his head. 'No, I wasn't thinking that, but a million in cash. You really will have to lie low or fuck off because everyone will be crawling out of the woodwork. Lance Ryder, for one. That man is pure genius. He came close to you so many times, but the idiot trusted me, or you would've been dead yonks ago. So, if he wants a million, it won't take him long to track you down.'

'Ryder is already tracking me down. He was fucking there when they captured me.'

Striker leaned forward, his face chalk-white in shock. 'You're kidding me? Fuck, it won't be long before he realizes that it's me running the fucking show ... Colin hasn't answered my calls either. Did you go and see him like I asked you to?'

'What? Are you fucking listening to me, Striker? The Regans and Zara have annihilated my family, so I couldn't give a shit about fucking Colin. I can't stand the poncey prick anyway, and, correct me if I'm wrong, but ain't that your job to deal with him?'

Striker grabbed his almost empty mug of tea and launched it across the room. The dregs flew up the cream walls, and the mug exploded into hundreds of pieces.

'You, ya stupid cunt, have been obsessed over the Regans when ya should've been getting ya nut down to fucking business. I swear to God, if you don't pull your head outta your arse, we'll both be locked up, and I'll fucking put a bullet through your head before I go to jail. That much, I can promise you.'

Torvic curled his top lip. 'Ya think I care about going to prison? Look at me, Striker. I couldn't give a flying fuck about anything anymore. Don't you get it? Once Zara Ezra and the Regans are dead and cremated, then I'll take over the manor. I'll have my business back, and you'll have your tasty earner ready for your long-awaited retirement. And another thing: fuck Colin. Ya don't need that prick. I'll go over to Poland meself and get the goods flown over.'

Striker glared with fire in his eyes. 'You really think that once Zara Ezra and the Regans are dead, the world will be a safer place?' He shook his head in disbelief. 'You just don't get it. You weren't the only man I had distributing the drugs. I've got men in France, Spain, and fucking Germany, all awaiting a delivery. So, now, d'ya see why I need to get hold of Colin? For all I know, Lance Ryder may already have got to him.'

Standing up to leave, Torvic gave Striker a sneering sideways glance. 'Me and you were like brothers once, until our enemies ruined that. You could've trusted me in Poland, not poxy Crawford, but they've killed my family and I won't rest 'til they're all dead!'

Striker lowered his gaze and wondered if Torvic was right. They had been close all their lives, and now the reason for them screaming at each other was about Regan and his firm and Ezra.

Accordingly, he moderated his tone. 'I know, mate. Look, I'm sorry about Tiffany, I really am, and I'm on your side. Believe me, I am.'

Torvic looked questioningly over at Striker to see if the man was being honest. A glimmer of hope in those hooded eyes told him he was.

'So, what's the plan?' asked Striker.

He was trying to keep a calm look about him, yet, inside, he knew that the tables had turned and Torvic's unpredictable character now had him by the bollocks. For his own self-respect, he wasn't going to have that. Be answerable to Torvic? Not in a million years. Having him out of the picture sooner rather than later would be a blessing and an answer to his own concerns.

His mind now devising his own plan that would be far more cunning than Torvic's ever would, he asked another question. 'Okay, mate, what car are you driving?'

'Well, mine ran out of petrol but I managed to get hold of Stephan's. That bitch, Zara, had it in her garage. Why?'

'I just wondered whether or not to take mine, but his is a faster motor.'

Torvic grinned. 'So you're gonna help me, then?'

Striker grinned. 'Oh yeah, I'll help you all right. I take it you've got the petrol, 'cos you smell like you've doused yourself in it.'

'I was in a fucking rush.'

'So, Torvic, do you have a plan in mind?'

Excitedly, Torvic replied, 'Yeah, we park the car in the farmer's lane right near the mansion. That's where my car broke down. Zara's CCTV doesn't cover that area and we can carry the petrol across the field. We'll need to make a few trips although it's only a short distance. I want that mansion like a towering inferno, hopefully with Zara Ezra and Mike Regan in it.'

'What about the farmer? Have you thought that he may call the police?'

'He's an old boy, a drippy twat, so he won't do anything. Trust me, Striker, I know what I'm doing.'

'And what's in it for me?'

Torvic laughed loudly. 'Me and you, Striker, we'll have a big piece of the pie. Once Zara and the Regans are out of the picture, we'll have access to far more than a few measly bits of business. We'll be able to take over the whole of the South-East and then the North. You'll have that condo in California. And as for me – well, I'll have my fucking revenge.'

Striker gave Torvic a conceited grin. He really didn't need Torvic to take over any manor; he was quite capable of mastering that himself. 'I'll bring my gun, then.'

Leaving the kitchen and making his way upstairs gave Striker the time to prepare a plan. It would include a strategy that would sort out Torvic and this mess once and for all. He opened his drawer and retrieved a gun, handcuffs, and chloroform.

* * *

Zara stepped out of the taxi and stood at the gates of her house, clutching the gun that rested on her hip. Her heart was pounding hard, and for just a moment, she shook with nerves, imagining being gunned down by the Devil himself, because, right now, that's how she saw her venture.

As she ran along the drive, she didn't take her eyes off the house up ahead, looking for any movement, from the lights, curtains, or anything that would suggest Torvic was there lying in wait.

As soon as she reached the front door, she paused. She couldn't hold the gun and keys with just one hand. And Torvic knew it. Instead, she hurried around to the rear of the house to the back door. As soon as she saw the broken window and smashed lock, she felt herself gasp and take a deep breath. She had to assume he'd either been here or was still here. Very cautiously, she pushed the door open, knowing that it didn't squeak. She stepped over the broken glass and controlled her breathing. With her gun in front of her, her finger was on the trigger. Careful not to tread on any creaky floorboards, she made her way to her father's office. Should Torvic be anywhere, he would be there, no doubt rifling through Izzy's files. It was so eerily quiet, which was not necessarily a good thing. But once she'd ascertained that he wasn't on the ground floor, her shoulders started to loosen up, and her breathing became steadily more relaxed, as her senses told her that for the moment she was safe enough. So where was he? Could it be that he was upstairs, lying in wait? Very slowly, she climbed the stairs, listening intently for any sound, however innocuous that would be, but there was nothing – nothing at all that signified danger. Her senses tuned in even to any whiff of cologne or sweat.

It appeared that the main part of the house was empty after all.

Zara was struck by something that drew her to the basement. Whether it was curiosity, or even intuition, she knew she had to go down those steps. As she crept down the stairs to the underground prison, she paused. *Shit! What if he was there?* She peered ahead, firmly gripping the gun. An appalling odour was drifting her way, and she instantly felt a sense of déjà vu from her time spent down here. As she stepped closer, the sight of vomit first caught her attention, followed by the chair that was no longer resting against the barred door but which instead had been cast onto its side some distance away. With her hand covering her mouth, she moved cautiously to the door itself, where she looked through the bars to see that Jackie was still sprawled out on the bed stone-dead. Now she understood. Torvic. So he *had* been here. And so was his last meal! He'd used the chair to stand on to get a proper sight of the body in the bedroom, hoping it wasn't Jackie – which would indicate his precious Tiffany was still alive. Zara grinned wickedly. Now he knew the truth. The broken windowpane, the chair that was tipped over on its side, and the puke, were evidence of that.

She remembered Mike saying that after he'd been to seek out his brother, he would come here to the house to check on Jackie. She rushed back up the stairs and out through the rear door and into the four-car garage where her other car was. An uneasy feeling swept through her. She was being underhanded, after promising Mike that she'd stay at the hotel, but there she was, jumping into her car. He would be here soon himself and would probably guess she'd been into the house, once he'd clocked that her vehicle was missing. Yet, Stephan's car was also missing, another clear indication that Torvic had been here. Still, she wanted to put right the mistake she'd made when she'd left the remote device behind in the hangar, and the only way to do so was for her to track Torvic down. After consoling herself with that idea, she started the engine and left.

As soon as she was on the main road, another thought entered her mind. When Mike reached the house and saw what had happened, he would almost certainly wonder why she hadn't called him to say that Jackie was dead. From the break-in, she hoped he would assume it was Torvic. She pulled over into a lay-by and tried to call his number. Twice she rang it, but it was engaged. She decided to continue on, hoping to call him later.

* * *

Mike and Staffie arrived at Eric's drum, both on high alert. Staffie was still reeling from the mess he'd found at his Uncle Mack's place and the fact that it had all been to do with Liam. The drive over had been quiet, with both men lost in their own thoughts.

Now, outside Eric's house, it was Staffie who broke the silence. 'If Eric is working with Torvic, will you kill him?'

Gripping his gun, Mike gave his friend a grim look. 'I just hope it won't come to that.' But he was shocked by Staffie's response.

'I fucking will!'

'What?'

'You heard me, Mike, loud and clear. I'm done with all this, mate. Here I am, hunting down fucking Torvic, when, really, I should be gunning for Colin. He's the man behind Liam's butchery.'

Mike stared at him grimly, in silence: Staffie was right.

'I know, Staff, I get it, but if we can take out fucking Torvic, we'll be strong-handed then to sort out Colin. If we don't, then Torvic will take us out, one by one. Er, please, Staffie, let me talk to me brother first, and, I swear, if he's working for Torvic, I'll shoot the bastard meself.'

Staffie's cold expression didn't change at all. His look at Mike was equally grim as he replied, 'You'd better, Mike, 'cos I will, I swear I fucking will.'

'Okay!' Mike raised his voice and then looked up at the house. 'We'll go around the back. I've got a key.'

Staffie followed Mike through the gate, and they both stopped before they got to the French doors. Staffie watched as Mike, slowly concealing his body, peered inside. He could see right into the lounge, but only his brother's arm, dangling off the sofa, was visible. He stared, watching for any movement, but there was nothing.

'He's in there. I can see his arm, but I think he's asleep or … Shit, get back, Staffie.'

Mike quickly inserted the key in the lock and pushed the doors open. Staffie was on his heels as Mike ran into the lounge and stopped dead in his tracks. 'Jesus!' He held his hand to his mouth and just stared aghast at the sight.

Staffie was no less shocked to the core. For there was one of his once closest friends with a hole neatly placed between his eyes. His gaping mouth looked grotesque, and his eyes were like a mannequin in a shop window.

Mike wobbled and leaned back into Staffie. They were silent, just staring, trying to take it all in. Staffie, for the moment, didn't know what to do. It was too shocking. Those words he'd expressed to Mike minutes ago about killing Eric felt like a sucker punch aimed at his best friend. Now he wished he could retract everything he'd said. It was clear that Eric wasn't working for Torvic; the evil bastard must have killed him and then answered his phone.

'I'm so sorry, Mike. Jesus, I feel fucking terrible. Poor Eric.'

Mike's whole body seemed to shake like an office block in the midst of an earthquake. The big man rocked on his feet, before falling in front of his brother in a heap. Staffie held Mike in his arms as he broke down and sobbed through salty tears.

'I didn't get a chance to ...' He broke off.

Kneeling beside him, they hugged one another, drawing strength from a lifelong friendship.

'He knew, Mike. He knew you loved him.'

'Christ,' he said. 'What am I gonna tell me muvver? What am I gonna do ...?'

'Mikey Regan, you're gonna get yaself together, right? We're gonna find this fucker and kill him!'

Mike rose to his feet, with a look in his eyes that Staffie had never seen before.

'Let's go to Zara's. I bet the fucking cunt's plotted up there. You drive, Staffie, 'cos I'm losing it. That bastard killed my brother, and I won't rest until the fucker is truly dead.'

* * *

Zara drove slowly along Tylers Green. She looked at the houses and guessed most of the occupants were elderly. The old-fashioned wooden front doors, with their polished doorsteps, and the immaculately presented front gardens lent themselves to typical pensioners' homes. She drove to the end of the road and took the next left into an overgrown alleyway, which ran the length of the garages that were attached to the row of cottages. As she crept along at five miles an hour, she noticed that the lack of attention to the garages, with their peeling paint and weeds surrounding the entrances, was a sure sign that these parts of the properties were neglected and probably not in use except for the next one to her left. This garage, with the green door, was exactly how Ismail had described it.

Looking at the garage and then up at the back of the house, she wondered if this was the place where Torvic had grown up. The lace net curtains and the trellises that separated the two houses were not something she would normally have associated with Torvic. This had to be his mother's house. The sound of the garage door banging in the wind pulled her from her gaze. The building wasn't locked. She looked ahead and then in her rear-view mirror, but there were no cars around. With her gun in her hand, she opened the car door using her little finger. It was amazing how strong her fingers had become. She had to use the one hand now for everything; luckily for her, she had mastered using it and was finding everyday tasks much easier.

She didn't close the car door, in case it made a noise, but crept towards the garage, still with her gun pointing forward. Cautiously, she opened the door to let in more light. The place was deserted except for an old rifle and boxes of bullets. Her eyes then focused on the door that obviously led into the house. If he was there now, he hadn't heard her, or he would have appeared.

Using her little finger again, she found she could easily turn the Bakelite knob to enter the house. *Strange*, she thought. *It should be locked*. Straight ahead of her was a kitchen. It was a small area with just the basics, consisting of an arrangement of Formica cabinets in between which were a free-standing cooker and a sink. It was spotless. Even the old floral tea towels that hung from the oven door were clean. Yet this was no man's place, certainly not a wealthy one's. This definitely must be Torvic's mother's house. The china chicken, the African violets in a pink pot, and the calendar on the fridge door all spoke volumes. Her eyes focused on the calendar with the picture of the Devonshire countryside; it was dated 1974. A cold feeling gripped her. So this wasn't so much his mother's home: it was his mother's shrine. She sighed to herself at the thought that Torvic had been loved as dearly as she had by her own mother.

The tick-tock sound reminded her of her father's grandfather clock. Leaving the kitchen, she wandered into the living room where a smaller version of her own timepiece stood. She tilted her head to the side; it just seemed so out of place, nestled between the two Dralon armchairs with the embroidered backrests. Again, the room was very dated, with the Winchester pattern carpet, the Chinese rug, and the glass top coffee table. For a moment, she was mesmerized as her eyes drifted around the room. Taking in all the knick-knacks and doilies on the side tables, and the small black-and-white photos, the eerie experience intrigued her.

In fact, she was so captivated by the character of the home, she wanted to look at the other rooms and decided to go upstairs, hoping that she would learn who Torvic really was. Would she discover anything by this visit to his mother's home? What had driven the man to be so evil? The staircase was steep. Leading off from the small square landing were four rooms, one of which contained a toilet, another a bathroom, and then just two bedrooms.

The largest was the room at the front of the house; inside was a double bed covered in a pink candlewick bedcover. A Tiffany lamp stood on one bedside cabinet and a spectacles case lay on the other one. By the bed, she noticed a pair of slippers, roughly size three.

His mother must have been a tiny woman.

Going into the other bedroom, she found it was marginally smaller, with a queen-size bed that dominated the room. Along the opposite wall stood a wardrobe and a chunky pine cabinet. Like the other bedroom, it was immaculate. A red throw and matching covers lay on the bed. Beside it, there was a small rug and above the bed was a framed photo, again in black and white, of a man leaning against a motorbike. She stared until she realized it was Torvic in his younger days. His cap and tatty shirt implied that he wasn't wealthy, and the look in his eyes suggested he was a sad young man.

She turned to face the cabinet and noticed that inside a silver frame there was a photo of a woman. Suddenly, her heart pounded. Snatching the photo, she stared at it. No! This couldn't be! But it was. It was of her mother. She'd never seen that photo before, but the evidence was there. No one had hair like hers. Holding the frame, she felt something behind it, and quickly, she turned it over to see an envelope glued to the back. Her curiosity was overwhelming, and she had to look inside. She needed to know the significance of the photo. At first, she felt a piece of paper in the envelope, but there was something else behind it. It was a chain. Placing the frame face down on the cabinet, she pulled the contents of the envelope out and stared at them once more. There was a ring on the chain. It was a dainty gold ring with a small diamond surrounded by sapphires. Then her eyes peered at the letter. *Was this from her mother?* she wondered. The discovery sent her into an anxious place, setting off a string of palpitations, which made her breathe erratically. As she opened the folded paper, she looked at the name at the bottom of the page and held her breath. It *was* from her mother. This was like stepping back in time, peering into the past.

Dear Vic,

Please stop sending me gifts. You really must leave me alone. I am returning the ring in the hope that you will finally get the message. I am to be married to Izzy, two days from now. What you and I did was wrong. As much as you are to blame for what happened, I was too. I should never have agreed to meet with you and certainly should never have taken a drink from you. So I know you drugged me, but I will not hold you entirely to blame, as it was I who drank the drink. Please leave me and my family alone. I will then keep what happened between us a secret and will take it to my grave.

Yours sincerely,
Isabel

Zara shook all over. This was her mother's handwriting, her dear mother, who this evil man eventually killed, all because he couldn't have her. It must have been why he hated her father so much because Izzy had what he wanted. He must have really loved her mother to have kept the letter, the photo, and the ring. She wasn't just a passing girlfriend, she was the love of his life, but he'd killed her. What Torvic couldn't have, he took, and in her mother's case, it was her life.

She looked at the date on the back of the envelope: it was the year she was born. Then she counted back the months. No! It was nine months before she was born, to be exact.

Suddenly, she spun around and stared intently at the enlarged photo on the wall, searching for any evidence that she looked in any way like that man. He couldn't be her father, surely to God! No way! An unexpected tear made its way down her cheek. But, quickly, she brushed it away and ground her teeth. This man wasn't her father: Izzy was. He had to be: no man would have loved her the way he did unless he was her father.

She calmed herself down and continued to search for anything else that would expose who Torvic was, and, more to the point, what he was about. What had made the man become a monster? Her eyes fell to a kid's piggy bank, which was covered in cracks. On closer inspection, she realized that it had been smashed and glued back together, piece by piece. That being the case, the money box clearly held some significance. Carefully, she held it in her hand and rattled it, but just a few loose coins jangled.

The internal door banged suddenly, the shock making her drop the piggy bank, which shattered into a thousand pieces onto the cabinet. She cursed and quickly retrieved her gun that she'd left on the side. The door banged again, and then she realized it must have been the wind. Her eyes returned to the broken mess and the old pennies that were strewn everywhere. Something told her to clean everything up and hide what she'd discovered. She quickly used her hand to sweep away the broken pieces and the coins behind the cabinet and kicked the pennies under the bed.

This room wasn't who Torvic was now: it was who he once was – a man filled with hopes and dreams, saving his money, loving a woman he couldn't have. The man in the black-and-white photo, who was leaning against the gleaming bike and holding a spanner, with grease up his arms, looked to be a tortured soul. That look, which she'd initially thought was just sadness wasn't sadness at all – it was bitterness. She glanced once more and then saw the small newspaper cutting pressed into the corner of the frame. She leaned in closer and tried to see who the subject of the picture was, but the image was too small to see. Underneath, though, was a short write-up. *Con artist Ralph Torvic Sobol was found dead on Saturday morning. His death was attributed to alcoholic poisoning.* She speculated on whether it could be his father.

As she headed back down the stairs, she took one last look in the living room and glanced at the photos; they were nearly all of his mother, and that's when she noticed that each one was torn in half. She could only assume the other part would have shown his father. The one photo that was intact was of Torvic with another much younger lad. They were grinning, with their arms around each other.

The sudden chime from the grandfather clock was sufficient to startle her once more; it reminded her that perhaps she'd been there long enough. Retracing her steps, she stopped when she reached the garage. The boxes of ammunition were all neatly stacked; he would be back for those, unless he'd enough already. Today, she wasn't taking any chances and searched for something to put them in. On the floor in the corner, she spied an old Army bag, covered in spiderwebs and dust. She checked outside before she got to work loading the bag. Once she'd cleared the shelf of the shells, she scurried to her car, wasting no time in pulling away.

The old Army bag lay on the seat next to her, and as soon as she was far enough away, she pulled over to catch her breath and take a proper look in it. Visions of her mother and Torvic sickened her. Worse, though, the germ of an idea filtering inside her mind that he might be her father made her want to puke. Nevertheless, she was drawn to that dust-covered Army bag.

The green canvas had two pockets sewn into the sides. She slid her hand inside the first one and pulled out an old cigarette case and a metal military disc with the name Ralph Sobol engraved on it. Next, she slid her hand inside the second pocket and retrieved the contents, comprising a photo and a note. The photo was of a tall, heavily built man and a young boy, approximately two years old, who she assumed was Torvic. Unfolding the note, she read the contents.

Dear Father,

It's been six months. I haven't heard how the business is going. I can send more money if you need it. I have just sold my bike. Please write back. I am anxious to know how our investment is doing. When can I move to Bristol to be with you? Mum's not well and so any good news will lift her spirits.

    I look forward to hearing from you.

Your Son,
Torvic

His story was unravelling, and now Zara was getting a clearer picture of who he was and why he had grown into such a monster. His real name was in fact Torvic, the man her father had referred to as the Russian, but he'd used an anagram – Victor. She wondered if her mother knew the truth. Nevertheless, she had called him 'Vic' in her letter – perhaps short for Torvic.

Chapter 15

Mike's head was in a mess. He'd tried ringing Zara, but the phone just rang off.

'Calm down, Mike. Please, listen. Zara is safe in that hotel room. No one knows where she is, okay? She's probably in the shower.'

'Nah, Staffie. I've had a missed call. It's from her. Something ain't right.'

Staffie suddenly came to a stop. 'Right, then. D'ya want us to turn around and head back?'

Mike wasn't listening; he was awash with sick thoughts of what Torvic would do to her if he got hold of her.

'Mike, try her again, and if she don't answer, then we'll head back.'

Mike redialled her number.

* * *

Totally absorbed in reading the note from Torvic to his father, Zara almost ignored the call when her phone rang.

'Hello, Mike. What's up?'

'For fuck's sake, Zara, I've been calling you for ages! Jesus, you had me worried to death. Where are you?'

Zara realized she couldn't lie so she sidestepped the question. The desperation in Mike's voice was more than worry. 'I'm okay, Mike. What's going on? You sound, er ...'

'Eric's dead. Torvic's killed him. Oh my God, Zara, he's dead, and that bastard will come for us, one by one. I thought when you didn't answer, well, you can imagine what ran through my head.'

Zara was uncharacteristically quiet; she just didn't know how to respond to that devastating news, although they'd both somehow expected it. With Eric dead, she knew it would break Mike. As much as the two brothers had their differences, she was aware that Mike was a loyal and devoted man, and he'd always loved his brother, no matter what.

'I'm so sorry, Mike.'

'So, can ya see why I need you to answer your fucking phone when I call?'

Normally, Zara wouldn't have taken that stroppy attitude from anyone, but today she swallowed it.

'Of course, love. I'm very sorry. Are you okay?'

He sighed heavily, soothed by Zara's contrite response. 'Yeah, just gutted. Look, me and Staff are gonna go over to see if Jackie's okay, and then I'll come back. Have you heard from Neil or anyone else?'

Zara paused before answering, her mind on Jackie and what Mike would find when he got there.

'Zara?'

'Er, no. Sorry, Mike, I haven't heard anything. Look, please be careful. Promise me?'

'Yeah, I'll call once I've been to your place, yeah?'

He didn't wait for an answer before he put the phone down.

She stared ahead and thought about what state Mike would be in when he returned to the hotel. With Eric now dead, he would soon see his ex-wife dead too. She didn't ask how Eric had died and wondered if Mike had walked into a torture scene. Her mind was still on trying to track Torvic down before he hurt anyone else – most of all, Mike.

Just as Staffie pulled away, Mike's phone rang. He looked at the caller ID. It was a withheld number. Taking a deep breath, Mike said, 'This might be Torvic.'

Staffie concentrated on the road ahead as Mike answered the phone.

'Mr Regan?'

'Yeah, who is it?'

'Detective Inspector Lowry. I've just been called to a fire. It seems that Torvic, the so-called Governor, is dead. The car, in his name and insured in his son's name, was found just a short distance from Zara Ezra's home. It had been burning for some time. The man inside, although now unrecognizable, is believed to be him.'

'How can you be so bloody sure?'

'Oh, trust me, Mr Regan, I'm sure.' His arrogant tone irritated Mike.

'No, Lowry. I wanna know how you are so fucking sure because the man has managed to fucking murder my brother, and I do believe he's on the warpath.' He paused and frowned. 'Lowry, how the fuck did you know he'd escaped? Because a message was sent to Stoneham to say that we had

291

captured Torvic, and I don't remember any of us telling you otherwise, or that he'd gone on the run.'

'Well, Mr Regan, I was briefed that you had him, but my informant told me he knows that he'd escaped because there's a million-pound bounty on his head. So, I assumed … Anyway, forensics are taking his body to the lab, although, to be honest, there isn't much left of him.'

'So you can't be fucking sure then, can you?'

'My informant was one of the men who watched him burn like Guy Fawkes, and I have no reason to doubt him, none whatsoever. You see, Mr Regan, you weren't his only enemy. Remember, there were many people who wanted that man dead.'

'I fucking hope to God you're right.'

'I wouldn't put you or your family in danger. So, trust me, when I say it's him. Okay?'

Mike felt his entire body tingling; maybe it was from shock or relief.

'I hope whoever it was, they burned him alive.'

'Apparently, he *was* burned alive, handcuffed to the steering wheel, so I know my informant was telling the truth because the handcuffs were there around the charred bones and so was a titanium ring on the remains of his right hand.'

Mike remembered seeing a ring on the man's fat, sausage-like fingers when they had him tied to the chair in the hangar.

'Do you know who did it?'

'A gang of Yardies, I believe. Torvic had disfigured one of their sisters before one of his sons raped her.'

'Which Yardies?'

'Mr Regan, I can't reveal that. I've told you enough.'

'Okay, Lowry. Cheers, mate.' He finished the call and turned to face Staffie.

'Torvic's dead. Some Yardie gang's set him alight.'

Staffie swerved. 'Christ alive. Are you sure, Mikey? This ain't no wind-up, is it?'

Mike rubbed his bristly chin. 'Nah, I think he's telling the truth. He's the DI, and what he said sounded convincing to me. That bastard Torvic would've had a lot of enemies. The bounty we put out there would've had people sniffing around. Maybe they plotted up near Zara's place, waiting to see if he would turn up, and then, bingo! I have to give it to whoever killed him – they were one step ahead of us. But, to be honest, I don't care, as long he can't hurt any of us now.'

'So, what are we doing now, Mike? Are we going to Zara's place or back to the hotel?'

'Zara's. I'd better check to see if Jackie's okay and if Stephan's car is missing. Remember, we had it parked up in Zara's garage. Then we'll get a look at this burned-out car. I should imagine it will be taped off by the police by now. Knowing Torvic's dead will certainly give me peace of mind and help me sleep at night. My only wish is that I had watched him burn.'

By the time they reached Zara's house, they could see police vehicles up the lane. Staffie decided to drive past the property towards the hive of activity. As he slowed down, they could see the area where the car had been burned out. Even the surrounding trees had been blackened by the flames.

Two men dressed in white suits and carrying cases stepped out of a black van.

As they watched, a police officer tapped on their window.

Mike lowered it and asked the officer what was going on.

'You'll have to turn around. We're closing the lane.'

'So, what's happened?' He pushed the officer to be more forthcoming.

The officer looked behind him and then back at the occupants in the car. 'It looks like we've a possible murder scene on our hands. There's a car burned out with someone still inside. But you can't drive on. As I said, they're closing the lane.'

Staffie nodded. 'Okay, Gov.'

As Staffie made a three-point turn, Mike continued to glare as the area was taped off.

'Let's hope that Eric meets him on the other side and gives him hell.'

Staffie wanted to laugh, but it wasn't appropriate. 'I'm sure he fucking well will do.'

'Staff, we need to get a move on. If the police start calling at any of the neighbours' houses, we'd better make sure Jackie's out of the way.'

'The police are hardly likely to go sniffing around Zara's house, are they?'

Mike shrugged his shoulders. 'Who fucking knows? This day is getting crazier by the minute.'

* * *

Now that Torvic was dead, Mike found no reason to go sneaking about with his gun on show. He used the key Zara had given him to let himself in. Staffie was close behind.

'Ya know what, Mike? This house still gives me the shivers. It's so fucking creepy. I dunno how Zara ever returned here.'

Mike sighed. 'She gets some comfort from being close to her farver, I guess. My Zara ain't easily spooked. That's what I love about her. She's a tough cookie.'

Staffie didn't need to be told how tough Zara was because he'd seen her in action, and those memories still made him go cold on their own. Perhaps she suited this house. The Devil's house and the Devil's daughter. He felt tired to the point his mind was all over the place.

They marched along the hallway to the door on the left and then hurried down the staircase towards the basement suite.

'Jackie, get the fuck up!' called out Mike, before he even reached the door.

Staffie stared ahead, the smell hitting him first before his eyes focused between the bars. He experienced another cold feeling, similar to the one when he'd entered Mack's house.

Mike swerved the pile of vomit and stopped and stared ahead. Jackie's blood had pooled onto the floor. Then, when he stood on tiptoes to get a better look, he found the source – the hole in her head. It was right between her eyes, just like Eric's execution.

'We're too late, Staff. Look, Torvic's shot her. Perhaps we should never have locked her in here. She didn't stand a chance, the poor cow.'

Staffie looked at Mike, who was just staring, and wondered how on earth he could suddenly go all soft on the woman who'd caused them all a mountain of heartache. He bit his lip before he said something he'd regret.

'I reckon DI Lowry was right, then. Torvic must have come here, shot Jackie, took his son's motor, and was then followed by the Yardies, who ran him off the road and set the bastard alight.'

Staffie nodded. 'So after all the running around to capture the man again, the bleedin' Yardies got to him first.'

'Well, to be honest, I couldn't give a shit who killed him. I'm just relieved that he's bloody dead,' replied Mike, in a flat tone.

Two loud, sharp knocks at the front door startled the men.

'Staffie, I'll go. You wait in the office. Let me deal with this.'

'D'ya reckon it's the Filth?'

Mike nodded. 'Yeah, I do.'

He was right. As soon as he pulled open the door, two officers in uniform, both looking wet behind the ears, gazed at him enquiringly.

'Hello, how can I help?'

'Sir, there's been an incident a mile up the lane. We're calling to ask if you've seen any suspicious activity?'

Mike noticed the other officer, a younger man, looking keenly past him along the hallway, his eyes taking it all in. And to any visitor, the grand entrance with its oversized gilt frames and gloomy appearance would, initially, be a surprise.

'No, I've been away. I've just returned to collect some clothes before I head back to London. Why?'

'An incident occurred a few hours ago. A body was found burned inside a car. We wanted to know if you have seen anyone hanging around or acting suspiciously. Can we take a look at your CCTV? We noticed you have cameras that might reveal something.'

Mike didn't expect the officer to ask that question.

'I'm afraid they don't work. We've had issues ever since they were installed. You can come and see for yourself.' His voice was loud enough for Staffie to hear.

The two officers stepped forward, which irritated Mike,

since they hadn't taken his word for it. He racked his brain, trying to think if the footage showed Jackie at the house, which would then set off another load of questions. His palms began to sweat as he nervously showed the officers through to the office. He looked at Staffie with trepidation, yet Staffie seemed very relaxed, with a smile on his face.

'Oh, hello, sir, I didn't realize ... Mr—'

Staffie stood up from the desk. 'Hello, Officers. What's the problem?'

The younger officer gazed around the room, his face pale. 'Er, who owns this house?'

Mike, now annoyed, answered coldly. 'Sorry, I thought you were here to ask about the incident along the lane?'

The officer's eyes met Mike's, and he realized he wasn't in a position to interrogate him.

'Oh yes, sorry, it's just that it's such an unusual place, I wondered who lived here.'

'And what makes you think I don't?' Mike's harsh and icy tone put the young officer back in his place.

'Sorry, sir, I didn't mean, I just ... it's just, it's so very grand, is what I was trying to say.'

The older officer was getting impatient. He had a bacon butty on order and wanted to get back as soon as possible. After all, this call was just a routine stop.

'The CCTV doesn't work, you say? I'm surprised, sir, because a house like this, with all its ...' – he pointed to the grandfather clock – 'its antiques, I would've thought you'd have made sure it's secure for insurance purposes, surely?'

Mike's chest was beginning to expand, ready to let rip, but Staffie intervened.

'Yeah, you're right, it's a nightmare. It was recently installed, but, for some reason, it doesn't work. Look, see for yourself.' He pressed a few buttons as they stared at the blank screen.

'So, what's going on? What's happened?' asked Staffie, drawing both officers' attention away from the security monitor.

'Oh yes, a car was found burned out with a body inside. We're just doing a sweep of the neighbours, asking if they saw anything suspicious.'

Staffie shook his head. 'We haven't been here for a while, ourselves, so, no, we haven't seen anything.'

Mike wanted to laugh as Staffie put on a feminine voice and even pouted his lips.

The two officers nodded, thanked them, and left. Once the men reached their car, Mike turned to Staffie.

'Fuck me, Staff, even *I* believed you were me boyfriend for a moment. You pulled that off too naturally for my liking.'

It was the first time that Staffie had chuckled in what seemed a lifetime. 'Well, think about it. I could see they were trying to imagine you living in this eerie time warp, and, Mike, it just doesn't go with your persona. But if you were gay, ya know, the theatrical type, then …'

Mike frowned. 'Theatrical type?'

'Well, yeah. You couldn't pull that off, so I thought I'd step in, with you being my bitch lover.'

'Fuck off!'

Mike laughed along with Staffie and then stopped when he stared at the screen. 'Did ya turn it off?'

Staffie smiled. 'Of course I did. Otherwise, they would've seen Jackie arriving, wouldn't they? And then there would've been even more fucking questions. Like we've said before, up there for thinking, down there for dancing, mate.'

Mike sighed. 'Cheers, Staffie. My mind's been all over the place. Me, I just couldn't think quick enough.'

Staffie rubbed his smooth head and yawned. 'I'm bushed, mate, meself. Let's go.'

Before they left, Mike checked all the rooms and then the back door, to find a broken window and a smashed lock. It confirmed what they'd both thought: Torvic had found a way in and killed Jackie.

'Staff, you go on ahead. I'll catch you up in a bit.'

Nodding, with a sad smile on his face, Staffie headed to the car. He knew that Mike needed time to register that his ex-missus was dead. The police turning up hadn't even given him a chance to absorb the situation fully. After all that Jackie had put Mike and the family through, she had still been a part of his life, and, of course, Ricky's. He wondered if she'd ever had any feelings for anyone, yet she wasn't his own ex-wife lying there dead – she was Mike's – and no one could dictate how his best friend should feel.

* * *

Mike returned to the basement. Why he felt the need to do so, he didn't know. However, he knew that he wanted at least to say goodbye. As he looked in through the bars of the metal door, he peered once more at Jackie's face. Perhaps he wanted to see an expression – anything, in fact, that would remind him of the woman he'd first met, but all he saw was the spiteful look, the selfish mother, his son's abuser. As hard as he tried to visualize a good time with her, all he could see were the fights they'd had over the wickedness she'd shown their son when he was a toddler.

His mind was now on Ricky. How would he take the news? That was his real concern: his boy. He looked away and sighed. The only sorrow he felt for Jackie was that she didn't live long enough even to attempt to turn her pathetic life around.

As he walked back along the passageway, he was pricked with annoyance. Jackie had always been a thorn in his side, and now, she had caused another problem – disposing of her body without it coming back to bite him on the arse.

Before he left, he made his way to the garage to check that Stephan's car had been driven away, just for peace of mind. But then he noticed that Zara's car wasn't there either. He scratched his head and thought back to the conversation he'd had with her a while ago. She'd never said she'd been back. However, the conversation had been very brief. He turned his head to look back at the house. Jackie was dead. A mad notion swept through him and covered his skin in goose bumps. Surely, Zara hadn't been the one who killed Jackie?

Pulling his phone from his pocket, he dialled her number. After two rings, she answered.

'Mike, I didn't get the chance to tell you that I've been back to the house to collect my car.'

He felt a sense of relief that she wasn't hiding anything from him. 'Zara, Jackie's dead and so is Torvic!'

'What? Oh my God! How? When?'

'It looks like Torvic must've come to the house and killed Jackie. Stephan's car isn't here, so Torvic must've driven it away. But he was run off the road and killed, apparently by some Yardies. Why did you come back to the house? Jesus, Zara – if he'd been here, he would've shot you.'

'I know I promised to stay put, but, Mike, I wanted to help. I felt …'

'Never mind. Listen, you're safe now. Torvic's dead, so we can at last breathe a sigh of relief.'

'I can't believe it. And you're sure it's him? How did you find out?'

'Lowry gave me the tip-off, and me and Staffie had a butcher's ourselves. The place was swarming with the Ol' Bill. The car was burned out and taped off, just up the road from yours, in the farmer's field. The evil bastard was burned alive by all accounts. Fucking good job an' all.'

'And what about Jackie?'

Mike sighed. 'If ya mean what am I going to do with her, well, I'll have to wait a bit. The police are scouring the area, so I can't do anything just yet. I'll meet you back at mine.'

He would have to wait until the police had finished with their business up the lane before he could make any kind of attempt to dispose of her, but he had a plan.

Chapter 16

Three weeks later

Arthur stood in his black suit with his arm around Gloria. The graveside was packed with mourners. From lawyers to villains, they came in their droves.

'He did have a lot of friends, didn't he, Arthur,' she snivelled.

Arthur looked around and recognized everyone, but he didn't have the heart to say to his wife, 'No, they're Mike's pals, not Eric's.' The truth was, Eric wasn't liked or even respected much. Arthur knew it, but he wasn't going to tell his wife that.

Arthur loved his son, and, once upon a time, he'd loved them equally, but as they grew into men, he knew there was a side to Eric that was so dark. He wished now he'd tried to understand him better. Maybe then he would have been able to get to the bottom of his son's secrets because he knew there were a hell of a lot. However, perhaps it was because he was such a straight-up kind of man himself that it caused him to turn away from Eric. His own belief was that family stuck together – whether it was good, bad, or ugly – and that they would always be honest with each other. Nevertheless, for some reason, Eric failed in those departments. In fact, he didn't just fail, he failed big time. Arthur looked over at Mike, who stood with his legs apart and his hands in front of him, linking arms with Zara, his fiancée. Arthur may be getting on in years, but he was savvy, and he'd sussed out early doors that probably the reason for Eric turning away from the family was Mike's intended: Zara. Two brothers loving one woman – the same one – was a car crash waiting to happen.

His eyes drifted to his grandson, Ricky, who stood just like Mike, with his feet apart, his shoulders back, and his head tilted slightly to the side. And there, on either side, were Arty and Liam. It really was history repeating itself. He was thankful that Ricky, being an only child, wouldn't have the same issues that Mike and Eric had had. He smiled to himself as he watched Arty place an arm around Ricky and squeeze his shoulder. Ricky was fortunate in having Arty, and Liam, of course. It was almost as if he had two surrogates – they would always be there for him.

Then his eyes focused on Big Lou Baker, Charlie Ritz, and Old Teddy Stafford, his pals in the old firm. Nothing had really changed much. They were just the same, all still part of the Regans' crew. He closed his eyes, and for the second time in his life, he prayed to God that they would all live in peace.

But then he opened them again and looked over at Willie, who appeared far from peaceful. Willie had a score to settle, and if Willie was anything like his father, then God help whoever was on the other end of it. And he wouldn't be on his own: the firm would stand shoulder to shoulder with him.

As the priest presided over Eric's body being lowered into the ground, Arthur wiped away a tear and took a deep breath.

He looked across at the mourners and beyond to the old oak tree, the largest by far in the cemetery. He blinked and desperately tried to clear his vision, blinded momentarily through his tears. He thought he saw a man hiding near the tree watching everyone, but then, he figured, perhaps his eyesight was playing tricks on him. He sighed, realizing, of course, that there would be all kinds of folk here. Some, no doubt, were hoping to catch a look at the many Faces who had come to pay their respects. Others, reporters, some from the main tabloids, were wanting to get a story in time for tonight's deadline.

As the mourners slowly left the graveside, Ricky walked purposefully over to Gilly, his other grandmother. She was very frail and needed her walking stick to hold herself upright. Quickly, he grabbed her arm. 'Nan, I didn't know you were coming. I would've stood with you.'

Gilly looked up and through tears she smiled. 'You're such a good boy, my babe,' she said, her travellers' accent apparent. She didn't hide it anymore, not in front of Ricky; she didn't need to. 'I thought it was only right and proper that I paid me last respects, ya know. Gloria and Arthur 'ave been a tower of strength, and you, my babe, 'ave always been the apple of my eye.'

'It's cold and damp, Nan. We would've understood if ya had stayed at home in the warm.'

She patted his hand. 'I know me and ya muvver … well, we didn't really 'ave a relationship, but I did give birth to her, and without her, I wouldn't have had you. So, I just wanted to see if her grave's been finished off proper, like.'

'Nan, I had it covered in peace lilies. I know she wasn't kind to me, but, like you just said, she was still me muvver, and I'll make sure her grave is regularly seen to – the gypsy way – always in full bloom.'

The lingering tears tumbled down Gilly's wrinkled face. 'And you won't forget me, my babe, will ya?'

Ricky put his arms around her, gently hugging her. 'I'll take oath that I'll always look after you, Nan.'

She chuckled at his gypsy accent, and the way he said 'take oath', as if he respected her heritage and recognized part of it as his own, even if it was just for her benefit.

Gloria trotted over to make sure Gilly was all right. The air was bitterly cold, and Gilly was such a thin, sickly woman. 'Come on, love. I'll get one of the lads to run you back to mine. We need to get ya nice and warm.'

Gilly shook her head. 'I'll be off home, Gloria, if ya don't mind. I feel a bit tired, ya know.'

Gloria walked her over to the cars and organized a lift home, knowing it must have been hard for the woman to come to the graveyard when her own daughter had been buried only a week ago.

The cortege of black cars finally made their way back to Arthur's house. Mike sat quietly, staring out of the window. His mind was on the past, when he was just a teenager. Eric, Willie, Staffie, and Lou were the up-and-coming firm. They laughed more than they cried back then. Life had been simple, and he'd been proud to have his brother by his side. He'd never been alone; they'd shared everything and would have died for each other. *Where had it all gone wrong?* he wondered. A tear trickled down the side of his nose and a lump rose in his throat. He would never know the answer, but no matter what his brother had done in the past, he had forgiven him. He hoped Eric knew that.

Christmas was approaching, but Gloria held off from putting the decorations up; she'd wanted to get the funeral over with before she would even entertain any festive celebration. It just didn't seem right somehow. All the close friends made their way back to her house, where she'd engaged caterers to put together sandwiches and fruit cake. She hated fruit cake, but it was the tradition on these occasions.

As she took her black fitted jacket off, Ricky made his way over and gave his grandmother a hug. 'Nan, I shouldn't really say it, but you do look lovely.'

She pinched his cheeks. 'Aw, Ricky, you're such a good boy. Now then, make sure everyone gets a brandy, and do us a favour. Keep an eye out. I don't want the old cronies thinking it's a party and getting pissed.'

Ricky raised his eyebrow. 'Ya know they're gonna anyway, don't ya?'

She smiled gently. 'Yeah, no doubt, but I want them to show some respect. I mean, I know Eric wasn't their favourite, but, still, he was my son.'

Ricky kissed her on the cheek and winked. 'Leave it to me, Nan.'

As the evening went on, the guests mingled and remained respectful. Ricky kept his promise by keeping a close eye. However, two men were really knocking back the drinks as if there was no tomorrow. Mike was in the dining room with Willie, Staffie, and Lou, remembering old times when they had their lads' nights playing poker or watching the footie. Telling stories of the heists that had seen them running around like headless chickens and finally counting their money had them roaring with laughter. Then they talked about Eric and the atmosphere became serious and respectful as they remembered why they were there.

Zara spoke with some associates while their wives took a back seat. Her reputation and power were respected and envied, but she dismissed the green-eyed monsters in the room; it was part of who she was, and, anyway, to her, it was like water off a duck's back.

Claudia Reynolds, the wife of the bank robber Gerry, sat next to Polly Roberts, the wife of Gerry's business partner George. Claudia leaned into Polly, gossiping away as always. 'She swans around like she fucking owns the place. Why the men kiss her fucking feet, God only knows, but I tell ya this for nothing. I won't be sucking up to her like a dog on heat. Just look at those men. They're like flies around shit.'

Polly laughed along. 'I dunno what Mike sees in her, what with one hand an' all. That man could have anyone he wants.'

As if Zara could hear, she turned around and held her head high and looked down her nose at the women. 'More drinks, ladies?'

The death glare had Claudia's face going crimson and looking down in shame, while Polly could only smile nervously. 'Er, no, thank you, Zara. We're just fine.'

As Zara turned her back on them to talk to the men again, Claudia looked up once more. 'See what I mean, Polly? She really thinks she's something, don't she?'

Polly was about to answer, when Gloria, from behind the sofa, leaned in. 'That, ladies, is because she *is* something, and if I were you, I'd watch exactly what you say, or you could just find you'll be attending your ol' fellas' funerals next. And this time, a word of warning to go with that advice: if you ever disrespect my family again, it won't be Zara's wrath you'll face, it'll be fucking mine. Now, smile sweetly and continue to act like the fucking money-grabbing tarts you two really are. And don't you ever forget where you came from. 'Cos if ya do, I'll give you two a swift fucking reminder.'

Claudia and Polly froze at that threat. Glued to their seats, they felt totally humiliated.

Zara listened to the men talking business, but her attention turned to the two men in the corner who were saying something to Ricky. She watched his stance change; he wasn't bantering and being his usual animated self. The look on the men's faces wasn't pleasant: they appeared cocky, as if they were trying to humiliate the lad. She wondered for a moment whether to let Ricky handle them or to intervene herself. Her heart was pounding as she watched one of the men poke Ricky in the chest. Breathing through her nose to calm herself, she made her way over but not so close as to get in Ricky's face. She stayed back, with her body turned to the side, listening intently.

'Do you know who I am?'

Ricky shook his head. 'Nah, I don't, but this isn't the time or place to get drunk.'

'You ain't got the fucking right, ya half pint, to tell me how much I can fucking drink. You don't know this family like I do. You weren't even in it for most of your life, so run along, lad, and leave us be.'

Zara was raging inside, but she knew she had to let Ricky handle it. She decided she would be on standby though, if it all kicked off.

'I might have been away from my family, but they are still *my* family. And this is my uncle's funeral, so I'm just saying, if ya wanna get bladdered, go down the pub.'

Zara was impressed with how cool Ricky was.

Fuelled by drink and feeling invincible, Gerry spat back. 'You're a cocky cunt, living off ya ol' man's reputation, ain't ya? Well, you ain't him, and one more word, boy, and I'll flip you right on ya bottle and glass. Now, fuck off, 'cos I'm 'aving a private conversation with me pal.'

Still keeping his voice low, Ricky bit back. 'I said, if you wanna act like you're at a wedding, then go and finish your jolly down the pub.'

Gerry had the crystal cut-glass tumbler to his mouth when he stopped and scowled at Ricky. 'Ya know what? Ya ain't gonna fucking give up, are ya, boy?'

With his hands gripped together in front of him and his head nodding rhythmically, Ricky, now having his daring hat on, replied, 'You heard me, and if you wanna argue the point, then me and you will politely take this outside, away from my grandparents.'

Gerry studied Ricky and then looked back at his mate. 'Did I hear the boy right? Was he offering me out or fucking what?'

George, who wasn't half as pissed as his friend, was still watching the expression on Ricky's face and decided not to get involved. If the boy was half the man his father was, then they'd both be in for a right good hiding, and there were enough men just in this one room who would back Ricky. 'Gerry, leave it, mate. He's just a kid, and, to be honest, I wanna get a move on. Me dogs need a walk and ol' Polly will be wanting her bed soon.'

Gerry placed his brandy on the coffee table, gave Ricky another hard look, up and down, and made his way towards the door. 'Come on, Claudia, we're going.'

Claudia didn't have to be asked twice; she was up on her stilettos, hobbling behind him.

Zara tapped Ricky on the shoulder. 'I'm proud of you, Ricky. You handled that with manly class.'

His face instantly changed. The eyes, which glinted like steel, revealing the man he would soon become, suddenly softened, and, at once, he became a lad again. Unexpectedly, he kissed Zara on the cheek. 'Well, I'm learning from the best.'

Just as Claudia passed Gloria, she gave her a filthy look and couldn't help herself in giving a final dig. 'Your precious son ain't nuffin now. Look at ya. Ya all walk around with ya nose in the fucking air. Well, there are men out there who'll eat your son for breakfast.'

Gloria was trying to act the perfect host; but listening to this blonde bimbo has-been talking out of her arse was giving her serious palpitations. She had to bite down hard on her back teeth to hold in the rage.

'My Gerry only came over here to have a nosey, to see who still crawls up Mike's arse. Well, it ain't us anymore.'

Those words hit Gloria like a concrete post and immediately her cool demeanour transformed into something more akin to that of a raging lunatic. In one swift movement, she swung her fist and landed Claudia a punch so hard that it knocked her against the wall. It didn't end there, as Gloria followed it up by gripping Claudia's long curls, and, despite her small stature, began to swing her full circle. Claudia screamed as she could feel all her hair start to come away from her head.

It was her pride and joy, probably her best asset, and she'd just spent over two hundred quid at the hairdresser's the day before to get it perfect for today's occasion. The room suddenly went deathly quiet. Zara and Ricky rushed over to find Gloria clutching clumps of hair amid flying arms and legs. Despite her one hand, Zara managed to pull Gloria away.

Gerry had reached his car before he realized that his wife wasn't behind him. He went back into the house to give her a mouthful only to see that Claudia had suffered a right mauling. Her hair was a matted mess, her right cheek was already showing signs of a large bruise, and both her lips were bleeding profusely.

Once the news had spread to the dining room – which was at the other end of the huge house – Mike, Willie, Staffie, and Lou rushed into the lounge to sort out the carnage. But they were too late.

As Gerry attempted to drag his wife away from this scene of humiliation, Gloria hollered after them, 'Say one more word about my family, ya fucking old whore, and I'll cut ya throat!'

Mike stood in front of his mother and stared at Gerry. 'What the fuck was all that about, and, more to the point, who invited you back to me muvver's house?'

'Go fuck yaself, Regan. You ain't nuffin now. And don't stand there all mouth and trousers. Your brother was more of a fucking man than you. At least he died holding his head high. He wasn't a snitch like you.'

No sooner had Gerry got the words out of his mouth than Mike was in his face. With one almighty crack to the head, Gerry stumbled back on his arse.

Lou, Willie, and Staffie pounced on Mike in seconds,

pulling him away before he got himself nicked. 'Leave the little prick alone. He's obviously had too much to drink,' said Lou.

But Gloria was livid and totally in the zone. It took a lot to wind her up, but when it happened, she was unstoppable. 'You, Gerry Reynolds, are nuffin but a big man in a fucking cheap suit with a bleedin' great chip on ya shoulder. Now fuck off while you still have two kneecaps.'

Mike took a few deep breaths as he surveyed the room. Everyone by this time had stopped talking, their eyes focused on Gerry, Mike, and Zara. It was like settling down to a front-row seat at a boxing match, although all bets would be on Mike as the winner. They weren't to know that this would get a whole lot worse, though, and Zara would be the one to beat.

The guests' eyes now focused on Zara. She was standing to the right of the door and glared with pure venom in her eyes. As Gerry wiped his mouth, he and Zara were at daggers drawn.

But Gerry was on an alcohol roll. The liquor in his system, mixed with the fresh air from walking outside, pushed him to yet another level of confidence. 'And you, ya one-handed slut, only live off your old man's reputation. Just so that we're clear,' he drawled, slurring out his words to everyone looking on, 'he was another first-class prick.'

The guests were having a ball. They knew when they'd been invited back to Gloria's home after the funeral, that they would receive the finest nosh and drinks that money could buy. But what no one had counted on was being there to witness the fight of the century.

Now the guests' eyes turned to Claudia, who tried to drag

her husband away, knowing only too well that once he started, he wouldn't stop. He just needed three or four brandies, and he thought he was the hardest man on the planet.

Without anyone seeing it happen, Zara launched herself away from the wall before Gloria or Mike had a chance to stop her. Gerry was in full view of the other guests, blatantly laughing at her. She, an Ezra. It was a total piss-take and it wouldn't be tolerated. And, even worse, the prat continued to laugh at her as she ran towards him. Yet she would have the last laugh. She might be slim, female, and have only one hand, but she could do a lot of damage with a raging mind and fire in her belly.

Savagely, she hurled herself at him. With her right leg pulled back and using all her strength and her skills in Taekwondo, she kicked Gerry directly in the solar plexus, knocking him completely off his feet. No one saw the rapid movement until he landed noisily, banging his head on the sharp edge of a glass coffee table. Like a beached whale, he struggled to get back up. But, before he did, her foot came up and slammed down hard on his face again and again until a high-pitched scream of terror let out by Claudia put a stop to the punishment.

Gloria realized that perhaps things had gotten out of hand somewhat and managed to pull Zara away. Mike, though, hadn't been able to slip through the throng of guests quickly enough before the beating was over. But, of course, she didn't need help. Gerry lay there, now a mangled mess. Gloria held Zara back, telling her to calm down, but Zara was beyond reason, and it showed in her copper-coloured eyes that were glowing red. 'You ever call my father a prick again, and I swear to God, I'll fucking gouge your eyes out and throw you into an acid bath.'

Those final chilling words had the guests – or more accurately, now, the onlookers – all standing there with their mouths open. Gerry was a Face. Not many people would ever have dared to upset him due to his volatile behaviour and his criminal connections, but those hadn't stopped Zara. And one-on-one, he was no match for this disabled woman.

Zara's eyes locked onto Claudia's. Zara deliberately stared at her and a cruel grin crept along her face as if to say, 'Don't ever underestimate me again.' The message was loud and clear for all to see.

Many guests had secretly questioned how Zara Ezra had so much authority, and many wondered if the stories of her past, regarding how she could take out a grown man, were actually true. However, the evidence was there – before their very eyes. Everyone had seen it, and everyone knew one thing: cross Zara Ezra, and you did do so at your peril. No doubt this spectacle would also become a talking point for guests for months to come, when exaggerating the gory dramatic details for effect. That cold look in Zara's eyes, those swift, precise movements, and the lack of fear were enough in themselves to put her up there with the likes of the hardest villains in London.

Most men would have been annoyed that their girl had taken up a fight with a man she'd been left alone to fight against, but Mike couldn't have been prouder of her, and, furthermore, he knew that if her father was up there looking down on her, he would be proud too.

'Get that piece of shit in his car and away from here. He should never have come!' shouted Zara.

Claudia pulled, tugged, and dragged Gerry into the

passenger seat of their Porsche Boxster. Just as he clambered into the front, she took one last look at Zara, and her mouth ran again.

'You won't get away with this. You'll see – when I tell Colin Crawford what you've done.'

Mike could sense Willie behind him and knew he had to stop him before he gave away their next plan.

'Stay back, Willie,' he hissed under his breath. 'Don't say a fucking word.'

Zara knew the score regarding Colin Crawford and was calm enough at that point to keep her mouth shut. She waved sweetly at Claudia and laughed as she witnessed her zigzagging down the drive.

Just as they all went back inside, Arthur appeared from the rear garden. He'd been down in his grand lodge, as he called it, where he'd taken up winemaking. 'Anyone like to try my home-made wine?' He was hit by stunned silence. 'What's going on? Have I missed something?'

Mike looked at his mother, who was casually straightening her dress. 'No, Arthur, we were just saying goodbye to Gerry and his missus,' she replied calmly.

Arthur frowned. 'What the fuck were *they* doing here?'

Gloria gave him a puzzled look. 'I thought you invited them, love?'

Arthur loosened his tie. 'Me? Why would I invite that twat and his so-called B-list actress? Calls himself a villain? He's nuffin but a ponce, a loud, brash one an' all. And as for his wife, well, don't get me started on her. Anyway, never mind, I've got this lovely home brew to try.'

Gloria waved her hands. 'Jesus, Arthur, get that out of here.

It bleedin' well stinks. I don't want my guests coming down with gut-rot,' she said, laughing.

Ricky stood in amazement at the whole mad scene. First his grandmother, then his father, and then, finally, the nutter of all nutters, his stepmother-to-be. They were all so handy with their fists, and as for the mouths on them – wacky didn't cut it.

Once the mourners left, passing on their good wishes, the rest of the family took to the dining room, ready for some serious talking.

Mike stood up first. 'I know this is me brother's funeral, but in the light of what's just happened, maybe we need to put this plan of ours into action more quickly.' He stopped and looked at his mother. 'Sorry, Mum, do you mind?'

Gloria had just settled herself heavily in a chair. Stretching out her legs, she sighed. 'I dunno. Today has been many things, and, to be honest with you, I'm not proud of scrapping like an old fishwife in full view of all our guests. I'm ashamed of meself, so what can I say, Son?'

Ricky suddenly burst out laughing. 'Well, I'll tell ya, then. Nan, you were brilliant. That well-deserved wallop, and you at your old age an' all. I'm one proud grandson.'

''Ere, less of the old, Sunshine.'

'And as for you, Zara, putting that old geezer on his arse, it was a right laugh.'

Instantly, Zara blushed with embarrassment as they all looked over at her with smiles and respect. And Ricky's words had lifted their spirits from the sombre and stifled mood. Moments later, they were relaxing and joining in the banter as if nothing untoward had happened. Soon after, though, it was back to business. It seemed that there was no point in asking Gloria to leave. She was just as much a part of the firm as Arthur, and always had been.

Zara stood up and looked at Willie. 'It's been three weeks since we found out that Torvic was murdered, so, now all that messy business is over with, it's time to sort out this Colin Crawford and his quack. Willie, this is your call. I'll step back and do whatever you ask, mate. I've my men willing to help. They can be pulled away from the restaurants, so they'll be at your disposal.'

Willie was stunned. He'd never been given so much respect and power. It had always been the case that he was further down the totem pole, and that was how he liked it. He wasn't a leader as such and would never want to be. So, although in theory it was his turn to call the shots, in reality, he wasn't the right man to decide the plan, which relied very much on Zara's smart brain. He turned his head to look at his son, who was still a little peaky. That troubled expression had bothered him, and now, in front of the firm, it was time to get to the bottom of it.

'Liam, tell us. We're family. What's worrying you, Son?'

Liam looked at all the eager faces, one by one, until his eyes rested back on his father's. 'I know what they did to me was bad, and yeah, the quack was hell-bent on finishing me off … Well, I do want him hurt badly.'

'Yeah, I'll chop his fucking hands off!' growled Arty.

'Yeah, well, if we can nobble him, at least he won't be able to do it to anyone else. But as for this Lucas bloke, I dunno if I want him hurt …' He paused and looked down. 'Ya see, he's me brother, or half-brother, maybe, but he's still me brother, and I think I wanna meet him.'

'To bash the fuck outta him, I hope!' said Willie, his voice now raised.

'No, Dad, I wanna just meet him,' replied Liam, in a gentle tone aimed at lowering his father's temper.

Zara intervened before a row kicked off. 'Let's not be too hasty, Liam, because, so far, this Colin and Lucas have no idea that we know it's them who've done this to ya. Staffie, by sheer chance, and then by using his brains, worked it all out. His uncles, Nicolas and Mack, have gone into hiding. They've vowed not to say a word, so no one knows except us. We need to keep it that way.'

Liam looked up and smiled. 'Oh yeah, I won't say a word. Not yet. You've no worries on that score. I just thought maybe it would be nice, though, to have a brother.'

Arty suddenly spoke up, annoyance in his tone. 'Liam, you *have* a brother. In fact, you have two: me and Ricky. This Lucas is an outsider. The cunt stole your *kidney*. His family left you to fucking *die*. Why, for Christ's sake, would you want to meet the bastard now? Me, I'd like to meet him and ram a knife down his throat – or gut him like a fish and take back your kidney. Jesus, Liam, you're going soft, mate.'

Zara raised her hand. 'Arty, of course you three are as close as brothers, but we mustn't forget this happened to Liam, and so we must respect his decision.'

Willie looked at his son and rolled his eyes. 'I don't get you, boy. The little shit is walking around merrily with your kidney. You could've died.'

'I know, Dad, I know. But, maybe, he didn't even know about me if he was really sick. Would he have planned it? Nah, I don't think so. The poor bastard wouldn't have had a clue. And,

Dad, don't you feel *anything*? I mean, this Lucas is your son as well, ain't he?'

Willie shrugged his shoulders. 'Fuck if I know. Son, he could be anyone's. I barely remember sleeping with the tart.'

Liam sighed. 'Dad, he *is* your son, yeah? Look, since we got back from Spain, I've been doing a lot of research on the internet, right? You can't just take out a kidney and give it to any old Tom, Dick, or Harry. You have to be a match. So, it follows, I must be a match. And besides that, Dad, he's definitely my brother.'

Willie jutted his jaw, now clearly annoyed with the way the discussion was going. 'And how the fuck can you be so sure? Tell me that?'

Liam looked at Arty, who looked away. This wasn't any of his business, but if he'd been asked his opinion, he would have told Liam that his dad was on the money. 'Because I looked him up on Facebook and he's just like you, Dad, and me.'

Willie raised his eyebrow, a smirk beginning to form. 'What? A good-looking fucker then, is he?'

They all laughed at that one and at once began to relax. Gloria brought in the bottles of drink and poured everyone a glass. 'Me, I'd find his mother. This Shelley sounds like a right thick prat. You could take her somewhere and ask *her* a few questions, like who knew about it, who was in on it, and who should rightfully pay the consequences.'

No one interrupted Gloria, not even Arthur. As the matriarch of the family, and a powerful personality in her own right, she'd been involved in a fair bit of skulduggery off her own bat, and, even at her age, she was still the woman behind the man and would give anyone who tried to hurt her kids a row.

Back in her youth and being the wife of Arthur Regan had brought with it expectations: to be ladylike, discreet, and classy. That was all well and good back in the day, and she'd pulled off the part very well, but after all they'd gone through, the requirement to be the perfect, classy wife had been superseded by the need to be the fighter, to protect her family, and if that meant fight like a wild cat, then so be it – she'd done it. She'd kill for her family and had done so not so long ago. The family had strongly suspected that she'd shot their archenemy Tracey Harman, the woman who'd severed Zara's hand off, but she'd always remained silent about that episode in her life, and the family had respected her for not only doing what she felt she had to do but for keeping schtum about it.

Zara smiled and looked at Gloria. 'I agree, Shelley should be the first person we need to get our hands on, and I think that it should be my job to do it, woman to woman. So, it's kind of ya, Gloria, but me and the firm are onto it. You've no need to bruise those pretty hands of yours. First, we need to know everything there is about this Colin and Shelley. That shouldn't be hard. The man has his fingers in a lot of dirty pies as well as legitimate businesses. As for Shelley, well, she'll be a creature of habit, no doubt, and from what Nicolas told you, Staffie, she likes to have her regular beauty routine. I think I could do with a haircut meself.' The look on Zara's face said it all: it was clear what she intended.

'That's not a problem. I bet me uncle will know where she goes.'

Zara tapped her chin with her forefinger. 'Hmm, and if he doesn't know – which a lot of men won't, will they – tell him to pull out her credit card records. I'm sure her regular beautician or hairdresser will be on there somewhere, and if she's that way inclined, her gym membership will be on there as well.'

It was left to Staffie to respond. 'Yeah, no worries. I'll sort it tomorrow, although, to be honest, Nicolas and Mack are shitting themselves at the moment. Crawford's men have made such a mess of Mack that it's put the wind right up 'em.'

A sad smile tugged at Zara's face. 'Yeah, no doubt. It's shocking what's happened to Mack. This Colin geezer really does need taking down a peg or two. He's just entered the realms of a new rule book, and, as far as I can see, when this gets out, his good name as a straight-up fella will go out of the window.'

'And once I torture the cunt, I can say, with me head held high, that it was 'cos he got personal, and I'd every right to fuck him up and take his money for my boy's future,' Willie said bitterly, with a mean look in his eyes.

Mike looked away; it wasn't his place to pull Willie back into line. And if Colin *had* orchestrated the kidney transplant, then his demise was guaranteed.

Lou sat listening, with thoughts of his own. As the man who always said the least, he felt he should mention the fact that Lance had been in on the capture of Torvic, having supposedly worked with Eric, and yet after his return from Spain, he hadn't been near or by. 'I thought Lance Ryder would've shown his respects. Why hasn't he shown his face, today of all days?'

There was stunned silence, all the men and Zara looking at each other.

'Do we even really know anything about the bloke, and, more to the point, should we be trusting him anyway?' remarked Lou.

Surprisingly, it was Liam who spoke up. 'Yeah, too right we should trust him. He was Kendall's father, and he was the first to help us. I like the man, and I'd put my life in his hands. Anyway, I ain't supposed to say this, but Poppy told me that her ol' man was called away on some mission. She didn't say much, only that he needed to keep underground or summat like that.'

Mike frowned. 'I don't really understand that bloke, ya know. I mean, who does he work for?'

Zara sighed. 'Look, my father always said he was a law unto himself and would work for the highest bidder. He keeps his cards close to his chest because the man was in the Services. He was in some special ops team.'

Staffie scoffed. 'Well, I don't know if he's that bloody good. He didn't find that Torvic geezer, did he? That was you, Zara, and when Torvic escaped, where was Lance then? He was in Spain, and as far as I know, he didn't find out anything about Liam's kidnapping either, so it makes me wonder if the man's a fanny merchant.'

'On the surface, I would normally agree with you, Staffie, but I know from Izzy that there is so much more to that man. And you know how much I trusted my dad's judgement.'

Staffie knew then she was serious because she rarely called Izzy 'Dad'.

She sighed and carried on. 'Anyway, he did us no harm, did he? Don't forget, he lost a daughter to Torvic's family, so I trust him. Anyway, if the man has other stuff to do, it's not for us to judge. We need to get our own house in order, starting with Shelley.'

That last remark was enough for Staffie to realize that he'd shot his mouth off without considering the individuals present in the room. He recollected something about Zara calling Lance 'The Machine', a man who'd been very useful to her father in times of real need. Accordingly, he lowered his head.

The discussion and further gossiping regarding a man who wasn't present was stopped dead in its tracks.

Chapter 17

After a night of drinking and listening to the men relive some poignant moments in their lives with Eric, Zara decided to head to her house. She didn't want to drag Mike away. Besides, she felt the men needed to reminisce over the fun memories and not the issues that had hung over them more recently.

She'd already been back, and with the help of her men, she'd had the basement cleaned up and Jackie's body disposed of in an adjoining field to her caravan site. One of Jericho's lurchers had found it. After the formalities were completed – the police were unable to discover who was responsible for Jackie's murder – she was laid to rest.

The back door had been made secure and the CCTV system had been repaired, so that when she turned it off, the electric didn't go off with it. Approaching the front door, she didn't think to be cautious, not now everything was back to normality, and the fear of Torvic returning was a thing of the past. She inserted the key into the lock of the front door and pushed it wide open. As soon as she stepped inside, using her backside to bump the door shut behind her, she found that the entrance hall was warm, which was a blessing, since the December air had such a nip to it. Yet she experienced a strange sensation as if someone was there watching her. Feeling for her gun, she slowly crept towards her father's office. Before she peered inside, a voice called out, 'Don't be alarmed, Zara, it's only me.'

She instantly recognized the voice as that belonging to Lance. Her first thought was automatically to greet him, but this was her house, so how the hell had he got in? He didn't have a key, and he hadn't been invited inside. On her guard now, she pulled the gun from her belt, and then appeared, holding the weapon in front of her.

With his shoulders square and his thickset neck, Lance stood there, looking more prominent than ever. He smiled and held his hands up. 'Look, don't worry. I come in peace.'

'How the hell did you get in?' she asked, clearly unhappy, and, worse, somewhat uneasy.

'Sorry, Zara, I had to come to your place. Don't worry, though. I haven't vandalized anything. I can get in anywhere, by the way. It was my job for long enough.'

Zara stepped forward, not taking her eyes off him. 'And, Lance, do tell me, exactly what *is* your job?'

'Are you alone? Is Mike coming?'

'I'm asking the questions, Lance. I thought you would've realized, considering there's a fucking gun still pointing at your chest.'

He nodded, looking totally unconcerned, and then he noticed the paperwork on her father's desk. 'He was a good man, your father. A man who you could trust, and the feeling was mutual, by the way.'

Zara glared, trying to work out his intentions. 'Look, you still haven't answered my questions.'

He slowly looked up with a sorrowful expression. 'Zara, I came here to talk, partly because you are the only person, and I *mean* the only person, I can trust. Like your father, I trusted him and vice versa. I didn't mean to startle you, but I couldn't call or knock. I had to get inside before I was spotted.'

Sensing Lance wasn't a threat, Zara placed her gun back into her belt and removed her jacket.

Lance followed her movements as she walked over to the drinks cabinet. 'Tell me, what was my father's favourite drink?'

He knew she was testing him and quite rightly so. 'Funny you should ask because, like me, as much as he liked his vintage brandies, he still favoured a good old-fashioned vodka martini, even with the glazed cherry.'

Zara spun around and actually laughed. Whether it was from relief that Lance was behaving to type or that he'd rekindled a memory of her father's, she didn't know. 'Yeah, he did, the silly ol' bugger.' Her shoulders relaxed; not many people knew that. Her father only let his guard down when he was wearing his carpet slippers and was holding his favourite tipple in his hand. So, she knew then that after all the underhanded acts that had happened to her and Mike's firm, and to various individuals along the way recently, Lance wasn't a fake. She knew he was the real deal.

'And yours, Lance?'

He blushed and took a seat by the side of the large oak desk. 'Me? I like a gin and tonic.'

'Good, then we shall enjoy a drink together. So, what did you want to talk to me about?'

'Well, I should imagine your father spoke a lot about me,

and I guess, from what you've seen of me, that impression would've seriously left you feeling let down, possibly questioning your father's sanity.'

Zara walked over to Lance, where she handed him his drink, after which she pulled up a chair to sit opposite him. He cast her a glance, observing how graceful she was. Anyone sitting here, but not knowing anything about this slender lady with her swanlike neck and serene movements, which were the epitome of ladylike, almost regal in fact, would most certainly form the wrong impression of her. He looked directly into her fiery eyes that reminded him of that stone, tiger's-eye, and noticed how very pretty they were. When he'd initially met her – at the hangar – she'd worn such a dark, almost foreboding, expression that he hadn't really seen the woman behind the cold mask.

'Lance, I'm not stupid, by any means. I was grateful for your help that night at the hangar and also for your loyalty in helping the youngsters in Spain ... But, as for not finding Torvic and leading us all to believe that that was your aim, well, I didn't believe it in the first place.'

He chuckled and sipped his drink. 'No, I assumed that would be the case, if, of course, you are anything like your father was.'

'So, I'm also guessing that your involvement at the hangar was just revenge for what Torvic and his two sons ...' She paused, not wanting to finish the sentence.

'Yes, that's partly true. I wanted to make sure Alastair was tortured, but I didn't want to interfere too much.'

Their eyes met in mutual understanding. 'So, Lance, I'm aware that you got involved with Eric with the aim of finding the person responsible for selling Flakka on the streets of South-East London, and that you claimed your mission was also to stop the gangs selling it. I also understand that your involvement was authorized by the same department that was overseeing the Police Commissioner's handling of the increased serious crime rate. But really, though, your role was just a front, wasn't it?'

'Very good, Zara. Yeah, you're spot-on there. It was indeed a cover-up. And, for the first time in my career, I got too involved. I was trained as a soldier, ended up in the SAS, and then I was sent off on various missions. I worked for whoever I wanted to because I owed no one anything. Yet when Alastair killed Kendall, it got kinda personal, and then discovering the twins were mine, it changed my whole perspective on things. Now? Now, I'm back on another mission.'

'I was right. My father told me bits and pieces about you but not everything. I was led to believe you were the guy who infiltrated the IRA and stopped the barracks from being bombed. That was just one of Izzy's bedtime stories.' She grinned. 'So, I'm not surprised. Can I know who this bigger fish is you need to fry?'

His sympathetic smile told her the answer.

'Oh, Lance, before you go …' She slid open the desk drawer and retrieved the listening device she'd found. 'Do you know anything about these gadgets? I believe Torvic planted this one in the grandfather clock.' She threw it to him.

Catching it with one hand, he turned the device over to scrutinize the serial numbers. 'Zara, may I take this?'

'Yeah, sure. Any ideas?'

He looked up and nodded. 'Yes, Zara, I do have an

idea. A bloody good idea, now, thanks to you. Right, I have to go.'

'Hang on. As I said, I thought Torvic planted it.'

'Zara, I'm sorry but I can't divulge anything.'

'Okay, Lance, I appreciate you coming over to see me. I guess, if anything, it confirmed my theory about you. Well, I hope whoever it is, you capture him ... or her.' She chuckled again. 'Unless, of course, he is one of my men.'

He shook his head. 'Absolutely not.'

With one more gulp of his gin and tonic, he placed the cut-glass tumbler on the desk and rose to leave.

Zara stood up to see him to the door. 'Tell me, Lance, was that all you came to say? I mean, you could've called me.'

Instead of going towards the front door, he headed for the back. 'I can't call you. In fact, I can't see you. I need to act as if my interest in the Torvic issue has been satisfied ... But the real reason I came is because I wanted to tell you face-to-face to never let your guard down. I liked how you handled me earlier with your gun always at the ready. Don't forget: always remain vigilant, and for now, try not to be alone.'

She gave him a deep, puzzled frown. 'And are you going to give me any explanation or anything?'

That sympathetic look adorned his face again. 'I can't, Zara. I wish I could, but it wouldn't be in anyone's best interests.'

As she held the back door open for Lance to slip away, there was one burning question in her mind that needed answering. 'This big fish. Was he or she Torvic's puppetmaster?'

Lance scanned the vast, open fields surrounding the property, pulled his jacket collar up around his neck, and then looked closely into her eyes. 'Yes.'

Zara gasped. 'Shit! So, then, there *is* someone behind that bastard. Does that mean they'll take revenge on us?'

Lance shrugged his shoulders. 'The short answer is, I really don't know. This person may have more pressing issues to deal with.'

'I take it you know who this person is then?'

Lance shuddered. 'I can't tell you that. Just stay safe, yeah?'

She watched as he sprinted across the fields. Within seconds he was gone, and a fierce wind, which was blowing through the back door, tore through her blouse, making her shiver. She quickly locked it and felt for her gun again. She had to rationalize the situation. Whoever this big cheese was, he was influential enough to have the special ops team after him, which surely meant he wouldn't have taken Torvic's capture personally. Besides, Torvic was dead now, and, in any event, would he have gone running to his boss to tell him or her the truth? How pathetic would that look? She focused her mind on the fact that whoever this person was they were probably male and almost certainly had international credentials. Torvic was just a big buyer and supplier of the dirty drug called Flakka. Yet her anxiety levels were suddenly raised. She wanted to run after Lance and demand more answers, but she knew that he wasn't the type to divulge anything unless he believed it was in his interests to do so. He hadn't got to live this long – bearing in mind what he did – by imparting information that was classified.

Chapter 18

Shelley lined up her son's tablets on the kitchen counter; the daily routine was now set in stone, and she would make sure he had the best care. She made his favourite drink, which was a latte with squirty cream and cinnamon. She placed the tall glass and the coloured pills on a tray, along with two slices of toast covered in peanut butter. She smiled, pleased with herself that she had created a smiley face in the peanut spread. 'There, that will cheer him up,' she said to herself.

Lucas sat in his latest gaming chair with a controller in his hand; he was fighting the Germans on his vast plasma screen. His mother entering the room irritated him. He was in mid-fight and could lose the tank he'd worked so hard to have as his weaponry.

'Here you go, babe. Your tablets are here, and I've made your special brekkie, as you like it.'

'Mother, fuck off, will ya? I'm busy. I'll come downstairs when I'm ready.'

Shelley ignored his moodiness and placed the tray on the small table directly next to his chair. 'Now, you know you have to take these tablets bang on time. The doctor said if you don't, you'll end up sick, so just put the controller down and take them. Eat the food, and then you'll have all day to fight the world.'

Lucas wasn't listening; he was intent on bombing the German tank. But what he didn't see was the other tank behind the mound. Bang! He was blown up.

'For fuck's sake, Mother! Now, you've got me killed. I worked hard for that tank. Why don't you just stop fucking fussing? Like I said, I'll come down when I'm good and ready,' he snarled at her.

Shelley tried to ignore his aggression, but once he was in one of his antagonistic moods, he wouldn't stop.

He jumped up from his chair and stood with his hands on his hips. 'Ya know what? I'm getting sick of you always in my face! Are you ever gonna leave me in fucking peace? Or are you gonna carry on fannying about? I ain't sick anymore, right? I'm well.' He held his hand out and looked down at his body. 'Look at me. I'm fucking fine now. If you keep on in my ear 'ole, I'll fuck off and get me own place.'

Shelley was dressed ready for the shops, her fitted black coat and long black boots with high heels giving her the look of a self-assured woman. Right now, though, she felt anything but. She adored her son, but he could be a right little bastard when the mood took him. 'Lukey, listen to me, I'm only trying to help. You nearly died, and I did everything to help you get better ...'

'Mother, you *didn't*! The kidney donor did that, so stop deluding yaself. Now, I'll take those damn tablets but only when I'm good and bloody ready.'

Shelley was itching to go to the shops. She'd let herself go over the last month, what with all the hospital visits and then flying over to Spain. But she wasn't happy leaving her boy unless she was sure that he'd taken his tablets. She knew that without them his body would reject the kidney and he would die, so all this tablet-minding was stressing her out.

'Lucas, I tell ya what. You take those tablets and I'll leave you in peace. I'll even stay out all day. How about that?'

What seemed like a very reasonable offer was turned on its head. Unexpectedly, Lucas lost the plot; with a quick movement of his hand, he wiped the small table clean. The tablets, the drink, and the toast covered in sticky peanut butter went flying across the room.

Shelley had to jump back quickly or she would've been struck by the plate.

'Fuck the tablets!' Lucas shouted at her. 'They make me feel sick.'

As Lucas got his breath back, Shelley scrambled around the floor on her hands and knees gathering up the pills. 'For God's sake, Lucas, what's wrong with you? They're just pills. One big gulp, and it'll be over. Please, love, do it for me.'

With flared nostrils, Lucas spat back. 'And why should I do anything for you, eh? You ruined everything for me. I could've had it all. Colin would've given me the business. I would've been driving around in a new motor, with money in me back pocket and a future to look forward to. But you put an end to my dreams! You had to shack up with that dildo, Nicolas, and ruin my fucking chances in life!'

Shelley stood up in shock, her hands to her mouth. How the hell did Lucas know all of that unless her father had decided to dig the knife in and tell him? She had to know.

'So, you've been listening to my father then, I take it?'

Lucas glared with eyes that would curdle milk. 'He told me enough, that's all you need to know. Then, he informed me that I was never to knock at his door again.'

'Tell me what exactly he said. Only, I wasn't aware that he'd even had a conversation with you.'

With a deflated tone, Lucas replied, 'His exact words were these: "I've taken a serious risk in getting you fixed up. Don't look at me as if I'm your grandfather. And don't get any ideas that you can come running to me for favours, 'cos this is the last favour I'm ever going to do for you."'

With a sorrowful expression on her face, Shelley sighed. 'He's an absolute bastard anyway. We don't need him, we've got each other, and as true as my word is, I'll make sure you'll want for nothing.'

'You just don't fucking get it, do ya? I don't want to be wrapped around you. Look at ya, a silly tart, thick as two short planks, and as for how you get your money …' He laughed. 'That's a joke. You wouldn't know how to earn a few quid unless it was selling yaself. All you've ever had is through men like Nicolas. You ain't worked a day in your life.' Even the horrified and hurt look on his mother's face didn't stop him from tearing into her. His voice was getting louder as he wound himself up. 'You must've taken after your mother, 'cos you ain't like your ol' man. But I am. I've watched him with his men, the way he walks and talks. That would've been me in a few years from now. But you've ruined any chance I had of being part of his firm. It's all your fault, and I won't forgive you for it. I could've been someone. He has the money, the respect, and it would've all been mine one day. So, fuck off, before I forget you're me mother.'

With his malicious words whirling around her brain, she was furious. And she attempted to slap his face, but he was too quick, and, in a flash, he gripped her wrist and leaned into her face. 'Touch me again, and I'll throw you through this bedroom window.'

Shelley shook her arm free and left the room. With tears of anger streaming down her face, she grabbed the car keys from the hallway table and her bag from the floor and left.

Her new GTI was her pride and joy, and once she put her foot to the floor, all her troubles would've normally been blown away in the wind, but not today. She drove around the streets, trying to calm down, until, finally, she stopped in the multi-storey car park, leaned on the steering wheel, and sobbed.

Her son, her only child, was a spoiled brat. She had raised a monster, and no matter how generous and kind she was to him, he just got worse. In her heart, she knew that he would belt her one someday – the evil glint in his eyes told her as much. She tried to dig deep and think what it was that made her protect him so much, to fuss and give in to his constant tantrums, but all she could think of was that he was hers. When everyone around her could dismiss her at the drop of a hat – Nicolas, her father – Lucas was the constant in her life, and she aimed all her love and affection in his direction.

She took a deep breath and pulled down the mirror and stared at her tear-stained face and the wrinkles that were deepening with age and worry. In the glove box was a packet of wipes. She pulled one from the packet and cleaned her face. There was no point in wearing make-up since she was off to have Botox and then her hair done. She tilted her head down and looked at the roots in the mirror. A few grey strands told her she wasn't a spring chicken anymore, and if she was to meet a decent man, she needed to tidy herself up.

She consoled herself with the fact that Lucas knew how vital it was to take those tablets. He didn't want to die; in fact, he was too selfish to harm himself. After taking a deep breath, she left the car and made her way through the shopping centre to the beauticians. Every last Thursday of the month, she would have a facial and a trim and dye if needed. But she'd been too busy during the last month.

As soon as she entered the salon, the girls all came over to greet her. She was a regular customer who gave generous tips.

'Shelley, how are you? Come over and take a seat,' said Piper, with an over-the-top sickly, grovelling smile. 'Now then, what did you have in mind for today? I see you've been booked in for most of the day. Lucky, really, because this time of year we're full to the brim what with Christmas and all.' She placed a gown around Shelley's neck. 'Er, Simone, lovey, please make Shelley a nice cup of tea and bring over some of those mince pies.' She chuckled and looked at Shelley in the mirror. 'Fortnum and Mason no less. So, how are you today?'

Shelley tried to smile and act her confident self but the last hour at home had really upset her. 'Yeah, I'm fine, thank you.'

'So, are you looking to have the same colour? Any highlights weaved in?'

'Yeah, why not. I think I'm due for a change. Is the Botox nurse in yet?'

Piper gave another saccharine smile, showing her bright-white veneers. 'She's on her way. Oh, and we have a new treatment you might want to try.'

Shelley was all for trying anything at the moment, anything

that was that would brighten up her tired face. 'Go on, then. Tell me about it.'

'Teeth whitening. Our Botox lady is also offering a special deal, two for one.'

Shelley's eyes lit up. 'Well, yes, then. I'll have that too.'

As Piper left to mix up the dye, Shelley looked around. A young woman was having her long hair bleached, an older lady was having her eyebrows dyed, and two seats along, there was another woman having a trim.

Shelley stared and wondered how old the woman was. She didn't look in her twenties, but her face and jawline were sculpted and tight. Her unusual coloured eyes dominated her face, and her long neck made her appear like a model. As the woman clocked her staring, Shelley looked away. Yet she was drawn back to the woman's appearance and wondered if that hairstyle and colour would suit herself. Then she noticed the woman was wearing black leather gloves.

As soon as she spoke, Shelley jerked. 'Oh, sorry, what did you say?'

'I said, does it hurt to have Botox?'

Now engaged in a potential conversation, Shelley turned to face the woman directly. Something about her fascinated Shelley. 'No, not really, but don't tell me you're thinking of having it done as well?'

'Yeah, why not?' She grinned. 'And this teeth whitening, I might go for that too.'

Shelley was drawn in by the smooth way the woman spoke. 'Well, I'm up for everything. I've let meself go lately, what with one thing and another, so it's an early Christmas present to meself.'

'And why not? Do you have much shopping left to get?'

Shelley had been so preoccupied with her son that she hadn't really given it much thought.

'To be honest, I haven't even started. Mind you, I only have my boy to buy for.'

'How old is your son?'

'Well, I say boy, but, really, he's a man. He's twenty-one.' Usually, when Shelley started talking about her son, she wouldn't stop. Yet today, she wasn't in the mood to spew out his praises.

'Do you have children?'

The woman gave an exaggerated sad smile. 'No ... My son died from organ failure.'

Suddenly, Shelley's ears pricked up. It seemed to her that they had something in common. 'Oh, bloody hell. That's so sad, and I know how you feel. I nearly lost my son. He had kidney failure but ...' She realized she might be seen as being somewhat insensitive. 'Well, he's okay now.'

'Tell me' – the woman asked, changing the subject – 'how do you get out of the car park? It's such a maze. This is the first time I've been here. I've just moved into the area.'

Feeling sorry for the woman, Shelley was eager to help. 'Yeah, it is a bit of a nightmare. Where are you parked?'

'See, that's the problem. I can't remember.'

Shelley then reached down into her bag and pulled out her own car parking ticket. 'Right then. You see that colour there? Mine's purple, which means I'm on the top floor. Yours will have a colour too. What ya do is take ya ticket to whichever floor you're on. Say it's orange, which is the second floor. Well, just before you go into the car park there's a pay-on-foot machine where you pay. The machine time-stamps your ticket. On your way out, you put your ticket in the exit machine and the barrier will come up. You have about ten minutes, I think, between when you pay into the machine and when you must reach the barrier.'

'Oh, thank you so much. I was getting anxious, worrying about it. So, do you live locally? Um ... sorry. What's your name?'

'Oh, it's Shelley. Yeah, me and me son just moved to Bickley. I left the ol' man and bought a nice little place just behind Bickley station near the cricket club. It ain't massive, but it does me and Lucas okay.'

The woman gasped. 'No way? I moved there too. What a coincidence. Which road?'

Shelley grinned. 'Pines Road, number fifteen. You should pop over for coffee one day.'

'I'd like that very much. I don't know anyone in the area, so that would be fantastic, of course, if it's no trouble.'

Feeling pleased with herself for making a new friend, Shelley positively beamed. What an improvement to what had been a really shitty beginning to the day. This would be a start to her new life: decent friends, a new haircut, and whitened teeth. She would ditch the bolshie bitch attitude and maybe start living a more relaxed way of life and begin by being friendly and polite to people.

The hairdresser returned with the dye and started taking over the conversation, by talking both women into buying more treatments. It wasn't long before Piper's sales pitch reaped the benefits. Shelley was under the dryer and only had a chance to wave as the woman, her potential friend, said goodbye. Shit!

She hadn't discovered the woman's name. But the stranger had her address, so there was a good chance she might call in for a coffee, and, hopefully, Lucas would be in a better mood when she did.

* * *

As Zara made her way into the Costa Coffee shop, she spotted Mike in the corner, reading the sports pages in the *Daily Mirror*. He smiled as soon as he saw her. 'Nice haircut, babe, so how did it go? Any good news to report?'

Zara squeezed through the tables and sat opposite Mike and sighed. 'I thought I would be in for a challenge, but I was thoroughly disappointed.'

Mike shook his head, in dismay. 'Shit! So, she didn't turn up, then?'

'Oh yeah, she turned up all right. It was a walk in the park. I didn't even have to work for it. She's parked on the top floor in the multi-storey car park, booked in until five, and she lives at 15 Pines Road near the cricket ground … and, oh yeah, she wants me to pop in for coffee. Her son, Lucas, who's just had an op, lives there too.'

Mike laughed. 'I told ya she's as thick as shit. Brilliant, so that's the first part of the plan in order. Shall I have Lou follow her?'

Zara nodded. 'Yeah, I think that's a good idea. We need to keep tabs on her, just to make sure she wasn't giving me a load of old flannel. But, I should tell you, I think she was overly honest, apart from the fact that she said her house wasn't massive because Pines Road has nothing but mansions, as far as I can recall.'

As Zara ran her hand through her shorter locks, she looked at Mike with a sudden self-conscious, almost bashful smile. 'Does my hair really look okay? I mean, I was looking at all the pictures in the salon of women with their hair curly and long. I was thinking for the wedding ...'

Mike grabbed her hand. 'You, my angel, are just perfect as you are.'

She blushed slightly. 'They can do Botox and teeth whitening and so much stuff, and I thought, maybe, I should perhaps just have ...'

'No!' He raised his voice. 'Sorry, I didn't mean to startle you. I mean, please, babe, don't start all that plastic shit. I can't bear it. When I said you are perfect as you are, I meant it. I ain't the type of man that goes for rubber lips and expressionless faces. Jackie went down that road, and fuck me, she ended up looking like the bride of Frankenstein.'

A young couple with bags of shopping sat at the table next to them. They were talking about all the presents they'd bought and how Christmas would soon be upon them.

'Mike, I haven't bought a single thing. Maybe, while we're here, we should at least buy your parents a nice gift.'

Mike glanced around at the hordes of shoppers. 'Shit, I hate shopping.'

She looked at the table and peeked below to see if he had any bags with him. She hoped that maybe he had at least bought a small present for her. It had been a while now since the proposal, and yet he still hadn't given her a ring.

No matter how confident she was about most things, he was still her weakness – her Achilles' heel. She wanted to press the issue but at the same time she didn't want to appear needy. After all, he hadn't said the wedding was off although he also hadn't set a date either. 'So, what shall we do about Christmas shopping then?'

Mike finished his coffee. 'Let's do it all online. Now Ricky has taught me how to use the computer, it's a doddle. All ya do is press "buy now", and it gets delivered, simple as. Anyway, babe, would ya like a coffee before we leave? I wouldn't mind another one.'

Zara shook her head and got up to leave. She was feeling a little flat, to say the least. Her mood had gone from feeling proud of herself for getting Shelley's address to a sense of sadness over the lack of Mike's interest in her and the wedding. This would have been the perfect opportunity to pick out that ring he'd promised her.

'Hey, wait up,' said Mike, as he grabbed her arm. 'What's the rush?'

'Like you intimated, we have business to attend to.'

He detected the coldness in her voice; it was a tone usually reserved for her enemies, and he didn't like it.

'Zara, are you okay? Is something bothering you, babe?'

She turned to face him, realizing she'd worn her heart on her sleeve. *Had he been reading her mind?* she wondered. 'I'm fine, Mike. I've just got a headache, that's all.'

He slid his arm around her shoulders, pulled her close, and kissed her forehead. 'Well, let's get you back home, and you, my sex kitten, can have a nice bath and relax. You did well today.'

She pulled away from him, now thoroughly narked. Hearing those words had really pissed her off. He'd spoken to her as if he was her boss. 'I did well? Really? Mike, I don't need a pat on the back. I'm not a rookie at an academy, ya know, so please, in future, don't treat me like one.'

Mike removed his arm and continued on, ignoring her moodiness, putting it down to her having a headache. He didn't mean to sound so patronizing; he just wanted to look after her, and yet his praises had been seen somehow as disrespectful. Women! He could never work them out, especially Zara.

As soon as they made their way out of the car park, Mike called Lou with all the details, only to discover that he was already at the same shopping centre, loading up with bags. The call was on loudspeaker, and so Zara could hear everything.

'Mikey, will Shelley recognize me? I mean, she knows us all from the past.'

'Wear sunglasses and a hat, then.'

Lou laughed. 'Yeah, I'll treat meself to a fake goatee an' all.'

'She won't notice you. Just follow her and make sure she goes to 15 Pines Road. If she goes anywhere else, let me know, but don't make contact. Zara's gonna do that.'

'Righto, chief.'

Zara sat facing the passenger side window, still annoyed, yet she couldn't tell Mike the real reason for how she felt. All kinds of thoughts ran through her mind, the main one being that she didn't have the third finger on her left hand. Her mind recalled the 1960s song 'Third Finger, Left Hand' by Martha and the Vandellas, which was now being played around in her head.

Mike noticed her looking down at her hand, and then as she pulled the black leather glove further up her prosthetic, his heart sank. Would she ever feel 100 per cent all woman? He knew in his heart that as tough as she was, that disability had knocked her confidence when it came to her appearance. It was just a shame, though, that she couldn't see that it never bothered him at all. He saw beyond the scars, yet he'd never dismiss what she'd been through.

Giving her back her self-respect, he asked, 'So what's the plan, Zara? How do you want to play this one out?'

Zara snapped out of her musing and smiled. 'I don't believe it will take much to get everything I need to know out of her. I agree. She's a first-class dope.'

Mike chuckled, and the ice was broken. He made a mental note not to talk down to her when business was being discussed. 'So, when are you going to make this visit to Shelley's?'

'Christmas Day.'

Mike was stunned. 'What? Why Christmas Day? I mean, what about the family? We've got dinner and …'

'I thought the most important issue was holding Colin Crawford to account? The only way I can guarantee she'll be at home or at his place will be on Christmas Day, and if she's just having a turkey dinner for her and her son, then that's the perfect time for her to call her father and invite him over. Wouldn't you agree?'

Mike felt a little awkward because she was right, of course, but she was putting him in a difficult position. Would the firm really want to be working on Christmas Day? He thought probably not. For all they'd been through, this was an occasion they would want to reserve for their families, and Willie had nearly lost his, so he had to think of a way of talking her out of it.

'Yeah, I know you're right, Zara, you always are …'

'Do I detect a "but", Mike?'

A pedestrian, who was laden with parcels, stepped out into the road; for a moment, Mike lost concentration and had to slam on the brakes. 'Er, sorry. Well, yes, maybe there is a but. It's just that this will be the first Christmas we'll all be together. Ya know, with you and Ricky. I've been looking forward to it, and I know my parents have as well.'

Zara was conflicted. She was right when she had her business head on, but Mike's point was a good one. The thing was, though, Christmas had never been special for her. Her vague memories of a celebratory time were only when her mother was alive. After she died, she would have counted herself lucky if she'd sat at a festive table or even enjoyed pulling a cracker. Once her mother was buried, Izzy threw himself into his work, and so her Christmas dinners were spent at restaurants. The food was great, but it lacked the atmosphere – all the laughter, the games, and the crackers that went with the occasion. She was always spoiled with presents; in fact, her father gave her whatever she wanted, within reason. So, having had years either alone or in a prearranged setting, Zara hadn't really given much thought to Christmas.

'Well, I'm sure Willie will want to use the opportunity to take his revenge, or am I wasting my time?'

Mike had arranged something special on Christmas Day, but maybe his surprise could wait. 'Yeah, you're right. Okay, Christmas Day it will be, then.'

* * *

The days leading up to the event were spent going over the plan. Lou made a daily trip to Pines Road to check if any cars came or went and watched from a safe distance unobserved, clocking the time the lights came on in the morning and went off in the evening. It was something he actually enjoyed doing. He preferred to be less hands-on, though, when it came to the violent stuff.

Christmas morning arrived, and Zara was up before Mike, taking a shower. She had all but moved into his house and had all the essentials there in his bathroom cabinets and her clothes in the wardrobe next to his. He'd asked her to move everything in, yet she'd felt she just couldn't completely tear herself away from her home. She considered that it might be perceived by Mike as one of her weaknesses – the link to the past and her father – but in many ways the house and his standing in the Jewish community represented symbols of what he'd accomplished in his life and what she knew he wanted her to achieve in the future. For her father and herself it was all about legacy and not sentimentalism.

As she stood in front of the long mirror in the dressing room, drying her hair, a pair of arms grabbed her from behind and pulled her close. 'Hmm, you smell nice, babe. Happy Christmas.'

Zara looked in the mirror at Mike peering over her shoulder. He had a glow and a cheeky glint in his eyes.

'Merry Christmas,' she replied, suddenly feeling guilty. She'd insisted on setting the plan in motion on this very day, without properly considering how her decision would impinge on the arrangements made by Gloria and Arthur.

Gloria had bought enough food to feed the street, and Ricky was having Arty and Liam over in the evening for drinks. But, for now, there would be no celebrating until this was over.

'Come back into the bedroom. I have a present for you. I wanted to give it to you tonight at dinner, but … well, anyway, you can have it now.'

Zara placed the hairdryer back in the drawer and allowed Mike to guide her into the bedroom. She smiled when she saw the red roses on the bed and the candles on either side. Mike wasn't a romantic as such, but he'd gone all out to turn the room into a honeymoon suite.

'What's all this about?' She could feel herself blushing.

Unexpectedly, Mike got down on one knee. 'I love you, Zara. I always have, and I always will. Will you marry me?'

Zara then saw the box in his hand and her eyes filled will tears. She'd never expected this. Now, it all made sense why Mike wanted to spend Christmas with the family. The decision to plan the downfall of the Crawford family at this special time speared her like a lance. 'Oh, Mike, I'm so sorry. I didn't know. I wish …'

His face suddenly crumpled. '*What?* You don't want to marry me?'

'Yes, of course, I do. But I'm just sorry I ruined today of all days.'

He stood up and pulled her close. 'Babe, just say you'll agree to marry me,' he whispered in her ear.

She pulled away and tilted her head in confusion. Then she saw Mike look towards the doorway at Ricky filming the proposal.

She laughed as the tears streamed down her face. 'Yes, of course, I'll marry you.' She took the box and slowly opened the lid. A gasp left her mouth when she stared at the bright stone twinkling in the morning sunlight. She remembered he'd once said he would buy her a diamond so big that an astronaut would see it shining. He wasn't wrong: the diamond was no tiny stone, that was for sure. It was a statement piece.

He took the ring from the box and placed it on the third finger of her right hand and then kissed her.

'Okay, you two, I don't need so much smooching on film,' said Ricky, laughing away.

Chapter 19

Mike, Willie, and Staffie parked their cars two houses along from Shelley's home and waited behind the tall bushes that fronted her property. Zara parked her car at the end of the road and winked at the men as she went past them. Dressed in jeans and a padded jacket to hide her weapons, she walked up to the door.

Shelley was in the kitchen basting the turkey while Lucas was upstairs playing on his new PlayStation games that she'd bought him for Christmas. She slammed the oven door shut, still angry with Lucas's tantrums over not receiving a car. Since he'd had his operation, his attitude had become worse. He was moody and aggressive and blaming her for him not having a relationship with his grandfather, when really it wasn't a relationship he wanted but a stake in the business. She reached for her glass of wine and took another big swig. It was her fourth glass, and she felt more than a little tipsy. After she looked back at the oven, she contemplated turning it off. She didn't like turkey anyway, and Lucas, as sure as hell, wouldn't sit at the table with her. As she wandered into the dining area, she stared at the fancy table setting for two and felt a lump in her throat. How had it come to this – a lonely woman going through the motions of Christmas with a bottle of wine as her only company?

The knock at the door made her jump, and for a moment, she hoped it was her father. At least it would give her a chance to introduce Lucas properly and maybe find some way of getting him off his arse and out to work, instead of continually sponging off her. She placed the wine glass on the table and checked the mirror. Her make-up was intact and her eyes, although glassy, didn't look like she was three sheets to the wind.

As she pulled the door open, her heart sank. It wasn't her father but some stranger. Just as she was about to close the door, assuming the person was a Jehovah's Witness, the woman said, 'Hello, Shelley. I hope you don't mind me calling.'

Shelley leaned forward for a moment, staring at the visitor, and then smiled. 'Oh, blimey, I remember you. We met at the hairdresser's.'

'Yes, you said I could pop in for coffee.'

Shelley frowned deeply. The Botox hadn't started working yet. 'What, on Christmas Day?'

Zara chuckled. 'No, sorry, Shelley. I was hoping I could wait with you. I've locked myself out, you see, and my brother is on his way over, but it's bloody freezing, and I don't know where to go. I was on my way over to his when the door slammed behind me. I don't have my keys in my pocket, so I'm bloody stuck.'

'Yeah, sure. Come in. I was only cooking a turkey. You can have a glass of wine with me.'

Zara followed her inside and glanced around. She could hear the sound of machine-gun fire and guessed Lucas was somewhere upstairs on a games console.

'Come into the lounge. I've got red or white, or would you

like something stronger? I might have a gin and tonic meself.'
Shelley was so busy walking and talking that she was unaware
of what Zara was doing behind her back. That was until she
turned around.

Shelley nearly fainted with shock. The fierce expression
on her new friend's face, standing with her feet apart and
pointing a gun straight at her, seemed totally at odds with the
person in the hairdresser's.

She nervously inhaled. Every hair on the back of her head
stood on end. 'Wh-what d-d'ya want?' she stuttered.

'Shelley, what I want is for you to be fucking quiet, or,
trust me, I'll take back from your son something that doesn't
rightfully belong to him.'

Shelley's mouth dropped open. 'What's he gone and nicked
now, the little bastard?' She couldn't believe that she'd let someone into her home who was actually brandishing a gun. Then
she wondered what Lucas had actually been up to because this
wasn't some young lads' squabble, surely?

'I said shut it. Just do as I say.'

Shelley nodded. Ashen-faced, she wanted to swallow, but
her brain had temporarily disabled all her reflexes. She was
stuffed and she knew it.

'Sit down!' Zara pointed to one of the dining chairs.

Shelley walked over and did as she was told, totally dis-
gruntled. Finally, she found her voice. 'For fuck's sake, what's
all this about?'

Zara noticed the change in Shelley's tone. She wasn't sweet
like before.

Placing the gun under her arm, Zara quickly pulled a roll
of duct tape from her pocket.

That was the moment Shelley went for the weapon. But she wasn't smart enough. Zara threw the duct tape, knowing Shelley's first reaction would be to catch it. It worked. Zara was onto her in a flash.

'Don't try anything stupid. Now, I want you to wrap the tape around you and the chair over there.'

The shock had Shelley sobering up and trying to get her thoughts into some logical order.

'Look, I dunno what all this is about but I reckon you may have targeted the wrong person. If my son owes you money, then you only had to ask, and I'll sort out his debts.'

'I said tape yourself up and shut up, 'cos, lady, I can easily put a bullet through ya mouth, and then the only noise you'll make is the splatter sound from your brains decorating the back wall.'

The expressionless face on this intruder made Shelley think twice about getting one over her. She remembered her father telling her once to be afraid of the calmest person in the room, and right now, she was staring at her.

She reasoned that there was no escape and began pulling the tape from the roll and tying it around herself and the chair. She stopped once she'd gone around twice and looked up to find the woman with a cruel, mocking smirk.

'Shelley, don't take the piss. I said tape yaself to the chair. Properly!'

Shelley curled her lip. 'My son is upstairs. What d'ya think's gonna happen when he comes downstairs?'

'Your son may just get a fucking surprise. Now, shut it. Carry on until I say you can stop.'

Once Zara felt that Shelley was secured, she rushed to the

front door, opened it, and gave a high-pitched whistle. Mike appeared, followed by Staffie and Willie. Willie was eager to take over and managed to bustle his way past Mike and head straight into the lounge-cum-dining room where he stopped dead in front of Shelley.

The shock at seeing Willie had Shelley's mouth gaping. All the pennies were dropping into place. She slowly turned and recognized immediately the other men. It was obvious they knew about her son. She couldn't pull a fast one, and, in any case, her brain just couldn't think quickly enough how to extract herself from this.

'You cunt!' spat Willie. 'You was gonna have my boy murdered, thrown in a fucking furnace, just so your kid could live.' Unexpectedly, Willie swiped her hard across her face.

She gripped her cheek and looked at him with terror in her eyes. 'Please don't, I'm begging you. I didn't know your son was supposed to be killed. I swear to God.'

Zara noticed how shocked Shelley was by what Willie had just said, and she wondered if she was actually telling the truth.

There was silence as Mike gripped Willie's arm. 'Shush. Just listen.'

Footsteps were coming down the stairs. The distant sounds of guns and tanks had ended. Staffie lunged forward and placed his hand over Shelley's mouth. He hissed in her ear, 'One word, and I'll break ya neck.'

The footsteps became steadily louder until Lucas entered the room. He didn't have a chance even to gasp before Mike had him around the throat and with his feet almost off the floor. 'You're gonna sit quietly next to ya muvver, and if you say one fucking word, I'll ram a knife right through your gut. Got it?'

Lucas's eyes bulged from his head as he tried to nod in agreement.

'Good!' said Mike, as he let him go. 'Now, you sit down and listen, both of you.' He turned to Zara and winked.

Willie was amazed at the resemblance between this lad and his own. They really were like two peas in a pod. 'So, you're the little fucker that has my boy's kidney?'

Having very little wisdom, Lucas assumed that since Willie must be his father, he would never hurt him.

'I thought you'd be pleased to meet me, Pops,' he replied, in a smug voice.

Shelley held her breath because she knew that although the two were related by blood, it meant fuck all to the likes of Willie. 'Please, Willie, he's just a lad. We never meant to hurt anyone. He was dying. Come on. You would've done the same. Be honest!'

'Be honest!' screeched Willie, as he flipped a chair up in the air. 'Honest! You don't know the meaning of the word. You never even told me you had a son by me. So fuck off about honesty. You had my boy kidnapped, operated on, and left to die.' His anger as he said those words made him flip another chair and lean in close to her face. 'Well you, ya skank, are gonna pay. I want me boy's kidney back.' He swivelled his diver's knife around in his hand.

Lucas felt the wrath of the man fill the room. The heavy breathing, and the hissing as he seethed like a monster, made Lucas recoil in dread. Was he serious? Lucas could only stare in horror at the madman. A fleeting moment of irony flashed through his mind as to how utterly pathetic he was in playing war games at his age, which was all they were, when here he was in the middle of a full-scale crisis in which his life was at stake and he was shitting hot bricks. Suddenly, his brash ideas of acting that way disappeared. It was the first time in his life that he was afraid. Growing up with Nicolas and surrounded by what he classed as hard-core villains was nothing compared to the men in the room. This wild-eyed bloke, who was supposed to be his father, appeared to be a complete lunatic, and his accomplices were no less evil-looking. As for the woman holding the gun, she didn't look to be that hard, but the weapon in her hand told a different story.

'Calm down, Willie, mate. We're here to get a job done.'

Her words and the firmness in her voice turned Lucas's eyes from his father to her. Whoever she was, she had his father stopping dead in his tracks. He wanted to laugh. A woman ordering them about – was she for real? The whole thing was absurd.

Willie stepped back. 'Yep, you're right. I've plenty of time. In fact, we've all day.' He sniffed the air. 'Ya know what? I think the turkey's burning.'

'Well, Willie, go and turn the oven off because I don't want the smoke alarm blaring.'

Willie suddenly turned from rage to laughter in a split second, which completely unnerved Lucas. This was so surreal, yet when he turned to face his mother, she didn't appear shocked at all. He sussed out that not only did she know the unpredictability of the man, she probably knew everyone in the room.

They all listened to the banging, crashing, and swearing coming from the kitchen. 'You never could bastard well cook! What, no fucking roast taters!' hollered Willie.

Zara turned her attention to Shelley. 'So this is what's gonna happen. You will get your father over here today. I don't care how you do it, but I want him here. I won't tell you what to say because only you'll know what it'll take to get him here, and I trust you value your son's life enough to cooperate.'

Lucas suddenly had hope. His grandfather would come with an army. From what he'd heard and seen of Colin, he wasn't a man to be threatened lightly by anyone. Lucas's mouth slowly creased up on one side and a smirk formed.

Staffie sneered. 'Take that look off ya face, 'cos when he gets here, things won't be pretty.'

With Willie still in the kitchen, Lucas put his arrogant expression back on. 'Do you even know who my grandfather is?'

Shelley cringed. 'Shut up, Lucas!'

'No, I won't shut up, you fucking stupid tart. They ain't gotta clue.'

Zara recognized the attitude as one that wasn't new. He was too quick to slate his mother, and if he treated her like shit, then he obviously had no respect for anyone. She wanted to put him to the test, just for her own satisfaction.

'Lucas, what would you say if I offered you a deal? Your mother's life for your own? 'Cos one of you is gonna have to pay for what you've done.'

Willie stood in the doorframe, almost touching the top. He leaned and listened, while he tore into the turkey leg.

Lucas looked from the woman to his father and speculated for a moment if this was some made-up dream. How could Willie go from being a complete nutter to someone who was casually tucking into their Christmas dinner? His eyes returned to the woman, and then, with a vindictive sneer, he looked at his mother. 'Go ahead. She ain't worth a wank anyway.'

With her heart beating faster, Zara felt her anger rising. He really was a little bastard. She had listened to Nicolas describing the boy but had considered at the time that possibly Nicolas was a little harsh because Lucas wasn't his son. But every word that came out of that man's mouth was on target. Lucas, it turned out, really was a nasty person. She looked across at Willie; for all his faults, he was kind at heart in a weird way.

She stared at Shelley. 'Looks like it's gonna be you then that takes the rap for what happened.'

Shelley was wide-eyed with terror. The woman spoke with such conviction that she had no reason to doubt her. Her mouth was dry and her heart was doing overtime from all the stress.

'Look, I ain't stupid. I know you'll kill me. I swear to God, I never knew Willie's son was left to die. That wasn't the plan, and as for Lucas, well, he never even knew he had his brother's kidney. He was too sick to know anything. It was only afterwards when I told him everything. But you have to believe me, I would never have wanted ...' – she looked at Willie – 'your son, Lucas's brother, killed.'

Willie pushed himself away from the doorframe and wiped his greasy mouth. 'Well, either fucking way, I want me boy's kidney back, and I'll take it. End of.'

Lucas laughed. 'I thought the woman with the gun said I could live if she dies.' He pointed to his mother.

It was Zara's turn to laugh. 'You're a complete prick, ain't ya? There's no love or respect for your dear ol' woman, apparently, is there? I wanted to see how bloody evil you were before I decided how your life will end.' She stepped closer.

'That is, if you and your mother don't manage to have Colin here before the end of the day.'

'Well, he won't come here, I can tell you that much. He hates me mother.'

Zara glared at him. 'Well, Lucas, he obviously doesn't hate you, to have arranged what I see as a very risky undertaking. So, I suggest you give him a call if you believe he hates your mother. Maybe you can work your magic and get him here. You see, the more you cooperate, the more chance you have of living. Or, failing that, at least you might die a less torturous death.'

Lucas looked at her unblinkingly, his head inclined. 'Who are you, exactly?'

Zara chuckled. 'The boss. Now, enough with the time-wasting questions. Start thinking about what you or ya mother's gonna say to entice your grandfather over here.'

Shelley butted in. 'He's right, though. Me father hates me, and to be perfectly frank, I don't care much for him either. So, I don't know what I could say to get him over here. He made it very clear he never wanted to see me ever again.'

'Well, I've done me homework, and let's just say I'm good at understanding the emotional dynamics of people … like your father. He arranged the operation, so the man does have feelings for you, both of you, and I would lay a million pounds on betting that if he thought either of you was going to have your fingers cut off, he would be here in a shot.'

'What? Are you *serious*?' croaked Lucas.

Willie gave his famous crooked smirk. 'Nah, she's joking. She'll cut off one of your hands and go from there.'

Understanding the interplay between the main players in the

room, Lucas was beginning to wish he could be a part of this crew. His father, although a little nutty-looking, was a man to be respected. The woman, he didn't care much for, but as for the men, they were right up his street. They were the type he wanted to be involved with. He didn't want to be the one ordered to sit on a chair. He longed to be the one dishing the orders out.

'Okay, listen, Dad. I'll tell you everything I know about Colin and—'

He didn't get a chance to finish before Willie was suddenly in his face, his hot angry breath almost burning his skin off.

'Don't you ever fucking call me *Dad*. I have one boy, and he can call me what he likes. You, though, ain't nuffin to me but a fucking leech, with a grandfarver who thinks he can fucking take what don't belong to him and toss the leftovers aside. Well, ya little creep, he ain't gonna get away with it. If it's the last bullet I shoot, I'll take that cunt down!'

Zara decided to stop Willie from saying any more. 'Willie, hold on. Don't be too hasty.' She put on her soft-spoken voice; it was a fake one that told him she was up to something.

'He is your son. Maybe we should listen to him. I mean, think about it. You don't know him yet, but, in time, you'll get to know him. After all, he has the same blood running through his veins.'

Willie backed off, trying to compose himself. But, inside, he was ready to rip the boy's head off. Nevertheless, he understood what she was doing and decided this time not to act so recklessly. 'All right, all right, I'm just upset. Liam could've died, that's all I'm saying.'

Not realizing a game was now in play, Lucas felt he was in

safe waters. 'Okay, I won't call you Dad, then, but the fact is you are me dad.'

Willie bit his lip but nodded equably enough. 'I guess so.' Those words stuck in the back of his throat, though. Lucas appeared to look like Liam's double, but there, the similarity ended. There wasn't a hint of niceness in his eyes – no cheeky smile or even a shy blush. It was as if he'd been born ugly inside and out.

Zara's eyes flicked to Shelley, who had a scheming expression on her face.

Not taking any chances, Zara sidled up to Staffie and whispered in his ear, 'Gag her and turn her around so that Lucas can't see her face.'

Without even blinking, Staffie cut the duct tape off the roll that was hanging from her chair and wrapped it around her mouth. 'There ya go, Shell. No gobbing off from you, now.'

Lucas's eyes widened. 'Er, what are ya doing?'

Zara smiled. 'I want your full attention, Lucas, with no distractions. Now, you seem to be a savvy lad, and I've no need to tell you where your bread's buttered, do I?'

He nodded with a conceited expression that grated on her; but, still, she held all the cards.

'So, about Colin. Tell me what you think we should know, and I'll see to it that you are initiated into the firm.' She chose her words carefully so that they would resonate with the young lad.

'Before I do that, what's in it for me?' he countered, with a sneer on his face.

Gotcha! Now, she knew she had his attention. 'That's up to you, Lucas. If we can trust you, then it will stand to reason that as Willie's son you'll be like the other boys and be a part of the firm. You'll help to run the business. I've got cocaine shipments coming in, and I need a trustworthy lad who'll oversee that, and, of course, you'll have a decent motor and money in ya back pocket, around five grand a week.' She paused and watched his expression. It was clear by the raised brows and open mouth that he was easily bought.

'And what about me own drum?'

'Don't push it, Lucas. One thing at a time. Our lads have to show their worth before they get one of my Dockland penthouse apartments.'

Lucas felt like he wanted to wet himself with excitement. He knew about the Dockland pads and would give his right arm for one. 'Okay, what do you want from me?'

That was it: it was all about greed and power with Lucas, and she knew then he would sell anyone down the river to get what he wanted.

Mike was laughing inside because Lucas was such a dork. As if he would ever get his hands on a single penny; still, he decided to take a seat and watch the show.

Willie looked at the small bar in the corner of the room and decided to help himself. He pulled the bottles of spirits from the shelf and offered everyone a drink, including Lucas, who nodded.

'A vodka and orange, Lucas? We all love a good drink. You'll get used to that.'

Zara smiled in relief that Willie was getting into character.

'Right, Lucas, tell us what you think would be useful for us to know regarding your grandfather.'

As much as Lucas found it hard to answer to a woman, it seemed that the others respected her, so she could be the person handing out the money. 'I don't know where he lives, but he owns a jet because he flew me to Spain, you know, to ...' He didn't like to say the words, in case he riled Willie up again. 'He has two men that act as his bodyguards. They're always with him, but they don't say much. I think they're called Raff and Gerry.'

Zara laughed. 'Gerry? Is he in his fifties, red face, and a beer belly?'

Lucas nodded.

'Well, your grandfarver is scraping the barrel if he thinks that wanker can handle himself,' Mike laughed, along with Staffie. Willie, though, remained silent, watching.

Lucas now had the impression that his grandfather, as much as he was rich, perhaps didn't have the clout he was led to believe, which only affirmed his allegiance to Willie's firm or this woman, whoever she was. Eager to get fully on board, he let his mouth run. 'And while I was on the plane, I listened to my grandfather talking to some geezer about drugs.'

Zara rolled her eyes. 'Lucas, if you're gonna play detective and listen in on conversations, you need to gain some actual hard facts, 'cos that means fuck all to me. He could be talking about the right dose of paracetamol, for all I know.'

Willie poured himself another drink. He needed it because right now Lucas was irritating the life out of him, and he wondered how on earth he could have spawned a kid so weak.

'He said something about this drug. I can't remember its name, but it was one I hadn't heard of. Flakes? Er, Flavel? I dunno, but he was getting heated with a bloke called Striker. At least I think that was his name.'

Zara shook her head. 'Jesus, there's a lot of "I don't knows", aren't there? Was the drug called Flakka, by any chance?'

'Yes! Yes, that's the one. It's Flakka.'

In wide-eyed surprise, Mike and Staffie looked at Zara as if she'd just uncovered a major plot.

Willie gulped his neat vodka and wiped his mouth, ready to speak. 'Did Colin mention the name Torvic?'

Lucas frowned. 'To tell ya the truth, I was struggling. I was so ill, I only remember small parts.'

Willie felt enraged when he thought about what Liam had endured, but he looked away so that Lucas couldn't see his flared nostrils and angry expression.

'And this Striker bloke, Lucas,' asked Zara. 'The one who Colin was talking to. Did you get the impression that your grandfather was in charge or did he seem beholden to the man?'

Lucas had to think carefully to understand what the woman was asking. 'Er, do you mean was this Striker bloke the boss?'

Zara nodded, forcing herself to be patient. 'Yes.'

Lucas tried to remember, but his memory was hazy. 'Aah, yeah, I think my grandfather said something like "I'll hold off the cargo from Poland, but can you let me know when you have a new buyer?" So, I'm not sure who was in charge, but I know he was more respectful to whoever this Striker fella was. Ya see, my grandfather is a moody man with no polite words for anyone, even me.' He looked down, feeling sorry for himself.

'It's a shame, Lucas, that your grandfather, with all his money, couldn't see his way to setting you up in business. He may have saved your life, but, really, that was nothing to him but just a gesture that would ease his conscience. Ya see, men like him hate feeling any emotion, and having your death around his neck would piss him off because he wouldn't have room in his selfish life for guilt.'

With an angry sneer, Lucas replied, 'Yeah, I know, he's a bastard. He wouldn't even give me the shit off his shoe, so what d'ya want me to do?'

Zara looked over at Willie who was now holding an address book. 'Is Colin's address in there?'

Willie shook his head. 'No, but there's a phone number for him.'

'Good. Right, Lucas, I want you to call him, and this is what I'm going to tell you to say, okay?'

Lucas looked at the men, who seemed to be ready for action. He wasn't going to argue; he wanted what they had, and he knew he wasn't going to get it from his grandfather. 'Yeah, sure.'

He listened very carefully to the plan and repeated to Zara everything she'd told him to say.

'Good lad. I can see you're gonna be an asset to the firm.'

With that, Lucas puffed out his scrawny chest and grinned.

Yet when Willie looked at him, he was sickened by the twisted smile. He wasn't even sweet, just pure nasty.

Willie turned away, and this time he looked at Shelley. He couldn't see her face, but he could see she was shaking. He had to stop himself from thinking about the past when he'd cared for her. That was a long time ago, and he'd changed, yet so had she. He could forgive her for not telling him she was pregnant with his child, but he couldn't forgive her for having Liam mutilated.

Mike handed Lucas the house phone, and as he took it, Mike pulled out a gun and then pointed it at Lucas's head. 'If you fuck up, boy, I won't hesitate to pull this trigger ...' He gave an exaggerated smile. 'Just a precaution, you understand?'

Lucas felt a little queasy. He'd never met a man so huge and ripped with such big muscles, not one in his late forties, that was. He wasn't going to argue.

Willie reeled off the numbers as Lucas punched them in. The phone rang seven times before an angry voice answered. 'Now, Shelley, I told you I never wanted to see you or hear your fucking voice again!' The phone was on loudspeaker so they could all hear the outrage in Crawford's voice.

'It's me, Lucas.'

'What do you want?'

Just as Lucas was going to reply as planned, Zara had a sudden thought. She quickly placed her hand over the receiver and then disconnected the call. Lucas looked up, surprised. 'What did I do wrong?' he spat, as if he was talking to his mother.

Zara raised her brow. 'Watch ya attitude. You did nothing wrong. I want you to wait. He'll call back.'

Willie glared at her. 'And how are you so sure?'

Zara smiled knowingly. ''Cos if he hated Shelley that much, he wouldn't have bothered to answer the phone in the first place, would he?'

Bang on cue, the phone rang. Zara held up her hand. 'Wait!'

Lucas didn't move, and then the phone rang off.

'What now?' demanded Willie.

'We wait, 'cos he'll either turn up or call back, and if he calls back, I want you, Lucas, to answer and just say, "They've taken Mum" and then hang up.'

Again, the phone rang. Lucas looked up, awaiting the

instruction, and then Zara nodded. Mike now held the gun to Lucas's head.

'They've taken Mum.'

Zara snatched the phone and listened.

'You what? Who? When? Lucas? Lucas!'

She replaced the receiver. 'Now, he'll come over, and when he does, then we'll know for sure that Colin cares enough to save your mother's life.' Zara then looked at Lucas. 'And yours as well.'

Lucas suddenly jumped up from his chair, fuming. 'You what? You said I could be a part of your firm.'

Mike stood in front of Zara, and with one fluid movement, he pushed Lucas back onto his chair. 'Jump up like that again, mush, and I'll fucking straighten your corrugated nose back into shape.'

Willie grimaced and ran a finger down his own nose, feeling every uneven bump.

'But you said I could be on your firm, I could have a motor, and ...'

'Oh, shut it, Lucas. I have *real* men on my firm, not snitches and backstabbers. You would've sold ya mother and your grandfather down the river in the blink of an eye and all for a fucking motor and a pad in the Docklands.'

Suddenly, Zara made her way over to Shelley. Tucking the gun under her arm, she ripped the duct tape from across her mouth.

Shelley's face was red where the tape had been; she appeared like the Joker out of the movie *Batman*. 'You heard all of that, didn't ya? Now, tell me why you would want to save a kid who doesn't give a flying fuck about you – his own mother?'

'Oh, fuck off. You wouldn't understand, so please don't try and turn me against him, 'cos it won't work.'

Zara laughed. 'Well, either way, you're both gonna fucking pay for what you did.'

The phone rang again, and Lucas stupidly thought he could reach it and warn his grandfather.

With a swift backhander, Mike stopped him before he'd even had a chance to touch the thing. The strike knocked Lucas off his feet and clean onto his back. 'Don't be a silly boy.'

Lucas wiped the blood from his mouth with the back of his hand and glared with utter contempt.

Mike laughed at him. 'You're a cocky little fucker, but, sadly, that bravado is all front. You've nothing behind it to back it up. Shame!'

'Oh, don't worry. My grandfather will fuck you all over. You just watch.' He looked at the small amount of blood on the back of his hand and shuddered.

Staffie and Willie grinned at each other, now with a few vodkas down their necks. 'He's a small man behind a lot of money to buy his muscle, that's all he is. The man can't fight, and neither can his minders. Still, you weren't to know,' said Staffie, mockingly.

The phone rang again but only three rings this time.

Zara smiled. 'He's on his way.'

No one asked how she knew. They just accepted her word as gospel.

Shelley's mouth was stinging as she glared with spite at the woman who exuded such confidence. 'Lucas is right. You won't get one over on me dad. He didn't get to where he is by being brought down by a load of shitty cunts like youse.' The tears of anger and frustration welled up.

Unexpectedly, Zara smacked her hard across the top of her cheekbone, using the handle of her gun.

'Aaahh! What the fuck did you do that for? Think you're hard, do you, 'cos I'm tied to a chair?'

'No, love. I think when your father walks in and sees you with a huge purple lump and your right eye dragged down, he'll feel sorry for you, and he'll then take your situation very seriously. You see, as much as you think your ol' man is tough, he's still your father, and seeing his little girl battered will lower his guard.'

Again, she smacked Shelley's other cheek, knocking her head back with dramatic force. 'Just setting the stage, darling, nothing else.'

No more words left Shelley's mouth. She knew she couldn't wind this woman up or get out of this mess if she got lippy again. Instead, she remained with her head looking at the floor, the tears tumbling down her cheeks. She guessed that fighting wasn't in her blood, and if she was honest with herself, she was only capable of a verbal catfight with a few scratches and hair pulling thrown into the mix.

Lucas slowly sat back on his chair, staring nervously at the woman; he wondered if in actual fact his grandfather would be a match for this lot. He mumbled something under his breath, which pricked Willie's ears.

'What did you say?'

Lucas peered up and grinned. 'I said everyone is a gangster until a real gangster walks into the room.'

Willie threw his head back and laughed. ''Ere, Little Lord

Fucking Fauntleroy's been watching *The Godfather*.' He narrowed his eyes. 'And what makes you think we're gangsters?'

Lucas's eyes twitched with nerves and anger. He hated being humiliated and it was far worse because this man was supposed to be his father. 'It don't take a lot of working out, does it? You come in here with guns, tie up me mother, and make all these threats ... What are ya, then?'

Willie leaned forward, gripping the two arms of the chair, and glared deeply into Lucas's eyes. 'We're a family that want to see justice served on a Christmas fucking platter.'

Lucas closed his eyes and looked down. Willie was a monster, and he decided it was best that from now on he kept his mouth shut and prayed that his grandfather would rescue him.

'Take him upstairs, Staffie. I'm sure Lucas would rather be playing on his PlayStation than being stuck in here with us talking boring business.'

Lucas didn't argue with the woman; he'd learned already that there was no messing with her. He got up and walked upstairs with Staffie, knowing there was no point in even shouting out if his grandfather turned up. He wasn't in a heroic frame of mind anymore.

'Draw the curtains, in case Colin decides to come in through the back. Leave the front door unlocked,' ordered Zara.

Willie did as she asked and then returned. 'He'd better hurry up. I'm still starving. I ain't had all of me turkey or the trimmings.'

'He'll be here,' said Zara confidently.

Chapter 20

Gerry scrambled into the front seat of Colin's Bentley. 'So what's going down, Boss?' He looked behind him to find Raff loading up his gun.

'I dunno, yet, but Lucas called. He said something like "They've taken Shelley." Who "they" are, I've no idea, but the boy sounded serious, and now he ain't answering the phone. I swear to God, if I get there, and he's playing some joke, I'll cut his tongue out so he can never speak to me again.'

Raff, a tall man in his mid-forties and dressed in a suit, looked up from his gun and into the rear-view mirror to catch a glimpse of Colin's cruel expression. He often wondered why his boss was so against his daughter and her son. He never asked because he was only with Colin for one reason – money. Colin paid well to have around-the-clock minders, although Raff couldn't understand why his boss took on Gerry. His only conclusion was that since Colin had climbed that wealthy ladder of his, over the years, with no attempts on his life, he felt he was invincible. He was a brash, hard-talking man, and he put the fear of God into people, but Raff was beginning to wonder why. Although the man gave the impression of being a Face because of the way he looked and spoke – he could frighten most souls – interestingly, Raff had never seen the man fight or even hold a gun for that matter. However, he was paid a whack and wasn't going to question his boss regarding that.

His only concern was with this drugs set-up that Colin was taking over. Cocaine supplies to Ibiza and other holiday resorts where the punters were able to party all day and night were all very well, but Flakka seemed a whole different ballgame, and if Colin had decided to ship the drug from Poland to supply dealers in London, then he would call it a day. Turf wars and druggies weren't his game, not from what he'd heard about the drug. He'd been surprised that Colin had even considered it, and it crossed his mind that his boss had somehow been put into a position where he didn't really have a choice.

'Boss, do you have *any* idea who Lucas was referring to when he said "they"?'

Gerry was still fiddling with his seat belt, trying to slide it around his fat belly, when Colin shouted, 'For fuck's sake, Gerry! *Ease* the fucking thing in. Don't yank it. And the answer to your question, Raff, is no. I have no idea, but I have a gut feeling that Shelley is up to something, so I'm going to find out what it is and put an end to it.'

Raff didn't believe Colin for one moment. He knew that his boss was worried and that he was just putting on a front.

Gerry finally managed to lock his seat belt in and the constant bleeping sound stopped. 'Raff, how many shooters did ya bring?'

The smell of booze on Gerry's breath had Raff rolling his eyes. 'Two, but by the fucking state you're in, I won't be handing one to you. You'll only end up shooting yaself in the fucking foot.'

'Oi, what d'ya mean?' asked Gerry, wheezing heavily and noisily.

'You're pissed, mate. That's what I mean.'

'No, I ain't. I've had a couple, 'cos it's Christmas Day. But what d'ya expect?'

Raff shook his head and looked out of the window, wondering what the hell he was doing. Was all the money really worth it now? For although he'd enough saved to set up a legitimate security firm, he had sacrificed his life working for Colin, which ended up with him not having kids or even a wife. He looked once more in the rear-view mirror at the man's beady eyes and felt his stomach churn. He wondered if his boss was actually turning evil. The last trip to Spain was pretty sick in his opinion. Snatching a kid and removing his kidney, what was that all about? He took a deep breath, closed his eyes, and asked God to forgive him.

As they approached Shelley's drive, Colin stopped the car. He stared up at the house. 'That boy had better not be lying, or I swear to God I will—'

Raff interrupted. 'You mean, you hope he *is* lying, or someone has got your daughter.'

Colin turned to face Raff, a flash of anger in his eyes. 'Don't fucking tell me what I mean – ever!'

Raff nodded in return. This wasn't the man he used to know. Colin Crawford had changed immeasurably over the past six months. He'd turned out to be a monster, so as soon as this situation was sorted out, he was going to leave the firm and get as far away from Crawford as he could.

It was now four o'clock. The house was shrouded in darkness. Colin knew where his daughter lived but had never actually been inside. He'd only followed the car that drove Lucas home after his operation.

'How d'ya wanna play this, Cole?' asked Gerry.

Colin, irritated, sneered. 'Gerry, don't call me Cole, okay? Me name's Colin. Right, you go and check around the back of the house, in case this is some kinda set-up. You, Raff, go and knock at the front door, with your gun.'

Colin, like the real coward he was, remained in the car at the end of the drive, watching the front of the house.

As soon as Raff was about to knock, he saw the door slightly ajar and gently pushed it open and crept inside, holding his gun in front of him. His hands were clammy as his heart raced. So many thoughts hurtled around in his mind. Whoever had taken Shelley must have a lot of front because although Colin was no fighter, he did have a dangerous reputation. He paid serious money to have people fucked up good and proper.

Slowly, trying to prevent even a floorboard from creaking under his feet, he made his way to the lounge. As soon as he got to the first doorway on the left, he lowered his gun and gasped. There in front of him tied to a chair and absolutely battered sat Shelley. He didn't think about who else would be in the room. Lowering his gun as well as his guard, he rushed in to help her. It proved a big mistake. When he was no more than three feet from her chair, someone from behind the door grabbed his arm and smashed it against their knee, making him drop the weapon. As he turned to see who it was, he was struck hard in the face with a vase, knocking him completely off his feet. Trying to get his senses back, he blinked and focused on a huge man, towering over him. He knew who it was: it was Mike Regan. He felt as though he was going to

376

shit himself. Regan was no stranger. Anyone who was anyone knew exactly who he was. Even though he'd been in the nick for years, Regan's reputation preceded him. Raff held his hands up in defeat. 'All right, mate, I ain't gonna fight.'

Mike's face was expressionless. 'No, you're right there. Who's with you?'

Under normal circumstances, Raff would have worked out a plan, but he'd had enough of the Colin Crawfords of this world and didn't care anymore. He'd lost so much respect for the bloke and certainly wasn't going to lose his life for him. And Regan was the type to kill *him* if he was on the wrong side of the argument.

'Colin's in the car and Gerry's outside somewhere, at the back, I think.'

'Just the three of you, then? Who's got the shooters?'

Raff pushed himself up into a sitting position. 'Just me.' As he looked around him, he noticed other people in the room. There was Willie Ritz and Teddy Stafford. Whatever the reason for their presence, Raff knew it had to be serious. Then Raff's eyes turned to the slim dark-haired woman.

Staffie snatched the man's guns from the floor and made his way to the back door. The kitchen light was off so whoever was outside couldn't see in. He listened to Gerry trying to open the door and instantly slid aside the bolt and ripped the door open. Gerry's face froze with shock at seeing Staffie, and he tried to make a run for it. But in his pissed state, he wasn't fast enough. Staffie smashed him on the head with one of Raff's guns and hustled him inside.

Gerry held his hands up and walked in through the kitchen with Staffie prodding the gun in his back. He knew he couldn't

377

argue, not with the weapon, and especially not with the likes of Staffie. The shock was sobering, and as soon as he reached the lounge, he knew it was game over.

Mike pulled Raff to his feet. 'You are gonna call Colin in!'

Raff sighed. 'Aw, leave off …'

The sudden punch to the back of his head made Raff wince, but he wasn't going to give in too easily. He had his reputation to consider. 'I'm not doing that, Mike.'

Mike was impressed with the man. The hard blows he'd given him didn't have Raff reeling in pain, and he was sure that he'd also broken Raff's arm. 'Yeah, you are, Raff, 'cos, mate, if ya don't, I'll blow your head off, and you know me. I fucking will!'

Raff stared into Mike's eyes and understood that either he did as he was told, or he'd be another casualty, and he didn't see why he should die for someone who didn't really give a toss if he lived or died. The truth was, he had more respect for Mike than Colin anyway. He nodded. 'Okay, I'll do it.'

'Good lad. You know it makes sense. And besides, Raff, there's no war between us, mate, is there?'

Raff frowned, questioning that statement.

'Mike, why would there be? I mean, what do you want Colin for?'

It was Willie who answered. 'Just get him in 'ere, and you'll fucking understand. But I promise you this: you fuck up, and I won't blow your head off, I'll fucking torture ya.'

Raff felt his mouth go dry. Willie was no pacifist, that was for sure. He nodded again. 'Okay.'

Gerry shouted out, 'You cunt!' and was swiftly punched in the mouth by Staffie. As the older man tumbled back, Staffie lifted his steel capped boot and kicked Gerry hard on the knee. Gerry instantly fell down on one side, knocking over the side table.

'Stay down, you mouthy prick!' demanded Staffie, pulling back the safety catch on the gun. 'One word from you and …' – he looked at the weapon – 'you'll be eating bullets.'

The front door was closed sufficiently enough so that Colin, who was still sitting in his car, couldn't see in. Mike followed Raff and told him to open the door fully, while he stood behind it, with the gun pressed into the back of Raff.

'Wave at him to come in, and if you so much as drop that smile, I'll kill ya.'

Raff did as he was told and watched as Colin got out of his car, straightened his suit, and walked towards the door as if he were some member of a cartel. Raff stepped back, allowing his boss to enter.

'So, what's going—'

He didn't get a chance to finish before Mike suddenly clutched him by the throat. He kept the gun levelled on Raff and then called for Willie, who appeared like a demon from the dead.

Mike let go of his grip on Crawford and waved the gun for Raff to return to the lounge.

'What the hell is this?' demanded Colin, although once he realized it was Willie Ritz standing there, everything was clear. All his bravado and threatening glances disappeared. He knew he was fucked.

Willie towered over Crawford with a look like a deranged lunatic, his eyes red and his jaw jutted forward. 'Get inside, you no-good cunt,' he said, clenching his fists tightly. He wanted nothing more than to kill the man with his bare hands, but he'd promised he would wait for Zara to interrogate Crawford first. She had something up her sleeve, and knowing her, it was worth paying attention to.

Colin felt his breathing increase as terror struck him in the chest. His palms were sweaty, and the hairs on the back of his neck stood on end. How the hell could he talk his way out of this one, and why had he been so stupid not to have brought more men? It was over. So, instead of squaring his shoulders and acting as a boss should, he meekly followed Raff into the lounge. He looked about, and in two seconds flat, he'd determined the set-up. Then his eyes fell on his daughter, who looked brutalized. For a moment, he felt sorry for her. She looked like her mother, his dear wife. Then he saw the tear that escaped her eye, and all he wanted to do was to put his arms around her. He assumed that he would be dead soon. The Regan firm were no idiots, and yet all he could think about was his daughter, his little girl. Why had he been so hard on her? Perhaps it had been misguided pride, but now, looking around the room, where exactly had that got him?

'Sit!' demanded Mike.

Colin was silent as he sat down at the dining-room table.

'And you, Raff, sit ya arse down too. It's gonna be a long night, unless we get some fucking straight answers.'

Colin looked at the back of his daughter's head. Her hair was a mess, and she was clearly suffering from sharp blows to her face. He looked up at the three men all ready to devour him and then wondered where his grandson was. Not that he cared that much for the boy. Firstly, he'd never really known him, and, secondly, what he did know, he didn't much care for. Lucas was a spoiled, arrogant bastard. Christian Bourne, his long-term friend, had said as much. The boy had been rude and disrespectful, especially to the nurses. Everything was now falling into place. Of course, the lad whose kidney they'd removed had recognized Christian; his friend had confirmed that. He wished he'd listened instead of calling Christian a paranoid twat.

This lot had played them. Leaving it for three weeks, they'd led them to believe that the boy hadn't known who had operated on him. It was a shrewd move that had sent them all into a false sense of security.

Just as he was about to open his mouth, a slim, attractive woman suddenly appeared. There was something icy about her, an evil aura, that he'd only ever seen in men like Willie Ritz. She walked with ease and class and sat down across from him.

The others were quiet as if she was the one in charge. He couldn't believe that some woman had the power to control the Regan firm. It wasn't possible.

'So, Colin, now we have your attention, I'll ask some questions. And, please, don't take me for a fool. It's Christmas Day, and, really, I have better things to do.'

'Who are you?' Colin was fuming that he was obviously being held at her say-so.

'I ask the questions. Here's the first one. What right did you have to take Nicolas's house from him and put it into your daughter's name when Nicolas had already given the bitch half in cash?'

Colin relaxed. So this was about Teddy Stafford's uncles. He could sort this out with no bloodshed, or so he thought.

'So, then, this is about Mack and Nicolas? Well, I took

the property off them because Nicolas only fucked and then married my daughter to get at me. We were enemies, and in my book, they took a right liberty, so I made Mack sign over the deeds. It was that simple.' He looked around at the seething faces. 'But, look, seriously, I don't want a war over that. I'll sign the house back over and offer a bit of compensation, if that's how you want it. How's that?'

Zara stared at the sudden confidence in the man. That was it: he bought his way out of trouble. She knew now she had the measure of Crawford.

'Now, the next question. What can you tell me about the imports from Poland?'

Colin clenched his hands together and frowned. 'What about my import business?' This was something he hadn't expected.

'Tell me all about it, and, before you begin, I know a lot already, so I'll realize if you're lying. Begin.'

Colin was flummoxed. What could she know and why would she even want to? he wondered.

'Are you the Filth or what?'

She shook her head. 'Answer the fucking question!'

'I dunno what you mean.'

Zara smiled wickedly. 'Willie, show Shelley your diver's knife. I think her father needs a little encouragement.'

With his hands in the air, Colin shouted, 'Stop! All right, listen. I import drugs, okay? It's not really my thing, but I do it ...'

Willie stepped back, still turning his knife around in his hand.

'Good. So, if it's not really your thing, then I can only

assume someone has put you up to it, and I wanna know who and fucking why,' grilled Zara.

Colin hadn't become a multi-millionaire without being smart. He smiled. 'I have property all over the world. I have an import and export company, mainly goods, all above board, and a few bits and pieces that make the real money. The Poles are good for business. They'll do anything for their euros and are happy to export drugs, so that's it, really. I'm not one for getting me hands too dirty but that little set-up is, shall we say, very lucrative.'

'And who's the man behind it?'

With an exaggerated frown, Colin replied, 'Me.'

Zara leaned back on her chair and looked at Willie. 'Show Colin what happens when he lies.' She sniggered as her eyes shot a callous glare at Shelley.

'No, wait! Don't hurt her. I *am* the man behind it. Who else are you talking about?'

Zara chewed on her lip. 'Who's Striker?'

Colin narrowed his eyes. 'Who?'

'Striker!'

Colin shrugged his shoulders in utter indifference. 'I've no idea who you mean.'

Zara started trying to work out if Colin was lying, but his face showed no emotion.

'And what about Torvic? I thought he was the dealer? The man who arranges the imports.'

Colin knew who Torvic was, and he hated him. A rude, aggressive bully, they had one thing in common, though, and that was their lust for money and power. Yet he was out of the picture, so he'd been told.

'Torvic? He's the distributor. Look, what is this all about? Perhaps we can work something out. If you want in on the deal, then ...' – he looked at Shelley – 'we can do it amicably. There's no need for this. I've enough business to go around, and, to be frank, I'm thinking of jacking in the drugs side of stuff. Just tell me what you want.' He hoped he sounded convincing enough to buy himself some time to get out of this mess without exposing the man behind the Flakka business.

'So you're the man who had that stinking drug that had half the druggies demented and the kids addicted in one fucking hit, then?' Her eyes narrowed as she looked Colin up and down, sickened by the idea that this lowlife, this scumbag, had the ability and the means to take Liam's kidney and export the terrible drug to half of the capital. Then, her eyes widened and her cheeks lifted into a smile. With Colin at their mercy, they would extract enough information to ensure that Flakka would never be sold in London again.

Colin had to think quickly because whoever this woman was, she obviously had morals and didn't take too kindly to kids getting caught up in drugs.

'Look, lady, whoever you are, you have the wrong man. I had nothing to do with what Torvic and his lot did to the drug once it reached England. As far as I'm concerned, it's as cheap as chips and far less harmful than cocaine.'

'Less harmful? Seriously?' She slammed her gun down on the table. 'It's evil and it's fucking cruel.' She glared with pure hatred in her eyes. 'Anyway, I wanna know what's gonna happen now Torvic's dead along with his sidekicks. So, tell me!'

Colin hadn't been told that Torvic was dead; he'd only been

informed that the man was out of action. 'Dead?' Just then, he wished he'd kept his mouth shut.

Zara suddenly laughed. 'Yeah, dead.'

Intrigued, he looked around the room, and he wondered if the man had died at their hands, but, at this point, he didn't want to know.

He threw his hands up. 'Well, that's it, then. Listen, I can promise you this: I won't be shipping any more of the stuff out of Poland. You have my word.' He looked at his daughter and shuddered, hoping he'd said enough to secure the family's freedom or their lives at least.

Zara stood up and smiled. 'Well, you won't be able to anyway. I just wanted to meet the man behind that devastating drug … Oh, and one final question. How the fucking hell do you think you had the right to take Liam's kidney?'

Colin's eyes nearly popped out of his head. 'What? What the fuck?' He was totally mortified. So they *did* know it was him. There and then, he was overwhelmed with fear. He'd met the feral eyes of Willie and knew his own death would not be pleasant. How much did they actually know?

He didn't have to ask. Willie lunged forward; with his hands around the man's throat, he growled, 'You ordered my boy to be burned in an incinerator.'

Colin felt his bowels move. He had no control now of his bodily functions, as terror struck him like a thunderbolt. The eyes of an enraged man burned into him, and he knew that he was about to experience hell on earth.

* * *

Mike took Raff outside the room to talk to him alone in the kitchen. He'd noticed the look of disgust on the man's face when Willie had mentioned that his son was to be burned in a furnace, and Mike was doubly sure that Raff was sickened by it. 'I knew you, Raff, years ago, and you were always a straight-up geezer. Did you know about this business with Lucas and Liam?'

Raff certainly wasn't going to lie. 'Yeah, but I swear I had no idea it was Willie's boy or that ...' – he looked behind him – 'that cunt would kill the kid. Now, I know you, Mike, and I ain't gonna lie, but for old times' sake, don't torture me.'

Mike looked him up and down. 'Why d'ya work for him?'

'He pays well – more than any other firm – but he's a nasty bastard an' all. If it weren't for the money, I would've killed him meself by now. He got lucky years back from a bank job.' He huffed. 'The man didn't even do the job himself. He had ol' McMasters killed and robbed the money from him. I only know because he trusts me, but I have very little respect for the man.'

'What do you know about Mack getting smashed up over a title deed to Nicolas's house?'

Raff inclined his head and appeared totally bewildered. 'What? Ya mean Mack, my ol' pal?'

Mike shrugged his shoulders. 'Were you mates, then?'

'Yeah, we 'ave been for a long time. Who bashed him up?'

Mike nodded his head towards the lounge. 'Your fucking boss had Mack beaten near to death.'

Raff let out a heavy sigh, in defeat. 'Look, I never knew about that, not that you'll probably believe me. I know why Colin didn't get me to do it. It's because he knew full well I wouldn't. I made it clear from the get-go that I wouldn't get involved in family matters. That ain't my way.'

A smirk crept across Mike's face. 'But ya helped him as far as his grandson was concerned, didn't ya?'

'And believe me, Mike, I wish I never had.' He paused and looked Mike squarely in the eyes. 'As I said, for old times' sake, will you give me a clean shot?'

Mike shook his head. 'Nah, I ain't gonna kill ya, mate. I want you to work for me. Starting today, I wanna know everything about his businesses before we clean the fucker out.'

Raff suddenly looked up, and his angular face beamed. 'Shit me, you really mean that, don't ya?'

Mike grinned. 'Yeah, I want everything that fucker owns. He's gonna pay for what he did. Now, do you know where this Dr Bourne lives?'

Raff nodded. 'Of course. He lives in Spain and over here. I can even get him on the blower … Listen, Mike, I'm really sorry, mate. It's gonna be in the back of my mind that you may do away with me, and I can live with that, but, I swear, I'll show you that you can trust me. In fact, I'll get a lot of satisfaction from seeing Crawford's business stripped from him.'

Mike grinned. 'It's a shame he won't, not when Willie's finished with him.'

'Where's the boy?'

Mike pointed upstairs. 'He's tied up for the minute.'

'They should've thrown the baby away and kept the after-birth with that one. He's one 'orrible bastard, he is. Can I ask, is Liam okay?'

Mike nodded. 'Yeah, he is now. He's a real diamond, that kid. Ugly as fuck but he has a heart o' gold.'

Raff chuckled. 'Like his father, then?'

A scream had Mike tearing back into the lounge. He knew Willie wouldn't have the patience to hold off hurting Crawford for long.

* * *

As soon as Mike clapped eyes on Willie, he shook his head. The diver's knife was out, and Willie was carving up the man's face.

'Hold up!' he hollered and then looked at Zara questioningly.

She shook her head and rolled her eyes. 'I couldn't stop him.'

Shelley suddenly cried out, 'Look, please don't hurt me. I swear, I won't say a word.' She shot her father a filthy look. 'I don't care what you do to him. Just let me and Lucas go.'

Zara stared at the woman's terrified expression – her bruised face and pleading eyes – and had a thought. She leaned into Shelley's ear and whispered, 'He was a right bastard to you, wasn't he?'

Shelley nodded furiously as she bit her bottom lip.

'So, what if we take a little chunk of his business and have it signed over to you, seeing that it should really go to you?'

Shelley's eyes widened and the thought of a Spanish dream home flashed through her mind. If her father wouldn't give her what was rightfully hers – in her eyes at least – then she wouldn't care how she got it. Looking over at her father for one last time, she saw the weasel for who he truly was.

'What do you want me to do?'

'Write a confession that you killed ya father and buried him in the back garden.'

'*What?* No way! Why would I do that? I ain't going to prison!' She lowered her tone when she saw the angry expression on Zara's face. 'Oh, come on. My liberty means more than a fucking poxy villa in Spain.'

'You have misunderstood me, Shelley. I want a confession, because if you ever double-cross me or my men, then I will have you behind bars. It's just a guarantee, and a gesture of good faith, that's all.'

Shelley nodded. 'Oh, right, so you ain't gonna make me kill him, then?'

Zara realized that she was dealing with a complete fuckwit. 'No, I just want you to write a confession. You don't need to worry about anything else. You are gonna stay with Nicolas until I have all the paperwork in place and a portion of his business in your name. Then, you are free to go off and sun yaself in Spain.'

Shelley had a stupid urge to try and call the shots. 'So, what if I say no?'

Zara held her gun and poked Shelley under her nose. 'Don't be a silly woman. Any more talk like that and I won't have any reason to trust you. I hope you understand exactly what I'm saying to you?'

Shelley nodded slowly. 'Yeah, okay, then.'

'Good. Now, Staffie's gonna take you to Nicolas's place, and I'll have that confession drawn up, just so we have a clear understanding. And you make sure your son keeps his mouth shut because I can sure as hell have him chopped up into quarters.' She looked at Willie and raised her chin. 'And we both know that wouldn't be pretty, would it?'

Shelley felt her stomach churn and quickly nodded. 'You have my word.'

Staffie began untying Shelley. 'No nonsense, right? You get your boy in my car. I don't wanna have to hurt him.'

'You won't have to. I'll sort him out.'

Zara looked down at Gerry, who had wet himself. She swiftly kicked him in the head, knocking him out cold. 'This fucker, you might as well dispose of, 'cos he's wasting oxygen as far as I'm concerned.'

'Okay, Boss,' replied Mike, as he winked.

She wondered if he was being serious or sarcastic, but then her eyes caught the sparkle of her ring. Somehow, it didn't matter anymore.

Chapter 21

Two weeks later

Zara sat at her father's desk and smirked at Michael Glover. The middle-aged man with thin, pointy features squirmed in his chair. When he had originally entered her house, he looked a confident, smug character with an air of superiority. That was until he realized that Zara was a very ingenious and dangerous woman. She had done her homework on him and Colin's businesses and had put it to him very bluntly that if he didn't work with her then he would be working against her and he really wouldn't like the latter. No one with that amount of money and so many businesses gained through illicit means would engage a straight lawyer. It really didn't take long to discover that Glover was as bent as a nine-bob note and she could prove it. And she had two strings to her bow because the company Glover and Glover was a joint business. Michael was the legal head, and Roger Glover was Colin's accountant.

To Zara it was like taking candy from a baby.

'I'll have all the company's assets assigned over to you by noon tomorrow,' he said, as he swallowed hard.

Zara grinned from ear to ear. 'And you do know that if

you have any ideas of running to the police, I'll make sure your name is connected to every dodgy dealing, including the import of the drug that is out there killing kids, don't ya?' She gave him a sarcastic smile. 'And we have a witness, Mack Marwood, who will testify that you were present when he was being tortured to sign over the house deeds.'

Michael raised his brow but remained white-faced.

'Oh yeah. I'll make absolutely sure that your implication in all this will stick like shit to a blanket. Are we clear?'

Without taking his eyes away from her, he nodded. 'Crystal.'

As he got up to leave, his legs still like jelly, he turned to face her. 'Hmm … You will need a good solicitor to work the business, won't you?'

Zara laughed. 'And, Michael Glover, do you know of any?'

His attempt at securing work fell flat on its face, and he left with his head hanging low in utter defeat. But at least he could leave with his reputation intact. He still had his company and more importantly his life. He was no fool and had learned a lot from working with Colin. There really was only one lesson: never mess with these kinds of people.

He passed Raff on the way out but didn't dare say a word. Raff had obviously defected to the other side, and he wasn't a man he would upset intentionally in any case.

* * *

As Raff joined Zara, he laughed. 'I don't think I've ever seen that man without his nose in the air. It's made my day.'

Zara smiled. 'Well, you did all the work. Without your help, I may not have had enough on him to ensure he kept his mouth shut and cooperated. Anyway, you were saying on the phone that Colin's secretary is asking questions.'

Raff nodded. 'Yeah, he had a bit of a thing going with her, and now she's angry because, obviously, he ain't answering her calls. I told her he's out of the country and hinted that he has another bird, but I'm not sure how long we can stall her. The lads are getting nosey as well. Ya see, Zara, Colin would always have someone with him and it would normally be me, so with me in and out of the office, they're getting suspicious.'

Dressed in a thick cable-knit jumper and her hair tied back, she looked more like a country toff than a businesswoman, yet he knew looks could be deceiving. He watched as she drummed her fingers on the desk, seemingly staring off into nothing.

'Do you think you could easily approach Colin's secretary and feed her false information?'

With a glint in his eye and a cheeky smile, Raff nodded.

'Good. Raff, do you know what Colin calls his secretary? I mean, like a nickname?'

Raff grinned. He guessed where she was going with this. 'Yeah, funnily enough, I do. He calls her Flossie.'

'Good. And I say that because I want her to believe that he's fine and he's selling on his business of his own accord. I need his computer, his hard drives, and everything else that contains information about his company.'

'How's the old bastard faring?'

Zara smiled. 'He gets three meals a day, clean clothes, and a gentle nudge from Willie every so often. You know, when his fingers won't grip the pen to sign the papers.'

'Knowing Willie, I'm surprised the fucker's still alive.' Raff laughed.

'No, Mike keeps him under control. He won't let him go too far. Although, one look from Willie down in the basement is enough to have anyone signing their soul to the Devil,' replied Zara.

'Are you gonna take everything?' Raff asked, eagerly.

'Don't worry, Raff, you'll get your fair share.'

'No, I wasn't asking for my own interest. I just think people will ask questions because Colin ain't the type of man who would just give his business away. He's obsessed with money. That's all he cares about.'

'Great. That means he has a lot of it, and, so far, I have bought fifty per cent of his companies with his own dirty money, but I want every last one ... Call it compensation for what that bastard did to Liam.'

Raff looked down in shame. 'I feel like shit that he was gonna let that kid die. Don't get me wrong, I ain't no saint, but what Crawford did, it goes against the grain for me. Liam was an innocent in all this.' He looked up. 'Sorry, did you say you bought his business with his own money?'

'Yeah, why?'

He shook his head and laughed. 'That's clever. He didn't deserve everything he had, ya know. He stole it in the first place ... from our own kind.'

'I know what he did was cowardly and fucking 'orrible. I've no time or respect for a cunt like that.'

Raff smiled. He was amused by Zara's choice of words. This classy woman using the c-word, it tickled him.

The door opened and in walked Willie, wearing an uncomfortable smile. 'Zara, I think I might 'ave gone a bit too far.'

'Oh no, Willie, I fucking told you I need that man alive. Jesus, will you ever listen?'

Willie turned his diver's knife around in his hand. 'Well, sorry about that, but he …'

She held up her hand. 'Stop! I know what he did, but I wanted to finish the job and take everything that man owned – for Liam!'

'I said "sorry",' replied Willie, like a naughty schoolboy.

Zara could only shake her head and sigh but there was a touch of humour about the situation which nevertheless made her smile.

The somewhat light-hearted moment was short-lived, though, when Mike walked in. 'You're lucky, Willie, he ain't dead. He's just fainted but leave off for now. The man is fucked all right. He's losing his mind now an' all. So, Zara, whatever you plan on doing, it needs to be done soon or he won't be coherent, especially if this great lummox keeps torturing him.'

Willie leaned against the wall and grinned at the blood on his knife. 'Okay, message received. I'll leave off, but once you've done what ya have to do, I wanna finish him off.'

Zara looked at Mike. 'Is he capable of talking, because I want him on the phone?'

'If someone plays a fucking nurse and bandages the cunt up before he bleeds to death, yeah, he should be okay. He needs a drink, though. A brandy should do the trick, I think.'

Zara handed Mike a bottle of Courvoisier. 'Liven him up. We need him to be able to talk … to his Flossie.' She laughed.

Mike and Willie returned to the basement cell.

Zara remained with Raff. 'Tell me about this Flossie. Is she a creature of habit, such as going to lunch at the same time every day?'

Raff nodded. 'She's a late luncher. She leaves at 2 and returns bang on at 3. She works until about 6, unless Colin asks her to stay on, and I can only guess what that's for. She's a stickler for routine and she's a terrific PA. Outside her job, she hasn't really got any interests. I guess she's a bit boring.'

'Perfect. And is she easily fobbed off?'

Shaking his head, Raff replied, 'No, but she listens to Colin, and to her, his word is gospel.'

Without another word, Zara got up from her seat. 'Can you wait here? I just need to assess the cock-up downstairs before I tell you what to do next.'

Watching Zara swan off, out of the room, Raff sat back, sipped his brandy, and smiled to himself. Colin had well and truly got his comeuppance. As for snooty Flossie, he was going to enjoy fucking her off. She'd always got up his nose, the way she'd looked down on him. Just because Colin was fucking the bitch, she seemed to think she was his boss as well.

He looked around the room and tried to match the décor with Zara; for some reason, he couldn't see a connection, but it wasn't his place to ask questions. As far as he was concerned, he was lucky to be alive, and the money she'd given him wasn't to be sniffed at. Mike Regan's and Zara's firms were more like a family. They were so far removed from Colin's idea of how an outfit should run, and he knew which he preferred. It certainly wasn't Crawford's, that was for sure.

Zara returned fifteen minutes later. 'Christ, Willie is a nutter. Anyway, back to the order of the day.'

Raff sat up straight. 'So, what's to do?'

'Colin is going to make a call to Flossie in her office at two-thirty. Hopefully, she'll be out at lunch because if he fucks up and doesn't do as I say, you can delete the recording on her answerphone.'

He nodded, not taking her eyes off her; this was sounding like an interesting plan. He could see now why Mike and his firm held her in such high regard.

'I want you to hang around, and when she hears the message, she'll no doubt question you, but, whatever happens, you're to leave with the hard drives. And, don't forget, he's terminally ill and wants to spend time with his family.'

Raff smiled. 'No worries.'

Zara looked at the time. It was eleven o'clock. She hoped that Colin would respond to the medication and be able to talk or at least string a coherent sentence together. If he came across as fatigued then that would actually increase the likelihood of the game plan being successful.

*   *   *

Mike ordered Willie to go home and take a bath; he was turning into a nightmare. Willie moaned and mumbled under his breath but left without too much to say. As soon as he heard the door close at the top of the stairs, Mike sat on the bed and looked at Colin who was tied to the chair.

Mike glared at the mess Willie had made. The man's eyes were swollen, his face was black and blue, and he cringed at the mess Willie had made where he'd sliced up the man. In fact, Colin's arms were dripping with blood, and his mouth was twisted at such an awkward angle, Mike wondered if the disfigured shape was because Willie had broken his jaw. He took a deep breath and a sip of brandy straight from the bottle.

If Colin's jaw was broken, then he wouldn't sound right when he made that phone call.

Colin muttered something, which had Mike on his feet. ''Ere, drink this. It'll help.'

Colin's head lolled sideways as he tried to focus. The brandy on his lips made him wince, but the cool amber nectar trickling down his throat made him realize he was still alive. The warmth as it hit his stomach provided some relief. A few more gulps and he felt his taut body relax.

As Mike gave Colin more to drink, he heard Zara behind him.

'Fucking hell, Mike, what's that smell?'

Mike stepped away and raised his brow. 'What d'ya think? Look at the state of him. Willie has scared the man to death. Anyway, I've sent Willie home.'

Zara nodded. 'Yeah, I said goodbye.' Looking at Colin, she said, 'We need to get him cleaned up before he drowns in his own crap. Christ, he smells rank.'

Mike tutted. 'I know. I feel sick.'

'Get him in the shower, clean him up, and stick some clothes on him. I want him *compos mentis*.'

Mike turned his head and glared at Zara. 'Hey, what's with the bleedin' orders?'

'Someone's got to see the plan through. So far, it's been me. Willie's just gone all ham, egg, and chips; you look like you need some sleep; and that bastard there, he won't last another twenty-four hours unless he gets rest, food, and …'

'And what?'

'He needs some serious drugs. I'll sort that out while you get him cleaned up.'

Mike laughed, now in a more relaxed mood, since it was clear that Zara was making sense. 'Leave the mess to me, why don't ya.'

Zara winked and left Mike to it. She knew that upstairs there was a box of morphine, enough to keep Colin out of too much pain. Aware that he was well beyond the point of no return, she assumed he'd probably welcome death. However, even to the bitter end, there was always that instinct to survive. She just hoped it was the same for Colin because the call he needed to make was vital to her plans.

* * *

Amanda Wells wandered around Colin's office fussing and polishing his desk. She looked at a blank computer screen, at his gold pens all neatly lined up, and felt another surge of frustration. Nothing made sense. In the early days, she would have freely admitted to herself that she'd been just his PA with benefits on both sides. He would screw the life out of her, and she would have her holidays paid for.

Nevertheless, that was a long time ago. Now, she hoped – indeed assumed – that in the last few years their relationship had moved on to a much more formal footing. He took her out for meals and … well, there really wasn't an 'and' as such. It was perhaps more to do with the way he indulged her. He gave her respect and he treated her with consideration – almost as an equal – although both knew that this 'relationship' was not based on anything other than mutual need. For there were no promises of anything serious like a marriage proposal or moving in together, but, still, he had become more attentive in a caring kind of way.

She stared out of the window and sighed. Perhaps it was all wishful thinking on her part. She had to assume he was in Spain working on the redevelopment because it wasn't as if he didn't make decisions on the spur of the moment. And he wouldn't confide his movements to her at the drop of a hat. He didn't answer to her. She wasn't his wife. Really, it wasn't any of her business what he did and when he did it. She was told that if he wasn't around, she was to use her charm and delay meetings and appointments. So, why did she have this awful feeling of dread in the pit of her stomach?

Her thoughts were dragged from the depths of despair when Raff walked in.

As soon as she laid eyes on him, her heart sank; she'd so hoped it would be Colin. 'Raff, where is Colin? I can't get hold of him, and he hasn't contacted me.' She choked on her words, trying not to get emotional. 'He didn't even call me over Christmas.'

Raff smiled, almost mocking her feelings. 'And why would he call his secretary, 'cos that really is all you are, ain't it?'

His words hit a nerve. She glanced up at him and saw the smile that didn't reach his eyes. Something about that remark and the look on his face made him seem different, less respectful. It was yet another sign that things were not all they should be in her life. Smoothing her dark hair that was so tightly pulled back in a bun that it dragged her eyes up at the sides, she pretended to be focused on her computer monitor.

Raff stared at her face and wondered how old she actually was. Probably around forty or maybe forty-five, he thought. She was too strait-laced for his tastes. And, more annoyingly, the bitch always looked at him with her nose in the air. But she definitely had one thing in common with old Crawford. Looking down at his desk, observing the precise arrangement of the pens, he knew her own office was just as tidy. They clearly had a touch of OCD.

With her face like thunder, she hissed, 'Raff, where is he?'

'He has some business to attend to, okay? I just need to pick up some files.'

Amanda looked him up and down as if there was a bad smell in the room. 'Well, he hasn't told me, so please leave his office until he gives me the okay.' She would have the last say; she had just made that clear.

Raff nodded. 'Right, I'll tell him.'

She rose to barge past him but stopped dead in her tracks. 'How exactly will you tell him, if he's not answering his phone?'

Raff laughed. 'Amanda, he has more than one fucking phone.'

'Well, can you give me his other number? I need to talk to him. I've had the staff asking where he is, and I've had a number of business clients on the phone. I've been by his house, but he's not there. So, Raphael, please just give me his number.'

Raff was enjoying the frustration in her voice, although he was seriously irritated by her calling him 'Raphael'. Only his mother called him that, usually when she was in a bad mood.

'Look, if he wanted you to have it, he would've given it to you. Stalking him won't do you any favours.'

Steeling herself, Amanda fumed, 'I'm not stalking him. I need to get *hold* of him. Now, Raphael, fuck off, and tell Colin to call me, or he won't see any fucking files.'

Raff gave an exaggerated wide-eyed look as if he was profoundly shocked at her language. Following her out of the room, he watched as she locked the door and stomped off back to her own office.

* * *

The clock in the downstairs main reception area showed three minutes to two, and if he was right, she would appear soon for her lunch break. The security guard was showing him some funny scene on YouTube. Raff had his back to the lift, but, right on cue, the lift doors opened and out she came. He continued laughing with the guard until Amanda was out of the door and on the high street.

'Snooty bitch,' mumbled the security guard.

Raff tapped his arm. 'I bet she's good in bed, though. That type always are.'

'She must be good at summat, 'cos ol' Mr Crawford's banging her.'

After ten minutes of bantering, Raff headed back up in the lift to Amanda's office and waited by the phone. Right on time, it rang. He listened for the six rings, his heart working overtime. On the sixth ring, the phone went straight over to answerphone. He listened carefully because he knew there could be no mistakes.

'Flossie, it's Colin ... When Raff arrives, give him all my files and the hard drives ...'

Raff held his breath; the man sounded very tired.

'Flossie, I ... I've sold the company ... Someone else will be taking over. I'm not well, so I want everything, um ... sorted out before I ... Just do it.'

The pause was long, and Raff wondered if that was the end

of the call. If so, something wasn't right because the message didn't sound very convincing.

'You and the others will get a payoff ... but I want to be left in peace ... I'm sorry.'

Good, Raff thought. *That was enough.* Now he was able to breathe more easily. Although Colin sounded tired and ill, if he himself hadn't been aware of the truth, he would certainly have believed the message left by Colin to be genuine.

Amanda returned precisely at 3 p.m. He could have set his watch by her.

Cross with herself for forgetting to lock her office before she'd headed out to lunch, she glared with spite in her dark-brown eyes at this hireling sitting at her desk. 'I thought I told you to leave. There's no need for you to be here if Colin isn't present. Besides, you're just his ... What are you, exactly, Raphael? A bodyguard, an arse licker? Tell me?'

Raff got up from her chair and sat on the edge of her desk. Looking through her diary, he grinned at her.

She snatched it from his hands and glared. 'I've told you once already. Now, just fuck off.'

'And I told you, I need his files. You might wanna check your messages because he said he would call you. But you were out shopping,' he sniggered, 'for a new personality, no doubt.'

Amanda was about to launch a verbal retort, but when she saw the red flashing light on her answerphone, she thought better of it and instead pressed the play button.

Raff stood up from the desk and studied her face intently as she listened. Instantly, she put her hands to her mouth and looked at Raff. 'Oh my God, is he really ill? Like, is he dying or what?'

Raff shrugged his shoulders. 'Who knows?' he said, casually. 'He wants to sell up, to retire. That's all you need to know.'

'But if he's sick, who will look after him? I mean, I need to see him.'

'Didn't you hear the message, love? He wants to be left alone, in *peace*. You'll have your redundancy, along with everyone else. But get the message, Amanda or Flossie, or whatever you wanna be called. Colin Crawford wants to be left alone.'

With a vindictive sneer, she replied, 'You have no idea about Colin and me. We go back a long way, and if he's ill then he will want me there.'

Shaking his head, Raff gave her a sympathetic smile. 'No, love. Ya see, you may have been his bit on the side, but he loved his wife, and when she found out about your little affair, she refused chemotherapy and died, and so, really, on the face of it, you killed her. He's talking with his daughter now, and so you need to fucking back off.'

With her hands shaking, Amanda dropped the diary on the desk. She tried to stop herself from letting rip, but the urge was too great.

'That little money-grabbing bitch is only after him for what she can get! Christ alive, he must be sick if he's letting her back into his life,' she yelled.

Raff laughed sarcastically. 'Yeah, I thought you'd hate that idea. But I guess, with Christmas good cheer and all that, Colin saw the light – a bit like Scrooge, I suppose. Anyway, enough talking about family reunions. Colin wants the hard drives and files pronto, or ...'

'Or what?' she squawked, now fuming.

'Or, Amanda, you'll receive the statutory state pension, and not a generous payoff. It's your fucking choice.'

The thought that Colin would do that to her had her upping her rant big time. 'What? What a devious fucking bastard. Well, bollocks to him and his conniving fucking daughter. I know enough about his dodgy dealings. I could have that man locked up for a very long time, so he can't threaten me with that shit!'

Raff shook his head and grinned. 'Amanda, you ain't nothing but an office worker, are ya? Seriously, you don't think Colin would tell you anything that would have him pulled in for questioning, do ya?' He laughed again as he continued to shake his head. 'I dunno, you silly office tarts really think you know it all. Look around ya. Take a good look, love. You seriously think he would own all of this and everything else if the likes of you could have it all taken away in less than a heartbeat. Well, do ya?'

Her mouth gaped open in shock. Suddenly, she saw the light. Of course, Raff was right. She tried to think what she really did have on Colin, but the truth was that it was only little bits and pieces that in the eyes of the law would amount to fuck all.

Without another word, she pulled a key from her pocket, opened a desk drawer, snatched a large bunch of keys, and threw them at him. 'The other keys to his cabinets and all the hard drives are in the top drawer in his desk. And you can tell him from me he was a useless shag anyway and I want a decent payout, or I'll do some digging, and, in fact, I'll make it my life's mission to bring that bastard down!'

She sat heavily on her chair, grabbed the phone, and stared at Raff. 'Well, what the hell do you want now?'

'What are you doing, Amanda?'

She returned his sarcastic grin. 'Calling Mr Glover. You honestly didn't think I'd take your word for it, did you?'

Raff felt uneasy. He'd never anticipated that. He just prayed that Zara had that side of the business taken care of. He waited and listened but was only able to hear her voice. He watched her facial expressions, though, trying to work out what was being said at the other end of the call.

'So the company *has* been taken over, then? And are you sure the money has gone into his account?'

Her face was white and her tone vicious as she growled down the phone, 'And you don't find that unusual?'

Whatever Colin's lawyer was saying, it was obviously pissing her off.

'I know it's not my business but … well, Colin never said anything to me and …'

The expression of being so insulted fixed itself on her face before she slammed the phone down and glared at Raff. 'What do you want *now*?' she hissed.

Laughing inside, Raff was impressed: Zara had pulled off a masterstroke. Using Colin's illegal money to buy his own businesses but in her name was pure genius.

'Oh, sorry, Amanda, didn't I tell you? He wants the staff, including you, to finish up today. The new owners will be moving in on Monday, and they have their own staff.'

With a face like a smacked arse, Amanda leaped from her chair, swiped the computer from the desk, snatched her bag and coat, and stormed off, slamming the door behind her.

Raff laughed. It was the best thing he'd seen in a long time. His mind went back to Mrs Crawford, the lovely wife of Colin's. She'd always been so kind to him as a lad, and the day she died – he knew why – it was the day he hated Amanda. He'd waited a long time to see her haughty face drop in humiliation. All in all, it hadn't been a bad day's work.

Chapter 22

As soon as Lance marched through the hallway into the lounge he paused and smiled. Poppy and Brooke were putting together a beautiful flower arrangement. They stopped and looked up, beaming. 'Dad, you're back. We were just—'

He laughed before Poppy could finish. 'Yeah, I get it. The lads are spoiling you rotten.'

Brooke got up from the table and dropped her smile. 'No, Dad, we were just going to the cemetery.' She pointed to the arrangement. 'For Kendall.'

He sighed. 'Oh, sorry, yes, of course. It would've been her birthday today.' He swallowed, trying to control his emotion.

Brooke unexpectedly linked arms with him. 'It's okay. You've been busy, and I guess we have too.'

Sitting down at the table, Lance admired his daughters. They had changed in a short space of time, from timid, geeky, and naive students to confident and positively glowing young ladies. He wondered if it was the influence from Arty and Liam, or the fact that they were out of their mother's repressive home. Either way, it was a joy to see.

'So, girls, it's probably time to think about going back to uni. What d'ya think?'

Brooke giggled. 'Well, we may have a really good opportunity lined up.'

Lance raised his eyebrow. 'Oh yeah, and what would that be?'

Poppy laughed and blushed. 'We will be working for the Regan firm.'

Jerking his head and pulling a tight face, Lance sternly asked, 'What d'ya mean?'

'Dad! Don't look so worried. It will all be legitimate. We are going into property development with Liam, Arty, and Ricky. I mean, what do they even know about business and accounts?'

Lance let out a relieved laugh. 'Well, I can see you two have been investing in a future. But, don't let the boys take advantage.'

It was Poppy's turn to raise an eyebrow. 'It might be too late for that, and, Dad, we aren't kids, you know.'

He looked from one to the other. 'You are to me, and you always will be.'

* * *

Shelley looked in the mirror at her yellow bruises and decided today that she would cover them up. Milking it, to gain sympathy from Nicolas, had worn thin. Being forced to stay at his house was initially an outrage, but she had to admit to herself that seeing him again had stirred feelings. She guessed he wasn't best pleased having her here, but from what she could gather, he didn't have much choice.

'Shell!' he called. 'Get ya arse down 'ere, babe. I've got some papers for you to sign!'

Shelley was working on her appearance at the dressing table in one of the many spare bedrooms in Nicolas's home. After adding another layer of foundation, and smoothing down her hair, she excitedly made her way downstairs and shimmied into the lounge. The smell of fresh coffee and bacon sandwiches made her mouth water.

''Ere she is, my shining glory.' Nicolas beamed.

Shelley rolled her eyes, knowing he was being sarcastic. She nodded at the man in the suit, surmising he was the solicitor.

'Shell, this is Brandon Miles, a lawyer. He has the deeds to that small complex in Spain that you wanted. All you have to do now, babe, is just scribble your name on the dotted lines, and it's all yours.'

Shelley dreamed of having her own business, and the fact that her father was signing some of it over to her was even better. Nicolas had already informed her that her father had seen the error of his ways, with a little help from Mike Regan, and wanted to turn things around. From what she'd been told, her father had offered to hand over a share in the business to Liam as well, for all the boy had been through. It was seen as a gesture that he was putting things right. After all, Lucas couldn't exactly give the kidney back.

Hesitating, she said, 'And this is all above board?'

Brandon gave her his most ingratiating smile and handed her a pen. 'Just sign there and there.' He pointed to the crosses in pencil.

Eagerly, she signed her name, and then he produced more papers. 'And this, too. I must say, this is most generous of your father. He seemed to me to be a very decent man,' said Brandon.

'Is he all right?'

Brandon nodded. 'Of course he is. He said he wanted to make sure you were taken care of.'

She scribbled her name again.

Brandon's smile almost reached his eyes. 'Now, I just need you to sign here to say I have witnessed it and then we're done.'

The formal business concluded, Shelley stood up, and in her tight blue dress, she started to walk away, wiggling her arse, no doubt trying to impress Brandon. She turned before she reached the door and gave them her sexiest smile. 'Right, Nicolas, I think I'd best be off to buy some new clothes if I'm to be the boss now.'

Nicolas, now sitting on the edge of the sofa, grinned up at her. 'You do that, babe, and why don't ya have a nice weekend at the spa as well. Let's face it, you're a rich woman now.'

Her face flushed with excitement, she skipped out of the room and went back up the stairs.

Brandon put his hands up to high-five his client. 'All done, Nicolas. She is now the proud owner of a development site in Spain that has no building plans. It was one of Crawford's dead-in-the-water ideas. Aah well, she doesn't look like the hard hat and hi-vis jacket type anyway.'

Nicolas laughed and patted Brandon's back. 'Oh yeah, but at least she will be out of my hair, along with that kid of hers. Er, that confession note she signed a couple of weeks ago. Is that all above board? I don't want her going off on one and shouting her mouth off.'

Brandon winked. 'Yes, I have a copy, and so does she, but my advice is you need to give her a reminder just so it sticks in the forefront of her mind.'

Nicolas laughed. 'Oh yeah, how did it go with Lucas? I was making the coffee. Did he sign everything?'

Brandon winked. 'He is one daft sod. He must take after his mother and not Willie, because I told him that there was no need to bother reading it as it was all legal jargon, which would take forever. In essence, as soon as I told him that he now owns half of his grandfather's estate, he just signed every paper I put in front of him. I have left him signed copies, and when he finally works out what's happened, he won't have a leg to stand on, and if he wants to go to the police, then he'll face being locked up. So that's all been tidied up nicely.'

'I must remember that if I ever have to sign anything that you shove under my nose, I read every bleedin' word. Staffie told me that you did the same thing to Jackie. How d'ya do it, Brandon?'

With a cheeky grin and a wink, Brandon replied, 'It's all about charm and who can be charmed. The likes of Jackie and Shelley, and even Lucas, are so full of themselves that they simply can't see beyond what they can gain, so you just use it to your own advantage.' He laughed. 'Honestly, does this face look as if it could lie?'

Fascinated, Nicolas took a good look and had to agree. Brandon's boyish looks and the twinkle in his eye could charm the eyes off a rattlesnake.

As Nicolas walked him to the door, he could hear the gunfire and bombs going off from the video games console. He shook his head. 'That boy won't even leave his bedroom unless he wants food or a piss.'

After he'd seen Brandon into his car and leave the

property, he saw another car pulling into the drive. Inside were two lads; it didn't take a genius to work out who they were.

Liam stepped out of the car first, followed by Arty. They waved to Nicolas while heading his way.

'Cor, blimey, Liam, if you ain't your father's double, and you, Arty, cor, you've grown a lot since I last saw ya. Give us a hug, boys.'

Arty embraced his great uncle and stepped back, allowing Liam to follow suit. 'Er, Liam wants to meet his brother.' He rolled his eyes. 'Me, I'd fuck him off, but this ol' softy won't have none of it.'

Liam looked at Arty. 'You're just jealous, Art.'

Arty tutted and shook his head. 'Uncle Nick, is it okay if we meet this prune?'

Nicolas stepped back. 'Come in. He's upstairs on that space station thingy.'

Liam laughed. 'Ya mean PlayStation.'

'Yeah, well, he should've grown out of it by now.' He looked the boys up and down; they were a far cry from Lucas. Arty was smartly dressed in a cashmere roll-neck jumper and a dark-grey fitted blazer, and his hair was gelled back. Liam was slimmer, but, still, he carried off his own style, and Nicolas had to give it to him – he did look smart in a beanie hat, polo-neck jumper, and a long overcoat. He smiled; if only he were thirty years younger.

'Go on, then. Surprise the lazy fucker.'

Liam was first up the stairs, heading for the sound of gun-fire. He was about to knock at the door but decided he would just walk straight in. Arty was on his heels, and as they closed the door behind them, they heard Shelley shout out, 'See you later, Lucas. Don't forget to take your tablets!'

So engrossed in his game, Lucas didn't see or hear the lads come into his room.

Liam stared at the lad who was supposed to be his spitting image, but what he assumed he would feel once he'd come face-to-face with him didn't happen. He felt nothing, no sudden affection, not even the long-lost brother sensation of completeness. Unexpectedly, watching Lucas's angry face as he shot the Germans on the screen, he had the urge to leave.

It was Arty who spoke first. 'Oi, d'ya wanna turn that thing off?'

Lucas slowly turned his head to the side to find two big fierce-looking young men, one giving him a cold stare. He paused the game and got up from his gaming chair. 'And you are?'

Liam stood with his arms crossed and his head tilted, weighing up his half-brother. 'Me, I'm Liam Ritz. This is Arty Stafford.'

Lucas, with his hair unkempt and three days of stubble, screwed up his face, and with a sense of sarcasm, chuckled. 'So *you're* the donor.'

Arty could feel his chest rise as he fought to hold back his temper. But this was Liam's business, not his, although, right now, he wanted to rip Lucas's head off.

'Your brother, mate,' replied Liam, wishing he hadn't said that.

Lucas smirked. 'I suppose you would say that. My guess is you wanna meet me now 'cos I'm fucking cako. Well, if you want, I can write out a cheque for the body part.'

Liam's face dropped in shock; this wasn't supposed to happen. He thought maybe they could go for a pint, get to know each other, have some kind of relationship – like he had with Arty and Ricky.

Lucas winked. 'What's up, Liam? Come on, that's why you're 'ere, ain't it? I mean, you never bothered to find me before.'

Liam was flummoxed. 'Hang on, I never knew about you until ya robbed me of me kidney.'

Lucas shrugged his shoulders. 'Whatever. So, what d'ya want?'

Arty could see the hurt written across Liam's face. He squeezed his shoulder and pulled him back. 'Come on, mate. You don't need this prick.'

Lucas laughed. 'Make that a rich prick.'

As if rage had suddenly twisted his brain, Liam spun around and lunged forward, grabbing Lucas by the collar, pushing him back against the wall. Nose to nose, he spat, 'You cocky bastard. I fucking stopped me ol' man from annihilating you for what you lot did to me. Now, I wish to God I'd never bothered.'

He let Lucas go and was on the point of walking away but was stopped dead in his tracks when Lucas replied, 'Your ol' man went over the top when he held a gun to my head, and he can go away for a long time. So, I suggest you don't ever touch me again or you'll be visiting him at Her Majesty's pleasure.'

The front that Lucas had shown was enough for Liam to do what he did best – unhinge his wild side.

Arty knew that look, and before he'd even had time to draw breath, Liam went for Lucas. The first fast crack to the nose had Lucas sliding down to the floor crying like a baby. Then followed a barrage of blows to Lucas's ribs. But it was the run-up kick to the head that finished off Lucas, who ended up sprawled out on the bedroom floor. Still in a temper, Liam ripped the PlayStation from the unit, held it high above his head, and smashed it down onto Lucas's face again and again until the console was smashed to pieces and Lucas's face was a mangled, bloodied mess.

'Wow, that's enough!' shouted Arty, as he pulled Liam away. He knew, with the side table now in Liam's clutches, Lucas would be dead, if he wasn't already.

Nicolas gasped in shock as he pushed the door open. Immediately, he dragged both Arty and Liam away. 'Get out, boys, for fuck's sake. Ya ain't killed the bastard, 'ave ya?'

Liam was panting hard, trying to get his breath. 'If I ain't, I'm going back in there to finish the slimy git off.'

'No! Leave it. That's all we need, a murder on our hands. Get off with ya, and I'll clean him up.'

Liam slowed down his breathing. 'He threatened to have me ol' man nicked.'

Nicolas winked. 'I can assure you, son, that that won't happen. He can't ever go to the Filth, not after he's signed his own arrest warrant. I'll make sure he reads it before he wants to make a nuisance of himself. Leave it to me, lads.'

As they all trooped downstairs, moaning and groaning sounds coming from Lucas's bedroom told them that they hadn't killed him.

Once they were both in the car, Liam looked at his bruised knuckles. 'Look, Arty, I'm sorry right? I don't need another fucking brother. You and Ricky … well, you're family, ain't ya?'

Arty started the car. 'Yeah, and from now on, we follow in our fathers' footsteps, yeah? We just stick to our own. Now, you get yaself cleaned up. I've got some baby wipes in the glove compartment there. You need to get packing, mate. We've got a business to run in Spain. That development over there needs a good look over, and now you're a rich—'

Liam laughed. 'Don't you call me a rich prick an' all.'

'Nah.' Arty laughed back. 'I was gonna say, a rich fucker.'

'I think, Bro – me, you, Ricky, and the girls all need another holiday, so before we get stuck into any business, get on the phone and book a villa, five stars no less.'

Arty whacked Liam's arm. 'Listen, you might be a rich fucker, but that doesn't make me your skivvy. The holiday can wait. And, Sunshine, we need to get ourselves clued-up and dressed for the part for this takeover. So are you gonna 'ave ya barnet cut and buy a new whistle and flute? I mean, us lads, the three musketeers, wanna look the dog's bollocks when we stroll into that posh office block.'

He gave Liam another quick once-over before saying, 'Especially you, mate, being the boss.'

As Liam chuckled, Arty beamed. He really didn't want another lad on the firm, and yet he understood why Liam had had to meet his half-brother. In fact, he would have done the same thing.

* * *

Nicolas helped Lucas onto the bed, and after fetching a bowl of warm water and a towel from the kitchen, he began cleaning him up. The bruising on his face was pretty bad, and yet he himself felt absolutely nothing. The arrogant sod deserved it.

'You need to take your tablets, Lucas.'

Lucas peered through slits. 'What? What I need is a phone to call the police. Look what that cunt's done to me. And as for his ol' man, I want him locked up an' all.'

Nicolas nodded. 'Yeah, all right, mate, but let's get you better first, eh? Now, like I said, you need to take your tablets.'

Lucas closed his eyes and nodded.

As Nicolas got to his feet, he stared down at the boy and shook his head. What a waste of space he truly was.

Scrutinizing Lucas's bottles of tablets, Nicolas opened his own medicine cabinet and took out his blood pressure tablets, his cholesterol pills, and the painkillers. It was an easy swap, if ever there was one.

He grinned to himself. Shelley would be so distracted now, what with all the money she thought she had to spend on her endless shopping trips, that she would never notice if the lad slipped into a coma.

* * *

Liam, Arty, and Ricky each parked directly outside the impressive tall building. The parking spaces were now reserved for their vehicles, and they stepped out of their cars with their shoulders pushed back.

The security guard smiled and welcomed them in. 'Did you

find the traffic okay, Mr Ritz?' Glen asked Arty, as he directed the question to the person he wrongly assumed was Liam.

Arty laughed. 'Mate, *he* is Mr Ritz, *I* am Mr Stafford, and *this* is Mr Regan,' he said proudly, pointing to his mates in turn.

Glen had been told that the new owner was young and not who you would imagine a property developer to look like. The description wasn't far off the mark. Mr Ritz, unlike his sidekicks, was a little scruffy around the edges, to say the least. A long grey military coat and a beanie hat didn't give the impression that he was the boss, but the sheer presence and size of Mr Stafford and Mr Regan did suggest that he was being accompanied by men who held sway.

'I'm told that most of the offices are empty now,' said Ricky, with a grin that confused Glen, as he was unsure if it was a smirk or a genuine smile.

Glen smiled back, showing his gold molars. 'There are a few guys who apparently have their own clients.' He shrugged.

Arty marched past Glen, determined to catch the staff siphoning off the business. He pressed the lift button three times before it finally opened. Liam and Ricky had to trot to keep up with him as they joined him in the lift.

'What's the sudden rush, mate?' asked Ricky.

'If Colin's old staff want the business, they can download all the information, effectively steal the files, and take the clients to another firm. Well, I want them searched before they leave the fucking building.'

Liam nodded in agreement. 'Yeah, let's start as we mean to go on. You take the lead, Arty, 'cos I know fuck all about computers.'

'Best you start learning, then, you crank. How are ya gonna run a business if ya can't use a computer?'

Liam grinned. 'I've got Poppy. She knows all that stuff.'

Arty rolled his eyes and looked at Ricky. 'I swear sometimes I could kick him up the arse.'

Liam sighed. 'Listen, it's good of Zara to give me this opportunity, but, seriously, Arty, what the fuck do I know? I would rather us all be equal partners, just so that ...'

'So that what, ya bloody great oaf?'

Liam gave them his most charming smile. 'So that we're always together.' He blushed and looked awkward. 'Look, I love you two as me own brothers, yeah, and, well, what do I know about business? I want us to be in this together. I don't wanna go me own separate way. It ain't who I am and it's also no fun.'

Arty put an arm around Liam's and Ricky's shoulders. 'All for one mate, then.'

'That's what I like to hear, d'Artagnan.' Liam laughed at that quip, now feeling more at ease. He knew that in the grand scheme of things he was no leader. He was much like his father in that respect – the backup. Ricky was the cute one with the face that would melt a girl's heart but with a temper that you wouldn't see coming. As for Arty, he was someone who was good with technology and would have sailed through an honours degree if he hadn't settled for a university of life certificate.

Just as the doors opened, there, looking flushed, stood Amanda with files that she could barely carry.

She stared at the three young strangers and demanded to know who they were.

Liam stepped forward and grinned. 'The new owner, and

I'll take those, thank you very much.' He snatched the files and handed them to Ricky.

Arty hissed in Amanda's face, 'You, lady, are coming with me before I call the police. Those files are not your property.'

Amanda felt her legs turn to jelly. 'Those are my private notes. They're nothing to do with this firm.'

Arty, dressed in a light-grey fitted suit, spun around. 'Listen up, lady. I don't know who you are, but you're trespassing. I have a list of all the files associated with this company, and if one of them, and I mean a single one, is missing, then I'll have every member of staff arrested and that includes you.' He stormed ahead towards the main administration room where there were eleven desks and computers, six of which were not occupied, but five men, all in suits, were busy doing something on their computers. Stacked up on the counters were box after box. Arty could see that they all contained files.

'Right, all of you, stop what you're doing! Do not touch any of the computers and step away this minute, or you'll all be arrested,' hollered Liam.

Nearly all of the men did as he instructed but were bemused that the order was coming from some young guy who looked as though he belonged to a pop group. Others stared at Ricky and Arty, who wore aggression like a well-fitted glove. One presumptuous lad, though, just ignored Liam and carried on.

In a flash, Ricky tore over to the desk, backhanded him, and pushed the man over. 'Did you not hear what he said?' He looked at the screen and could see that information was being sent to a personal e-mail address starting with the name 'Jim Garcia'.

'Arty, this geezer's downloading stuff.' He glared at the young man. 'Is that your name?'

Nodding, Garcia jumped to his feet and pushed Ricky to get his hands back on the keyboard.

Ricky reacted in way that had everyone shocked. In a flash, Garcia was grabbed by the throat and dragged over to the large window. With one hand, Ricky opened the window; with the other, which was still throttling the bloke, he forced him over the windowsill. The strength of Ricky was enough to have the top half of Garcia's body leaning out over the pavement twenty-one floors below.

The silence was palpable: no one moved for fear that they would be next to feel this young man's wrath. Garcia, who was hanging backwards, clutched Ricky's arm for dear life. 'Please, please, I'm sorry.'

Still keeping the blubbering guy in the same position, Ricky turned to face the others. 'If any of you other wankers even think of mugging us off, then I'll drop this cunt like a bag of shit.'

It was Arty who now took control. He was actually afraid that Ricky might lose the plot and drop the bloke. 'Right, you thieving bastards, all of ya line up, one by fucking one. You're going to open your e-mail accounts and delete the e-mails that you've just sent, and you can empty your pockets. What you guys are doing is theft and sabotage, a serious fucking offence, so unless you want to spend a few years in the nick, you'd better do as we say.'

When Ricky pulled Garcia back, away from the edge, and threw him to the floor, everyone felt a huge sense of relief.

Liam watched his mates with pride, as the suited and booted

men acted as though they'd a gun to their heads. Each man complied with the orders, and within an hour, all the e-mails to personal accounts were deleted.

Having been well briefed about the company by Zara, Ricky confidently stood back and demanded their attention. 'You were all going to get paid a very good redundancy package at our discretion; however, I've changed my mind. We've looked over your employment contracts.' He gave an exaggerated laugh. 'And what a joke they are. In truth, they aren't even legally binding, so all your dismissal notices will be sent to you in the post, and you'll now receive only statutory redundancy …' He laughed again. 'I am sure, lads, that will buy you a decent meal at McDonald's. Now, fuck off!'

The files were returned, and Colin Crawford's ex-staff were left looking dejected and broken, except for Garcia, who'd needed a backhander to stop him from working on his computer.

He waited until his colleagues left the room before he spoke. 'You underestimated me. I was deleting files that would incriminate this company.'

Arty rested his eyes on Garcia, staring him out.

Garcia, though, wasn't at all bothered. 'Colin trusted me with his other business, and I needed to get rid of all traces, but I guess that's your problem now, and it won't be me in jail but you guys. Good luck!'

He was about to squeeze past both Ricky and Liam but was instantly stopped.

Ricky grabbed his shoulder. 'Wait up, you ain't going anywhere. You're gonna tell me exactly what you're talking about.'

With a cold feeling ripping through his bones, Garcia nervously replied, 'Please leave me out of it.'

'I don't fucking think so, Jim Garcia. Me and you need to have a little talk in me new office.'

Garcia felt intimidated, and by the look of the man and the tone in his voice, he really wanted to get away from them as soon as possible. This wasn't the way businessmen spoke. It was bordering on gangster speak. He didn't want to get involved.

'No, thanks. I need to be off home. I'll take the statutory redundancy and be out of your hair.'

Ricky wagged his finger. 'No, you won't. I said, me and you will have a chat in me office, and I don't like to be contradicted.' He looked at Arty. 'Do I?'

Arty could see Ricky as a replica of Mike and acted in response. He straightened his shoulders and replied, 'That's right, Mr Regan.'

Their intimidating manner alone had Garcia shitting himself. He decided to do as they demanded rather than suffer the consequences. Nodding to all three men, he followed them into Colin's former office.

'Sit down, Mr Garcia!' said Arty.

Knowing Liam would prefer to stand back and not do the talking, Ricky sat in the coin seat, with a confirmatory nod from Arty.

With a forceful hand from Arty, Garcia took the chair opposite and tried to stop his knees from bobbing up and down. 'What is it exactly that you want?'

Ricky clasped his hands together and leaned forward. 'Everything you fucking know. I want names, places, times, and dates.'

Swallowing hard, Garcia asked, 'Are you the police?'

Liam laughed. 'Ol' Bill? I tell ya what, mate. You'll fucking wish we were, if you don't answer the questions!'

Garcia appraised them all. He had a good measure of what they were all doing and his astute brain thought of a way of turning this situation to his advantage.

He leaned back on his chair and grinned with satisfaction, although, inwardly, he was still nervous. 'I'll tell you everything you want to know on condition you take the statutory redundancy off the table and replace it with something worth my while.'

Ricky nodded and laughed, impressed with Garcia's audacity. 'Yeah, not a problem, so start talking. The property business is just a sideline – we know that. What do you know about Flakka? Who's behind it? And, just so you know, we're aware that Colin Crawford shipped it over from Poland.' He lowered his voice and gave Garcia a grave look. 'And we fucking know by what means.'

Garcia's mouth dropped open. How the hell did they know that? As far as he was aware, there were only two people from the office who knew that level of information and that was Colin and himself. Yet he couldn't deny anything because, however these three young men had managed to get their information, they knew the score.

Ricky had been given all the facts by Zara, so he knew exactly what questions to ask. She didn't want any of the lads going in blind. Liam, though, had found it a bit difficult to understand the inner workings. However, Ricky was different; he'd grasped everything she'd told him and was well equipped to interrogate Garcia.

Liam locked the door. 'Just a precaution, you understand. We don't need any distractions.'

Garcia looked from Liam to Arty and saw the smart man's suit jacket shift slightly to the side, revealing a gun. 'Um ... er ... yeah, sure. I know all about that. Colin had mules sent over on a weekly basis, but then it all stopped. The man who took delivery suddenly disappeared.'

Ricky frowned. 'Er ... you mean he's dead or what?'

Garcia shrugged. 'I don't think he's dead. All I know is that the drugs were being held up in a factory, awaiting the go-ahead, but we had a date for the next shipment, so that's why I was so stunned when Colin sold up everything and I couldn't reach him.' He looked questioningly at Ricky. 'Colin *is* dead, isn't he?'

Ricky shook his head. 'No, he ain't dead. He's retired due to a sudden serious illness. Anyway, he's sold the company to us, but that's not your fucking business. You, Mr Garcia, are going to answer my questions, and if you're honest, then you'll get ya decent payout, or Mr Ritz, 'ere, might even keep you on. But treat this as an interview, yeah?'

Garcia knew then not to look a gift horse in the mouth. It really was a no-brainer.

Chapter 23

Zara snuggled into Mike's arms and looked down at her ring. 'So, Mikey Regan, it's all well and good having that rock on me finger, but shouldn't we be setting a date?'

Mike kissed the top of her head and felt a sudden feeling of sorrow. The love of his life had been to hell and back and was still running a risky empire. He was so proud of her, and yet, she should be enjoying all the pleasures other women experienced in life.

'Yes, indeed, my rosebud. What about June? Here or abroad?'

Zara felt a surge of excitement, and it showed, because she blushed, and her eyes sparkled. As Mike held her in front of him, he drank in the excitement radiating across her face and dancing in her eyes.

'June! That will be perfect. I want your father to give me away, if he won't mind, and I want Ricky as your best man. I would love Joshua's little girl to be bridesmaid and ...' She stopped. 'What are you looking at?'

He was absorbed in her delight. 'You look like a little girl, Zara. You're so excited, and it's so refreshing, babe. This is what life's about, the good stuff. And if wedding planning puts that pleasure in your heart, then we should get married every year.'

She pulled him close to her and gently kissed him on the lips. 'It's all I've ever wanted. Me, Mrs Zara Regan.'

'And don't you forget it.' He cupped her face and kissed her again.

Their intimate moment was cut short when the light in the office suddenly dimmed as if there was a power dip. Zara turned to look at the blank screen on the monitor, and her shoulders dropped.

'I swear that bloody thing's cursed. It's gone off again. Mike, would you get the engineers over to sort this out once and for all? I'm going to have a quick shower.'

'Yeah, sure. Why did it do that?'

Zara sighed. 'I dunno. I think it's to do with the electrics. If Torvic was still alive, I would swear it was him.'

As soon as Zara reached the top of the stairs, she heard a bang at the front door. On edge, she peered down from the landing window to see Ricky standing there, looking frozen, and behind him a taxi disappearing down the drive.

'I'll get the door, Mike,' she called out, hoping Mike would get on the phone and give the engineers a real earbashing.

As she opened the door, she stepped aside for Ricky to come in. 'Jesus, it's freezing out there, Ricky. Where's your coat, love?'

Wearing only a thin fitted jumper, jeans, and his cheeky grin, Ricky leaned forward and kissed her on the cheek. 'I have some padding underneath this top.' He winked as he pulled away.

'Aw, what was that for?'

He blushed. "Cos you care, and it's nice that you do.'

Zara felt her heart swell. Ricky was eighteen and no boy. The feedback from Arty and Liam on how Ricky had conducted himself with the takeover at Colin's offices had put a proud grin on her face. She had given them the tools to take on the business and free rein to do it their own way. In the home, Ricky, Liam, and Arty were just boys, but outside, they were as fearless and dangerous as their fathers.

She closed the door and opened the small box in the wall that held all the reserve keys. The code was simple: it was 1944, the year her father was born.

Retrieving some spare keys, she handed a set to Ricky. 'Take these, in case I'm not in. You can let yourself in. Besides, after I'm gone, all this will be yours ... although I should think you'd want to sell it.'

Ricky looked up at the high ceilings and the huge framed pictures. 'Aw, I dunno, Zara. I kinda like the place. It's like a castle.'

As she turned to lock the box, she tutted; something seemed amiss. On close inspection, she realized that there was something actually missing. In fact, quite a few keys were not there. Yet it had been a month of Sundays since she'd opened that box; there hadn't been any need until now. Taking a deep breath, she stopped her brain going off on one, worrying about who had them. They may have gone missing when Izzy was alive. She snapped the door shut and followed Ricky into the kitchen.

He rubbed his cold hands together. 'Do you want a coffee, Zara?'

She nodded. 'Yeah, a strong one, please. Ya dad's in the office. We've some tittle deeds for you.'

Ricky placed a cup under the espresso machine and raised his eyebrow. 'Deeds?'

'Yeah. We're just sorting through the business, making sure everything is hunky-dory and squeaky clean. There are two properties that are now in your name: one's in Spain, a nice villa by all accounts, and the other is a flat in West London.'

Ricky held his breath in anticipation, yet the surprise was written all over his face.

Zara beamed. 'The keys are in the office. They're all yours.'

'What! But I can't. I haven't earned it. I mean, how can I just be given a London pad and a holiday home? I don't deserve either.'

Zara's eyes filled up. 'Oh, Ricky, you are such a good lad. Most lads would grab them with both hands and run. They are *yours*. You *do* deserve them. I can't make up for what Jackie put you through, I know that much, but your dad and I can make sure you're set up for the future.'

Unexpectedly, Ricky threw his arms around her and hugged her tight. 'You should've been my mum. I wish you were.'

Caught off guard, Zara replied, 'There's nothing to stop me from adopting you.'

Slowly, he pulled away, with a tear trickling down the side of his nose. 'Really? What? Then I can call you Mum, can I?'

The word 'mum' had her eyes overflowing with tears that cascaded down her cheeks. 'You can call me Mum, anyway, and the day I don't act like it ... well, it's the day you should call me Zara again, but, Ricky, I will do my best by you, I promise.'

'What's all this?' came a voice from the doorway.

Both Ricky and Zara turned around, teary-eyed.

'Mum was just telling me about the deeds.'

Mike froze for a moment. Did he hear that right? Did Ricky actually call her 'Mum'? He looked at them both, wondering if it was a slip of the tongue, but it was her reaction that shocked him the most. He watched her as she walked over to him and put her arm around his waist.

'I said that as his parents, we will make his future brighter, starting with the deeds.' She smiled and winked at Mike, who was still gawping.

'So, after coffee, let's get those papers signed. Go on, Ricky, you go with your father. I'll make us some sandwiches. I've got some fresh salmon in.'

Mike felt his life was complete. At long last, he had his family, his future, all together. With his arm around Ricky's shoulders, he whispered, 'I'm so proud of you, Son. While you were taken from me, Arty grew into a man that we thought would take over. He's a good lad. He takes no shit. Mind you, neither does Liam.'

'I know, Dad, and I like working with them. Honestly, I feel like I belong. I never liked the travellers' way of life. Working with you, my uncles, and the lads is where I fit in.'

Mike turned Ricky to face him. 'Fit in? Son, you do more than fit in. Arty was so humbled by you that his exact words were: "Mike, I was just keeping Ricky's seat warm until he returned."'

With a lump in his throat, Ricky replied, 'Then I must be a chip off the old block!'

* * *

As Zara buttered the bread, she heard a rustling sound by the back door and paused to listen. Then the sound of a fox snapped her from her paranoid thoughts. From the kitchen window, she looked across the field and noticed the thin white layer of snow. It shouldn't have been a surprise, for the last few days had registered below freezing temperatures. Something made her look again: the farmer's house in the adjoining field appeared lifeless. Twisting her head to the side, she realized that on this cold day there was no smoke billowing from his chimney. That was odd because the old boy always had his log burner on the go. She had known the farmer all her life and wondered if something was amiss. A cold feeling crept over her, but the sound of the fox starting up again pulled her from her thoughts. She looked at all the salmon left over and thought maybe it would be a nice treat for some animal out on a day like this. She chopped up the remainder, placed it on a plate, and unlocked the back door. The cold air kissed her cheeks like spears of ice. Just as she stepped forward to put the plate down on the ground, a sudden recollection hit her. Like a stack of dominoes tumbling down, one thought after another jolted her – the old farmer – his lifeless house – the car burned out in his field – the body burned alive, and now, finally, the most crucial thought of all: foxes are normally nocturnal.

Then, out of the corner of her eye, she saw a vapour cloud to her right and heard the distinctive click of a gun being cocked. She didn't need to look to see who was holding the weapon. She knew. Whether it was the way he breathed or his familiar smell, she knew he was her worst enemy. All she could think of was Ricky, his sweet innocent face beaming with love. The way he hugged her, it felt like she really was his mother. And now she had Mike, her man, the person she'd thought about every waking hour. Love had reached such depths that it went beyond passion. She would die for these two men. Never would she subject them to this evil man's cruelty.

Without looking to assess where exactly he was positioned, she instantly flung her right arm and connected with the cold metal. The shock caused Torvic to fire and gave Zara a chance to grab his arm. In his attempt to shake her free, he pulled his fist back to punch her in the face, but, as he did so, he slipped back on the ice and fired the gun again. The force at which he hit the ground pulled her down too. Yet she wouldn't let go of his wrist. And he couldn't point that gun at her all the time she forced his arm away. With his other hand, he ripped at her hair, trying to pull her head back so that he could release her grip, but her knee came up and caught him between the legs, as he fired once more. Like a German Shepherd in a fight, she held onto his wrist and tried desperately hard to knee him again. But Torvic managed to pull himself upright and back onto his feet, despite the pain. Zara, not letting go, used his arm and hauled herself up. Fiercely, she fought to reverse the gun barrel around. For his part, all he could do was punch her on the side of the head. She wavered but didn't let go.

The sound of gunshots had Mike up on his feet, with Ricky behind him, running through the kitchen and out of the back door where he found Torvic smashing Zara in the face, as she tried hard to twist the gun barrel and aim it at her attacker.

The second Torvic clapped eyes on Mike, he fired another round, but, again, he missed his target. Zara was desperate to stay focused although the force of his punches to her head had almost knocked her out.

But with Torvic's mind distracted for that vital split second, Zara managed to pull herself towards his arm, and, using all her strength, she sank her teeth into his flesh. She caught his reflex tendon, which made his gun recoil, and his finger systematically pulled the trigger again and again. She desperately wanted him to empty that magazine.

Torvic bared his teeth and fired yet another round, catching Mike in the shoulder. The force of the bullet threw Mike backwards and into Ricky, who was directly behind him.

'No!' screamed Ricky, terrified that his father had been shot in the chest. He couldn't bear to see his father die, not now, not ever.

Gripping his shoulder in complete shock and in abject pain – for Mike had never actually been struck by a bullet before – he nevertheless tried to recover his balance to help Zara, but the moment he was stable on two feet, Torvic had a firm hold of her by her hair and the gun barrel now pressed against her temple.

'No! Okay, don't shoot!' cried Mike.

Ricky tried to back away to call for help, but Torvic eyed him very quickly. 'You move, and she dies. Your choice.'

The pain shooting down Mike's arm made him want to cry out. He could feel all the blood gushing out from the wound, but he couldn't move. 'Stay behind me, Ricky,' he whispered, under his breath.

Ricky, relieved that his father was not critically injured, remained motionless, his eyes fixed on Zara. Her face was battered, one eye was half-closed, and she looked drained. Crying inside, Ricky knew that Zara had put up one hell of a fight. If he could smash the life out of the old man with his bare hands, he would, but there was nothing he could do. He'd never felt so helpless in his entire life. All he could hope for was that Torvic wouldn't pull the trigger just yet.

Mike and Ricky could only watch as Torvic leaned into Zara's ear and whispered, 'If you even think about making the wrong move, I'll kill them in a way that'll make you turn inside out with repulsion.'

As Zara's senses began to return, she tried to put a mental plan into place; yet she was powerless. He still had his cold weapon pressed against her temple. Even if she decided to fight him, he would shoot her and then her family. She needed another strategy, one that might catch Torvic off guard.

'Get inside. Any funny business, and I'll blow her fucking head off!' he bellowed, almost deafening her.

With great difficulty, Mike held up his hand. 'All right, all right, just don't hurt her. You can shoot me, just not her.'

For the first time in almost a month, Torvic smiled from ear to ear. This was what he had dreamed of, planned for. His revenge would be sweet as he savoured their fear and soaked up their pleas before he carried out the ultimate in revenge.

For the vision of what she had made him do to his own son would haunt him for the rest of his life unless he could replace that hideous image with something so much more palatable – their gruesome demise.

Still gripping Zara's hair, Torvic cautiously stepped forward, in case he slipped again on the ice. 'Back up, Mike. Turn around and walk slowly to the lounge. And remember, one false move, and she dies.'

Mike turned around and pushed Ricky into the kitchen. With his back to Torvic, he nudged Ricky, whispering, 'No heroics, boy. Just do as he says.'

Ricky was shaking but not through fear. He was angry, and

it took all his willpower to stay calm and show no expression of rage.

Once they were inside the lounge, Mike and Ricky turned to face Torvic.

Mike felt sick when he saw how one of Zara's eyes was now completely closed, the swelling having mushroomed in size within minutes. Yet she was not like any other woman; she still held that fearless expression and unyielding darkness that emitted from the one eye she had open. He assumed she'd got all her faculties back – she was one hell of a strong woman.

There was silence except for the sound of Mike's blood dripping onto the parquet flooring. The pain had gone; now there was just a throbbing weak feeling emanating from his arm.

Although he looked tired and dishevelled, Torvic hadn't lost that fierce look in his eyes or the evil smirk that made his bottom lip curl at the edges. Both were prominent outside the old wino guise.

'Now the tables have turned, you are gonna feel what it's like to have been in my shoes.'

His sick, demonic tone made Mike shudder. He knew this was going to be his worst nightmare.

'Take a seat, you two. It's gonna be a long day. Ya see, Zara, here, is gonna decide who I kill first, and I'll make her watch, even if I have to staple both her fucking eyes open.'

Mike stepped back, grabbing Ricky's arm.

'I said fucking sit down! Now!' bellowed Torvic.

Mike's heart was beating so fast, it was like nothing he'd ever experienced before. He wasn't afraid of anyone – until now. He looked at the gun – a Kimber 1911 Raptor 11 – and he stared at the magazine. If there was one thing he knew about, it was guns. Mentally, he tried to count the number of gunshots he'd heard before confronting Torvic and of course receiving one in the shoulder. The magazine had the capacity to hold just seven rounds in the magazine, plus one in the chamber ready to fire. If his calculations were right and the magazine was fully loaded then there was just one bullet left. But if he was wrong, then there were two. Either way, there was a serious risk of at least one of them being killed and he prayed it would be him.

'Sit!' demanded Torvic, as he pressed the gun deeper against Zara's head.

Mike immediately sat on the sofa. Ricky followed suit.

Torvic laughed. 'Now we're all nice and cosy, Zara will make her choice.'

Mike froze. *Was he hearing right? Was Torvic saying that he had no more than one round left?* Because if he had three – unlikely – then he could kill all of them ... slowly ... one at a time ... and then get away. But if he only had two rounds – or maybe just the one – his options were severely limited. Someone would survive and kill *him*.

Torvic put his arm around her shoulder and squeezed her as if they were old buddies. 'So, what's it to be, Zara? Who will you stomach watching getting executed, eh?'

'Let them go and just kill me, Torvic,' she pleaded.

He coughed and then laughed, pretending to be choking with shock. 'Oh, dear me, Zara, that's not what I want ... Well, yes, of course, I want you dead, but I want you to witness what I had to do. Ya know what I'm talking about. You remember, you were there.' He raised his voice. 'You dished out the fucking *order*.'

Zara felt the vomit rise to the back of her throat. She looked at Mike, who was bleeding profusely, and who must be in excruciating pain, but there he was, trying to put on a brave face. The man who owned her heart, how could she choose him to die? A tear ran down her cheek. Then she looked at Ricky, the boy who was supposed to be her own, the kid she loved so dearly. His sweet boyish face was so full of kindness and tenderness. She couldn't do it; she just couldn't bear to choose between either of them. It would have to be her. Then she saw the terror in Mike's eyes, as he pleaded with her, knowing what was in her mind. He knew her so well … too well.

She flinched when Torvic hissed in her ear, 'Yeah, that's right, Zara, you made me watch my son scream in agony, and there was nothing, and I mean nothing, I could do about it.'

She felt the tension in his body tighten like an elastic band being stretched.

'Come on, Zara. Who's gonna die? Ricky or Mike? It makes no difference to me. It's all down to you. And I know, my darling, how that choice feels. It eats at you; it rips into your innermost dreaded thoughts and brings them to the surface. It's a feeling as if nothing on earth could ever be worse. And, trust me, when I say you would rather die yourself than have to choose between the two people you love so dearly.'

He was so right. She did want to die herself rather than make that choice. Desperate to do something, she tried to remember everything she'd seen in Torvic's mother's house. She closed her eyes and tried mentally to recap everything, every last detail. The photo of her mother, the letter. That was it, she could take him down memory lane. It would at least bide her a little time, and hopefully, it would be long enough for someone to turn up.

'What does it matter, Torvic? You will kill us all anyway.'

With that evil grin, Torvic looked at Mike. 'You know, Mike, I saw you eyeing up my gun – well, actually, Izzy's gun. I found it taped under a cabinet. I knew the old bastard would have plenty lying around. And, yeah, I'm fully aware that you're an expert, so we both know that I have just the one bullet left, don't we?'

What? Mike couldn't believe it. Torvic had actually done him a massive favour – he'd done the maths for him. So only one bullet left then. That certainly made things easier, although he knew they weren't out of the woods yet. Not by a long stretch.

Avoiding Torvic's gaze, Mike looked at Zara who nodded. She knew he was clued-up about the gun. This one was one of five: the others had been shipped out to the Lanigans a long time ago. Izzy, the ol' git, had obviously decided he would hold back one for himself.

'So, the truth is, Zara, one of your loved ones will live, and one will fucking die, and you will be the decider.'

Zara knew she had to think quickly. She could feel Torvic's body becoming tense and his breathing increase.

'It's a shame, Torvic, you weren't truthful with me. I mean, we could've built an empire. Together, we could've had it all.'

She sensed him hold his breath. 'What the fuck are you on about?'

'Aah, I think you know. And I have known for a very long time. I just didn't know you by your full name. You only told me your name was *Victor*.'

She felt his hands trembling as he fought the tiredness to take in the meaning of what she was saying.

'Stop talking in fucking riddles. You ain't Izzy. You're just his pathetic daughter.'

'Am I, Vic? That's what my mother called you, wasn't it – "Vic". But, am I his daughter? Really, if you believe that then Izzy and my mother lied to you too.'

Mike stared, watching Torvic's face falling, as if he was suddenly experiencing a revelation, but Mike had no idea what she was talking about. However, Zara was an intelligent woman. Whatever she was saying, it was certainly having an effect on the man.

Just as she was about to say more, the sharp, shrill sound of her phone rang.

Torvic froze and waited for it to ring off. 'None of you move,' he said.

Then, Mike's phone began to ring. They waited, but as soon as it stopped ringing, Ricky's phone started.

The continuous ringtones made Torvic sweat, and he began to lose his concentration. Too much was going on: the phones, the strange thoughts, and now Mike's smirk. He could just pull the trigger, but not now; there were too many unanswered questions.

Suddenly, there was silence, and Torvic took a deep breath.

Zara could sense the apprehension and decided to carry on, dragging him away from the idea of firing that gun. 'You know what I'm talking about, don't you? My mother.' She stopped and waited for a response.

'Shut up!'

'Why, Vic? I want answers before you kill me … or could you ever do that? I mean, you had so many chances before, but you never did. I think we both know why, though, don't we?'

'You think you're clever, but you ain't as clever as me. I know your game, and it won't work.'

'I ain't playing a game. I want to know as much as you do. Was my mother telling me the truth about you and her?'

Instantly, she felt his body go rigid. She almost tasted the astonishment in the air.

'So, it's true then, ain't it?'

'I don't know what she told you, but, whatever it was, it makes no difference now. You made me kill my boy!'

Mike and Ricky were now totally perplexed. Mike even wondered for a split second if he really knew her. What was she talking about?

'And how the hell did you think I felt when you killed my mother? I grew up believing that it was some mad Russian guy, when, all along, it was you, the one man who would've only stooped to such a shit level for revenge on Izzy. Is there not a tiny piece of you that can forgive me for what I did?'

Torvic was stunned into silence. It was true he'd killed her mother, all because she didn't want him and she married Izzy. As much as he was trying to focus on the task at hand, he had visions of the day she died. That sad questioning look as she realized he'd poisoned her. He swallowed hard and tried desperately to get the vision out of his mind. 'Shut up!'

Zara knew she was getting to him. 'But you loved her, so before you kill either Ricky or Mike, or even me, I want to know the answers to these very important questions. Why did you have to kill her? And was it truly down to jealousy?'

'No. Shut up, Zara. You don't know what you're talking about!'

'Oh, but I think I do. Tell me, Vic. Did my mother ever tell

443

you the truth or did she just send you packing, claiming she'd made a mistake?'

Suddenly, Isabel's words swirled around in his head as if she were in the room and talking to him. Yet it wasn't her: it was Zara's voice. She sounded so much like her mother. 'I said shut up. She never left me. I left *her.*'

'No, Vic, she said she'd made a mistake and told you that she never wanted to meet you again.' Of course, Zara was guessing her mother's exact words. She was speculating and using the information she'd read in the letter, which she'd found in Torvic's bedroom.

Mike was feeling hot under the collar. Beads of sweat peppered his brow as he prayed she would shut up. He could see that Torvic was getting more and more wound up. Any minute, he would pull that bloody trigger. She was deliberately antagonizing him so he would kill her. He had to stop her.

'Your sons deserved to fucking die!' shouted Mike, trying to distract Torvic's attention away from Zara.

'At least I had sons who were my own flesh and blood.'

Mike was stunned when he noticed how Torvic's face took on a self-satisfied look.

'You, though, Mike Regan, never had a son, did ya?'

Right away, Zara knew what Torvic was saying. She needed to shut him up. Mike could never know the truth. 'You loved my mother, Vic, I know you did, and look at me. I am just like her. We can—'

'Shut it, Zara. I'm talking to Mike.' He smirked at Mike again. 'Ya know what, Mike? You walk around with ya shoulders back as if you're the dog's bollocks. Ya think you have it all: money, respect, and ya son … your treasured boy.' Torvic's high-pitched laugh made them all jump.

Desperate to shut Torvic up, Zara returned to her conversation. 'You have me, Vic. Come on. Izzy may have raised me, but we both know—'

Cutting her off once again, he turned to her with a vicious hiss. 'I'll do a DNA with your blood when you're fucking dead. Now, unless you want me to take a pot-luck shot at either Mike or Ricky, you'll shut your mouth. I'm having my fun.'

'Fun, *fun*? You sick motherfucker, I hate you. I fucking hate your guts.'

Mike was wide-eyed. His girl was definitely losing it big time. He'd never seen her talk like that. She was always so controlled, but now she was like a kid in a school playground, hurling insignificant swear words. With his mind in turmoil, he tried to fathom out why she was behaving in this way. Maybe the blows to her head had sent her loopy. Then the penny dropped: she was acting in desperation, trying to shut Torvic up.

'What are you saying, Torvic?'

'Aahh, you want to know what I have to say, do you?'

Mike nodded.

'No!' yelled Zara.

But Torvic was grinning. He intended to savour this moment forever.

'As I was saying, Mike, you thought you had it all, but you didn't. Your brother …' He laughed. 'Eric took you for a right fool. He worked for me. I bet you didn't know *that*.'

Mike nodded again. 'Is that the best you can do, Torvic? Because that doesn't surprise me. I had an inkling.'

With his face deflated, Torvic shot his jaw forward in anger and the words flew out like bullets. 'Well, I bet you didn't know he was fucking your wife, did ya? And as for your precious boy, well, he ain't yours. He was Eric's son!'

The room fell deathly silent. Zara's shoulders slumped, feeling overwhelmingly gutted. She simply couldn't look at Mike or even bear to see the pain on his face.

Mike gripped Ricky's arm, squeezing it tight to let him know he loved him.

The silence was broken when Mike replied in a slow voice, 'Blood or not, Ricky is my boy. He always was and always will be.'

Torvic realized just then that Mike wouldn't be hopping mad; he was far too self-controlled. 'So, Zara, now you know the truth, who is it to be? Is it the bastard or Mike?'

Zara slowly turned to face Torvic. His gun was now pointed at her face.

'Don't move, Zara, or I'll kill you. All I need is one excuse, and that'll cost you your life, because, right now, I don't care. My Tiffany is dead, my boys are dead, and—'

'But you have me though, Vic, don't you? *I'm your daughter.* It's an undeniable fact.'

At last, Torvic was distracted, and Ricky knew he was fast. He'd been trained well by the gypsies. Not that he was proud of that, but he knew what he was capable of. He also had something on him that Torvic was unaware of.

The shock of what Zara had just said was written across Torvic's face. It caused him to stumble back. As soon as he did, Ricky leaped up from his chair and into the air. He could jump high. He'd had enough practice.

Partially stunned, Torvic's reaction was delayed, but his thumb was heavily on the trigger, and, in an instant, he fired.

The leap in the air saved the bullet from passing straight into Ricky's head. Instead, it blasted him in the chest, knocking him back onto the sofa. In utter shock and disbelief, Mike threw himself on top of Ricky, screaming in grief.

Zara assumed Torvic hadn't been bullshitting them about how many rounds were in the magazine so the gun was only as good as a dead weight. She pulled her head back, and with one almighty crack, she headbutted Torvic in the temple and then kicked him hard in the groin. He tried to fight, but it was no use. He was an old man now, and she was a martial arts expert. Each deliberate blow was proving to have an effect, and the savagery of her assault meant he was unable to take care of himself, let alone take control of her. As he fell to the floor, Zara kicked and kicked until she was almost out of breath. 'You stinking fucking vermin. Die, you bastard, *die*.'

Mike was suddenly dumbfounded when Ricky pushed him off. 'Dad ... I'm ... okay.'

Mike looked at his son's chest. There was no blood, yet he'd seen the gun being fired and Ricky catapult onto the sofa. On impulse, he pulled the jumper up over his son's chest and stared at the black jacket underneath. Yanking it up, he saw the enormous red swelling.

Mike wanted to cry with ecstasy. He struggled up from his seat and did his best to hurry over to see to Zara, whose face was now splattered with blood. But Torvic was in a far worse state: his head was a bloodied mess – his body virtually lifeless.

'Christ, I thought we were gonna die.' He half laughed, pulling Zara away.

A noise from the kitchen made them all freeze to the spot and listen. They heard footsteps, and before Zara had a chance to grab her own gun, there, in the doorway, wielding another serious tool, was Detective Inspector Simon Lowry.

Mike's and Zara's shoulders relaxed. 'Fuck me! You should've got here sooner. He nearly killed us,' said Mike, as he wiped the sweat from his brow. He glanced over at Torvic, who was moaning on the floor.

Zara stared questioningly at the detective, who still had his weapon held in front of him. 'It's okay. There's just him and us.' She pointed to Torvic.

'Good. Now, I want you to stand back, away from him.'

Mike's eyes widened. 'Hey? What the fuck's going on?'

Torvic coughed up more blood from his mouth. 'You took ya fucking time, Striker.'

'What!' screeched Zara. 'But you're a … I mean, how do you know …?' As if someone had turned a light on, she stared at the detective with incredulity. It was *him*, the other lad in the photo, standing next to Torvic.

'Stand away from him!' ordered Lowry, 'or I'll have you all nicked for attempted murder.'

Zara's phone rang again. As she began to move, Lowry stopped her in her tracks. 'Leave it!' he demanded, as he flicked his gun for her to get back from the device.

Mike reached for her hand and gently drew her back, not taking his eyes away from Lowry. 'So, you know Torvic?'

Lowry smiled. 'I warned Stoneham not to take on you lot. Everything would have been fine if you'd just kept your noses out of our business. But no, he wouldn't listen. You see, Regan, no one will rid the streets of drugs because it's what the kids want today, and far be it for me to stop them. I was a copper for years, slogging my guts out, trying to nick any scallywag for breaking the law, and you know what I discovered? It makes no fucking difference. D'ya get it, Regan?' He didn't wait for a response before he carried on. 'Putting in all the hard work, I was just laughed at by the next dealer, robber, mugger, or any other shitbag who thought themselves above the law. There they were, driving around in their flash motors, living in their flash drums, and eating in fucking flash restaurants. And, what was worse, they were flaunting their money right under my fucking nose. You can imagine how soul-destroying that really was at the time, so you should actually see me as not a bent copper but as a man like yourself. Far cleverer, though, wouldn't you say?'

Mike couldn't believe how different Lowry's persona was outside the police station. This cocksure bastard was nothing like the fat, dopey, lazy detective he always thought he was. It seemed as though Lowry had been given a personality transplant overnight.

The phone rang again but no one uttered a word until it stopped.

'Do you know something, Regan? I fucking can't stand you. You really thought you were so hard, even talking down to me, but look at you now. You're not that tough now, eh?'

Torvic moved, trying to get up. He moaned and attempted to talk, but Zara had well and truly battered him.

Annoyed, Lowry huffed, 'For fuck's sake, Vic. Did you find Colin?'

Torvic shook his head and spat out a mouthful of blood. 'Nah.'

'Where's Colin?' asked Lowry, glaring at Mike.

Mike tried to shrug his shoulders and realized only one shoulder would move; the other was obviously shattered inside from the gunshot wound.

'Liar! Where is he?'

'Who's Colin?' asked Zara.

Lowry's eyes slid from side to side, quickly surveying his surroundings. 'Don't play games. You know who I'm talking about.'

Zara's lips turned down as she shrugged. 'No. I've no idea who you mean.'

Lowry felt uneasy, uncomfortable that his notion of Regan capturing Colin was merely that – a notion. His mission was to find Colin, kill Regan, and then get his lucrative business back on track. He glanced down at the state of Torvic. For a moment, he wondered what the hell he was going to do. Torvic had fucked up, by doing what he did best – teasing and torturing his victims before he killed them. However, he could see that this time his little plan had failed, and now it was left to him to pick up the pieces. It would usually be Stephan or Alastair, not himself, who would do the heavy lifting. He wanted to kick Torvic for being such an idiot, but he didn't have the time to start having a row. He had to get this mess cleaned up and quickly before whoever it was who was calling the house decided to turn up.

With Torvic incapacitated – as useless as a knitted condom – all he had was himself to take control.

Again, the phone rang, and it was joined by Mike's; as before, the noise was distracting.

Zara suddenly became aware of another movement inside

the house. She knew every creak in the old mansion; someone else was inside.

'Get back against the wall,' ordered Lowry, now beginning to sense something was awry.

Mike gripped Zara's hand and glanced at his son, who was still seated on the sofa. He prayed that Ricky wouldn't pull the same stunt, in case this time it didn't work. But then he came to the conclusion that his son was in no position to do anything. The swelling he'd seen when he'd lifted the flak jacket told him that some of Ricky's ribs were broken.

Lowry's light-blue shirt, peeping through his jacket, was wet with sweat; it was obvious to everyone that he was nervous, and his eyes, flicking around, showed he was on edge. 'Get up, Vic.'

Torvic was fucked, but he tried to get onto his hands and knees.

'I said, get up, will ya, for fuck's sake.'

Zara looked behind Lowry to see a shadow cast from the hallway light, which was permanently on. She knew then that someone else was present.

Lowry clocked her looking behind him, and in his nervous state, he stupidly did the same. That's when Zara spotted the red laser light appear on Lowry's head. *Who else was here?* she wondered. She realized what was about to happen and held her breath. As soon as Lowry turned his head back to face them a sound like a whistle went off. In a split second, Lowry hit the floor next to Torvic, who wasn't slow to react. He may have been badly beaten up, but he still had the wherewithal to grab Lowry's gun.

But he wasn't quick enough. From nowhere, a man, dressed

entirely in black, entered the room and shot him cleanly in the head – twice.

For the first time in his life, Mike was wholly stunned. All he could do was stand and stare.

The man dressed in black combat trousers, a padded black jacket, and a balaclava covering his entire face, grabbed both the dead bodies by their collars and dragged them to the front door.

Mike was about to follow, but Zara pulled him back. 'No, Mike, don't.'

'But, who the fuck? I mean, what's going on?'

'Mike, just stay here with Ricky and me, okay?'

Mike looked at his son, who was washed out. 'Are you all right, my boy?'

Ricky slowly nodded. 'Me chest hurts but at least I ain't dead.'

Zara sat next to him. 'Sorry, Ricky, I should've told you when I gave you Izzy's jacket, that it will stop a bullet penetrating, but, fuck me, it does hurt. You'll be fine in a few weeks, darling.'

Ricky knew then that she'd been shot at some time in the past. His eyes lowered in sadness. What had Zara really endured in her life? He wondered if she'd been through far worse than she'd let on. Perhaps that explained their close bond.

They listened as the front door opened and closed. Zara got up and looked out of the window to see a black van making its way down the drive.

'What the hell was all that about? Who were they? Jesus! It was like a fucking James Bond film.'

She smiled. 'That's "The Machine".'

Mike's eyes nearly popped out of his head. 'What? As in Lance Ryder?'

She nodded. 'It all makes perfect sense now. Lance was after the big fish. Lowry was the one he was after. I gave Lance an old listening device that I thought belonged to Torvic and he recognized it, I guess, from his line of work. It must have been one issued by the police and no doubt planted by Torvic but given to him by Lowry. Torvic was a sideshow as far as Lance was concerned. He helped us out only because Torvic killed his daughter, but it was never about him. It was always about the top guy. Lance told me to stay safe – always. That's why I gave Ricky my father's flak jacket.'

Tears welled up in Mike's eyes. 'You wanted to protect my son even though you knew you would've been the target?'

Zara smiled. 'You got that slightly wrong, Mike. He's *our* son, Mike, our son.'

Ricky chuckled. 'And that prick really thought I was Eric's son. Jeez, what a dick.'

Zara thought her heart was about to stop functioning. 'You didn't believe Torvic, did you?'

Mike heard the hesitancy in her voice. 'No, and I won't ask why you thought it. Whatever the reason, it's all in the past.'

Zara swallowed hard. Perhaps Mike had guessed the truth – that Jackie had told her and that's why she'd killed her. 'Yes, it's all in the past. Ricky is your boy.'

Mike pulled up his sleeve and pointed to the tattoo that read 'RICKY MY BOY'. 'Do you know why I had that tattoo done?'

Ricky was smiling, but Zara, confused now, shook her head.

'I knew about Eric and Jackie. That's why sometimes I was

hard on him, and when my boy was born I wondered. Not that it would've made any difference. When Ricky was five, I decided to have a DNA test done, just to put my mind at rest.'

Astonished but relieved at the revelation, she gasped in surprise.

Ricky joined in. 'I remember it well. You took me out for dinner that day, didn't ya? And you showed me the tattoo. I remember. I ran my hands over it, thinking how sore it must have been. But most of all, I remember Dad saying that no matter whatever happens, or whatever's said in the future, he had a letter that stated I was his son. I never knew it was a DNA test, I was too young, but I remember feeling proud that he was my dad.'

Mike ruffled his son's head as he'd always done.

'Jackie made me believe my dad was dead, and my memories were fading fast, but ...' He was choked up and had to pause for a second. 'But that day in the prison when I was being held at knifepoint and this big man lifted his sleeve and showed me that tattoo, everything came flooding back. I knew he was my dad, so, just now, I didn't believe anything Torvic said.'

The phone rang again, pulling them out of this poignant moment. Zara smiled gracefully, indicating that she should take the call. As soon as she answered, the voice on the other end brought her back down to earth.

'Zara, listen. We're on our way.' Neil's Irish accent was unmistakable. 'Torvic isn't dead. Get out of the house, Zara!'

'Neil, it's fine. He's definitely dead now. I watched his demise with my own eyes this time.'

Neil slowed his car down from 140 miles per hour to 80. 'Are you sure he's dead? 'Cos that fecking monster seems to have a way of coming back from the grave.'

She laughed. 'Oh, he's definitely dead, and so is Lowry. He was in on it all the time. Where are you?'

'On my way to yours. Your cousin Josh tried to call you and then he called me. He saw Torvic driving his own fecking car towards your home. I thought when no one answered the phone, he'd killed you. Jesus, you had me fecking worried there.'

Zara looked up at the large painting of her father. 'Not in my house, he wouldn't have.'

As Mike helped Ricky to remove the flak jacket, Zara left the room to get cleaned up. She walked up the stairs, past her bedroom, and stopped at her mother's room. She stared at the bed and imagined her mother sitting up and smiling at her. A tear appeared and plummeted down her cheek as she whispered under her breath, 'Sorry, Mum. I just had to pretend that he was my father, but only for a minute.' She looked down at her bloodied hands. 'I hope, Mum, that you and Dad will now rest in peace.'

She didn't hear Mike behind her. 'Who are you talking to?'

'Oh, just ghosts, I guess.'

He gently slid his arms around her waist. 'Um, Zara, Izzy *was* your farver, wasn't he?'

She smiled with her eyes. 'Of course he was. Where else do you think I got my eyes from?'

He stared for a while and watched the colours change from amber to dark brown, like swirls of tiger's-eye. How could he have even questioned it? In that respect, Zara and Izzy really were alike.

Chapter 24

Two weeks later

Shelley kneeled by her son's bed; his face was grey, his cheeks were sunken, and scabby sores covered his lips. She stroked his hair and allowed more tears to flow.

'Come on, Shell, leave him alone. The doctor's on his way,' said Nicolas, with a touch of compassion. It wasn't for Lucas but for Shelley. She had been his love for many years, and, as thick as she was, she doted on that nasty child of hers.

'We should've taken him to A&E,' she said, sobbing. 'I bet that fight with his no-good bastard brother caused this fucking setback.'

'But, Shell, love, we couldn't do that. You, me, and Lucas would've been locked up. The only quack that can see to him, as well you know, is that Dr Bourne fella.'

She sniffed back the tears. 'I suppose you're right. How long will he be? Because I really don't think Lucas will last much longer. I mean, I just don't understand what's going on. He was taking his meds, so why is he so ill?'

Nicolas took her downstairs and led her into the kitchen. 'Sit there, babe. Let me make you a cup of tea. I don't know what's wrong with him. Perhaps his body has rejected the kidney. I mean, are you sure he's even Willie's son?'

Shelley threw him a spiteful glare. 'Of course he is, and they did all the tests before the operation.'

Nicolas poured the tea and sighed. 'Babe, these transplants don't always work, ya know.'

Shelley ran her hands through her hair and then wiped her tear-stained cheeks. 'For fuck's sake, I just wish that doctor would hurry up. The plane landed four hours ago. It ain't that far from Gatwick. He should be here by now.'

Nicolas felt for Shelley because he knew damn well that Dr Bourne wasn't going to arrive, and if he did, it would no doubt be in black plastic bags.

'He did say he would pop home first to collect his medical bag.'

'We should've taken Lucas to his house then and met him there. Fucking 'ell, I wish I hadn't gone away on holiday and left him alone.' She glared up at Nicolas. 'You should've taken proper care of him.'

Nicolas sighed. 'Shell, let's get things straight, yeah? We ain't together anymore, he ain't me fucking son, so don't go on at me. All this ain't my fault. And another thing. You extending your stay here don't mean that me and you will get back together.'

Shelley wiped her nose on the back of her left sleeve and sipped the tea that Nicolas had put in front of her.

'When Lucas is better, I'm off anyway to Spain. I've got a business to run. Oh yeah, I tried to draw some cash out from the machine, and all I got was a "card declined" message.'

Nicolas turned his back on her.

'Nick, why would my card be declined?'

Biting his lip, Nicolas wondered if now was the right time to tell her about the legal papers she had signed. He took a deep breath before he said quietly, 'Listen, Shell, there *isn't* any money.'

'What!' she gasped, as she lurched to her feet. 'What the fuck d'ya mean there isn't any money?' She tugged on his arm. 'Answer me!'

Reluctantly, Nicolas turned to face her, the confused look turning to deep anger in her eyes. At that point, every ounce of sorrow he'd felt for her dissipated into thin air. He hated that expression and the selfish, cold side to her.

'The deeds to the Spanish development you signed weren't really worth much and certainly won't be bringing you in any money.'

Her eyes widened in disbelief. 'What the fuck! Have they done me over? 'Cos I swear to God, I'll have 'em all behind fucking bars. They won't get away with this!'

Nicolas watched as her eyes turned dark and her face flushed bright red.

'You can't do that either, Shelley, because, my sweetheart, you'll be behind bars with them. Remember, you signed a confession.'

Her eyes flicked from left to right as she tried to comprehend what had taken place; it was a complete piss-take.

'What the fuck *have* I inherited, Nicolas?'

Uneasily, he shifted from foot to foot, because he knew that once she read the papers, she would go ballistic. Yet there was nothing she could do about it. His reluctance to answer Shelley sent her tearing from the kitchen into the lounge where the legal documents were. With her hands trembling, she frantically trawled through the papers.

Shivers were running up and down her spine as she looked at the other documents, and, specifically, the deeds to the property in Spain. She glared at the picture of the waste ground and the stamp across it that said: 'Permission for development declined'. Shocked, Shelley felt her legs buckle. She had been well and truly fucked. She looked at Nicolas standing there in the doorway. 'You bastard, you fucking bastard!'

'Shelley, you did some shit things, and I didn't deserve it. I loved you. I took you and your kid on. You wanted for nuffin. I threw you out because all you cared about was that kid. I gave you half, more than you should've got. You bought a grand house, and yet that still wasn't enough, was it? You had me brother nearly killed and my house put into your fucking name. So, Shelley, you're the bastard, not me. Now, my lovely, you've no choice but to keep ya fat gob shut, or you'll be inside for a very long time, and trust me, babe, they don't have boutiques, hair salons, and spa baths in the fucking nick.'

She sat down on the sofa before she fell down. The reality hit her like a brick around the head: yes, she'd been well and truly fucked over. All she had was her house, and no doubt her father was buried somewhere in the back garden. A sneaky grin curled her lip. 'And this place, Nicolas? Is this still in my name?'

The audacity of the woman had Nicolas's eyes twitching. 'No, it fucking ain't, you cheeky bitch. You signed that back over to me. And, Shelley, it's all above fucking board. Brandon Miles is one of the best lawyers this side of the country, so fuck you, ya money-grabbing, emotionless cunt.'

Raff sat nervously next to Willie; he'd never seen a man look so incensed. 'Willie, don't get too close up his arse, mate. He'll have a reason to look in the fucking rear-view mirror.'

The high-pitched chuckle leaving Willie's mouth made Raff jump.

'Don't fucking worry about that, me ol' son. He'll see my fucking face soon enough, and I'll make sure it's the last fucking boat race he ever sees. You're sure it's him, though, ain't ya? I'd hate to do over the wrong fella.'

'I wouldn't mistake that pompous prick. Oh, it's definitely him all right.' Raff sighed and shook his head. 'I can't believe I ever got involved, and I promise you, Willie, if I'd 'ave known it was your kid or the fact that they were gonna kill him, I never would've got involved. I tried to talk Colin out of it, ya know.'

Willie slowed down, dropping off from Dr Bourne's Maserati. 'Did ya?'

'Yeah, I did, but he was adamant that he would go through with it. I know he still loved Shelley because he knew the truth. What really killed his wife wasn't Shelley shacking up with Nicolas, it was Colin fucking every tart in sight. When she found out about his PA, she made a decision not to start her chemotherapy. I reckon he had to blame someone, and Colin being Colin, he'd hardly lay the blame at his own feet. Anyway, mate, I did try.'

Willie unexpectedly took his hand from the steering wheel and put it around Raff's shoulders and pulled him close. It told Raff that he was forgiven.

'Raff, mate, you've done good since, and I know Mikey wants you on the firm, but ya know what it takes, so be prepared to get ya hands dirty, starting with that poncey prick in front.'

As they followed the Maserati, they noticed how the properties in the country lanes were getting larger. Long drives, huge conifers, and grand mansions were prominent.

Tired from his early start, followed by the uncomfortable last-minute flight, Dr Bourne didn't notice the Mercedes behind him until he pulled into the drive. As soon as he stepped out of the car, he glanced back to find two men standing there and smiling at him.

'Can I help you?'

Raff had his sunglasses on and a beanie hat; it looked so wrong on every level. However, it was enough for Dr Bourne not to recognize him.

Willie calmly walked over to him with what looked like a leather holdall. 'Yeah, Doc, you can. Go inside and we can talk.'

Raff kept behind Willie, trying to hide his face before Dr Bourne realized who he was.

'Look, I'm sorry, but who are you and what do you want?'

His sharp tone pissed Willie off. 'Just go inside, will ya?'

The doctor shoved his nose in the air. 'No, I won't. In fact, if you do not leave my property now, I will call the police.'

Willie laughed. 'Oh yeah? Good, 'cos I think the police will have a fucking field day with you.'

'What? What do you mean …?' His voice faltered as soon as he thought he recognized the deranged-looking man.

Willie wasn't interested in having a conversation with this

stuck-up prick on the front drive of his mansion. He gripped his face, pushing him against the door. 'Now, listen to me. You'll fucking open that door because me and you 'ave some business that needs taking care of, don't we, *Dr Bourne?*' He let the doctor go and then pulled his gun from his pocket and pushed it under the doctor's chin. 'I think you'll wanna open that door now, won't ya?'

Dr Bourne's eyes bulged as he held his breath. He knew there and then that he had to open the door and let them in because the wild-looking man had 'fearless' written all over his face.

His hands shook as he tried to find the right key.

'Move it!' Willie urged.

Fumbling and shaking, Dr Bourne finally managed to enter the house. Willie pushed him in and looked around. The hallway was grand and every inch was immaculate. *The marble floors, the spotless paintwork, it was such a pity*, thought Willie. He grinned to himself. He knew it wouldn't look like this for much longer.

Waving his gun, he gestured for the doctor to go into the dining room. Although the room had the same marble floors and pristine white walls, it looked nothing like as finished off as the entrance to the house. Just a large dining table and eight chairs comprised the total contents. Willie could only imagine the mess to the place when he'd finished.

'What do you want?' asked Bourne, less confident now.

Willie was grinning like a sick nutcase. 'Your fucking kidney, mate, seeing that ya took me boy's and ...' – he jumped forward and spat in Bourne's face – 'ya left him to fucking *die!*'

Bourne felt his stomach churning and his bowels moving,

yet he didn't feel the warm liquid run down his leg until he heard it drip onto the floor. He looked at Raff, hoping for any kind of help, praying that the big guy with the olive skin was in charge of the raving lunatic. However, all he saw was mirrored sunglasses that reflected himself.

'Look, please, I can give you money.' He knew he couldn't deny what he'd done. He'd previously just hoped that the kid hadn't recognized him. He hadn't considered the man at the hospital – this giant – who was obviously the boy's father.

'Money!' screamed Willie.

Bourne nodded. 'Yes. I'll offer you a lot of money in compensation.'

Willie was on edge and jumping about all over the room. Cocaine always fuelled his appetite for violence, and he was pumped up now, ready to do some serious damage. He wanted to hear the man scream.

Surmising what was about to happen, Bourne tried in desperation to make a run for it, while the nutcase was delving into his holdall. But he hadn't noticed the chunky guy's hand gripping a metal bar, and as he shot past, trying to make his way to the front door, a hard whack to the back of his head knocked him completely off his feet.

Willie shook his head in disappointment. 'Raff, I wanted that cunt awake when I started on him. Shit, never mind, I'm sure he'll wake up soon.'

Raff looked at the axe in Willie's hands and suddenly felt light-headed. *Surely not*, he thought. Taking a massive intake of air, he looked away.

Dr Bourne was out cold with a nasty gash in the back of his head. Lucky for him, he didn't see the terrifying vision as that axe came down and instantly chopped straight through his right wrist.

As Willie lifted the shaft high above his head for a second time, the doctor stirred and his eyes opened. Seconds later, as the axe came down again, severing his other hand, he felt the most excruciating pain. Holding up his two mutilated wrists, he screamed in terror.

'Now, you'll never operate again, you no-good cunt!' shouted Willie.

Willie took pleasure in watching the man writhe around in disbelief and pain.

Gasping and screaming in utter terror, Bourne just couldn't comprehend that his hands were missing. 'Jesus, Jesus!' he screeched, as he watched the blood shooting out like water pistols from his two stumps.

Willie stood up straight, stared down at the man, and smiled. 'Oh, fuck it, the show's over.' With that, he held the axe above his head, and with all his immense strength, he swung it and completely beheaded Bourne. Moments later, the twitching stopped.

Raff threw up instantly. Bent over and gagging, he tried to catch his breath.

Willie, however, was as cool as a cucumber, just staring at his final deed. 'No one hurts my boy and lives to tell the tale.' He stared at the severed head. 'He was an ugly fucking bastard, anyway.'

Once Raff had caught his breath, wiped his mouth, and straightened himself up, he looked at Willie. 'Are we done now?'

'Nearly, mate. We've just gotta clean up.'

Raff looked at the blood everywhere. 'Fuck, I hate cleaning up blood. Anyway, I guess we've got all day, assuming we don't get any visitors to turn away.'

Willie smiled. 'If my info is correct, mate, we've got forever. From what Kirsten the nurse told me, he only pops back once every couple of months. He's got no kids, no missus. He's just a lonely money-grabbing cunt.' He looked around and shook his head. 'Colin only had to ask Liam if he would donate his kidney, but, no, the sly bastard didn't think for one minute that Liam would say yes.'

Raff frowned. 'Oh, come on, Willie. If Liam had said no, then you would've known right away what had happened to him. And who would've been responsible? You see, Colin believed everyone was like himself.'

'Well, he was wrong, because my boy said he would've given his brother a kidney if he'd only asked.'

* * *

Shelley paced the floor, watching out of the window for the doctor to arrive. 'Aw, for fuck's sake, where is he?' she muttered to no one.

Nicolas appeared and stared at the woman he once loved but not anymore. Yet he did feel some sadness for her. 'Shell, love, listen: it's too late.'

She spun around, with her head inclined. 'What? … No! He can't be!' she screamed, as she ran past him and flew up the stairs.

Nicolas listened to the screams and then the apparent silence. He guessed she was sobbing. He wouldn't interfere now: this was her grief, not his.

466

Chapter 25

A year later

Mike was fidgeting in his suit.

Gloria gave him a nudge. 'Stop it, will ya? Stand still, for Gawd's sake. That lovely girl will be walking down the aisle soon. You men have no patience. The drinks will be flowing the minute this is over.' She looked around, and the other men, including her own husband, looked bored. She, however, had her tissues at the ready.

Willie was the only man not so restless. He decided today was not one for snorting cocaine. He'd even had his hair cut and a proper barber's shave with a cut-throat razor. By his side was Kirsten, the English nurse, who had risked her life for his son. He had carried out his promise and made sure she was set up in a nice flat, conveniently nearby his own house. Despite his scary appearance and wild ways, Kirsten soon realized that, along with those closest to him, she was one of the lucky ones to see the soft and loving side of Willie.

Ricky and Arty stood side by side, both as tall as each other and just as muscular. Mike peered at his son and smiled with pride. His boy, handsome and smart, was dressed in his best suit, alongside a young, pretty girl, a friend of the twins, there on his arm.

Arty had Brooke glued to his hip. She was hanging onto him as if her life depended on it, yet Arty remained still and reserved with his hair immaculately gelled back.

Then Mike glanced at Liam, and an unexpected tear filled his eye when he thought back to the day they'd all believed he was dead. There he stood, with his face beaming and his cheeks glowing. Mike had to blink because, for all the years they'd joked about his looks, today they'd been transformed. Maybe it was the new-found confidence in him. Who knew? But one thing he was sure of: Liam was a diamond.

The registrar stood behind the table in the grand registry office and announced the congregation to be upstanding for the bride. As Mike looked around, he wondered if there was a dry eye in the house. Staffie was rubbing his nose and wiping his face. Mike knew he'd been crying. Lou shuffled from foot to foot, obviously emotional, and Gloria had her handkerchief in her hand.

The music played Michael Bublé's 'Close Your Eyes', and then the real snivels began.

As Mike turned to see Poppy in her beautiful princess wedding dress, he felt a lump in his throat. She looked stunning, breathtaking in fact. He nodded to her father who was positively beaming.

Then he felt Zara sniff. As he peered down, she clung to his arm. 'Aah, Mikey, don't she look lovely? And Liam. What a proud boy he is.'

As Poppy passed her bouquet to Brooke, she turned, and a tear left her eye. Liam was the man she'd fallen in love with the moment she'd laid eyes on him, and with their little one on the way, she was thrilled to be walking up the aisle with her father – her real father, Lance – by her side. With their money, the wedding was booked and paid for with no expense spared.

Brooke walked back to Arty, clutching the bouquet. 'That'll be us one day soon, Arty,' she whispered.

A sudden look of horror spread across his face. 'What? Are you expecting an' all?'

She giggled. 'No! I meant getting married.'

Arty rolled his eyes. 'Yeah, babe, but not just yet, eh? Maybe in five years.'

'Two.' She nudged him.

'Three and we have a deal.'

The claps and whistles as Liam and Poppy said the words 'I do' were almost deafening.

'I'll tell ya what, Zara,' Mike whispered to her. 'She looks stunning, but I have to say you were still the best bride I've ever seen.'

Zara cuddled into his arm. 'You're just biased, Mikey Regan.'

'No, I'm not, Mrs Regan.'

As everyone began to leave the room and head for the reception, Mike pulled Zara away from the crowds. 'I saw your face, Zara, when you watched Lance walk Poppy up that aisle, and I know you were gutted when we got married that it was my dad who accompanied you and not Izzy. Look, I just wanna say, he would be so proud of you. Like I am, you know the day Torvic ...'

'Don't talk about him, Mikey. It's all over now.'

'No, please, listen. He forced you to make a choice: either me or Ricky to die, but you couldn't choose, could you? You would've sacrificed your own life for us.'

Tears filled her eyes and tumbled down her cheeks. 'I know, but, please, we're all safe now, and, well, I don't want to think about it anymore.'

'Zara' – he cupped her cheeks as he always did with so much tenderness – 'I hear you in your sleep. It haunts you.'

She held his wrist and kissed his hand. 'It's still my worst nightmare, but, hopefully, I'll get over it. It's finished now. We'll carry on with business and …'

Mike shook his head. 'No, no more, Zara. The lads and I have agreed: it's time to retire.'

'But …'

He tapped her nose. 'No buts, babe. We don't need the worry anymore. We've enough money to live a life of luxury. World cruises – you name them – we can afford as many as you like. I always thought that it was in my blood and in yours to be a villain. Well, no more. I never want you or Ricky to be in that position again. And, let's face it, we've no need to be.'

He looked at the guests, all excited and laughing, making their way to the reception party. 'Look! That's what life's about now.'

She looked on and saw Ricky with his arm around his new girlfriend, his whole body moving up and down, laughing at something she'd said.

'You're right, Mikey. I've proved my worth, and I'm not going to do anything that would ever put us in that position again.' She looked up and smiled. 'And, yeah, my dad would be so proud.' She chuckled, as her face blushed. 'And he would be so proud of you too, Mike. He knew one day we would be married, and he knew the only person he could trust with my life was you. He was right.'

'Remember, Zara, when your dad, all those years ago, made me make a choice? To work for him and you or …?'

She nodded. 'He was a persuasive man. I'm glad you chose the first option.'

'Me too, my babe, me too.'

Acknowledgements

Robert Wood, my editor, who never lets me down.

My good friend, Deryl Easton, and all the members of the NotRights book club for all your encouragement and support.

A huge thank you to all the readers. You give me a reason to write and the will to do my best.

Turn the page for an extract from Kerry
Barnes' gripping crime thriller, *The Hunted*...

'Riveting'
Anna Smith

'A gripping read'
Dreda Say Mitchell

She's playing them
at their own game...

THE HUNTED
Kerry
Barnes

PROLOGUE

South London, 1968

A lamp cast its soft glow onto a round table positioned in the middle of the room. The closed, heavy red drapes gave the room a daunting – almost eerie – feel, as if the assembled group was about to engage in a séance.

Dread twisted around Ronnie's stomach. For a moment, he didn't want to speak, so afraid his words would come out as just a mere squeak, and that he would look less than a worthy man. The eyes that glared back at him were narrow and beady, silently interrogating him, or perhaps posed to intimidate. Either way, he was now in the lion's den, entirely at their mercy.

Was his fiancée really worth it? Her beautiful face and long shapely legs popped into his head – yes, she definitely was. So, he had either to prove his worth or be fucked off by her brother and his close allies. Until now, he hadn't quite grasped the power of these collective Jewish men. Sensing the intense atmosphere that pervaded the room, he knew they were more than just unassuming businessmen.

He presumed this first meeting would be a case of proving himself. After all, he was going to marry their queen, their worshipped sister. Now, he surmised that this meeting wasn't all about giving him the rundown on how to treat his wife-to-be. It was more than that – something much more profound, almost cultlike.

The way in which they sat side by side with their hands clasped on the table symbolizing an unspoken bond between them, did it mean more than honour among family? After all, the two men who were scrutinizing him weren't brothers by blood, they were brothers in a different sense. He suspected that they were united by a pledge.

Ronnie could feel that they were going to initiate him into something – whatever it was he would soon find out.

The silence, which was perhaps a mere few seconds, seemed to linger. They were sussing him out, trying to read his thoughts.

He almost jumped when the taller of the two men, his future brother-in-law, spoke. 'I understand you are a man who wants to earn money …' He paused and glared, waiting for affirmation by a nod or a yes.

Ronnie twisted his head slightly, questioning their statement.

'We have a common enemy,' the speaker continued.

Ronnie raised his brow and waited, hoping he would get to the point.

'Arthur Regan!' He hissed the name through gritted teeth.

Ronnie's eyes widened. Yes, it was true: he and his brother Frank hated the Regan crew; in fact, they loathed them with a passion.

Arthur Regan was only nineteen and had already taken charge of all the knocked-off gear that entered Bermondsey.

His little empire was strong-handed and growing fast. They may be just out of nappies, but they were taking over the manor and earning good money.

The business that had once been run by the Harman family had now been taken from under his nose just because the Regans had more muscle, and, worse, more front. The dealers, the robbers, and the pretty women were all being drawn in by Arthur's success.

So what was he left with? Fuck all, that's what.

He nodded and remained silent.

'You are aware, I trust, that when you marry my sister, you and your brother become an integral part of our family? With that comes accountability!'

Ronnie frowned. 'Of course, but what's that got to do with Arthur Regan?' With the menacing expression staring back at him, he wondered if he should have been a little less direct.

Ronnie watched in fascination as both men looked at each other and silently rolled up their sleeves to show a mark on their right wrist.

Still oblivious, Ronnie shrugged. Again, he wondered if his body language was really doing him any favours. 'Sorry. Am I missing something?'

'You have a reason to take out the Regans' firm. Although it may be very different from ours, it amounts to the same thing. We want Arthur Regan and his men hunted down for the scum they are. His home, his business, his family, and his fucking name will be ripped away, piece by fucking piece. That bastard and his followers shouldn't be walking the streets, making money, or even breathing the same air as us. So, if you want to marry my sister and enter our family, you must agree to be on our side, no matter what it takes to ensure their pathetic lives and those of their children are tortured and tormented until they are living like worms under a rock!'

A million thoughts tumbled over themselves as Ronnie tried to digest what the Jew was saying. Then, once again, his words were direct. 'What have they done to you?'

'Those cunts killed my brother, my beloved sister's twin.' The tall Jewish man looked to his left at the man seated beside him. 'And they killed his brother too.'

Ronnie glanced at the shorter man. A sudden shiver ran through his body, and for a second, he thought he was staring at the Devil himself. Portrayed in those dark, expressionless eyes and lopsided grin was a cruel streak.

Leaning back in his chair, Ronnie grinned. This was it. He didn't have to consider pledging himself to this pact, cult, or whatever the fuck it was. He was in. The Jews had money and a tight, nasty firm, and he had the prize bride. He had a gripe with the Regans, and so what better way to take over the manor than to do so with the help of a bunch of wealthy psycho Jews? Even better, he would take back what he believed was rightfully his.

He gazed down once more at the strange marks on their wrists and was startled by a rustling sound from across the room. He could just make out a brooding figure in the shadows. Something in his hand gleamed from the soft light of the lamp. In a sudden rush of panic, Ronnie's forehead formed beads of sweat and his mouth became as dry as a horse's salt lick. As the daunting man approached the table, the side lamp shone a light on the tool he had in his hand. Ronnie's heart rate levelled as soon as he realized it was only a tattoo gun.

Chapter 1

Kent, 2002

The summer evening was drawing to a close. Mike could just soak up the last of the pink shimmer in the sky before he would have to face the cold, hard-faced bitch he called his wife. As he stepped out of his Porsche and felt his feet crunch under the newly laid gravel drive, he sucked in the warm air and braced himself.

Sacha, the housekeeper, opened the door before he had a chance to put the key in the lock. Her sweet round face was loaded with anxiety. It made Mike bite down on his lip and flare his nostrils. 'Go on, love, tell me. What the fuck has she been up to now?'

Sacha lowered her gaze and shook her head. 'Sorry, Mr Regan, but I just can't do it anymore. I am handing in my notice ... I can't, I just can't.' Her voice cracked, as she tried to hold back the tears. Mike held out his big meaty arms for his housekeeper to fall into. He'd known she wouldn't stay in the job for much longer. Sacha was too sweet and inoffensive. Dealing with Jackie was just too much for her.

He held her tight and stroked her long black hair. 'Come on, love. Don't get yaself upset. It's okay. I understand.'

She gently pulled away. 'I'm so worried about little Ricky, he is so … well, affected. Yes, maybe that's the word. I will come back tomorrow, Mr Regan, to take him to school, but after that, I have to leave. She's too …' Sacha looked into Mike's compassionate grey eyes and gave a smile loaded with sorrow. 'She's just hard work.'

Mike heard the cab driving up towards the house. He nodded and winked for her to go. He would deal with the aftermath.

As Sacha bustled herself into the taxi, she looked back to see Mike disappear inside the house of misery. Gutted she had to leave, she knew, nevertheless, that Jackie was becoming utterly out of control. The last straw was when she took a slap from her, for ushering little Ricky away before Jackie could say another cruel thing to him. Sacha would have loved to have swapped places with Jackie. Mike was perfect in her eyes, a Gerard Butler lookalike, rich and generous too. However, he was also faithful to his wife.

Mike stepped inside, gently closing the door, hoping that Jackie was crashed out somewhere. The house was quiet, so he crept up the curved staircase and walked along the corridor and into Ricky's room. He gulped back the lump that had lodged in his throat. There, asleep, still hugging a pillow, was his little six-year-old son. The curtains were drawn, and his night light was just bright enough to show that his face was still moist from crying. There, among the child's dreams, he witnessed another sob. Mike's heart ached for his son – his sweet little chubby boy, with the biggest eyes, button nose, and wayward floppy fringe. He wanted to pull him into his arms and hug him tight, but he didn't want to wake him. Quietly, he closed the door and walked back down the stairs and into the lounge. His shoulders relaxed when he realized he was alone. Loosening his tie, he went to the bar and poured a brandy, slowly allowing the bitter bite to warm the back of his throat. He held the bottle in his hand and rolled his eyes. Thank God she didn't like brandy, or his vintage collection would be consumed by now. Jackie was content with a litre of vodka each day and didn't care if it was called Grey Goose or Mother Goose, as long as it got her pissed.

Mike took his weighty crystal tumbler, with a double shot of brandy, out through the French doors and onto the patio, where the garden lights automatically came on and flooded the pool area.

With Sacha handing in her notice, and the concerning call he'd received earlier regarding his arms import, he really needed to think about what to do, now that both work and home were a mess. He shuddered and gulped back the drink. If it was true, and his deal had been intercepted by the government agents, he was looking at going down for a long time. *Christ, what would happen to Ricky?* He had to keep his head straight. First thing tomorrow, he would call a meeting at which only his trusted men would be present. He stared as far as his eyes could see and surveyed the walled perimeter. For a second, he thought he saw something glimmer, and his heart stopped beating. *I am getting fucking paranoid now.* He had to get some sleep; the last few days had been intense, and he needed a clear head for the morning.

As he went back into the house and upstairs, the inebriated snoring from their bedroom made him pass by silently, hoping his wife wouldn't wake up. The last room on the left, the blue room, was cool and inviting. He removed his clothes and slid between the sheets, allowing the fresh cotton to engulf him. Just as he was about to drift off, a loud bang woke him and rattled his nerves. There she was in the doorway.

'Where have you been, ya fucking wanker!' spat Jackie, full of piss and vinegar.

Mike sat up and rolled his eyes; she was off on one again. For a second, he stared and wondered why the fuck he was still with her. Half-dressed in a designer blouse and just her knickers, she looked like a streetwalker. Her hair was a mess with knotted extensions and her oversized, collagen-filled lips were twisted in an ugly fashion to match her tight, beady eyes. Botox, boob jobs, and a fake tan had done her no favours. She was only twenty-six and could have passed for eighteen a couple of years ago. Why she'd had to have all that shit done was beyond him. He didn't recognize her anymore, but that wasn't the issue. It was her wild personality that had truly changed beyond recognition.

'Well, where 'ave ya been?' she demanded, standing there swaying with her hands on her hips. Even the sleep hadn't sobered her up.

'Fuck off, Jackie, and leave me alone, will ya!'

'You don't know what it's like for me to be stuck in this place all fucking day with that brat whining!'

Mike felt his blood rushing through his veins. If she'd been a man, he would have leaped from the bed and smashed her head straight through the window. He clenched his fists and flared his nostrils.

'Leave it, Jackie, and go back to bed,' he said calmly.

Jackie wanted a row; she needed to vent her anger, but he wasn't having any of it.

'Oh, that's it, Mike. You just bury ya fucking head in the sand ... Look at ya. Think ya better than me, acting like I don't even fucking exist.' With her face screwed up, she egged him on, eager for a fight. Anything to get his attention – any attention.

'I'm warning you, Jackie. Go back to bed, or I'll forget you're a fucking woman.'

His deep raspy voice would have turned her on a few years ago but not anymore. She hated him – she hated everyone. Now she saw a change in his expression; it was a coldness that crept across his face. She hadn't seen him like that before and thought perhaps she'd pushed him too far, but the drink fuelled her on and she lashed back again. 'Oh yeah, fucking hardman. Well, you lay a fucking finger on me and you just watch. You'll be seeing that kid of yours from behind bars, and only if I fucking say so. I have so much on you, Mike, that you'll go down for a long time.'

That was the last straw. The thought that she could grass, and even worse have control over their son, incensed him, taking him to a pitch that would see the red mist come down. In one fluid movement, he leaped from the bed and lunged towards her, grabbing her by the hair and throwing her to the floor.

Her cheek caught the corner of the bedside cabinet, causing her to let out a dramatic scream.

Sucking in a deep lungful of air, he slowly calmed down and glared at his wife, who was squirming around on the floor.

'You bastard!' she yelled with a wilful jeer.

He sighed with relief that he hadn't killed her. But when he clocked her malevolent expression, he wished he had. No woman had ever pushed him as far. Wife or not, no one would make threats concerning his son. Yet hitting her went against everything he stood for. Things would have to change.

He had only been with Jackie for seven years, having met her at his twenty-seventh birthday bash. She was stunning back then, a natural beauty. Her confidence was what had attracted him to her. The party was a big affair with friends and wannabe mates all trying to buddy up to him. He had money and a reputation, but he wasn't stupid; he kept only a handful of close friends who were his business colleagues.

Then Jackie arrived with his brother's girlfriend. Tall and slim, with blonde waves tumbling down her back and shrouded in assurance, she swanned over to him and gave him a birthday kiss. He remembered the sweet smell of some expensive perfume, and how he'd decided to engage in conversation. Little did he know that all the bull she plied him with that night was just to get that fucking great diamond on her finger. She was a wild spirit and had no intention of sticking to one man. Her subtle make-up and sweet expression were deliberately aimed at getting what she wanted. She wasn't sweet at all, but by the time he realized what she was all about, he was up the aisle saying 'I do' and little Ricky was on his way.

He should have listened to his head when he saw the subtle changes; after all, no one can hide their real persona for very long. Perhaps it was the age gap, for she never settled down, always wanting to party and get pissed. But he was firm and put a stop to her antics with frustrating consequences. So she turned to drinking indoors during the day.

She got to her feet and shot him an acid glare. 'You, Mike, will wish you'd never done that.' She wobbled away, back to their bedroom, leaving him wound up and needing another stiff drink.

As he made his way down the stairs, his phone vibrated in his trouser pocket. He checked his watch; it was 2.30 a.m.

It was Eric, his brother. 'What's up? It's fucking early doors, mate.'

'You best get back over to the lock-up. We've discovered something you might wanna see.'

Mike ran his big thick hands through his loose waves and then scratched his bristles.

'Okay, mate. Give me half an hour.'

He didn't ask what. He didn't like to talk too much on the phone, just in case. He dashed back up the stairs two at a time and retrieved his shirt from the back of the chair in the spare room. Jackie was quiet, her mumbling and cursing having died off, so he assumed she'd gone back to sleep. Outside was deathly quiet. There wasn't even a sign of a breeze. So, when he clicked the key fob to his Porsche, the sound of the locks releasing, although expected, still made him jump. He was tired, the lack of sleep taking its toll on his nerves. As he drove towards the entrance, the gates automatically opened. Deciding to have one last look in the rear-view mirror, he gave a sigh of relief. Apart from the outside lights, the house was in total darkness.

Good, she was still asleep.

His lock-up was in the middle of West Kingsdown in Kent, cleverly hidden in a place called Knatts Valley.

Centuries ago, the area had been divided up into plots of land for smallholdings. Over the years, the residents had turned the dwellings into large houses with stables or workshops, and some even had log cabins for holiday retreats. Through the middle ran a narrow lane, hardly wide enough for two cars, so if any police vehicles travelled along it, the residents, most of whom lived on the wrong side of the law, would be instantly notified. The lane was dark and just up ahead was the turning onto his land. From the front it looked like two large log cabins, and behind was a workshop cleverly disguised as an average-looking garage. Smaller cabins surrounded it, and so for anyone passing through, it would appear as a holiday let. However, it was a carefully secured place of business that only a very select few knew about.

He turned off his headlights and parked behind the first log cabin and slowly crept towards the side door of the workshop. He had a gun in his hand, in case this was a set-up. But then he saw Eric appear and look around. Eric spotted Mike and waved his hand, beckoning him to come in.

From the outside, the lock-up looked small, but once inside, the space seemed to open up. In fact, it was large enough to house twelve cars, a small office, and a kitchenette. The building was lined with steel shutters inside and almost impossible to break into.

There in the middle of the room, under a spotlight, bound and gagged, was Travis, their new recruit. Surrounding him were overwhelmingly daunting men. Willie Ritz – tall, lanky, mean, and hard-faced – Ted Stafford or Staffie for short – who looked as though he was made of plasticine, with a bobbly nose and oversized biceps, and Lou Baker – who looked a little like Johnny Depp – greeted Mike with a nod. Then they looked at Eric to announce the news.

Mike put his gun back inside the belt of his trousers and

kept his eyes on Travis. In a firm and controlled voice, he said, 'So, Eric, what's all this about?'

Eric was livelier than Mike, but being only ten months apart, they could have passed for twins when they were younger. Mike, the eldest, commanded more respect and his cool demeanour earned it. Whilst this six-foot-seven giant, weighing around twenty-five stone, was an intimidating sight, it was the intensity of his eyes that could strike terror into anyone who was brazen enough to front him out. Eric, though, didn't have the same presence about him, being slightly shorter and with a body that had once been muscular but had now turned to fat. Even his voice lacked authority, and when he spoke, he did so in a less measured way, often allowing his mouth to run away with him.

History was repeating itself. Like their parents, who had created the Regans' firm, Mike and his friends were also inseparable. As close as brothers, they worked together, played together, and more importantly trusted each other. Their criminal activities had earned them enough to move away from Bermondsey and they now lived in the cleaner surrounds of Kent.

By the time the boys reached adulthood, they were notorious. Living the straight road, paying taxes, and working for a boss just didn't appeal, not when they saw how their parents could earn a banker's annual salary from a single overnight job. So, it stood to reason that they would all follow in their fathers' footsteps – and what better teachers than parents? Like being an apprentice, they learned the art of safecracking, ballistics, reading architectural drawings, and negotiating. As for understanding the tools of the trade for crafting their work, they were masters at extracting information and handing out punishment.

It was a rule that they had each other's backs, come what may, like their fathers before them. They wouldn't trust anyone outside the firm, especially once they were taking on bigger moneymaking crimes, like the import and export of firearms. Inexplicably, however, their activities had somehow come to the attention of the authorities.

'I think I'm right in assuming you've found the grass then, Eric?'

Eric gave his brother a cocky smirk and a nod. 'Oh, Mikey, my dear bruvver, I've found a lot more than that.'

Mike was intrigued. 'Oh yeah, and what's that then, Eric?'

'Well, ya see, we were under the assumption that there was a little spy in the camp, an informant for the Ol' Bill. But we were wrong, Mikey. See, Travis 'ere, ain't working for the Filth ...' He kicked Travis's chair. 'Are ya, Travis?'

Mike inclined his head and stepped closer. 'Oh, is that so?'

The others were holding their breath, waiting to see if on this occasion Mike would lose the plot and rip Travis limb from limb. But they should really have known that was unlikely, given his track record. Mike was a strategic thinker, rarely losing his cool. He had twin gifts. Whilst there were not many men who could take Mike on one-on-one, he also had an innate craftiness about him. It had eased them out of trouble on many occasions, enhancing their firm's credibility.

Even his father and so-called uncles saw him as a force to be reckoned with. He'd always been the same. As a ten-year-old, he seemed to have more balls than the others and was lethal with his fists or any weapon at hand.

Nevertheless, their new venture took them into the realm of possible breaches of national security – it was Mike and his firm's biggest challenge to date – and their major concern was MI5 becoming nosy.

Their latest worrying matter was one of their more secure lock-ups in London getting turned over by the police. The cars were ready to be stripped and refitted, with all the gun parts carefully concealed in every orifice inside the car panels, before they were shipped to Ireland. But, two days ago, the police had surrounded the lock-up and turned the place over.

So there had to be a snitch. Luckily for Mike, though, his own inside man, DI Evans, had tipped them off. Mike was livid because that little tip-off had cost him more than the poxy guns were worth. Nevertheless, it had saved him from serving a big lump inside. But there was still a problem. There was a grass. And it wouldn't be the Irish buyers because they had no idea where the lock-ups were. And in any case, why would they want to sell the Regan firm down the river? It was a complete head-scratcher.

'So, who are ya working for, then, if it ain't the Filth?' asked Mike, in a menacing tone that would put the wind up any grown man.

Travis knew he was small fry in comparison to the men surrounding him. Right now, he was shitting himself. He knew it was over: there was no mercy showing on Mike's face. Those icy, emotionless grey eyes made his bowels move of their own accord.

It was true. Mike did have a look that was like death calling, a deadpan steely expression that unnerved many a man.

Staffie, the shortest of the five men, at five foot seven, with no neck, and a goofy, childlike grin, stepped forward holding a torque wrench. ''Ere, Mikey, ya don't wanna get ya hands all messy, now do ya, mate?'

Mike put his hand up. 'Hang on a minute. Before I smash the granny out of this geezer, I wanna know all the facts.'

Staffie nodded, chuckled, and then placed the wrench back on the tool rack.

'Take that gag outta his mouth. I think he wants to talk.'

Travis's eyes glistened as he nervously clocked the blowtorch that was resting on the long wooden bench. Terrifying thoughts pierced his mind. Jesus! A childhood memory of catching his arm over the steaming kettle reminded him of the pain, but he knew that would be nothing in comparison to a naked flame. He swooned and felt the warm liquid run down his leg. Totally consumed by fear, his muscles became flaccid and his bowels relaxed. He wasn't cut out for this work and stupidly he hadn't looked beyond the actuality of getting caught. However, now he was facing the consequences head-on.

Willie Ritz, the big meathead with the scar that ran from his forehead down to his chin, cut the gag from Travis using his diver's knife, his favourite tool. None of the firm ever understood why it was still his weapon of choice, even after an older gang of thugs had taken it from him in a street brawl and run that evil-looking jagged blade down his face. But Willie still turned that knife around in his hand and even kissed the blade. As tall as Mike, but with less meat on his bones, Willie liked to snort cocaine, especially if any violence was to be had. It raised his level of anger and sent him screwy and a little unpredictable. Whenever Willie's eyes were like saucers, and glared a piercing blue colour, Mike knew his friend had gone over the top, and so he would remove the supply that Willie kept in a pouch shoved down the front of his trousers. Only Mike could get away with it – no one else would dare.

With trepidation, Travis took a few deep breaths and stared wide-eyed, waiting for the inevitable.

'I think you'd better tell me what you've been up to, and, more importantly, who the fuck for.' Mike didn't shout or even raise his voice.

Travis looked at Eric and then back at Mike. 'No, listen, please, ya got me all wrong. I, er ... I was just taking pictures for meself, no one else, I swear.' He knew it sounded stupid. Really, he had no excuse.

Mike looked at his brother. 'Well, Eric, this prick ain't playing ball, so you'd best tell me what happened.'

'Gladly. We all thought that the Ol' Bill were tipped off, yeah, and I dunno, I just had this sneaky suspicion that it was this little weasel, and so I followed the rat to his house. But, see, Mikey, Travis, 'ere, ain't too clever. He left his phone right there on the dashboard of his car with the doors unlocked. So, I thought I'd just have a little butcher's, ya know, to see if the little fucker had any numbers that I would recognize. Well, fuck me, lo and behold, on the screen was a photo of the London lock-up, and so, after 'aving a mooch through the other pics, I found what I can only describe as incriminating evidence. So, I ran in through his back door and there he was in the kitchen, taking his boots off. The shit-licker only had one of our guns tucked inside his fucking Timberlands.'

Mike looked back at Travis, who, in turn, looked as though he was going to pass out. 'So, how do you know he ain't working for the Filth, Eric? 'Cos I'm guessing you ain't completely sure on that score.'

Eric smiled confidently. 'I ripped the shirt off his back and he wasn't wired. I tied him up, and the boys and me ransacked his pad. There was no sign of the Ol' Bill being involved. So, we shoved him into the boot and brought him back here.'

Mike shook his head. 'Eric, Eric, you have a lot to learn. I dunno, I still think he's an informant, but I'll let Travis tell me the facts.' He turned back to Travis with a sneer. 'You will, won't ya, Travis? You'll be only too pleased to tell me bruvver 'ere exactly who you are working for, eh?'

Willie sniggered. He knew exactly how Mike worked and braced himself for claret flowing everywhere when Mike set to work on their captive.

Travis watched through eyes of terror, as Mike removed his own shoes, his shirt, and then his trousers. 'Hold me clobber, Eric. I've just had them dry-cleaned, and, well, I don't want them stained, do I?'

Like a boxer ready for the ring, Mike stood in just his underwear. His legs were as thick as tree trunks and his chest was as wide as a standard doorframe.

'Staffie, hand me a screwdriver. It's only fitting, since this prick wants to screw me to the fucking wall.'

Travis let out a high-pitched scream like a girl. Then he began to wriggle and writhe about as if he'd been electrocuted. Mike looked at the others and laughed. 'Fuck me, I ain't even touched the knobhead.'

'No, no, all right, I'll tell ya. Please don't hurt me, pleeaasse,' he begged. The tears were streaming down his face and snot was bubbling from his nose.

'Getting covered in claret, it's pretty disgusting, don't ya think?'

Travis nodded furiously. 'Please, Mike. I'll tell ya everything ya want to know. Just don't torture me.'

'Torture? Who said anything about torture? No, Travis, it's called negotiation. Or do I mean interrogation? Well, let's hear it, then. Who's paying you?' He tilted his head to the side and gave a sarcastic grin.

Gulping back the fear, Travis thought about the firm he was just about to grass up. Either way, he was a dead man. If only he hadn't dated the sister. But how could he not? She was such a good fuck he couldn't get inside her knickers quickly enough. And then he'd had to prove himself worthy of her affections. Really, though, it was her brothers he needed to impress. He was sucked in; before he knew it, they had him planted in among the Regans' firm. He wasn't cut out for all this hard-core bollocks.

He stared at Mike's lifeless eyes, took another gulp of air, and said, 'Harry Harman.' Then he lowered his head and waited for the backlash.

Mike looked at each man with a deep furrowed frown, searching for some explanation. They either shrugged or curled down their lips. No one had a clue who this Harry Harman was.

'Mikey, do you want the screwdriver or the mallet? What's ya flavour?' asked Staffie, now eager to see the carnage.

With his eyes blinking away the sweat, Travis peered up and winced. 'Look, Mike, I don't know much, but I'll tell you everything. Just … please, don't use a tool.'

In an instant, Mike snatched the screwdriver from Staffie

and plunged it into Travis's left kneecap. No one saw it coming, not even Travis. The pain was slow at first, until it reached every nerve in his leg and forced a demonic scream to leave his mouth. Lathered in sweat and writhing, he couldn't clutch his wound because his hands were tied to the chair. Mike waited for the blood-curdling cries to die down before he handed back the bloodied screwdriver.

'Mike, please, please don't torture me. I'll tell you everything, I swear ...' His cries tailed off, as his head flopped down from the unbearable pain.

'And, Travis, me old son, I am a man of my word. Ya see, that weren't torture, that was a dig. Now then, when you get yaself composed and stop the blubbering, I'm ready to listen.'

Eric started to laugh but was instantly silenced. 'Shut it, Eric. This is no laughing matter, and you, ya silly git, took this rat on the payroll.' He shot his brother a deadly glare and bit his lip.

Eric was on the point of defending his actions. Being chastised in front of the men was a piss-take. Furthermore, he wanted to be seen as an equal in command. Ideally, he would have loved to have been the main man, but Mike took that position. He always had – at school, at work, and at home. But it was worse when it came to women. Eric's mind wandered, as it often did, to the one woman he'd wanted more than anyone – except Mike had got in there first. He was furious that when he'd expressed an interest in the woman, his brother had then dated her himself. Mike insisted he had already been seeing her, but Eric never believed that for a minute. However, he had the last laugh when she left the country, and Mike ended up with Jackie the tramp instead of his one true love.

'So, Travis, from the beginning, what the fuck are the Harmans doing nosing around my business?'

Travis tried desperately to put up with the pain and concentrate before Mike stabbed his other knee. The Harmans had sworn they had his back. Come what may, he wouldn't get hurt and when the business came their way, he would have a hefty cut of it. All he had to do was to find out where the lock-ups were, who their supplier was, and to record the evidence. The rest was up to them. Now, he wished he'd never agreed to any of it. It was no secret as to who he was doing over or how hard these men were.

The history of the Regans went back decades. The old man, Arthur, ran the firm with an iron fist. With his crew, they controlled the streets in Bermondsey.

Mike and Eric were Arthur's pride and joy. He brought them up to be a pair of chips off the old block, and they were – to the extent that they were even more fierce and reckless. Learning everything they knew from their father and his contemporaries, so they wouldn't have to learn their criminal trade within the walls of Wormwood Scrubs, it was almost an early baptism, except it began when they were aged thirteen and twelve respectively.

Travis often drank in the local haunts frequented by Eric and Mike. For years, he was just there mooching in the background, dealing a bit of cocaine and weed or selling knocked-off merchandise. It was Eric who had taken him on board, totally unaware that he was colluding with the Harmans. Yet, Eric wasn't as sharp as Mike, and had royally fucked up this time, by not doing his homework on Travis.

'So, tell me then, Travis, because I ain't got all night, see. Are you gonna be the problem or the solution? It's your choice.'

'Harry Harman wanted me to take pictures of your lock-ups and stuff.'

Mike's blank expression spoke volumes. Travis had to put more meat on the bones to satisfy Mike's hunger for information.

'I was seeing their kid sister, Paris. I swear, I didn't want to get involved, but they … Oh my God, they're gonna fucking kill me …'

'No, they ain't, Travis, because—'

No sooner had Eric opened his mouth than Mike spat, 'Shut it! Eric, I do the talking, if ya don't mind.'

Eric took a step back and bowed his head to hide his clenched teeth. It was outrageous. Mike was really getting in his face now.

'Sorry about that, Travis. You were saying?'

'I didn't want to work for them, but they saw it as payback for seeing Paris. They said I owed them for taking liberties, and the only way to pay them back was to take poxy photos … That's all I know, I swear.'

Mike held his hand up for Travis to stop talking. He paced the floor and then spun around. 'Staffie, give me that screw-driver.'

In a sudden panic, Travis screamed, 'Please! No! They know all your lock-ups and how you're transporting the guns.' His breathing was fast, and he was tripping over his words. They left his mouth like a pisshead on the run with his pants down.

Mike twirled the screwdriver around with his huge fingers. 'You missed out the part about our supplier, Travis.'

Travis shook his head. 'No, they don't know, Mike. I swear, because I don't even know.' His round puppy-dog eyes looked over at Eric, urging him to say something.

'Is that right, Eric?' demanded Mike.

Eric snapped out of his sulk and mulled over the past events, trying to work out if there was any way that Travis would have known. He thought he'd been careful. But, had he been careful enough, though, by Mike's exacting standards?

'Yes, Mike. That's right.'

Mike wasn't a man to take unnecessary risks. 'What I wanna know is this: what the fuck are they intending to do with that information, Travis? Oh, and don't leave anything out. I want to know every last detail or … Well, let's just say I can replace those fucking guns with your body parts.'

Travis eagerly nodded. 'Oh, please. Come on, Mike. I don't know. They wouldn't tell me, would they?'

Mike held his hands up. 'Tell me this, then. Did the Harmans grass my lock-ups to the Filth?'

Travis nodded. 'Yes. They want you outta the picture, by any means, even if it means grassing. I swear, if I knew then what I know now, I would never have got involved.'

'Get the man a drink, Eric. It's gonna be a long night. Travis, I want everything you have on these Harmans.'

Gripped by these thrilling stories?

Want more?

**Then don't miss out on more books from the
Governor of Gangland, Kerry Barnes**